The Ruby Brooch

The Celtic Brooch Series, Book 1

Katherine Lowry Logan

Cover art by Damonza
Interior design by BB eBooks

Website: www.katherinellogan.com

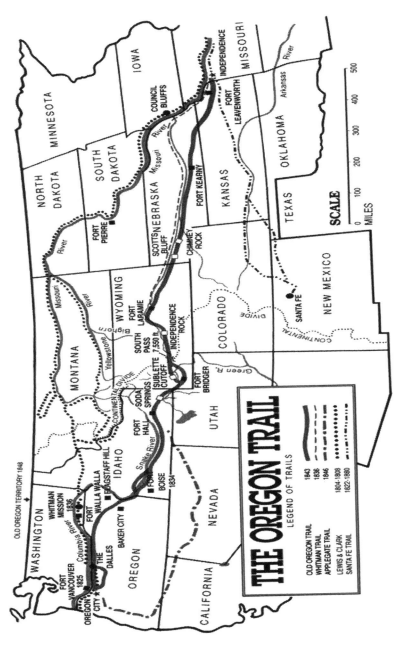

US Department of the Interior Bureau of Land Management

Chapter One

Independence, Missouri, April 4, 1852

IN A SUNLIT corner of the cluttered Waldo, Hall & Company freight office, Cullen Montgomery sat tipped back on a chair's spindly rear legs, reading the newspaper and scratching a rough layer of morning whiskers.

Henry Peters slumped in a leather reading chair and propped his legs, covered in faded cavalry pants, on a crate marked *textiles* and bound for Santa Fe. "What you learning 'bout in that gazette?"

Cullen chuckled at what little real news the paper printed. Since he no longer lived in Edinburgh or Cambridge, he needed to lower his expectations when it came to the local press. Every word of the *Independence Reporter* had been read and reread, and although he couldn't find mention of a scientific discovery or notice of a public discussion with a famous poet, he knew Grace McCoy had gotten hitched last Saturday. Reading the paper's recitation was unnecessary. He'd escorted the bride's widowed aunt to the nuptials and knew firsthand that the bride had swooned walking down the aisle. Virgin brides and widows. The former didn't interest him, the latter lavishly entertained him.

He gave the last page a final perusal. "There's no mention of our wagon train pulling out in the morning."

The old soldier took a pinch of tobacco between his thumb and forefinger and loaded the bowl of his presidential-face pipe. "We ain't got no more room anyways. No sense advertising."

The day had turned unusually warm, and Cullen had dressed for cooler weather. Sweat trickled down his back, prompting him to roll his red flannel shirtsleeves to his elbows. "Mary Spencer's not going now. We can take on one more family."

Henry dropped his feet, and his boot heels scraped the heart-of-pine floor. "Dang. Why'd you bring up that gal's name?"

"It isna yer fault she disappeared." Although Cullen hadn't said anything to his friend, he believed the portrait artist he'd seen making a nuisance of himself at the dress shop had sweet-talked the porcelain-skinned, green-eyed woman into eloping.

"Maybe. Maybe not." The joints in Henry's bowed legs popped and cracked as he stood and stepped to the window.

Cullen pulled out his watch to check the time. Before slipping the timepiece back into his vest pocket, out of habit he rubbed his thumb across the Celtic knot on the front of the case. The gesture always evoked memories of his grandfather, an old Scot with a gentle side that countered his temper. Folks said Cullen walked in his grandsire's shoes. He discounted the notion he could be hotheaded, with one exception. He had no tolerance for liars. When he unveiled a lie, he unleashed the full measure of his displeasure. "We canna worry about yesterday, and today's got enough trouble of its own."

"Rumor has it John Barrett needs money. Heard you offered him a loan." Henry wagged his pipe-holding hand. "Also heard he got his bristles up, saying he wouldn't be beholden to nobody. Got too much pride if'n you ask me. You get down to cases with that boy and straighten his thinking out."

God knew Cullen had tried. "If I canna find a compromise, our wagon train could fall apart before we get out of town."

"You're as wise as a tree full of owls, son. You'll figure it out."

The newspaper had served its purpose so he tossed the gossip sheet into the trash. Then he stood and stretched his legs before starting for the door.

Henry rapped his knuckles on the windowsill. "Where're you goin'?"

A queue tied with a thong at Cullen's nape reminded him that his shaggy hair hadn't seen even the blunt end of a pair of shears in months. "To the barber. Afterward, I'll figure out how to get yer wagon train to Oregon. There's a law office with my name on the door waiting at the end of the trail. I dinna have time for more delays."

Henry's bushy brows merged above his nose. "There's more than work awaitin' you."

"To quote an old soldier: Maybe. Maybe not." With the picture of a dark-haired San Francisco lass tucked into his pocket alongside his watch, and the keening sound of his favorite bagpipe tune playing in his mind, Cullen left the office to solve today's problem before it became tomorrow's trouble.

Chapter Two

MacKlenna Farm, Lexington, Kentucky, February 10

K IT MACKLENNA TOOK the brick steps leading to the west portico two at a time. When she reached the top steps, she slipped on a patch of black ice. Her arms and legs flailed rag-doll like, giving her some kind of weird location never intended for a human body. Forward motion ended abruptly when she collided with the farm's marketing manager exiting the mansion wearing three-inch heels and her signature pencil skirt. Tucked under Sandy's rail-thin arm was Thomas MacKlenna's 1853 journal. Both women screamed. Sandy's arms went up and the book hit the floor. And for the second time in less than thirty minutes, Kit landed on her ass.

"Oh, I'm so sorry." Sandy helped Kit to her feet. Then she picked up the leather-bound journal, brushing ice crystals from its cover.

"My fault. I wasn't paying attention." Kit rubbed her sore butt. "That's old Thomas's journal, isn't it? Did you read the proclamation to the staff?"

Sandy's normally animated face brimmed with heartfelt concern. "The forty-day mourning period is officially over. But I'm not sure it will make your life any easier."

Kit unbuckled her helmet and tugged on the dangling chin strap. "I woke up believing I'd feel better today, but I guess that's my character flaw."

"What is?" Sandy asked.

"Believing the impossible is always possible." Kit slipped her hand into the pocket of her plaid bomber jacket and fingered a crumpled letter. "Every once in a while, impossible is just what the word means."

Sandy squeezed Kit's arm. "I know it's hard, but you'll get through this, too."

Kit removed her helmet and shook her hair, pulling out a few long blond strands and a clump of mud. "Days like today make me wonder."

Sandy gave her another reassuring squeeze. "I wanted to ask you something." She opened the journal and pointed to a line in the proclamation. "This mentions a great-grandson born on the fortieth day? Do you know his name?"

Kit read the line above the marketing manager's manicured nail. "There's no record of a birth. Daddy said old Thomas was senile when he died. He probably imagined a grandson."

"I wonder why no one ever made a notation in the journal?" Sandy snapped the book shut. "Whatever. Oh, by the way, I left the sympathy cards that came in this morning's mail on the table in the foyer."

A salty tear slid from between Kit's eyelids and down her face, leaving behind a burning sensation on her wind-chapped skin.

Sandy pulled a tissue from her pocket. "Here, take this."

Kit wiped her face and silently cursed that she no longer had control over her emotions.

"Everyone on the farm misses your parents and Scott. We're grieving with you."

"I know." Kit blew her nose. "It's made the last six weeks easier."

"Well, call me later if you want to go to lunch or talk or cry. I don't have broad shoulders like Scott, but I can listen."

"I miss him bugging the crap out of me." Kit scratched the scar on the right side of her neck, something she often did when she thought of her childhood friend.

"I can bug you, if you want. Since I don't have your dad to pester, I feel sort of useless." Sandy grasped the railing and made her way down the stairs. "Hey, what happened to your stick?"

Kit stooped and picked up her broken whip. "Stormy went one way. I went the other."

Sandy cupped one side of her mouth as if sharing a secret. "Don't tell Elliott. He worries about you enough."

"The way news spreads around here, I'm sure the old Scotsman has already heard. He'll find me soon enough and ream me out."

"Don't let anyone hear you call him old. That'll tarnish his reputation." A crease of amusement marked Sandy's face. "Hey, did you hear what happened to his latest fling?"

Kit covered her ears. "TMI." Half of Lexington's female population gossiped about the sexual exploits of the serial dater. The other half made up the membership in the Elliott Fraser Past & Present Girlfriends' Club.

Sandy eased her long legs into an electric cart. "Oh, I forgot. I returned your copy of *Palm Springs Heat*. Loved it." She depressed the accelerator then gave a beauty-queen wave good-bye.

Kit mimicked the wave.

The former Miss Kentucky and marketing guru laughed. "A bit more wrist, sweetheart."

"Pshaw." Kit glared at the offending wrist that had been broken four or five times. She wasn't the beauty queen type. She could ride a Thoroughbred bareback, but put her in a pair of strappy sandals and she'd get stuck in the mud. It wasn't that she was clumsy. Just the opposite. Silly shoes couldn't compete with her penchant for practical footwear. She lived on a farm, for God's sake.

Before entering the house, she ran the soles of her tall riding boots across the blunted top edge of the boot scraper. Then she turned the brass doorknob and gave the heavy oak door pockmarked with Civil War bullet holes a quick shove. It opened on quiet hinges into an even quieter house.

The scent of lemon oil permeated the twenty-foot wide entrance hall. Even as a child, she'd loved the smell. The room cast the appearance of a museum with a vast collection of furniture from the eighteenth and nineteenth centuries, each piece darkened by countless waxings. Now that Sandy had read the proclamation, the cleaning staff could remove the black linen shrouds that draped the family portraits dotting the oak-paneled walls.

Kit dropped her helmet, crop, and muddy jacket on the rug, and pulled off her boots, leaving everything piled by the door.

The letter.

She grabbed it from her jacket and stuffed the note inside her shirt pocket.

The side cabinet held a stack of sympathy cards. She blew out a long breath. People from all over the world sent condolences. Their thoughtful words tugged at her heart, but she couldn't read them right now.

An official-looking envelope from the Bank of San Francisco piqued her curiosity. It was incorrectly addressed to *Mrs. Kitherina MacKlenna.* She pried her nail beneath the sealed flap. Then the phone rang. *Elliott?* Avoiding him was impossible. He'd continue to call until she answered. She dropped the mail on the edge of the table and hurried down the hall.

On the second ring, she entered her father's office. On the third, she plucked the receiver from the cradle. "MacKlenna Farm."

"Do ye have a cold, or are ye crying?" Elliott asked in a voice that held only a hint of his brogue.

She propped a hip on a corner of the mahogany desk. "I strained my vocal chords last night singing all of Scott's favorite songs."

"Heard that squawking. Almost called the police."

A faint smile eased the tension in her face. "You're in rare form today."

"I've been at a meeting with the board of directors."

"Well, that explains it. Where are you now?"

"Driving through the main entrance. Stay put. We need to talk." The line went dead.

"I need to talk to you, too," she said, sassing the handset before dropping it into the charging cradle. The dang thing tumbled out and landed on the desk next to a Jenny Lind doll trunk. The bread-loaf-shaped trunk held that closed-up-for-a-long-time smell that made her nose twitch. "Achoo."

She smacked the lid closed and somehow pinged her finger on one of the brass nailheads that held a metal strap in place. Droplets of blood pooled beneath the tip of her nail. The injured digit automatically went to her mouth.

My accident-prone morning finally drew blood.

She shoved off the desk and paced the room. When she heard the door knocker, she veered into the hallway. The canvases were now uncovered. *Welcome back.* Just as she'd done since childhood, she patted each one, saying their names in a singsong manner: Thomas I, Thomas II, Sean I, Jamilyn, Sean II, Sean III, Sean IV, Sean V. She usually kissed the portrait of her father, Sean VI, on the cheek, but not today.

At the ripe old age of five, Kit had decided she wanted her portrait to hang alongside Sean I's twin sister, Jamilyn, who died while sailing to America. Kit didn't want her great-great-great-great-aunt to be the only woman in the MacKlenna Hall of Fame. So she drew a self-portrait then nailed it to the wall with wood screws she found in her daddy's toolbox. She'd never forget explaining to her pony that she couldn't ride for a month because she damaged the wall. She patted the blemishes between the portraits, still visible to those who knew they were there. Punishments and tragedies had never diminished her ability to take it on the chin—until now.

Elliott was visible through the front door sidelight, standing on the porch wearing a green Barbour jacket and khakis with the usual knife-edge press. His aviators were tucked into the collar of his polo shirt. A MacKlenna Farm ball cap covered all but the sides of his freshly barbered hair. She kicked her boots and muddy jacket aside and opened the door. "Why'd you knock?"

"Door was locked. Didna have a key."

"Sorry. I must have done that when I came in."

Her godfather crossed the threshold, favoring his right leg. His expression was solemn and severe. She knew the old injury to his calf was especially sensitive to the cold. He removed his cap. As he raked his fingers through the gray hair above his temples, he sniffed the air. "Cleaning day."

"Sandy just read the proclamation."

"It's done, then."

Kit pointed over her shoulder. "Mom's portrait is uncovered. All the shrouds are gone."

He glanced at the portrait hanging over the mantel. An equal measure of sadness and anger registered on his face. "That's Sean's best work. It never should have been draped."

"I had to follow MacKlenna tradition. Daddy would have come back and haunted me if I hadn't. The last thing I need is another one of those see-through people."

"Sean MacKlenna as a ghost. That's an intriguing thought." Elliott hung his jacket and cap on the hall tree. When he spied her coat and boots on the floor, he clucked his disapproval. "Let's go into the office and ye can tell me why ye came off yer horse this morning. That's twice this week."

She held her breath a moment waiting for the lecture.

"Yer horse showed up at the barn without ye. Scared the grooms and trainers. If a hot-walker hadn't seen ye cutting through the tree line, every alarm on the farm would have sounded."

She twisted a corner of her shirttail that had come untucked when she fell the first time. "The ghost spooked me at the cemetery. Stormy planted his feet and I went over his shoulders. Then I had to walk home with a sore back, a bruised ego, and that handsome apparition shadowing me. Again." She glanced out the sidelight to be sure the ghost wasn't still hanging around. "Today he looked like a nineteenth-century lawyer all decked out in a double-breasted frock coat. What's up with him anyway?"

"I'm sure yer ghost didna intend for ye to fall."

She elbowed Elliott in the side. "Get your tongue out of your cheek. I never know whether you believe me or not."

"I believe ye. But if ye fall and break yer back again, ye might never get up."

She rolled her tongue along the backside of her teeth to give it something to do instead of blurting out that she didn't want Elliott or a ghost or anyone else hovering over her. She was a paramedic. The Lexington Fire Department trusted her. Wasn't that proof enough she could take care of herself? "If you're done with the lecture, tell me what the board of directors wanted."

His face tightened. "It was a heated meeting. Hazy Mountain Stud wants to buy a controlling interest in Galahad. I dinna want to decrease the farm's percentage of ownership in the stallion, but as CEO I only have one vote."

"That means he'll shuttle to the southern hemisphere every year. Daddy didn't have a problem with that. I guess the board feels—"

Elliott reached over and patted her twice on the shoulder. "Dinna worry about it."

She folded her arms, stiffened, then followed him down the hall. "If I had a dollar for every time Daddy told me not to worry, I'd have more millions than his estate."

"And more Apple stock than me."

"Ha-ha," she said, glowering at his back.

They entered the office. Elliott headed straight to the full-service wet bar located opposite a wall of floor-to-ceiling windows. "I suppose it's too early for scotch."

As if on cue, the long case clock in the corner sounded the hour.

"Nine o'clock is a bit early for me, but you might want a drink to wash down what I've got to tell you."

He poured a cup of coffee instead and pointed it toward the desk. "What's with the trunk? I've never seen it before."

She lifted the lid. Small leather pouches filled with diamonds, gold nuggets, and coins lay on top of a bloodstained lace shawl. "Jim Manning's office called late yesterday. He wants a copy of the 1792 land grant for probate. No one could locate the original. I searched the desk this morning and bingo. It was with this trunk."

"I didna know there was a drawer that big."

"There's a secret compartment. Daddy showed it to me when I was a kid." She framed an imaginary headline with her hands. "*Heir learns secret at age of ten.*" Her shoulders sagged. "He said never to open it until I was the farm's mistress. Now I am and I still felt guilty doing it."

"Thanks to that MacKlenna brainwashing, ye feel guilty about everything. So what'd ye find in the treasure chest? Gold doubloons?"

"Sort of. And a journal. And a letter from Daddy." Her voice teetered on the verge of cracking. "He said he found me on the doorstep when I was a baby."

Elliott muttered, shifting uneasily on his bad leg. "We both"—he cleared his throat—"found ye asleep in a Moses basket."

The heat of confusion burned through her. "You knew?"

A wistful expression deepened the fine lines on Elliott's chiseled face. "Sean asked me never to tell ye."

"Don't you think I had a right to know?"

Elliott stared into his coffee and pulled his lips into a tight seam.

She pointed her finger at him. "You know what's in the trunk, don't you?"

"Did he save the shawl?"

The confirmation in the form of a question stung her far beneath the skin.

"I thought ye were hurt, but the blood was on the shawl, not ye." He set his cup on the desk and picked up the ruby brooch Kit had taken from the trunk earlier that morning. "This was pinned to yer dress. I havena seen it since we found ye. I didna search the basket. Sean said he would do that."

"I found a book on Celtic jewelry in Daddy's library. That's a fourteenth-century brooch. The letter said it's magical. Do you believe that?"

Elliott picked up a portrait miniature of a blond-haired, nineteenth-century man, studied the face, set the painting aside, and then ran a finger across the two-inch ruby set in delicate silverwork.

"I've studied our folklore most of my life, Kitherina. I believe there're forces in the universe we canna see or understand. If Sean said this is magical, I have no reason not to believe him." Elliott turned the brooch over and studied the back of the stone. "My grandfather used to say, 'Some see darkness where others see only the absence of light.'"

She drew in a breath. "Meaning?"

He placed the brooch in her hand and curled her fingers around it. "Keep an open mind."

"That's what Daddy said in his letter *before* he said this thing took him back to 1852."

Elliott's face lost its color. "Where's the letter?"

Kit pulled it from her pocket and nudged his arm. "Here."

Lines formed between his eyebrows. "Ye made a paper airplane out of it?"

She glanced at the blister on her knuckle. "With sharp creases, just like you taught me. Then I flew it into the fireplace. It crashed on its side or the whole thing would've caught on fire." She walked over to the wet bar to grab a bottle of water. "My grief counselor would probably call it a form of disassociation. Burned my finger when I pulled it out." Her finger hurt like hell. "Read it out loud. It might make more sense hearing it from you."

Elliott smoothed out the folded letter and began with a quick throat clear. "Dear Kitherina, I'm writing this knowing ye may never read it, but I canna risk dying without telling ye the truth of yer birth. Please keep an open mind as you read.

"Ye were only a baby when I found ye on the steps of the west portico, wrapped in a bloody lace shawl. At first, I thought ye were bleeding, but ye weren't. Ye had a ruby brooch pinned to yer dress and a portrait miniature clutched in yer hand. Both the portrait's gold frame and the shawl have a monogrammed *M* worked into their design."

Elliott carried the letter and cup of coffee across the room and sat in a tufted, hunter green, velvet wing chair situated just so in front of the fireplace. He took a sip and continued. "Not long after yer second birthday, I discovered whoever made the brooch had split the ruby and hinged the halves together. Engraved inside is a Celtic inscription: *Chan ann le tìm no àite a bhios sinn a' tomhais an gaol ach 's ann le neart anama.*"

Elliott lowered his hand to his lap and she could tell he was thinking hard. Then he said, "'Love is not measured by time or space. Love is measured by the power of the soul.' At least that's my best translation."

Kit dropped onto the ottoman in front of him. "I wondered what it meant."

He took another sip of coffee. "When I read those words out loud, I was instantly propelled toward amber light. I found myself in Independence, Missouri, in the spring of 1852. The city was a major jumping-off point for those traveling the Oregon Trail. That year alone, there were over fifty thousand people heading west, so ye can imagine the crowds in the city. Since I was there for several weeks, I painted portraits to earn money for room and board. I also painted from memory the face of the man in the portrait miniature and showed it to everyone I met. Although a few people thought he looked familiar, no one was able to identify him.

"When I decided to return home, I repeated the words. I had no way of knowing if the brooch would take me home, but neither did I understand why it had taken me to Independence to begin with, although I am thankful it did. The brooch is, however, yer legacy, not mine."

Elliott leaned forward, pressed his elbows into the arms of the chair, gripped the letter between his hands, and continued reading. "I've spent over twenty years researching 1852, Independence, and the Oregon Trail, but I've found no mention of a missing ruby brooch or a disappearing baby. If I had discovered evidence of one or the other, I would have gone back. If a lead existed, it has been lost to history by now.

"I had the bloodstains on the shawl tested. The DNA profile was compared to a sample of yer DNA, and there is a genetic match. The blood belonged to yer birth mother. I'm sorry I canna offer ye more to help ye understand where ye came from, but I know where ye belong, and that's on MacKlenna Farm." Elliott's hands shook as he ended the letter. "Even though ye weren't born a MacKlenna, ye are one—the ninth generation." He dropped the paper on the table next to the chair. Color drained from his face. "I'll have that scotch now."

Kit picked up the letter and slipped it between the pages of the journal. "You and Daddy were friends for over forty years. You believe this is true, don't you?"

Elliott poured two fingers of scotch and tossed them back in a single swallow. "Sean never lied to me."

"Well, he lied to me," she said, her voice cracking. She dropped the journal on the desk next to a photograph of her show jumping at the 2010 World Equestrian Games in Lexington. The tips of Kit's fingers traced the smooth edges of the frame. "If I had died in the crash, too, this information never would have surfaced." The normal steel in her voice melted into a gray puddle at her feet.

Elliott shuffled to her side and wrapped his arms around her—arms that had held her through boyfriend breakups and broken bones and burials.

"Daddy raised me to believe in a code of honor. Keeping a secret like this goes against everything he taught me." Her eyes filled with drowning grief. "I hurt, Elliott. I hurt because my parents and Scott are dead. I hurt because my parents didn't tell me about this. I hurt because I don't bleed MacKlenna blood. My life has always been about bloodlines and pedigrees. We know our stallions' dams and sires." She thumped her chest. "Who sired me? Who?"

The winter wind ceased, and the skeleton branches no longer thrashed against the side of the house. "Damn it," she said, breaking into the silence. "It would have been so different if I'd known all my life that I was adopted. I wouldn't have bought into this two-hundred-year-old family legacy if I'd known I wasn't really one of them."

Elliott punched his fist into his palm. "Ye're wrong, young lady. Ye're as much of a MacKlenna as those old men whose pictures are hanging in the hallway."

She grew quiet as a dozen thoughts bunched up like racing Thoroughbreds along the rail. "You don't get it, do you?"

His deep brown eyes held a puzzled look. "I get it. I'm not sure ye do. Ye're still Kit MacKlenna. It doesna matter who yer birth parents were. Ye're now the heart and soul of this farm."

The wind started up again, blowing hard and swirling around the house with a mournful cry. Kit pushed away from him and faced the window. Her fingers dug into the thick drapery panels. She pulled them aside, allowing a shaft of outside gloom to peek through.

"What's in the journal?" Elliott asked.

Glancing over her shoulder, she offered him a smile—a tense one, without warmth or humor. "After I read the letter, I couldn't read anything else."

He swept his hand toward a pair of sofas that faced each other. "Let's sit and look through it. There might be something in there to make ye feel better about this news."

From her position at the window, she could see her mother's winter garden—stark and bare. "That's unlikely."

He put his arm around her. "Come."

They settled into the thick cushions, a signal to Tabor, a brown tabby Maine coon, to jump up between them and perch on the back of the couch. "Get down, Tabor," Kit said. The cat jumped to the floor and sauntered over to a corner of the room.

"Yer mom spoiled him. I'm surprised he listens to ye."

"He doesn't. He's scared of you. He thinks Dr. Fraser is going to give him another shot."

"Memory like an elephant." Elliott gave Tabor a thoughtful glance then flipped to the first page of the notebook where Sean had written *1852 Independence, Missouri*. The next pages contained pencil sketches. Shops on the right, a grid of roads around a town square on the left.

She pointed to one of the buildings. "Look at the woman in that window. Who does she look like?" Kit opened the drawer in the table next to the sofa, rifled through the contents until she found a magnifying glass, and then held it over the picture. She gasped. "*Good God.* It's Mom. Why'd he sketch her there?"

Elliott grabbed the glass and squinted through it, then regarded

Kit with narrowed eyes. After a moment, he returned his gaze to the drawing and said, "Sean drew Mary's face when he doodled, just like ye draw Stormy."

Kit turned to the next page and began to read. With a gulp of surprise, she grabbed Elliott's hand and demanded, "Listen to this. 'I met Mary Spencer the day I arrived in Independence.'" Kit could barely move, feeling as if her joints had frozen where she sat. "What's he saying, Elliott? That Mom was from the nineteenth century? But that's *impossible.*"

He placed his other hand over hers and squeezed. "Ye're the one who believes the impossible is possible."

"Yes, but—"

"If we had told ye we'd found ye on the porch, ye would have wanted to know what steps were taken to find yer birth parents. Sean wasn't going to tell ye that he'd found a way to travel back in time. If he had, would ye have believed him?"

"An act of omission is still a lie and MacKlennas don't lie." The revelations stripped away the bare threads of her self-control. She jumped to her feet and whipped her head around so fast her ponytail smacked her in the chin. The room folded in on her. If she didn't get air she would suffocate. She staggered to the French doors, pushed them open, and stumbled onto the portico.

Elliott stood in the doorway. "Come back in here. Let's talk about this."

The fingers of her right hand tensed into a fighting fist. "Go to hell."

A moment later, the doors clicked shut.

She pounded her fist on the railing as she stared out over the rolling hills covered with frost-tipped Kentucky bluegrass. Her stomach roiled, but she kept down the little bit of food she'd eaten at breakfast. *Why has this happened?* She closed her eyes, but darkness couldn't halt her father's words from flashing strobe-like across her brain.

When her eyelids popped open, she spotted her ghost. He stood under the pergola in the garden, rubbing his thumb across the front of his watch case—a gesture she'd often seen him make. He stretched out his arm, beseeching her to come to him.

"What do you want?" The panic in her voice reminded her of the little girl she had once been, sprawled on the ground after falling from her horse—scared, but not of him. A sob tore from her throat. "There's nothing you can do."

He slipped his watch into his pocket, gazed once more into her eyes, then faded away.

Sometimes life is nothing more than a photo album full of good-bye pictures. She stepped back into the house, an empty house, where unlike her ghost, the hurt and the heartache would never fade away.

THAT NIGHT, BAD dreams woke Kit from a fitful sleep. She flipped on every light switch between her bed and the kitchen, where she listened to Bach and made a pot of herbal tea. The cup rattled against the saucer as she walked to the office with Tate, her mother's golden retriever, leading the way.

"Where were you when I was fighting the bad guys in my dream?" she asked the dog.

He gave a little whine and lowered his head. Drops of tea splattered to the hardwood floor, and he licked them up.

"I don't like the bad guys any better than you do."

He barked.

"Okay. I'm glad we're straight on that."

When she entered the office, she spotted the trunk still sitting open on the desk—a trunk full of clues to her identity that led nowhere. Could she, like her father, spend twenty years searching historical records? No, she couldn't. She'd chew off all her fingernails. Patience was a limited commodity in Kit MacKlenna's world.

She sat in her father's chair and opened the journal. There were pages of research notes; tangents he'd followed and later abandoned, others he'd clung to for years. From all his research, he believed her birth parents had traveled the Oregon Trail in 1852, but he couldn't prove it. He couldn't find that one piece of evidence that linked her to a family. No missing ruby brooch. No missing baby. His exhaustive research had ended five years earlier.

Five years. Did Daddy stop looking before or after the attacks? She rubbed the scar on the left side of her neck. *Probably afterward.*

Kit sat back and pressed her warm palm against her forehead, hoping the pressure would supplant the tension headache. Wasn't there more information on the web now than years earlier? Of course there was. Well, if she was going to continue her father's research, all she had to do was dig into the time period between when he stopped working on the project and now.

How long will it take? She sighed, unsure of anything other than her losses were wavering at an emotionally dangerous level. What she desperately needed was a sense of control and a good working plan. Quickly, feeling ideas germinating, she snatched pen and paper from the desk drawer.

Step One: Send an email to the professors and historians listed as contacts in the journal. They would know of any new diaries or letters.

Step Two: Email historical societies.

Step Three.

She sat straight in the chair. *Forget step three until one and two are exhausted.*

After bringing order to her thoughts, she fired off a group email to her father's contacts, then went back to bed, praying she wouldn't have to outline Step Three.

LATER THAT DAY, Kit checked her email. There was a response from the Oregon-California Trails Association. She held her breath and opened the email.

> *The Barrett family donated an 1852 Oregon Trail journal to the Portland Historical Society three years ago. To read the online version,* **click here**.

She took a deep breath then clicked the link.

The author, Frances Barrett, wrote in sloppy print as she described the weather, food, and breath-stealing dust. Halfway through the June 1852 entries, Kit read:

June 16, 1852 South Pass. Mr. Montgomery found a wagon train full of murdered folks. Mr. and Mrs. Murray's baby girl is missing.

Kit's heart pounded in her ears. The monogram on the locket and shawl had the letter *M*. What were the odds of finding parents with a missing baby and a last name beginning with that letter? Her insides were frantic now, unnerved by information that slashed through her composure.

It took several minutes to rein in her thoughts. Finally, she typed a return email and copied it to all her contacts asking for information about the Murray family who had traveled west in 1852. And she specifically requested information about a wagon train full of murdered people discovered in South Pass in June of that year.

All she could do now was chew her thumbnail and wait.

KIT SLUMPED IN the desk chair, twirling the end of her ponytail around her finger, frustrated that none of her emails two days earlier had provided answers. In her periphery, she spotted Elliott standing in the doorway. She hadn't spoken to him since telling him to go to hell.

"We need to talk." He shuffled to the wet bar. "Do ye want some coffee?"

"I'm off caffeine."

"Still having nightmares?"

"Yep."

He poured himself a cup, stirred sugar into the brew, and said, "I know ye're upset, but Sean asked me not to tell ye."

"A course of action you *obviously* championed."

Elliott's chest rose with a deep inhale, but his steady gaze never faltered. "I'm yer godfather, Kit. Not yer father."

She continued twirling her hair.

"So what's kept ye locked up in here? Research?"

"You know exactly what I've been doing. You've been here late at night reading my notes." She pointed to an empty mug on the desk. "You could have cleaned up after yourself."

He tossed the stir stick onto the counter. "Ye left the notes out for me to read."

"So what do you think?"

"None of yer trail experts have read another journal mentioning murdered people in South Pass—"

"They call the entry an anomaly."

"I call it possibly fabricated."

"That makes no sense. Not when the rest of the entries are consistent with what others wrote in their journals. And why"—she straightened to give depth and conviction to her voice—"would Frances Barrett make it up?"

He arched his brow, seeming to look right through her.

"Stop looking at me like I'm crazy."

"I'm not—"

"I want to believe her, dammit, even if no one else does. And because I believe her, I think it's unfair that people were killed and there's no historical record. The gold and diamonds in the trunk probably belonged to the Murrays and should go to their heirs."

"Let's say the story is true and ye're the Murrays' missing baby. Legally, the treasure would belong to ye."

"I don't care about it. I just want answers." She stood and paced the room, stomping her feet on the hardwood floor. Finally, she said, "If I had a picture of Mr. Murray I could compare it to the portrait."

Elliott took another swallow of coffee then studied the contents of his cup as if he were reading tea leaves. "Go take one. Sean went. Why don't ye? I'll even go with ye."

She gave him a dry laugh. "You want a nineteenth-century wife, too?"

"No, thanks. I like being a bachelor." He sat on the arm of the sofa while she continued to pace in small circles. "Look...I dinna ken whether the Barrett journal is true, but I know yer father's story is. If ye're looking for a logical explanation, ye're not going to find one. The Barrett journal is what it is and the brooch holds an ancient Celtic secret. That's hard to grasp."

"I've had a ghost following me around since I was ten. The natural and supernatural coexist in my world."

"Look at the way yer parents raised ye. Ye've been attending pioneer reenactments yer entire life. Ye can ride, shoot, and yoke the oxen as well as yer father. Why'd he insist ye learn to do that? Why'd he direct ye toward the medical field? Why'd yer mother teach ye how to cook over a campfire? Ye probably never noticed how yer speech pattern changes when ye're out on the trail. Ye turn into a nineteenth-century woman."

He sipped his coffee and they were quiet for several minutes. "Ye may not want to hear this, but yer father raised ye to make this trip, or more accurately, to make a return trip. Sean would have told ye the truth when he knew ye were ready. Knowing him, I suspect he intended to go back with ye someday."

Elliott picked up a legal pad and thumbed through the pages. "When did Frances Barrett say those people were killed?"

"June sixteenth. Why?"

"Well, look, if ye went to South Pass—"

"Have you ever been to South Pass, Wyoming? It's a wide-open space now. Can you imagine what it looked like in 1852?"

"No. But if ye could get there by June sixteenth, ye could see if anyone matches the little painting, get a hair sample for DNA, and then come home. Ye're a paramedic. Dead bodies dinna bother ye."

She shuddered and tried to block out the memory of her parents' vacant eyes staring at her moments after the crash. "I've seen my share. They've all bothered me."

"That isna what I meant."

She paced the room, biting her nail. "If I went back in time—and I'm not saying I'm going—but if I did, the tricky part would be arriving in South Pass by the sixteenth."

"When did Sean go back?" Elliott moved to the desk and put his feet up. "Sometime in the spring, wasn't it? If ye go back in March or April that would give ye plenty of time to get to Wyoming, assuming the brooch takes ye to the same place it took him."

She turned again and headed toward the window. "Do you really think I could do it?"

"Well, ye canna change history or what happened in South Pass. That might obliterate yer life in the twenty-first century. But yes, ye're physically able to handle the journey."

Kit stopped pacing and stared at Elliott. "Okay, I'll get the brooch and go."

"Whoa." He put his feet on the floor. "Ye canna go off unprepared. We know from the journal that Sean returned with Mary and a covered wagon. So it seems logical that ye can take supplies and emergency equipment with ye."

"You make it sound like I'm going off to a third-world country."

"Ye've been on the trail. Ye know how primitive it can get. This isn't a reenactment. It'll be worse." He leaned forward and put his elbows on his knees. "Look, I know ye. Ye'll never be settled until ye have the truth. If ye go, I'd like to go with ye."

"If I decide to go, you can't. You'll need to cover for me, especially with Sandy."

"And let ye go off and have all the fun? That *isna* going to happen."

She'd sneak off without him, of course. As much as she'd love to have Elliott along, she wouldn't put him through a rigorous trip while he was recuperating from his fourth leg surgery in five years and facing another one before the year ended. If she went, she'd go alone.

KIT MULLED OVER her predicament for several weeks while devouring every word of her father's journal. Then in the early morning hours of April Fools' Day she rolled out of bed drenched in a cold sweat. In a dream, she'd heard the voice of a young woman crying out for help.

Unable to go back to sleep, Kit wandered to the kitchen and steeped a cup of tea. Tate trotted into the room and whined to go outside. She opened the back door and stood there, arms folded, watching the sun peek above white-planked paddocks. The air smelled of horses and freshly turned earth. Tears slipped down her cheeks. It didn't seem fair that their stallions could trace their line back over three hundred years to three foundational stallions, but she couldn't draw a line back to her roots. She didn't know where they were. *Somewhere in 1852. Maybe.*

The not-knowing tied her up tighter than the twine wrapped around the bundle of old newspapers stacked at the door. As she wiped away a tear, she recalled a quote by Anaïs Nin. The words swirled inside her mind and tasted sweet on her tongue.

And the day came when the risk to remain tight in a bud was more painful than the risk it took to blossom.

She slapped the door with the palms of her hands. Not knowing her identity was more painful than the risks she'd take going back in time. And at that singular moment, she knew what she would do. Not what she had to do, but what she chose to do.

KIT HUSTLED OUT of the house shortly before sunrise for her usual horseback ride around the farm. This morning, though, she rode straight to the old tobacco barn where her supplies were already stowed in the covered wagon. After yoking the oxen used in the annual Old Kentucky Farm Days Celebration, she tied Stormy to the tailgate, slipped a nineteenth-century-style yellow gingham frock over her jeans, and shoved her flannel shirt into her carpetbag. A shiver of anxiety coursed through her as she removed the brooch from its velvet-lined box and tucked the jewelry into her pocket.

She climbed up on the wagon's bench seat with her to-do list in hand. One item remained unchecked: tell her parents good-bye. She snapped the whip over the heads of the oxen and the team lumbered across the pasture toward Cemetery Hill.

At the crest of the knoll, pockets of a shimmering blue fog rose from the ground, leaving only the tip of Thomas MacKlenna's monolith visible in the predawn light. Kit gathered her shawl around her, warding off the strong current of air that lifted dead leaves in upward spirals.

Something wavered in the tree line. She gasped. *Why is he here now?*

Her blue-eyed ghost carried a shovel. Another apparition who resembled the first Sean MacKlenna appeared and together they glided across Cemetery Hill. Then her ghost rammed his shovel into the ground surrounding old Thomas's monolith, marking the burial site as if it didn't already exist.

"What're you doing?" Kit asked.

Her ghost held his hand out toward her, but she shook her head and kept her distance. The Sean MacKlenna look-alike put his arm around her ghost's shoulder and together they faded into the mist.

She shivered. *This is probably a good time to leave.*

When she pulled the brooch from her pocket, the stone warmed both her palm and her mother's wedding band she had worn on her right hand since the funerals. A notation she'd made in her notes popped into her mind. *Getting help will be easier if I pretend to be a widow.* She switched the ring to her left hand, feeling a twinge of guilt. *How can this hurt anyone?* It probably wouldn't, but it was a lie. Once she started down that thin edge of the wedge, as her Granny Mac used to say, telling the next one would be easier.

She opened the stone as her father had described in his journal and read the Gaelic words aloud. *"Chan ann le tìm no àite a bhios sinn a' tomhais an gaol ach 's ann le neart anama."* Tendrils of mist, carrying the scent of heather and peat fires, wrapped her in a warm cocoon.

Tate barked, the wagon jerked, and dog tags jingled.

A swirling force propelled the wagon forward into amber light, taking Kit who knew where with six oxen, a Thoroughbred, and a high-spirited golden retriever.

Chapter Three

Independence, Missouri, April 4, 1852

K IT KEPT A white-knuckled grip on the bench seat until the frantic ride ended as abruptly as it had begun, cutting her loose in a fog. Fuzzy shapes appeared all around her.

Who's out there? What's out there?

Whatever or whoever it was, she wasn't about to face the unknown without protection. She reached into the carpetbag at her feet, wrapped her fingers around an 1850 single-shot Henry Deringer pistol, one of the weapons she'd pilfered from her father's gun collection, and slipped it between the folds of her skirt.

One shot. One chance. Not particularly good odds.

The fog lifted with the dramatic flair of a curtain rising on an opening act. The unfolding scene could easily be a refugee camp. Smoky campfires and hundreds of tents and wagons covered acres of land in a nineteenth-century version of uncontrolled urban sprawl.

Then, *wham*. The stench of garbage, manure, and burned coffee hit her nostrils, disturbing her already queasy stomach. A hammer's clang rang from the blacksmith's forge and reminded her of Hemingway's *For Whom the Bell Tolls*. Not a good omen.

Kit's gaze followed the haggard women's faces as they cooked and tended to children. Men huddled in small groups with maps spread open on makeshift tables.

No one's pointing at me. I just dropped out of the sky and no one cares. Tension unknotted in her shoulders, and her trigger finger relaxed.

The six oxen remained quiet, apparently undaunted by their journey through the time portal. Stormy had his tail up, ears pricked forward, and eyes focused. Tate jumped over the trunks and burlap bags, climbed up on the seat beside her, and licked her hand.

"Are you okay?" She dug her fingers into his dense, reddish-blond fur and scratched his neck, jiggling his dog tags. The collar had to come off and with it his flea protection. "Sorry, buddy, but I don't think anyone would understand what this is."

The weather felt warm against her skin but not hot, and sunlight filtered through a few wispy clouds in a deep blue sky. A Renoir sky, her art teacher would say. The beauty beyond the smoky campsites warmed an urge to draw that had been stone cold since the crash, but now wasn't the time. As soon as she found a wagon train bound for Oregon, she could sketch until she wore her pencils' graphite tips to nubs. When she returned home, she'd have notebooks full of sketches and a lifetime to paint them.

Tate nudged her arm.

"You're ready to go, aren't you?"

His dark, deep-set eyes said, "Yes."

Based on her research, she would begin at Waldo, Hall & Company, a freighting business operating out of a two-story brick building near Independence Square. If they couldn't lead her to a wagon train, her next stop would be Hiram Young's wagon shop.

A quick spank with the whip and the oxen lumbered up the hill following an old road toward town. When she spotted the freight office's rusty sign swaying over an oak door, her hands turned cold and clammy. She gave herself a mental kick in the ass. *I'm a first responder. Fear has never held me back.* She stood on the edge of a panic attack.

Breathe. Breathe. Breathe.

It took a couple of minutes, but by the time she halted the team in front of the freight office, her breathing had returned to normal.

Can I leave everything unattended? Certainly not something she could do in her century.

With a nonchalant air, she glanced up and down the street. Some nasty-looking men were hanging around, and never-met-a-stranger Tate didn't amount to much of a watchdog. The freight office, though, was only ten or so feet from the wagon. If she stayed close to the door, she would hear him bark if someone approached the wagon.

"*Stay.*"

He wagged his tail.

"I mean it, Tate. Stay. I'll be back in a few minutes."

The door barely creaked when she pushed it open on a paper-cluttered office smelling of apple and cherry pipe tobacco. In a sunlit corner of the room, a man reading the *Independence Reporter* sat tipped back on a chair's spindly rear legs, the heels of his muddy boots looped over the chair rung. A head of thick, black hair peeked above the newspaper. The man rustled the publication, turning pages slow and easy with long slim fingers.

Kit cleared her throat. "Can you help me? I want to join a wagon train heading to Oregon."

The deep burr of a Highlander's voice came from behind the newspaper. "We set out in the morning and have room for one more family."

Kit stared at the newsprint still blocking the speaker's face. "I don't have a family." She paused for a shaky breath. "Could I—can I still join up? I'm a widow." Her tongue caught on the lie, and a heated blush spread across her cheeks.

The chair dropped to the heart-of-pine floor with a heavy thud. The man unfolded his long, lean body and stood. She guessed him to be about six-one, one eighty. She was good at sizing up people whether they were standing or lying on a gurney.

Ropy veins in his forearms pulsed below red-flannel shirtsleeves rolled to his elbows. The loose shirt did little to disguise the broad expanse of his chest. He tossed the newspaper to the pedestal desk and turned toward her, glaring with vibrant blue eyes curtained by thick lashes. A rough layer of dark morning whiskers covered his square-jawed face.

The downy hairs on her neck stood upright. *Impossible.*

She couldn't take her eyes off him. Even facial scruff couldn't hide the face as recognizable as her own. The face of her ghost.

The floor fell away from beneath her feet, and she swayed, but somehow remained standing. The man began to whistle the unmistakable strains of Bach's "Jesu, Joy of Man's Desiring." A Bach-whistling ghost look-alike. No. Her ghost always appeared clean-shaven and impeccably dressed, not scruffy like this Highlander.

Think logically, Kit. This man is on his way to Oregon. If he's going west, he can't be at MacKlenna Farm selecting Thomas's gravesite when he dies on January 25, 1853.

He wasn't her ghost, but whoever he was, he had an unnerving effect on her. His close proximity and the look of puzzlement in his eyes sent her heart drumming to a loud, irregular beat.

Worry about getting to South Pass. Nothing else matters. She didn't even know for sure she'd arrived in the right year. A quick sideways glance at the newspaper caused an inward laugh to bubble up.

April 4, 1852. Good God. I did it.

Granted, the paper could be a week old, but assuming it was a reasonably current edition, she could estimate the number of travel days she needed.

She mentally calculated. The distance from Independence to South Pass was 914 miles. Traveling an average of twenty miles a day, the trip would take forty-six days. April 4 to June 16 totaled seventy-three days. That gave her twenty-seven days for layovers and river crossings. If she left Independence soon, she could arrive in time.

The Highlander shook the shoulders of a man sleeping in a chair with his legs propped on a crate marked *textiles.* "Henry, the widow wants to join our wagon train, but she's got no family."

He opened his eyes and peered at her beneath droopy eyelids. Deep grooves etched his leathery, wind-burned face. Faded cavalry pants and an unbleached cotton shirt covered his burly frame.

Graying hair fell short of his collar. He dropped his feet and his boot heels scraped the floor. Then he put his hands on his knees and stood, grunting under the effort. The joints in his bowed legs popped and cracked with each step he took. He skirted the desk and drew to a standstill in front of her.

"Sorry for your loss, ma'am, but we got rules. Single women ain't allowed 'less they're traveling with family."

A swell of outrage surged through her. She leveled her best you've-got-to-be-kidding glare. "*Why?*" The question eked out in a shriek, and she wanted to snag it and reel it back in. First impressions were important, and she didn't want to appear to be a shrew.

"Three reasons." He ticked them off on stubby fingers. "One— pretty little things without a man around cause trouble. Two—you cain't do the work. Three—you ain't strong enough."

Kit puffed out her chest. *Never mind first impressions.* She mirrored his three fingers. "I can take care of myself, my wagon, and my animals."

He gave her a one-shoulder shrug. "You ain't going. Not by yourself."

"Then I'd like to speak to your supervisor."

He screwed up his face. "Ain't nobody else. Just me."

The Highlander's eyes held a quickening of interest, but he didn't intervene. She tapped her foot. Maybe she could buy her way onto the wagon train. Smiling, she directed a question to the old soldier. "What will it take for you to…uh…reconsider?"

He picked up his pipe and tobacco pouch off the desk and leveled a smile, cold and unmoving, that didn't match his warm brown eyes. "Ma'am, I'm sorry. Single women ain't allowed. That's all I'm saying 'bout it."

"But—" She stopped herself. Arguing would not change their minds. Their *no single women* policy reeked of blatant discrimination, and there wasn't a thing she could do. Or was there?

The smoke in the room settled over her in a choking cloud. She coughed.

If she donned the shorthaired wig and britches she often wore during the Annual Old Kentucky Farm Days Celebration, she could pass herself off as a boy. The disguise would fool the old codger. She chewed her nail as she devised a plan.

I'll change my clothes, lower my voice, put some dirt on my face, then come back and try again.

She gave them her best just-you-wait smirk, turned on her heels, and left the office.

Chapter Four

CULLEN MONTGOMERY WATCHED the blonde-haired beauty gather her pride and walk out, leaving behind a hypnotic vanilla scent. When she'd first spoken, her dulcet voice had glided across his skin, soft and silky like early morning dew on his Highland hills. Although tempted to lower the newspaper and glance at the woman, he didn't want to be disillusioned when he discovered the voice of his dreams had the face of his nightmares. Then she spoke again, announcing she was a widow, piquing his curiosity even more. But he'd still refrained from gazing at her until she stood so close he could feel her warm breath on his skin. Finally, he relented and looked her way.

The enigmatic beauty stood caught in a beam of light streaming through the partially opened slats on the shuttered window. Stunned, his breathing had stopped, his step had faltered, and words had abandoned him. Unable to speak, he whistled as he gazed into emerald green eyes that burned with intelligence and something else. A spark of recognition.

Impossible. He didn't think he'd ever seen the woman. If he had, he certainly would have remembered, but the look in her eyes still puzzled him. He rubbed the crook of his index finger across his chin, musing—a beautiful widow. The heated rush of sexual desire coursed through him.

With a breath of regret, he slapped Henry's shoulder. "Ye're all horns and rattles, old man."

The old soldier remained silent while he took a pinch of tobacco between his thumb and forefinger, loaded the bowl of his presidential-face pipe, lit it, and drew on it several times. "You know dang good 'n well I only wanted to change her mind 'bout travelin' alone."

Cullen looked into his friend's glum face. "The lass brought up memories of Mary Spencer, didn't she? Ye're not to blame for her disappearance."

Henry wagged his pipe-holding hand. "I told her she could join up, and then she vanished. If I'd sent her packing like the little missy just here, she'd still be alive. She would have gotten back on that boat and gone home instead of hanging around town waiting on the wagon train."

Cullen strode across the room to the window and opened the wooden shutters to a square shaft of sunlight. "Ye dinna ken she's dead."

"I know she ain't around no more. Neither is her wagon."

Miss Spencer was gone, and he couldn't help her, but he could help the widow. "Maybe there is a solution."

"You're as wise as a tree full of owls, son. You'll figure it out."

Cullen fixed Henry with a stare, and then headed toward the door and opened it.

"Where're you goin'?"

The words to one of Cullen's favorite poems came to mind, and he elocuted, "To help my lady with the gold o' morning sun shimmering in her hair. The saints be with the Highland lass who rides her mighty steed, beyond the heather she brings the glory light for my soul too dark to see."

Henry feigned a coughing spell.

"Ye wander far across the loch, oh lads o' Callander..." Cullen continued. Then with the keening sound of his favorite pipe tune playing in his mind, he went to help the bonnie lass.

WHEN KIT RETURNED to her wagon, she found Tate sitting on the bench seat doing his best imitation of a sphinx. Sitting next to him doing his best imitation of a junior sphinx was Tabor. "*You came, too?*" Although the dynamic duo's charm was disarming, she sagged all the way through to her feet. Tabor leaped into her arms. "What am I going to do with you?"

Tate tilted his head, waiting for a report or more likely a reward for staying put.

"I struck out," she muttered under her breath. "They won't allow single women traveling alone." She set down the cat. "Y'all didn't notice a phone booth where I could change clothes, did you?"

Tabor scratched his chin with a hind paw, and Tate barked.

"Guess not." As she silently watched an array of Indians, Mexicans, and bullwhackers walk in and out of the groggeries surrounding the public square, Kit's hand eased into her pocket and clasped the Derringer. The weapon provided only a small measure of security. She seriously doubted it would scare off a man threatening her with a bullwhip or bowie knife.

The freight office door opened behind her, and she heard the Highlander quoting poetry. Then the sidewalk creaked under firmly planted footsteps. She shot a quick glance over her shoulder. He swaggered in her direction as if he were on a mission to mark an item off his to-do list.

"Ma'am," he said, walking until he stood close to her. "My name's Cullen Montgomery."

She grabbed the wagon wheel and laced her fingers between the spokes. Surely he wasn't *the* Montgomery in Frances Barrett's journal? She cleared the nervous knot from her throat. "I'm Kitherina MacKlenna."

He placed his hands on his hips and tapped out a silent rhythm with his fingertips. "I might be able to help ye, Mrs. MacKlenna, if ye're interested."

Mrs. MacKlenna? That was her mother's name, not hers. But the wedding ring she twisted on her finger said the name now belonged to her. "What'd you have in mind?"

He searched her face so intently that heat spread across her cheeks. "Do ye have funds to pay someone to drive your rig?"

"Do you know someone I can hire?"

"I canna make promises before talking with John Barrett, but his lads are old enough to hire out. He might be willing to let one work for ye for reasonable wages."

"Barrett? I...I'd like to meet him." Were these random events coming together to form a grand design or just plain old coincidences? If she had to place a bet, she'd go with a grand design, and she found that unnerving.

Cullen scratched under his chin with the backs of his fingers. "Barretts are camped outside of town. Stay here. I'll be back."

She gulped. No way was she letting him out of her sight. "I'll go with you."

Tate barked, and Cullen turned toward the dog. "Pretty. What is he? Never seen the breed before."

Oh great. She cleared her throat and told her next lie. "He's a mix. He's also a stowaway."

The dog had jumped into the nineteenth century uninvited, and his ancestors wouldn't come along for another ten years.

Cullen issued a playful growl. "Stowaways have to earn their keep." Then he spotted the cat. "And what do we have here?"

The pressure of questions she couldn't answer hovered in the air. "That's Tabor. He's a stowaway, too."

Cullen scratched the cat's head and gave Kit's Thoroughbred an appreciative glance. "Ye have quite a menagerie."

A menagerie was exactly right. How was she going to keep them healthy? She'd prepared for Stormy and the oxen but not the little ones. Why couldn't she have snuck out of town without them? Maybe she should take them home and start over. But what if the brooch operated like a revolving door and left her spinning between two worlds?

Oh, that's a scary thought.

Cullen placed warm hands at her waist and lifted her to the bench seat, then climbed up beside her. His clothes carried the pleasing apple and cherry aroma that had been present in the office. She bounced her leg and refrained from chewing her thumbnail. Stacks of sketchpads lined the shelves in her bedroom closet. Each pad had drawings of the ghost who resembled the man beside her. Every line on his face seemed familiar to her, but he had no scar below his right ear.

"Get up." The animals moved out on his command. "Ye've got a well-trained team and larger than other oxen around here. What'd yer husband feed them?"

"My *husband* fed them Kentucky bluegrass and hay." The lie sank her feet deeper into the proverbial hole, caking her boots with thick Missouri mud.

Cullen weaved the wagon through the crowded street, wearing a tight-jawed look of concentration. When they reached the edge of town, he halted the team and pointed to a group of wagons nestled in a grove of oak trees. "The Barretts are camped there."

She stood, intending to go meet them.

He stretched out his arm, blocking her movement. "Whoa, lass. It'd be best if ye stayed behind."

Stay? Is he kidding?

He climbed down and walked away from the wagon.

She swung her leg over the side, but stopped abruptly when her annoying internal voice reminded her that she was out of her element and needed to be patient. "Damn." She plopped down on the seat and twiddled her thumbs.

Cullen forged his way through the overcrowded campsites, shaking hands and slapping backs. Children hugged his legs and women offered plates of food. Kit had seen politicians work crowds, but this part-Highland bard, part-American cowboy seemed to have disarming charisma. She stopped twiddling and watched the ease at which he moved—relaxed, yet with an air of confidence.

She shook her head, baffled not only by the Highlander but also by the magical stone. Why didn't the brooch send her directly to South Pass instead of putting her through an eight-week journey that forced her to impose on people she didn't know? Granny Mac would tell her if she stayed preoccupied with the questions, she might never discover the answers.

Oh well. She went back to twiddling and hummed a little rock and roll.

Cullen reached the Barretts' campsite and assisted a broad-shouldered, barrel-chested man heaving sacks into a wagon. When the work was done, the two men leaned against the tailgate and crossed their arms across their chests. The man she assumed was Barrett lit a pipe. As he smoked, he occasionally pointed in her direction with his pipe-holding hand.

Jeez, she'd love to be a hub in the wheel and hear the conversation. *I bet Montgomery is telling him I'm a helpless widow.* The thought sparked a kick-ass reaction—a need to prove she was the least helpless female she knew. She tapped her foot and twiddled so fast her thumbs rammed together. *As soon as I secure a spot on the wagon train, I'll set Montgomery straight.* She'd wager a sack of gold coins that she could shoot straighter, ride faster, and hum Bach concertos he'd never heard before. "Helpless. Pshaw."

Then it occurred to her that Barrett might think she'd be too much trouble if she were so helpless. *Then it's time to set them both straight.* She swung her leg back over the side, but reined herself in when a woman and a teenage boy wearing an out-of-control cowlick joined the two men. The stocky youngster had to be Barrett's son. His coloring, facial structure, and broad shoulders bore a striking resemblance to his father.

The woman scrunched her brow and glanced in Kit's direction. Then she said something that made Cullen laugh.

And what's so damn funny?

He placed his hands behind his back and perused the small group. Although she couldn't hear him, she could tell from his audiences' rapt attention that he was speaking slowly and deliberately to each one. What was he saying? She watched his full lips, hoping to pick up a word or two. Where did she get the notion she could trust him to plead her case? He'd been no help at the freight office. Just because he volunteered to assist her now didn't mean he had her best interest at heart.

Her foot pounded against the floorboard, rocking the wagon. "Come on. Come on. What's taking so long?" She fingered the brooch in her pocket and wondered if Elliott knew she was gone yet. Did she make a mistake not including him? If he had come, she wouldn't be sitting there feeling helpless.

While she was second guessing herself, the powwow concluded and Cullen sauntered back to her wagon with the man and boy in tow. If body language cues remained constant throughout the centuries, then in Cullen's pointed gaze she read success. From all appearances, she was on her way to South Pass. She loaded a smile with a spoonful of conjured-up confidence, gathered her skirt, and climbed from the wagon.

"Mrs. MacKlenna, this is Mr. Barrett and his son, Adam. We talked about yer predicament and worked out an agreement that will satisfy Captain Peters."

It didn't matter what the terms were; Kit would agree to anything. Then she remembered the way she'd been treated in the freight office and decided to listen, evaluate, and then make a decision. The terms might be more restrictive than she could live with.

She folded her arms across her chest. "What are they?"

"Adam will drive yer wagon and take care of yer stock for a salary of one hundred dollars. He's to be paid twenty-five dollars now, twenty-five when we reach Fort Laramie, another twenty-five when we reach South Pass. The balance when we arrive in Oregon City."

"Sounds"—she gulped back her surprise. Ten times that amount wouldn't be enough—"reasonable." She wasn't sure what else to say.

"Ye'll be responsible for yer own food," Cullen continued. "Mrs. Barrett invited ye to contribute to their supplies and take meals with them." He pulled a piece of paper from his vest pocket, pursed his lips, nodded, then shoved the note back into his pocket. "If these terms are suitable, a handshake will seal the deal."

Barrett squinted his dark brown eyes at her. "Never shook hands with a woman afore." He removed his hat and threaded the brim through his fingers. Sun-streaked brown hair fell across his forehead. Full eyebrows, wrinkles at the corners of his eyes, and a square jaw framed a rather nice looking face, except for the sour expression. "My boy will work for you, but if'n he needs discipline, you leave that to me."

Discipline a strapping young man a head taller? Not likely. "Yes, sir," she said, in a respectful tone.

He stuck out his frying-pan-sized hand with blunt-tipped fingers. His tender grip surprised her, and she couldn't reconcile his touch with his displeased expression.

"I'll be glad to pay you the entire amount in advance," she said.

His eyes flickered, and he seemed to consider the offer. "The deal we struck is twenty-five dollars today."

Cullen clapped Barrett on the shoulder. "Believe my work is done." He held Kit's gaze. "If ye need anything more, Adam can find me."

"I'm very grateful for your help." Looking into his face now, she noticed slight differences between him and her ghost. Maybe it was a trick of the afternoon sun. Maybe not. Cullen had a fuller face and a sexy twinkle in his eyes. Her ghost always had sad eyes, sunken cheeks, and appeared twenty-five pounds leaner.

He tipped his hat and ambled back toward town, whistling Bach again. This time, "Violin Concerto in A Minor." She knew classical composers and was curious if his repertoire, like hers, extended into the Renaissance and Baroque eras, too.

Tate pointed his nose to the sky and howled.

A smile flashed across Adam's face, a wrinkle-free version of his father's. "Guess your dog don't favor that kind of music."

Kit patted Tate's head. "He's partial to banjos and guitars."

A woman and two boys approached Barrett. They had remained a short distance away during the negotiations. "Mrs. MacKlenna, this here's my wife, Sarah, and my other boys, Ben and Clint."

The woman smiled, crinkling the corners of her light brown eyes. Where Barrett seemed off-putting, Mrs. Barrett seemed as sweet as a breath of spring air, radiating a similar calm spirit as Kit's mother. A knot formed in her throat, and she twirled the ring on her finger.

"If you've a mind to, come sit a spell. We'll talk."

"That'd be nice," Kit said.

Barrett gazed into his wife's eyes. "While you ladies are visiting, I'll borrow a buckboard to carry you to the mercantile." He checked the time on his pocket watch. "I'll be back in an hour." He trailed the curve of his index finger down the back of his wife's hand. The look in her eyes spoke to the love she had for him.

Kit glanced away and tried to swallow the knot growing to obstruction size in her throat. Her father always said a woman in love was like a blooming rose. She'd never bloomed, but then again, she'd never tried. Scars wrapped her heart inside a thorny thicket, and it would take someone with a machete to hack their way through.

Chapter Five

KIT AND SARAH returned to camp from their trip to the mercantile driving Kit's newly purchased buckboard. After loading the covered wagons with a few pieces of furniture, food, and supplies there'd be no room left for people, and she didn't want to walk to South Pass or put extra stress on Stormy riding him every day.

A little girl with soft brown curls and big brown eyes chased Tate around a stack of burlap bags. She laughed, the dog barked, and she laughed some more. Kit couldn't remember the last time she played with him.

"That's Elizabeth. She's ten." Sarah stood on tiptoes and stretched her neck, searching the adjoining campsites. She pointed toward a child walking in their direction. "There's Frances." A note of relief sounded in Sarah's voice. "She just turned eight."

Frances Barrett is a child?

Kit climbed to the ground and swayed again. Quickly, she grabbed the side of the wagon with one hand, then pressed the other against her queasy stomach. *I'm here because of an eight-year-old's journal.* The possibility existed now that Elliott had been right when he said, "I call it fabricated." But Kit had wanted to believe in Frances. And now? She honestly didn't know.

Sarah whispered to Kit. "I fainted with each of mine. Let me fix you some fennel tea to settle your stomach."

Each of mine. Kit gasped. "Oh, I'm not pregnant. I just haven't eaten much in the past few days."

"You need to eat. Let me—"

"Thank you, but there's no need."

Sarah pursed her lips.

"I'll eat in the hotel dining room tonight." Kit worked up a smile, but it didn't relieve the concern written on the woman's face.

Frances folded to the ground at Kit's feet like a marionette when the puppeteer sets the crossbar aside. Tabor jumped into her lap, and she giggled when he danced his long tail in her face. "Adam said you're traveling with us. Will you be my sister like Elizabeth?"

Kit sat beside her on the ground, curious about the child. "I could be a sister or a friend."

"Do you have brothers?"

"I'm an only child," Kit said.

Frances placed her warm, tiny fingers on Kit's hand. "Don't be sad. One day you'll have a baby and you won't be alone ever again."

What an odd thing for her to say. Not even a baby would fill the loneliness that swam just below the surface of Kit's life.

"If we're going to be sisters, will you help me read the books Adam reads?"

"I'd love to help you."

A smile touched her pretty, heart-shaped mouth. "Will you help Elizabeth, too?"

"We should ask Elizabeth what she wants."

"She wants the same as me. To be smart and go to university. Do you think girls can go to university?"

Intelligent and intuitive. "I suspect you have the tenacity to go wherever you want and knock down doors if they won't let you in."

A frown crossed Frances's face. "Then I'll need Papa's hammer."

As a little girl, Kit's father's toolbox, full of wooden handles worn smooth and shaped to his grip, fascinated her. Several of the old tools were stored in the wagon with her supplies. "In case he won't give up his, you can have mine. It was one of my father's."

A hint of mischief gleamed in Frances's eyes, and Kit realized at that moment, the child was capable of anything.

HOURS LATER, KIT entered the Noland House dining room wearing a green silk taffeta dress with a deep neckline and white lace under-sleeves. Tan ribbons edged the matching jacket. Her mother had created the gown for the previous year's Old Kentucky Farm Days Annual Gala. Kit and Scott had danced the quadrille under a canopy of stars until an emergency called him to the hospital. The next time they'd danced had been during the party on New Year's Eve. She shivered as thoughts of the crash and the drunk driver who killed her parents and her friend punched through her fragile protective wall, leaving her edgy and on the verge of a panic attack.

Wearing the dress tonight added to the eerie sensation that she was crawling across a bridge spanning two worlds. The quicker she got to the other end, to South Pass, the quicker she could go home and attempt to rebuild her life—an alien thought.

The maitre d'hôtel seated her in the busy dining room's front corner between a drafty window and a fire blazing up the chimney. She looked about. From her vantage point, she could see most of the diners in the room and the crowded sidewalk outside. He handed her a menu and lit the candle in the center of the table. After a quick glance at the bill of fare, she decided to pass on the pig head, buffalo tongue, boned chicken a-la-happy-family, and settled for roasted venison and a bottle of Mumm's Cabinet champagne.

With a glass of wine and dinner on the way, she opened her journal to jot down a few notes and rein in her distressed thoughts. Instead, she drew caricatures of the people she'd met.

An hour later with an empty plate, a full stomach, and another glass of wine, she returned to her drawing of Cullen, draping him in a Montgomery plaid.

"Did ye enjoy your supper?"

She jerked her head back, settling her gaze on a distinguished-looking man standing beside the table. Amusement played across his face. "Mr. Montgomery?" She blinked once then twice. Finding a measure of composure, she closed her journal, hiding the caricature that exaggerated his shoulder-length hair and scruffy beard. The drawing no longer seemed apropos since he'd obviously been to the barber. Not only was his hair shorter, but the sexy, three-day whiskers were gone as well as the flannel shirt and work trousers. A black, double-breasted frock coat and gray wool trousers hugged his body as if the tailor had stitched the garments on him.

How will he ever get them off?

Her eyes remained fixed on him, and she scrambled for words. After a beat or two of silence, she pointed to the empty chair on the other side of the table. "Would you care to join me for a glass of wine?"

He studied her for a moment. Had she committed a *faux pas?* When he gave her an approving smile, she relaxed a smidgeon.

"I'd be pleased." He eased his long, muscular frame into the chair and signaled the waiter. "Mrs. MacKlenna has offered to share a glass of wine."

The scent of bay rum wafted across the table and settled in her lungs. The smell would later wrap her in thoughts of the man and his doppelganger. "I didn't realize you were in the dining room."

He glanced across the room. "From where ye're sitting, ye would only have seen my back. I didna notice ye until I got up to leave."

The waiter set a glass on the table and poured. Cullen picked up the crystal stemware and leaned back in his chair, his expression thoughtful. He sipped, rolled the wine in his mouth, swallowed, and saluted her with the glass. "My compliments." The wine appeared golden in the candle's flickering flame. "The Barretts are fine folks. Ye'll get on well."

She folded her arms on the table and leaned forward. "I can't thank you enough for the introduction."

"I've known for some time they needed help. Yer coming to town was providential."

Another liar's blush spread warmth across her face, and she glanced away. When she turned back, she found him watching her intently. "I'll have to find a way to repay you."

He scrunched his brows in mock thought and lifted his glass.

"This is repayment."

A young waiter cleared their table. When he turned to leave, he accidentally bumped into a tall, redheaded army captain. Cullen jumped up in time to steady the waiter's tray. The soldier brushed his jacket as if he'd been shot at and wasn't sure whether or not he had been injured.

"Quick action, Montgomery."

"I'd hate to see yer uniform sullied by the remains of Mrs. MacKlenna's lemon pie." A smile ticked at the corner of Cullen's lip.

The soldier relaxed his rigid stance and said in a lighter tone, "It appears I survived unscathed."

Cullen stepped aside, and Kit saw the captain's sharp, angular face. Piercing dark eyes rested on her, sending an involuntary shiver to her fingers, causing her glass to shake and spilling wine onto the white tablecloth. The pieces of her father's chess set were Civil War officers, and she'd studied history while playing the game. The carved features on one of the wooden pieces matched the face of the man standing before her.

General William Tecumseh 'March to the Sea' Sherman.

"Mrs. MacKlenna, may I introduce Captain Sherman," Cullen said.

The captain bowed. "It's a pleasure to meet you, ma'am."

Her mouth turned dry, and all she could do was return a faint smile. She'd grown up going to galas and fundraisers and sitting on Millionaires' Row at the Kentucky Derby with movie stars and politicians. Famous people had never rendered her nervous or speechless—until now.

Sherman straightened. "If you'll excuse me, my dinner guests are waiting." He nodded to Kit, and then turned to Cullen and said, "I'll see you in San Francisco in a few months."

"I'll look forward to it. If ye need legal advice before I arrive, I hope ye'll call on Mr. Phillips. He'll introduce ye to our partner, Braham McCabe."

"I'll certainly do that." The men shook hands, and the captain left.

Cullen sat and pulled his chair to the table. "The captain resigned his commission and is moving to San Francisco to open a branch of a large St. Louis banking house. I hope to get his legal business."

Kit raised an eyebrow then spoke in a calm voice, not wanting her surprise to appear overly dramatic. "You're a lawyer?"

"I earned a degree in law from Harvard."

"But you said you were leading the wagon train with Mr. Peters."

Cullen leaned back in his chair and stroked his chin. After a moment, he answered. "I met John Barrett several weeks ago. He told me he'd joined up with a large extended family from Indiana. Issues developed among the group and the organizing member quit, leaving them without a leader. They had guidebooks but no one had enough confidence to govern a wagon train. I brought Henry and John's group together. Henry had one condition that nearly brought the negotiations to a standstill. He wanted me to sign on as guide. After a sidebar conversation that was actually more arm-twisting than discussion, I agreed."

She discerned nothing in his voice that indicated he regretted his decision, but still it seemed like interlocking pieces from two different puzzles. "Lawyer. Guide. I don't get it."

A laugh came from deep in his throat. "I've made this trip before. That's why I agreed."

Kit sank into a panic. A lawyer was going to lead her to South Pass. Not that being a lawyer and having a good sense of direction were mutually exclusive, but... "One trip? Don't you need more experience than that?"

"Road's well marked."

I'm relieved.

"Wagons will be ahead and behind us."

Help won't be far away.

"We willna get lost, if that's got ye worried."

Damn right, I'm worried.

The long, thin fingers she'd noticed earlier caressed his glass and swirled the wine in tiny circles. He stopped and studied the streaks rolling down the wine-coated sides. "Why are ye going to Oregon?"

She sat very still and stared into the fire. "I'm not…I mean, I didn't plan this until—"

Crash!

Along with the sounds of shattering crystal and silverware clanging against metal came the terrorizing memory of colliding cars. Shards of stemware scattered across the floor. A small piece flew up and scraped her cheek. She touched her face, then rubbed the scar on the right side of her neck. Numbing sensations rushed to her arms and face. Afraid she'd faint, she whispered, "Please, get me out of here."

Chapter Six

FROM THE CORNER of Cullen's eye, he spotted the waiter's unbalanced tray and watched as the young man fumbled with the teetering stemware. There would be no rescue for him a second time. Glasses and plates crashed to the floor and shattered into dozens of pieces. A few shards landed on their table, pinging against Mrs. MacKlenna's glass.

"Ah." A collective gasp erupted from the diners in the crowded room.

Cullen shook his head, feeling pity for the waiter who would lose his job. When he returned his gaze to the widow, he stiffened at the sight of fear-glazed eyes. He noticed a tiny scrape on her cheek, and he reached out to touch her.

"Please, get me out of here."

Her whisper stayed his hand. He stood, knocking his chair against the wall.

"I can't breathe." She grabbed the table's edge, stood, and then leaned her trembling body against him.

"We'll get some air." He took hold of her arm and threaded a path between the tables, escorting her toward the front of the hotel. The cooler air in the lobby seemed to revive her. The rise and fall of her breasts returned to their hypnotic rhythm, and a pink flush colored her face.

"Thank you. I'm not sure I could have walked out on my own." Her small hand with trimmed nails fiddled with her diamond-encrusted gold wedding band.

Was she reliving her husband's death? Regardless, she needed something to settle her. "Could I offer ye a glass of sherry?"

"No, thank you." Her tight voice held remnants of the fear he'd seen in her eyes. "I think I'll visit Stormy before it gets dark." She walked away from him with a slight wobble in her step.

He grabbed his hat from the rack before hurrying after her. "Allow me to escort ye. Ye're not steady on your feet." He shoved open the door, and as they crossed the threshold, he took her arm once again.

"You keep coming to my rescue." The evening air relaxed her face, allowing a semblance of a smile.

He settled the hat on his head. "Stormy must be the Thoroughbred, or else you've given a stowaway a new name."

"He's my mighty steed, oh lad o' Callander."

Cullen chuckled, delighting in her sense of humor and recall. "Yer steed must have belonged to yer husband. He's more horse than ye need. If ye're interested in selling him, I'd be happy to assist in finding a buyer."

"*I* raised Stormy," she said, puffing her small frame. "And if you'd like to race, I'm up for the challenge."

"My Morgan would give yer Thoroughbred a good run. But I wouldna want to be responsible for yer death if ye came off yer horse."

"Ha." She poked his arm with her finger. "It would probably be you coming off your horse, not me. And I wouldn't want to be responsible for your death either."

The imprint of her finger lasted in his mind much longer than on his arm. He studied the widow closely, puzzled by her forwardness and unconventional beauty. She appeared to be quite different from the lovely Abigail Phillips of San Francisco, who would never ride a spirited mount.

The racing challenge died on the balmy breeze blowing in from the river as they strolled down the rickety sidewalk in silence. By the time they reached the end, the western sky had turned lavender with approaching dusk.

"In Scotland they call the meeting of the day with the night—"

"The gloaming," Kit said. "Do you believe the time of two-lights is mystical?"

He lifted his eyebrow. "According to Scottish folklore, encounters between the visible and invisible worlds occur then."

"That must be why ghosts sometimes appear at twilight." Her eyes were as dark and full of mystery as they had been when he first met her.

"And dawn," he added. "That's the time of day I saw the lady riding her mighty steed—"

"Excuse me, Mr. Montgomery." Mr. Nieland, an older member of the wagon train, stepped to the sidewalk and motioned Cullen to join him at the railing.

"Give me a moment." He released Kit's arm and joined Nieland at the edge of the walk.

"I wanted to let you and Mr. Peters know that Mrs. Nieland and I decided this trip's too risky. We're going back home. We're much obliged for what you've done and wish you well." Mr. Nieland batted away tears in his eyes.

Cullen patted the man's shoulder. "Maybe next year." Traveling to Oregon stood as a risky proposition for the young and healthy. For older folks, age added additional burdens as they crossed the trail hemmed by disease and bad water. Cullen didn't want to pressure the man. Instead, he watched him walk away, noticing the downward slope of his shoulders. Nieland loved his wife more than he loved his dream.

Cullen shook his head and reclaimed Kit's arm. "My apologies."

"I hope you were able to help him. He looked defeated."

"Nieland was leaving with us in the morning, but he canna accept the risk." Cullen shot a quick glance over his shoulder at the man trudging down the sidewalk. "Ye might discover this is too great a risk for ye, too."

She put her thumbnail to her mouth and tapped the tip against her teeth. "I know the road won't be easy, but neither is waking up every day without my husband. I appreciate your concern. Really, I do. But you don't know how capable I am." She dropped her hand and lifted her chin. "I can take care of myself."

He doubted she could. The only evidence he'd seen were manicured nails, with the exception of her thumb, and a flawless complexion. Those spoke of elegance and privilege, not ability. If she made it as far as Fort Laramie, he'd be surprised. "For yer sake, I hope ye're as capable as ye claim to be."

Her green eyes narrowed. "I need to go, Mr. Montgomery. Good night."

"I'll walk ye—"

"That's not necessary." She hurried away, dodging freight wagons careening through the street.

"Mrs. MacKlenna." She either didn't hear him or chose to ignore him, most likely the latter. Did the widow not have a lick of sense? Couldn't she see the streets were dangerous and no place for a woman alone? He shuddered. If her behavior was indicative of how she'd act on the trail, he'd have his hands full keeping her safe from the elements and from herself.

The back of his neck prickled as it often did when the jury entered the courtroom to deliver his clients' verdicts, especially the clients he knew were lying. He began to whistle Bach's "Toccata and Fugue." The dark, eerie melody seemed appropriate for following the mule-headed female.

THE SUN HAD just crested the horizon when Kit crossed the hotel's threshold and stepped out onto the sidewalk, carpetbag in hand. Her head hurt and greasy eggs weren't sitting well in her stomach. Either her equilibrium was messed up from zapping backward a hundred-sixty-plus years or the half bottle of champagne she'd consumed had made her sick. Did her drinking partner feel as bad? Probably not. Almost twice her size, he could handle a full bottle of wine.

Cullen's questions had lulled her into his confidence. She couldn't allow that to happen again. She cringed at the thought of the ramifications if he discovered where she was from.

He had followed her to the Barretts' campsite and back to the hotel. His covert pursuit had irritated her, but on reflection, she knew concern had motivated him. In hindsight, she should have said something. But what? That she had a brown belt in karate and could beat the crap out of anyone who threatened her? That wouldn't be smart. She needed him, but didn't need him to hover. He was an intelligent man and could easily become suspicious.

"Mrs. MacKlenna." Adam took the hotel steps two at a time. He slid to a winded stop in front of her, his broad hat hanging about his ears. "Pa sent me to fetch you. He feared you might not find your way back. I didn't tell him you checked on your horse last night 'cause he'd be madder than a bobcat with his tail tied in a knot. You don't argue with Pa."

"Thanks for the warning, but I don't think we'll argue. Do you?"

"No, ma'am. Like I said, you don't argue with Pa." He smoothed down his unrepentant cowlick and then grabbed her carpetbag's handle. "I'll carry this for you. If I hadn't been late, we wouldn't have to rush. But once I start reading Mr. Montgomery's books, time goes by faster than potatoes at suppertime."

Her eyes gazed up and down the street, taking in the stevedores and soldiers from Fort Leavenworth and whooping riders galloping their ponies through the mud. "What were you reading?"

"*The Merchant of Venice* by William Shakespeare."

A dress shop window at the end of the sidewalk drew Kit's attention, and she only halfheartedly listened to Adam's response. The similarities between the shop and her father's drawing were unmistakable. How could she have missed the building the night before? She dropped Adam's arm and made her way through a group of cigar-smoking men arguing over the fastest, safest trail to Oregon. She felt tempted to tell them what they wanted to know, but kept walking. Life had to happen without her interference.

She reached the dress shop, placed her palms on the cool glass, and peered inside. Had her mother worked in this store? How far away would her father have been to see her inside the shop? She turned, searching for his vantage point. Independence Square was diagonally across the street with benches nestled among the trees. He could have watched from there. Her father wasn't sitting there now, but Cullen was. Hat tipped back, one leg crossed over the other, and a newspaper spread open in his lap. His eyes weren't on the paper. They were on her, gazing this way and that as if she were a painting on display.

Adam tugged on her arm. "Ma'am, we need to hurry."

"What? I'm sorry. What'd you say?"

"We need to hurry. Pa's waitin' on us." He hooked her elbow, and they headed toward the Barretts' camp, but her gaze remained fixed on Cullen. He was visible now only in profile as he talked with a man who had approached him. *Does he ever have a moment's peace?*

With her eyes still on Cullen, she said, "Tell me again what you were reading."

"*The Merchant of Venice* by William Shakespeare." Adam must have sensed a receptive audience of one. He proceeded to recite the part of Bassanio extolling Portia's virtues to Antonio. Kit pushed thoughts of Cullen and her parents to the back of her mind and gave the young thespian her attention, enjoying his enthusiasm.

By the time they reached camp, her stomach had settled, and her headache had subsided to only a mild throb. Then she saw John glaring at his pocket watch. She apologized for being late, and told him it wouldn't happen again. She followed Adam's lead and ducked out of the way.

Frances found Kit while she was grooming Stormy. The child stepped under the horse's nose.

"Be careful, Frances."

"I'm always careful. He's a big horse, isn't he? Can you ride him? Do you fall off? Are you 'fraid you'll get hurt? Do you—"

"Whoa, young lady. Give me a shot at the first question before moving on to the rest."

Frances crossed her arms and remained planted as if Stormy were only a statue. "Ma said your horse is dangerous. I'm supposed to stay away from him. You're not scared, and you're not much bigger than me."

Kit gave the child's bonnet strings a little tug. "But I'm a lot older."

"I'm eight. How old are you?"

No one needed to know Kit's age. By their standard she qualified as an old maid. What would Cullen think if he knew she was twenty-five? And why did his opinion matter? "Stormy is five. He'd just been born when I saw him the first time. Not much taller than you are now."

"Did he walk?"

"On shaky legs." Stormy's birth was a slippery issue, and she didn't want to talk about it. "I'll ask your mom and dad if you can ride with me sometime."

With the innocent face of an acolyte, Frances asked, "Do you mean my ma and pa?"

Kit snapped her fingers like a magician pulling surprises out of the air. "That's exactly what I meant." Pretending to be a nineteenth-century widow wasn't going to be easy with a precocious child posing questions faster than Tabor could skedaddle from a room. "I'm going for a ride this morning, but this afternoon we can read, if you'd like."

"Can Elizabeth read, too?"

"Sure." Kit hoped Frances's reading was better than her writing.

With a bubble of excitement, Frances ran off with Tabor pouncing on her heels. The cat needed more attention than Kit had given him. Maybe he would be over his depression by the time they returned home. Maybe she'd feel better, too.

She finished grooming Stormy, slipped on a pair of wool trousers under her dress so she could ride astride, and then helped Sarah prepare picnic baskets with the family's lunch. When all was ready, Elizabeth and Frances, along with Tate and Tabor, climbed in the back of the buckboard.

"We're ready, Ma," Elizabeth said.

Sarah glanced at Kit. "You ready?"

"I'm going to take Stormy and ride ahead. I'll meet you in a couple of hours." Sarah wore disapproval in the tight set of her jaw, but before she could voice it, Kit escaped again.

NOT FAR FROM town, Kit found a bluff overlooking the trail. A breeze rustled the underbrush along the switchback she followed to the top. A twig snapped. A tree fluttered its budding branches. A bird sang. Nature's quiet symphony.

Turn down the volume on the silence.

If that wasn't a song, it should be. At least it wasn't the eerie silence she'd heard the night Scott died in her arms. No other sound in all of creation compared to the last whisper of breath. A shiver rolled up the length of her body. She shifted in the saddle. If she fell into an emotional quagmire on her first full day living in 1852, she might as well quit and go home because she'd be of no use to anyone.

She stiffened her spine and focused on the scene unfolding below her.

The wagons' white bonnets shimmered in the morning sun, and the wind blowing across the long grass created an illusion of schooners sailing over the ocean. The view made her drawing fingers itch. She grabbed her pencils and journal from the saddlebag and within moments became lost in her work.

"If a man's dream could be painted, ye're looking at a masterpiece."

Adrenaline exploded in her body. The journal and pencils flew from her hands. She jerked around to find Cullen reining his horse alongside her. "Damn, you scared me."

His expression changed from surprise to smoky in a single heartbeat. "Ye shouldn't be up here by yerself." He dismounted, slow and easy. "It isna safe." He picked up the journal and pencils, and handed them over.

"I appreciate your concern, but—"

"—ye can take care of yerself."

"Exactly."

He withdrew a cheroot from his pocket and put a match to the cigar. "Out here we need each other. Where we're going, we'll need each other more."

A flock of honking geese, flying in V formation, pulled their gazes toward the sky.

Cullen puffed, and wisps of smoke formed a halo around his head. "There're lessons to learn from geese."

"What? Fly high enough not to get shot?"

The corner of his lip twitched. "That's one."

They remained silent for a moment or two before he said, "The flock works as a team. If a bird falls out of formation, he soon realizes he canna fly by himself and gets back in line. If one gets sick and drops from the flock, two others fly with him to the ground and wait until he gets better or dies."

She cocked her head, giving him a sideways glance. "Is that true?"

"The birds share a common goal, Mrs. MacKlenna, a common direction. And they'll get where they're going quicker than one bird could get there on its own."

"I sense you're not just talking about birds."

He returned her gaze. The look in his dark blue eyes grew intense.

Her heart beat faster than normal. The pencil in her shaking hand tapped lightly on the page. "What'd you say about dreams? If a man's dreams could be painted…"

"Ye're looking at a masterpiece."

She wrote the word *dream* then drew a faceless woman. "All those folks on the wagon train are filled with dreams, aren't they?"

"Just like ye and me."

"I wonder how many will give up on theirs."

He took a long, slow pull and blew out the smoke. "We've got close to a hundred strong-willed folks traveling with us. If they stay healthy, most will make it to Oregon. But some of their dreams will be shattered along the way." He rolled the cigar between his fingers. "Dinna let one of them be yers."

THE VAST EXPANSE of the landscape stretched out before Kit in rolling swells. A carpet of bluestem grass peeked through the prairie thatch. The occasional turkey buzzard gliding through the air broke up the repetitiveness of the plains. From the eye of an artist, beauty abounded.

The wagon train's destination for the day, the Blue River, lay only twelve miles from their starting point. They had to do better than that if she was going to reach South Pass in time.

When they stopped for the nooning, she unsaddled Stormy to let him graze. She had promised Frances they would read, and she didn't want to disappoint her.

As Kit and Sarah repacked the buckboard with kids and lunch supplies, Kit watched a little boy jump from his family's wagon. "That's so dangerous." Out on the trail, mistakes and stupidity killed people. "Have there been any accidents you know of?"

"Every day fingers or toes go missing," Sarah said. "Folks are careless. John's on the boys all the time to pay attention, but they're children. Tend to get distracted. Why?"

"Guess I've seen too much bad stuff."

Sarah let out a hefty sigh. "The girls are my biggest worry. They're still innocent. Don't know about death and dying. I've tried talking to them, but—"

"Hold on a minute. I have an idea. I'll be right back."

"Don't go riding off now. It's time to leave," Sarah said.

Kit rushed back to her wagon and rearranged boxes until she found her guitar. A few minutes later, she put the case in the buckboard.

Frances's eyes lit with anticipation. "Can *you* play the guitar?"

"I thought we might sing this afternoon," Kit said. "Would you like that?"

Frances rubbed her small hands along the black guitar case. "Yes, ma'am. What songs do you know?"

Kit did a quick rat-a-tat-tat on the case with her fingers. With a final tap on an imaginary ride cymbal, she said, "I thought we might write our own."

Chapter Seven

T HE SUN SAT low in the western sky by the time Sarah pulled the buckboard into camp with the wide-eyed *von Barrett* children singing the song they wrote to the tune of "Yankee Doodle."

Little boys and little girls from wagons never jump.
   We turn around and climb to ground to safety on our rump.
Caution always on our mind so carefully we leap,
   and stay away from rocks and caves where creatures go to sleep.
We wash our hands and eat our food that we prepare and cook,
   and stay in sight of Ma and Pa for us they never have to look.
We pick up twigs out in the sun and never fire a big bad gun,
   and stay on watch all through the day until the evening's done.
When dark announces time for bed, we gladly go along,
   for rest is what we need tonight to get to Oregon.

Kit couldn't help but feel that beneath each line a disaster waited to happen. Could she keep the Barretts from becoming victims? Could she even keep herself safe?

After unloading Sarah and the children at their campsite, Kit drove the buckboard to hers to unhitch the team. The men had already pulled the wagons into a circle and fastened them together with ox chains, creating a corral to protect the animals. Tents and campfires would ring the corral.

"I'll take care of Stormy and the mules," Adam said.

She handed over the reins. "Then I'll go wash up and help your ma."

"I reckon she's got the biscuits cooking, but let her know her boy's got tapeworms hollerin' for fodder."

That was a new one. She had started a list of his colloquialisms, but didn't think a thousand miles would give her enough time to figure them all out. He was right, though. By the time she washed up and returned to the Barretts, the dining tent was up and the biscuits were in the cookstove.

"What can I do?"

"Mix up another batch," Sarah said. "We've got a hungry crowd tonight."

Frances slouched over to her ma. "What can *I* do?"

"Why don't you help your pa pull the chairs to the table?"

The child turned a slow circle, frowning. "I can't find him."

John walked up behind her carrying a long bench. He sat it down and placed a hand on her shoulder. "There's my helper. Are you going to stand still to Sunday or help your old pa?"

"You're not old. Not like Mr. Peters."

John's face crinkled. "Mr. Peters wouldn't appreciate hearing you say that about him."

"He says he's old, Pa. Why can't I?"

John rubbed his nose to cover a smile. "It's not polite. Now take hold of one end of this bench and help me out."

"Where's Mrs. MacKlenna gonna sit?"

"She can sit on the bench between you and Elizabeth."

"That's Mr. Montgomery's place if'n he's taking supper with us."

John patted his daughter's head. "Believe we have room enough."

Sarah carried a pot over to the table. "Call the boys. Food's ready."

John struck the large steel triangle with a mallet, and its clang peeled out over the campsite. Three freshly washed boys and Cullen appeared as if they'd been hanging out in the wings waiting for a curtain call. The lawyer look was gone. The scruffy look was back. Kit didn't mind the scruffy look at all.

"Sit here, Mrs. MacKlenna, Mr. Montgomery." Frances scooted to make room.

"No wine tonight?" Cullen asked.

His whisper came so close she felt the warmth of his words on her neck. He smelled of sun and summer heat and freshly washed cotton. Although the thought of drinking made her sick at her stomach, the thought of drinking with him—

"Bless the food, John. The boys are hungry," Sarah said.

Before he said amen, pots and pans flew across the table along with seven different conversations. Kit watched with wide-eyed fascination. Cullen chewed his food slowly, his eyes hazy with thoughts or perhaps the pleasure the food gave him, or like her, he was simply following multiple willy-nilly conversations. He didn't have enough room for his long legs and kept bumping his thigh against hers.

When had her leg become an erogenous zone?

Adam's eyes strayed toward something behind her. She glanced over her shoulder and saw two young girls strolling past, heading toward the river. Adam's lips curled into a puppy-love grin. "May I be excused, Pa?"

John pushed back from the table. "You can all be excused, but don't forget your chores."

Kit watched Adam run off with his brothers, completely ignoring the girls. It tickled her, thinking back to her own adolescence. She turned to the older Barretts. "You have a precious family. You must be proud of them."

John packed his pipe with tobacco. "We're mighty proud, aren't we, Ma?"

"I think Adam's got a bit of spring on his mind," Cullen said, putting a match to his cigar.

John lit his pipe. "I noticed that a few days ago. Believe the girl's a Baue. Her pa's got no sit in his ass."

Kit lifted her hands in a gesture of confusion.

"Baue canna sit still," Cullen interpreted. "He's always up doing one thing or another, making a racket when folks are trying to sleep."

"If Adam's interested in courting their girl we should be making a call soon." John slipped his pipe between his teeth and closed down on the stem with a click.

"She's a pretty girl," Sarah said.

"It'll take more than a pretty face to keep that boy's interest. He's got plans," John said.

Sarah turned to Kit, giving her a worried sigh. "Mr. Montgomery's been talking to him about going to a university, but I don't know where the money would come from."

"Money will work out." John pointed his pipe toward Kit. "The boy did fine work today. If you have problems, go to Adam directly. If he don't do what you ask, you come to me."

"He's a fine young man. I can't imagine having—"

"*Pa.*" Elizabeth ran toward her father with arms flapping like a baby bird unable to fly. Tate trotted at her heels.

"*Pa.*" Frances mimicked her sister's scream, but instead of waving her arms she half carried a dangling cat. Tabor's paws pushed against her tummy, trying to either hold on or make a quick escape.

Alarm spread across John's face. "What's got you two so riled up?"

"*Indians.*"

He pulled the girls into his arms. "Nothing a'tall to be scared of. Indians around these parts are friendly."

Elizabeth wrapped an arm around her pa's neck. "Are you sure?"

"Yep."

"Have you seen Indians before, Mrs. MacKlenna?" Frances asked, nestled against her father.

Kit caught Tabor's bottom half just as the cat slipped from the child's hold. "I've seen Indians, but to be correct, we should call them by either their tribal name or Native Americans."

John tapped his teeth with his pipe. "That's an odd name to be calling 'em."

Kit gulped. "That's…ah…that's what my father used to say."

"No matter what you call 'em, they're still Indians, and I hope none of 'em tries to steal that stallion of yours."

"He's a magnificent horse. Take a special mare to be bred to the likes of him." Cullen brushed her thigh again as he stretched his legs.

She didn't think it was intentional, but it was disconcerting, and her leg tingled. When Sarah stood and gathered up a handful of dishes, Kit snagged two pots and ran from Cullen's errant leg, but she couldn't run from what his touch did to her insides.

AN HOUR LATER, with the dishes scraped and scoured, and the beans put on to soak for the next day's meal, Kit took a moment to stir some thoughts. What an exhausting day, the first of seventy-three. Could she—

"Folks will be dancing tonight at the Camerons'," Sarah said.

"I'm sorry. What'd you say?"

Sarah poured out the dirty dishwater. "Dancing at the Camerons'."

Dancing? Even if she had the energy, she didn't have a partner. "What time?" Kit asked, trying to show some enthusiasm.

"Young folks will gather soon as the old ones start yawning."

"Don't think I'm up for dancing, but I'd enjoy listening to the music."

Sarah dried her hands on her apron and gave Kit a sympathetic look. "You can mourn that man you lost, but you can't quit living. Music fills up inside of you and spills out all cool and bubbly. Makes folks feel good. Saw that today. Saw joy on the girls' faces. Saw joy on yours."

"Well…"

"You get yourself up there to the Camerons'. One of those young men will ask you to dance, and you say yes. And don't give a thought to what your husband would say. He's gone now, and you need to get on with your life."

"Are you going, or are you sending me off by myself?"

"John and I'll be there soon enough. You run along. You'll be welcome as family. Now, git."

Kit wiped her hands down her skirt to smooth away the wrinkles. "Speaking of family, I hope Tate and Tabor won't be a bother. They seem to have attached themselves to the children."

Sarah's laugh rolled into the small fine lines around her mouth. "I don't see you sitting still and petting animals for hours on end. Those girls have begged their Pa for two years to get a cat or a dog. He's never been inclined. Those critters are good for them. Teach them to care for something other than themselves."

"Tate and Tabor are very demanding. The girls might decide they don't want the responsibility."

"I don't think that will happen. Now stop dillydallying. Maybe Mr. Montgomery will ask you to dance. He's the favored partner, even though all the young girls know he's thinking of marrying a woman named Abigail when he reaches San Francisco."

Marriage? Abigail? That didn't fit him any better than wagon train guide. The news stung for a moment, but why should it matter to her? In a few weeks, she'd be on her way home. She had no time for complications, and no time for a Highlander.

Chapter Eight

A S KIT WALKED toward the Camerons' wagon, a cannon-sounding rumble rattled the sky, and her feet literally left the ground. Was she tense or what? She hurried toward the music, passing a screen of willows. Her breath hitched at the sight of a man's silhouette lingering between the trees and the river. When she reached the other side of the willows, he was gone. She glanced back to be sure she wasn't followed.

Yes, she was tense. No doubt about it. Why would anyone follow her? No reason she could think of. It wasn't like she was out walking in a dark and dangerous part of town. She tied her shawl around her shoulders and walked faster. She wanted to stop by her wagon first and change from boots to moccasins. Not that she intended to dance, but just in case.

If she had made a list of rules to follow, no fraternization would be number one. The Barretts were an exception, but they were the *only* exception. She screwed up last night when she invited Cullen to share a glass of wine, but she was curious about the man who resembled her ghost.

Another rumble, another shudder.

Close behind her, a growling voice demanded, "What are ye doing?"

A double shot of adrenaline surged through her. She responded to the threat defensively with a donkey kick to the man's chest. She turned and prepared for a palm-heel strike to the nose, but her hand froze inches from his face. "*Cullen Montgomery.*" She inhaled deeply to control her breathing. "That's twice today you've snuck up on me."

He groaned as if he'd been mortally wounded. "Why'd ye kick me?"

"You scared me."

"Why didna ye scream?"

"If you intended to hurt me, a scream wouldn't stop you."

He poked at his chest. "I think ye broke my ribs."

"Your chest is like a brick wall, and I didn't kick you *that* hard."

"I've seen Japanese warriors do that move."

"It's called karate."

He looped his thumbs through his suspenders. "Mrs. MacKlenna, I find ye perplexing."

Was he hitting on her? Surely not. "Will you please call me Kit? Or is that improper?"

He laughed. "I dinna believe ye've ever been governed by propriety."

She feigned a gasp. "Why would you think that? Because you've seen me drink, curse, and walk off unescorted? I'll have you know I'm fully cognizant of socially appropriate behavior."

"Maybe ye are, but from now on, walk closer to the wagons."

"Guards are posted."

"It still isn't safe."

"I'll bring Tate or Tabor next time. They've been known to bite and scratch."

He shook his head. "Ye've lost yer animals to the Barrett girls."

Kit laughed and it shocked her. How long had it been since she'd had anything to laugh about? Weeks? And now twice in one day. "I don't think even Stormy is safe. It wouldn't surprise me to find Frances sneaking him out for a ride."

When she was Frances's age, she'd mounted a horse in the pasture for a leisurely ride. Normally, that wouldn't have been a problem, but the horse she rode was a multimillion-dollar Derby winner. Her punishment was no riding for two months, which for an eight-year-old lasted *forever*. She never knew if her father's consternation arose from his concern about her safety or the horse's. The remembrance was bittersweet.

Neither Kit nor Cullen said anything for a few moments while her laughter faded into the soft breeze blowing through the leaves.

The sound of a fiddler playing "My Dark Hair'd Girl" broke through the silence. "I told Sarah I'd meet her at the Camerons'. I need to hurry or she'll worry."

"I'm going there, too. I'll walk with ye."

She wanted to say no, but what harm would there be in a short walk? It would give her a chance to tell him what she didn't tell him the night before. "You followed me after dinner last night. I didn't say anything, but you needn't watch over me. I—"

"Can take care of yerself."

"Yes."

"When ye prove ye can, I'll stop watching." He hooked her elbow, turned her toward the Camerons', and began to whistle.

"Violin Concerto in D Minor," she said.

His eyebrows shot up. "Put yer lips to work and join me."

She caught a glimpse of his dimples. His remark was a double entendre. He *was* hitting on her. *Watch out. He's probably a nineteenth-century version of a player.*

They arrived at the Camerons', where a crowd had already gathered. Firelight from pine resin torches unfurled and flickered, bathing the dark corners of the prairie's dance floor in warm rose-gold shadows. One quadrille set was dancing to the music of a fiddle and flute. Three other couples stood by clapping, waiting for a fourth couple to join them to make another set.

"There's Mr. Montgomery," someone yelled. "He'll be our fourth."

Cullen turned to Kit. "Do ye know the quadrille?"

"Yes, but—"

"May I have this dance?" He whisked her onto the dance floor, ignoring her protests.

They formed a square with the other three couples.

The caller announced the steps, and they crossed over and started back to their original places. She missed a step, and he smiled. They returned to their starting position, facing each other. She gazed into his eyes, soft and warm.

"Swing your partners, swing them around, swing them clear up off the ground."

Cullen did as prompted, and she laughed, feeling her skirt swish through the air. The fragrance of wild flowers wafted through the air and the spongy buffalo grass cushioned her steps.

"Gents to the center, then back to your wall," the caller yelled.

She'd never danced with a man over six feet tall. He had a light step and natural rhythm, and his warm hand on her back held steady and firm.

"Do-si-do and on you go. Promenade home."

The figure repeated four times before the caller called, "All *chassez.*"

Sweat dripped from her forehead, but she couldn't stop dancing long enough to wipe it away. When she glanced at Cullen, a warm sensation passed through her. She was hot—inside and out.

They faced each other again then crossed over four times. He passed to her outside and back, and they finished with a bow and curtsy. He led her off the dance floor into the shadows of the sputtering light. "Ye have music in yer soul."

She panted, pulling more air into her lungs. "Music is my life." His hand was gone now, but the heat of his touch lingered on her back.

"Bach must be the favorite part of it." He pulled a handkerchief from his vest pocket and wiped his forehead.

"I do love Bach, but my taste in music is very eclectic."

A young man wearing a sheepish grin approached Cullen. "My sister"—he pointed his thumb over his shoulder—"she's standing back there, would like you to join our set."

Kit wrapped a loose strand of hair around her finger, an annoying habit she thought she'd outgrown as a teenager.

Cullen glanced at a giggling, pug-nosed girl. "Will ye excuse me?" he said to Kit. "I need to do this." He wore a pinched expression of one who'd eaten a sourball. When he offered his arm to his new partner, Kit's insides tightened, but she stayed rooted where he'd left her at the edge of the dance floor, watching. When he swirled the giggling girl, Kit wiped the feel of his warm, lingering touch from her back. But she was unable to erase the touch from her memory.

Stay away from him. He is a player—predictable and dangerous.

Chapter Nine

A HORN BLASTED, pulling Kit from the fog of sleep. Where was she? Heavy weights pressed against her, making movement impossible. Her scratchy eyes refused to open, but her nose was fully alert to the smell of frying bacon and burnt coffee. Slowly, her wayward cognition returned, but too late to give her more than half a second to cover her ears with her pillow before the second blast of Henry's horn invaded camp with a sound as terrifying as a screeching herd of horses. Three times every morning he blew the damn horn. He was either deaf or a sadist. The only way to stop the racket was to either shoot Henry or steal the bugle. Both options were under consideration.

Tate stood and stretched, and then without bothering to bark good morning, jumped out of the wagon. Tabor stuck around for hugs. She pulled him to her and buried her face in his fur. "At least one of you still appreciates me."

During the three days they'd been on the trail, the animals stayed with the children most of the time, but during the night, they always found Kit's bed. She wanted to believe they came to protect her, but she knew her bed was probably the most comfortable place they'd found to sleep.

She rubbed Tabor's neck. "Let's get up. Sarah's waiting." The cat just stared at her, purring, and she hugged him again. She was sleeping well, something she hadn't done since the crash, and she resented waking up, especially to Henry's noise pollution.

She grabbed a Theraworx premoistened cloth from her trunk and began her first of two full-body baths of the day. The lack of sanitation and bathing topped the long list of concerns she had about traveling to the past, and the cloths were the next best thing to a hot shower. Actually, she realized, a hot shower had no *next best thing*.

Outside her wagon, camp quickly filled with the sounds of clanking pans, whispers, and footfalls of the men and boys heading off to the woods for their morning constitutions. Well, at least she and Sarah had solved their sanitation concerns by insisting the men erect a latrine tent for the women. During the day, nature's call occurred *al fresco* behind billowing skirts, but at least at night and in the early morning they had privacy.

She finished bathing, dressed, and climbed down from the wagon. The sun was barely up, throwing long shadows on the ground. She headed in the direction of the Barretts' wagon located on the other side of the circle. Sarah would already be at the cookstove frying bacon.

When she reached the Barrett campfire, Sarah was dropping more bacon onto the skillet. Sizzling fat popped and splattered. "What can I do?" Kit asked.

"We need more biscuits."

The Barretts ate more carbs than any family Kit had ever met.

Sarah poured two cups of coffee and handed one to Kit. "How'd you sleep?"

Kit covered a yawn. "Well enough, I guess."

Sarah glanced over the rim of her cup. "A wagon's heading this way. Henry and John are walking out to meet the driver."

Kit watched as a crowd gathered around the wagon.

Sarah pulled the skillet off the burner. "Let's go see what's happening."

"…it's spilled over the bank," the man was saying when the ladies walked up.

"Did you see it?" Henry asked.

The man shook his head. "A rider just rode up to our camp. He seen the river. Says it's bad. I didn't sign up to kill my family. We're going home. Good luck to you." The man snapped his whip over the heads of his team and the wagon rolled away.

"Go-backer—giving up at the first sign of trouble," John said.

Henry scratched his chin. "Cullen left a couple hours ago to check out the river. He'll be back this evening to tell us what he's seen. Just 'cause we're starved for news don't mean we have to believe stories told third and fourth hand."

"John and I've talked about those river crossings,' Sarah said to Kit. "They scare me, but I don't want him to know. It'll taint his decision if one needs making. He needs to do what's best for the family without worrying about my silly fears."

To Kit, Sarah's fears weren't the least bit silly. People died crossing rivers.

John put his arm around his wife's shoulders. "Henry said he'll call a meeting tonight when Cullen gets back. We'll talk about what we know, not some scuttlebutt spread by a go-backer. Come on now. Day's wasting. Let's eat breakfast and get on the road."

Kit saw a nervous tic around Sarah's mouth and knew the up-coming meeting wouldn't mollify her fear.

HENRY CALLED AN after-supper meeting. The rumors about the swollen river had floated around the wagon train all day. When Kit and Sarah arrived at the Camerons', the fire-lit torches illuminated dozens of tense-jawed faces. Calming this crew would take some powerful rhetoric.

Henry didn't blow his bugle to get folks' attention. He fired his pistol, which didn't bother Tate curled at Kit's feet, but scared Tabor right out of her arms. She knew the cat would find Frances, who would comb and quiet his standing-on-end fur.

Henry removed his hat, holding the brim with both hands, and looking like a preacher presiding over a funeral. "You folks know we'll reach the Kansas tomorrow." His slow and laborious voice, however, sounded like a preacher. "You heard that go-backer this morning. Well, don't let him scare you. Cullen went to the river and talked to folks firsthand. He's here now to tell it to you straight."

Cullen stepped forward, planted his feet, and put his hands on his hips. "Crossing willna be easy. Spring rains have swollen the river and water's pouring over the bank. The current's stronger than usual. That makes it dangerous." He paused, but Kit sensed it wasn't for effect. His deep, controlled breathing, along with an intense look in his eyes, told her he was softening up his listeners, but not in a manipulative way.

"What ye havena heard is that Pappan's Ferry broke down this morning." There was a collective gasp. He gave the crowd a moment before holding up his hand to demand attention. "If the ferry's not operating by the time we arrive, we'll have to float the wagons."

A heavyset man standing a few feet from Cullen shouted, "You know what that means? Some of us will get drowned for sure—or lose our wagons." His tone raised a black cloud of uneasiness, and murmuring among the crowd increased.

"Folks have been crossing the Kansas for years." Cullen grew quiet and looked around the circle of men, making eye contact with each one. "If we stay determined and work together, we'll get across this water, across the mountains, and we'll make it to the Willamette Valley."

His words instilled a heightened sense of urgency. In the dim torchlight, Kit wondered if she was willing to risk her life and her animals. But wasn't that what she'd already agreed to do? The entire trip was a risk, not just this river crossing.

"We can lay over a few days," Cullen continued, "wait for the water level to drop or the ferry to get up and running, or we can float the wagons. Keep in mind, every day we delay is one day later we get to the mountains. If we run into snow, the weather could kill us like the Donner party."

The river crossing debate went on and tempers flared. Cullen listened to arguments and concerns until finally he said, "When the time comes, ye men will make the right decisions for yer families. I canna decide for ye. I can advise ye, but the decisions are yers alone."

The crowd disbursed, and Cullen and Henry joined the Barretts and Kit for coffee. John passed a plate of chewy molasses cookies. "What do you think we should do, Cullen?"

He chewed a cookie, rested his elbows on his knees, and leaned forward. "If the ferry's not running, I think we should float across."

John squeezed Sarah's hand. His face held no smile. "We'll do what you decide is best."

Later, as the Barrett family sought their beds, Cullen asked Kit if he could walk her to her wagon.

"That's not necessary. I promise not to wander far." She glanced up into the night sky where thready clouds darted across the full moon's face. "Meet me by moonlight—"

"Alone, and then I will tell ye a tale." He sang the ballad's first line with a lusty tenor voice that made her tingle.

"Your taste in music is as varied as mine." She nodded toward her wagon. "Come on."

He fell in step beside her. "No dancing tonight? Yer suitors will sorely miss ye."

She gave him a teasing one-knuckle punch in the arm. "Haven't you noticed? I'm Ben and Clint's shill. They dance with me so they can ogle the other girls." She laughed, thinking of their sweaty palms. Then she remembered dancing with Cullen and the warmth of his hand pressed against her back. She breathed deeply, hoping fresh air would cool the heat building inside her. She retreated to safer thoughts—teenage boys and sweaty palms. "Soon enough they'll get up the courage to ask their secret sweethearts to dance, and I'll be left without a partner."

He removed his dusty black fedora, swept his fingers through his hair, then put his hat back on. "Several wagon trains are already camped at the river. I'm sure we can find ye a dance partner, one without sweaty palms."

Was he reading her mind or recalling his own teenage years? Cullen as a gangly young man with raging hormones wasn't easy to imagine. She searched his face. Something weighed heavy on his mind, and she'd bet a pouch of coins it had nothing to do with dancing. "The crossing will be difficult, won't it?"

Beneath his black hat sitting low on his forehead, shadows covered his face. "I watched several wagons float across. Men stood at the shore, scratching their arms, hoping to scrape away their fear. Men on this train can take hard work, but the thought of putting their families in danger will cause them to question how much risk they're willing to take."

He tilted his head. With his face no longer shadowed, the stern set of his jaw told her what she needed to know. He was afraid, but not for himself.

"How much risk are ye willing to take?" he asked.

"I'll do whatever it takes to get to Oregon." She said Oregon without stumbling over the word, but felt guilty for lying. "If I have to dismantle my wagon and float it across, I will."

"It's dangerous—"

She held up a hand, interrupting him. "I appreciate your concern. If I need your help, I'll ask."

Several moments of silence hung between them.

"Well, good night, then." Cullen tipped his hat and walked away maybe ten paces then turned back to face her. "I'd like to dance with ye one last time when we reach Oregon City. I canna do that if something happens to ye. Be careful out there."

She gave him a wistful smile. "You've got a date."

He walked off into the night, whistling.

Tabor rubbed against her leg. She picked him up, and he nuzzled her with his wet nose.

"We're not going to Oregon City, Tabor. And I've already had a last dance."

Chapter Ten

THE WAGON TRAIN reached the Kansas River crossing in the late afternoon as the sun melted on the horizon. Kit stood beside John near the river's edge. Her churning stomach mirrored the swirls and eddies in the muddy water that spilled over the bank. *Is this an acceptable risk?* Her resolve seemed to fade as fast as the daylight.

"Cullen's lost his ever-loving mind if he thinks we can cross this river in a wagon," Kit said.

Tension puckered John's face. "We're not. We're crossing in a boat."

She pointed a shaky finger toward the long line of prairie schooners moving into circle formation. "Those are wagons, not boats. Removing running gear and caulking seams aren't going to turn pigs' ears into silk purses."

His eyes darted up and down the bank. "Now's not the time for doubts."

"Doubts are spreading faster than a California wildfire. Cullen's a lawyer, for Pete's sake. What does he know?"

"More than you. More than me. We already agreed on what to do." John shifted nervously, kicking at the stiff-bristled brush growing alongside the river. "Here comes Sarah. Don't go worrying her with your doubts."

"Worry her, or worry you?" Kit's words bounced off his thick chest and landed with a thud at her feet.

The wind skidded across the water's surface, whipped against her skirt, and entangled her legs in yards of useless cotton. She always paid attention to signs and omens. Something made the back of her neck itch, and it wasn't the scratchy fabric.

KIT PEERED OUT the back of the wagon to watch the morning's sun rise in a swirl of pink and yellow. Her first thought was not to shoot Henry for polluting the air with the god-awful sound he produced with his bugle. While she no longer worried she'd turn into a murderess, she did worry about the lies that poured out of her mouth like sour milk.

The temperature hovered in the low sixties, comfortable enough for early April if she wore a fleece jacket and gloves, but she hadn't packed either one. So she piled on layers of clothes and looked and waddled like the Michelin Man's wife.

Suddenly, knee-slapping, hoot-'n-hollering tore through camp. "What the hell…" She followed the noise, stopping at the Barretts' camp where she found Sarah putting on a pot of coffee. "What's going on?" Kit asked.

Sarah put more fuel on the fire. "Maybe God parted the sea during the night."

Kit refrained from rolling her eyes. "Where's John? He'll know what's happening."

"He went looking for Cul—"

"*Sarah. Sarah.*" John ran an obstacle course filled with tents and animals and children, waving his wide-brimmed hat high above his head. When he reached his wife's side, he scooped her into his arms. "Pappan's Ferry is back in business."

With more enthusiasm than Sarah usually exhibited, she clapped him on the back as if he were solely responsible for the ferry's repair. "The Good Lord answered our prayers, John."

He kissed her, and she kissed him right back.

The heat of embarrassment spread across Kit's face. She ducked behind the wagon, wrapped her arms around herself, and sniffed back a tear or two. Were her hot cheeks pink embarrassment or green envy? Neither. She'd watched her parents' public displays of affection her entire life without reacting, and she'd never admit to envy. Instead, she settled on relief that a crisis had been averted.

With a quick swipe, she dried her tears and glanced around camp. Her gaze went immediately to the one person who always appeared heads above everyone else in any gathering, large or small.

Cullen stood so close to the water that it lapped his boots. One hand bracketed his hip; the other rubbed the back of his neck. He appeared to be deep in thought. She watched him with a hunger she wanted to ignore, but it gnawed at her, biting off small chunks of her protective coating.

Within a minute or two, he must have come to terms with whatever was troubling him. He stepped back, brought both arms to his chest, then pulled his arm back, and threw a fist-sized rock. The stone sailed through the air at major league speed and hit a piece of driftwood floating in the river. The accuracy astounded Kit. She expected some sort of nineteenth-century equivalent to an end-zone dance or chest bump, but he didn't celebrate. He did, however, stare in her direction. Her face flushed again, but she didn't drop her gaze.

The resemblance to her ghost was uncanny. She half expected him to reach out his hand to her. He didn't, but he did check the time on his pocket watch. Before he returned the timepiece to his pocket, he rubbed the case cover with his thumb in the exacting manner she'd witnessed dozens of times.

She felt like a player in one of Shakespeare's play and hoped to hell it wasn't a tragedy.

WITH A FEW HOURS to herself while she waited her turn to cross over on the ferry, Kit sat by the water with her journal. The memory of Cullen throwing the rock continued to play in her mind. He moved with the grace of a dancer and the power of an athlete. Keeping her eyes off him, her mind clear of him, and her fantasies free of him were damn near impossible.

Tate trotted over and laid his head on her lap, ears relaxed. She rubbed his neck. "Well, look who's here. So you want to spend time with me now, huh? Where's Elizabeth?" He lifted his head and looked back toward the wagon. "Surely you're not hiding from her. Has she worn you out?" He nudged Kit's hand with his muzzle, dog speak for, *rub me again*. And she did. "I need both hands to draw. If you want to sit with me, be still."

He rolled over and went to sleep.

"Bless your dirty paws, Tate."

During her teen years, her dad had nurtured her passion for painting. He had been a dynamic artist who painted abstract shapes with vivid shades of red, green, and yellow, while she preferred muted colors and comforting landscapes. He had encouraged her to be more expressive and passionate.

"Close your eyes, stretch, capture the world through other senses," he had said. "Paint what you taste and smell and hear, not only what you see."

"You paint your way. I'll paint mine," she had told him. But she could no longer paint her way, nor could she paint landscapes in muted color tones. Not anymore. Not since the crash.

Her eyes closed, and she chewed on the end of her pencil. *Stretch and capture the world through sight and sound and smell.*

She opened her eyes and watched the activity on the river. On the opposite bank, an army officer and his command waited for their turn to cross. On her side, the south side, prospectors and pioneers heading west lined up their rigs and waited. What was she not seeing?

She closed her eyes again. The faces of the men flashed one by one in her mind. John, the boys, Henry, Cullen. They all held the same subtle fear. While tension reflected across their taut faces, the fear they tried to hide from themselves and each other clouded their eyes.

She looked down at her journal. In the top corner of the page, she drew an eyeball. Then she concentrated on blocking out the hype and hooey and catch-me-if-you-can laughter. Underneath the discordant surface sounds, she discovered the fragile, melodious song of a wren.

Kit sketched a bird next to the eyeball then focused on the overpowering smells in the air—coffee cooking in fire-blackened pots and bacon frying in cast iron skillets. She sniffed again for the elusive smell she knew had to be there. Breathing deeply through her nose, she caught a whiff, a faint whiff of sweet-scented verbena.

The sights, the sounds, the smells all simmered together in her mind, and then as if her graphite drawing pencil had a mind of its own, it slid across the textured paper, pulling timbre and melodic details from her imagination. Her hand glided with the fluidity of a symphony conductor's baton.

After an hour of drawing and blending and sculpting shapes out of light and shadow, she set the pencils and erasers aside. Tears streamed down her face as she gaped at the finished drawing. Although the sketch included only shades of gray, there was a level of realism and depth she had never mastered.

From one side of the page to the other a rope bridge dangled inches above a river flaunting white-capped waves. One half of the bridge bore frayed ropes and rotten planks. The other half had a solid wood floor and triple-knotted ropes.

In the top corner, she had reworked the nondescript bird she had originally drawn into a house wren perching on the side of a nest built into a broken limb's crotch suspended precariously above the river.

Dying verbena covered the ground and merged into river waves. On the far bank, the verbena rose from a calm body of water and crept in full bloom up the slope.

At the bottom of the page, she'd drawn a man with a two-sided face. Horror blazed in the shadowed eye on one side, and warmth in the other. Captured in the center of both eyes were reflections of herself that she hadn't consciously drawn. Blood drained from her face, stealing the energy that had fueled her imagination.

"Mrs. MacKlenna, are ye ill?"

The sound of Cullen's voice yanked her with the force of bungee cord recoil. She closed her journal, and after a moment's pause to gain composure, she said, "I've heard that the pain of losing loved ones lessens with time. But I don't believe that, do you?" She squeezed her hands into tight fists. Her nails left half-moon prints in her palms.

He sat beside her and folded his legs Indian-style. Her pencils lay on the ground between them. He scooped them up and rolled them across his palm. As he studied the Prismacolor Turquoise Drawing Pencil imprints, a chill settled uncomfortably along her spine.

"Never seen pencils like these. Especially the one that looks like a beaver attacked it."

She raked the pencils together like pickup sticks. No point in lying, so she didn't say anything.

"I'd like to see yer drawing, if ye've a mind to share it."

She rolled in the corner of her lip and held it between her teeth while she tapped her fingernails on the journal. "Maybe someday."

"Then someday, I'll ask again."

They sat quietly watching people, but after a couple of minutes the silence made her fidget. She pointed toward the ferry. "Do you think it's safe?"

"The ferry?"

Even though she wasn't looking directly at him, she was sure his gaze never left her face.

"Best option we've got. If the wagon wheels are well seated in the center, there shouldn't be a problem."

He picked up a pebble, held the stone in the crook of his finger, and tossed it side arm, low, and parallel to the water. It sank.

A soft laugh relaxed her shoulders. "Don't you need a calm body of water to skip rocks?"

"I'll have ye know," he said, lips twitching, "I was a rock-skipping champion when I was a lad."

"I don't doubt that." A peal of laughter rolled out. When it subsided, she said, "I needed that. You knew it, though, didn't you?"

"No, ma'am. I was only skipping rocks."

"In a turbulent body of water?"

He raised his shoulders in a what-can-I-say shrug. "Occasionally, ye do things knowing yer efforts might not get ye what ye want."

"Why would you do that?"

He threw another stone, and it too sank. "I represented a man I knew was guilty of murder. As a lawyer, I wanted to win the case. As a law-abiding citizen, I wanted him to spend the rest of his life in jail or hang. But I did my job, and he walked away with a not-guilty verdict. Next day the victim's family shot him dead."

"What happened to them?"

"Law looked the other way." He made the statement matter-of-factly, but the regret was evident in his visibly tightened lips.

"Vigilante justice."

"Not sure the killing made the hurting ones feel better." He turned and captured her face again with his gaze. "Which brings us back to yer original question: Does a person ever recover from grief? I'll start out by saying *no* and finish with what I hope ye'll remember."

His stoic expression gave no hint of his thoughts. He seemed to be going through a mental exercise preparing for what he was about to say. She imagined he did the same exercise before starting a trial, much as Scott had done before he performed surgery.

"The summer before I turned twelve"—he stopped and cleared his throat—"my sister and I were swimming in a loch near our house in the Highlands. My father had tied a swinging rope to a tree. He told us to swing out and drop away from the bank because the roots could catch us. What he said made an impression on me. I canna say the same for my risk-taking sister.

"I swung out, dropped, swam back to shore. Kristen climbed on the rope, swung out, dangling with a one-handed hold. Her hand slipped and she dropped too close to shore." His voice broke.

Kit knew the memory had swallowed him whole.

"I waited for her to come back to the surface, but she didna. I yelled for my father, then I dove in after her, swimming faster than I ever had, but I was too late." The words burst out in an explosion of breath that sounded like he'd held it inside his lungs for years. "Roots entangled her foot. I couldna get her loose. I tried, but I couldna. I swam up for air." He gulped in a gasping breath.

Kit knew his mind swam in the dark water of the loch that had defeated a twelve-year old. She knew because she often swam in a similar kind of dark water.

"I waved to father, then dove again. He reached us and sent me back up for air. I took a deep breath and swam back toward the bottom. By then he was coming up with Kristen in his arms. I'll never forget the look in her eyes. I should have saved her, but I'd waited too long."

Kit touched his arm and felt him shudder. She yearned to hold him, to let him know it wasn't his fault. But she offered only words that he'd probably heard a thousand times. "You were a child. The accident wasn't your fault." How many times had she heard the same words spoken to her in the midst of her grief and guilt?

"Kristen was a wee lass and my responsibility. Her death *was* my fault." He planted his elbows on his knees and dug his thumbs into his eye sockets. "Ye dinna get over that. Ye try to outrun the pain, but ye canna shake loose from the roots that tie ye up in knots. Eventually, the hurt becomes who ye are. Ye learn to live with it. My mother told me if we didna love the people we lose it wouldna hurt so much. I've learned one thing for sure in thirty years. Loving comes with risks. Ye make choices based on how much risk ye're willing to take."

"*Cullen*," Henry hollered from the far side of the ferry. "Need your help."

Cullen cupped his hands around his mouth and yelled, "Be right there." He unfolded his legs and stood.

Kit watched his pulse beat in his neck. Hers, not surprisingly, mirrored his.

His slow smile appeared as a warning. "Always know what ye're willing to risk, lass. And, if ye decide to jump, stay clear of the roots."

Chapter Eleven

WITHOUT A WATCH, Kit relied on her stomach to tell the hour. Telling time based on the position of the sun was like finding her way around a Super Walmart without aisle signs. Tate abandoned her for some canine pursuit that probably involved food, while she stayed put at the riverbank to watch people, one tall person in particular. After Cullen's heartfelt confession, she understood his overprotectiveness. She couldn't make any guarantees, but she'd try to be more tolerant.

Unable to shake loose the images of a frightened Scottish lad frantically ripping out roots to save his entangled sister, Kit opened her journal and fell into another drawing frenzy. She drew a grown-up, rain-soaked, and bleeding Cullen stuck in thick twining vines, hacking at tendrils with the ragged edge of a sheared-off piece of plank fence.

"Mrs. MacKlenna." Adam's voice calling from over her shoulder barely provoked a ripple in her artistic trance. The pencil swept across the page.

"Mrs. MacKlenna?" He touched her shoulder with an impersonal tap. "Mrs. MacKlenna." He tapped again and finally broke through the spell.

She set down her pencils and curled and uncurled her drawing hand, releasing the tension. "Are we next?" Her voice sounded disconnected, as if it hadn't yet caught up with her body.

"Yes, ma'am. I thought you might want to stow supplies. They'll get jostled when we hoist the wagon down the slope."

"Have I told you lately how much I appreciate your help?"

He blushed. "No, ma'am, but you don't have to tell me nothin'. I'm just doing my job."

"You do much more than I hired you to do. Look for a bonus when we get to Fort Laramie."

He straightened, squaring his shoulders. "Yes, ma'am."

Kit closed her journal and gathered her pencils. After disentangling from yards of fabric, she dug her boots into the sandy soil and pulled herself to her feet without tripping over her dress hem.

The wagon had nothing that need stowing away. Her minimalist lifestyle created a clutter-free environment, the complete opposite of home with books stacked floor to ceiling, a collection of guitars, paper airplanes, and stacks of dirty clothes. Little black dresses and business suits hung in a walk-in closet she rarely visited.

If her wagon crashed into the water, the airtight trunk holding the money and paramedic supplies she pilfered from the farm clinic would float. If she tumbled into the water wearing boots and a heavy dress, she wouldn't.

She changed into a lightweight skirt over a pair of trousers, and switched from boots to moccasins. If she went into the water, she could ditch the skirt and the slippers.

Within a few minutes, she returned to her spot on the riverbank and watched the Springers drive their wagon onto the ferry. The family climbed down and stood alongside the rig as two strong men on the gunwales thrust long poles against the river's bottom. The ferry slowly left the dock. When the boat was about twenty-five yards from the bank, a rope attached to the opposite shore broke loose.

"*Watch out*," men yelled from both sides of the river.

"Straighten it out. Come on, you can do it." Kit was too far away to be heard by anyone close enough to help.

The two polemen frantically thrust their poles into the water, but the ferry jerked in the current. The motion sent the wagon rolling forward, forcing the right front wheel off the edge. The unbalanced boat shifted with a violent jolt and knocked the passengers to the deck. A small child rolled into the water.

Mrs. Springer screamed, "Somebody get my boy."

"Throw me a rope." Mr. Springer tied one end of a rope around his waist. The other end was tied to one of the ferry's support posts. He dove beneath the surface, popped up, looked around, then dove again. Although men lined both banks, they were unable to do anything more than knit their fingers and watch with wide-eyed terror.

"*Get my boy.*" The mother ran along the length of the ferry, waving her arms high over her head, screaming in a pitiful, high-pitched wail.

A small arm reached above the surface. Kit marked the spot in her mind as she kicked off her moccasins and dropped her skirt. Snippets from rescue training flashed through her head.

Rescue rule number one—never jeopardize yourself.

Rescue rule number two—never attempt anything you haven't done before.

She plunged into the frigid river, ignoring both. Hypothermia would come quickly. Long, determined strokes moved her against the current. When she reached the spot below where she had last seen the child, she stopped, and treaded water. He broke through the surface to the left, sputtering. Tiny fingers clawed the air, trying to climb an invisible ladder to safety. Then the current dragged him under again.

Kit dove. *Where was he?* She shot back to the surface. There. A red plaid shirt. With a big gulp of breath, she dove again and snatched at a shadow in the murky water. Her fingers hooked the shirt. She drew the child under her arm and kicked to the surface with the current swirling around them. Without fins, her legs already ached. One strained arm wrapped under the boy's chin, and with the other, she angled toward shore, not more than fifteen yards. Panic threatened her, but she could make it. Couldn't she? Two lives were at stake.

"*Kit, catch the rope.*"

The lasso spiraled above the water's surface and landed inches from her outstretched arm. She grabbed it then rolled onto her back so Cullen could pull her against the current. The hemp cut into her palms. As soon as her feet touched ground, he ran into the water and snatched the child.

"We don't have much time." Her teeth chattered around words caught in a rush of deep, heaving breaths.

He placed the boy on dry ground and touched his neck. Cullen shook his head. "There's nothing ye can do."

"Get out of my way." She dropped to her knees and tilted the boy's head. The child was a frightening shade of blue. She covered his mouth with her own and blew her breath into him. Then she placed the heel of her hand in the center of his breastbone and compressed over and over, counting. "Twenty-eight. Twenty-nine. Thirty."

A chorus of murmurs rippled through the crowd surrounding Kit in a claustrophobic circle. "One, two, three, step back, four, five, give me room, six, seven…" She gave the child two more deep breaths, then resumed compression.

Cullen's strong hand grabbed her upper arm and squeezed. "*Stop.*"

She jerked free.

Mrs. Springer fell to her knees beside Kit, wringing her apron in her red-weathered hands. With calm desperation, Kit repeated the cycle of breaths and chest compressions for a third time. "Come on, you can do it. Don't give up on me now."

The boy's eye twitched. Did she imagine the slight movement? She put her head to his chest. Nothing. "Come on, come on." More compressions. "Don't quit on me." His long black lashes fluttered. That wasn't her imagination. Relief spiked through her veins. She pressed fingertips against the pulse point in his neck. Thready.

Thank God.

Mr. Springer stood over his boy, running his hands through his thinning hair. Cold river water poured off his clothes and puddled at his feet. His teeth chattered behind purple lips. Gray eyes appeared clouded with disbelief.

Mrs. Springer's hair had fallen loose of the tight knot normally worn at her nape and formed a frizzy halo around her head.

Kit shook the woman's arm to gain her attention. "Help me get him out of these wet clothes." Several other women appeared, offering blankets. "Wrap him up, rub him. Don't stop until his color returns."

Mrs. Springer's hopeless wailing turned into sobs. "Will he be all right?"

Kit wasn't one hundred percent sure the child would survive. "We'll need to watch him for the next twenty-four hours. But right now he needs to get warm—quickly."

Cullen pulled her to her feet. "*Ye* need to get warm."

Adam shoved a handful of blankets toward her. "Ma sent these for you. Can you teach me to swim like that?"

Cullen brushed Adam aside. "Not now." Kit grabbed a blanket and pulled away from Cullen, but her frozen feet offered no support, and she collapsed. Cullen caught her before she hit the ground, then picked her up, and cradled her in his arms.

Her teeth chattered, sounding like castanets on steroids. "Cover my head."

"Adam, get yer ma. Bring her to Kit's wagon. She'll need help."

"I don't need help."

The veins in Cullen's neck pulsed. "Ye think ye dinna need anyone." He was a volcano on the verge of erupting. Steam actually rose off him. "Ye almost drowned. What the hell were ye thinking?"

"That I could save him." Craving his heat, she nestled into his chest. Every kettledrum beat of his heart resonated against her cheek. She didn't want to be near the explosion set to detonate. "Put me down. I can walk."

"Ye canna even stand. How the hell can ye walk?"

"You're cursing at me."

"And ye'll hear more before this is over."

She ignored the muscle now ticking in his jaw.

He carried her to her wagon, where he dropped her on its tailgate with enough force to sting her shivering butt. If a spanking had been his intention, he succeeded. White-hot anger burned off the chill.

He wrapped a death grip around the tailgate's edge. "Get out of yer wet clothes, and do not step outside this wagon. I want to know where ye are every minute. Do ye understand?" The staccato voice punctuated his demand. "Heed my words, or I'll damn well put ye on the first wagon heading east." He pushed away, leaving her with a parting glare.

Sarah arrived, carrying Kit's skirt, moccasins, drawing paper, and pencils. "Let's get you into dry clothes before you catch cold. Come on, now. Stand up, and we'll go change."

"I can manage."

"Of course you can, but I'm going to help anyway."

Although colder than she'd ever been in her life, Kit moved rapidly and focused on what needed doing. She removed one of the blankets. "If you'll hold this, I'll stand behind it and take off my clothes."

"Not the time for modesty, dear," Sarah said.

"Please."

Working with the men at the fire station and long weekend survival treks had bred modesty right out of Kit, but she sure couldn't explain her thong or sports bra to Sarah. And God only knew what she'd think of the butterfly tattoo.

A few minutes later, dried and dressed, her heart rose and fell in its complex rhythm, reminding her how close she'd come to drowning.

"What you did was the most selfless act I've ever witnessed," Sarah said. "You shamed a few men who stood by kicking the dirt. My John was one of them." She enveloped Kit in a warm hug. "I'm proud of you. Folks will be speaking about this for a long time."

Kit had known Sarah only a few days, but she had discovered from long conversations riding in the buckboard that the woman could go from parochial to profound in very few words. She had more to say and it wouldn't be complimentary. Even-tempered Sarah was definitely nettled.

"However, you didn't come on this trip to get yourself killed. If you ever do anything like that again, John will send you packing with the next go-backers we see."

Kit felt a consuming embarrassment. "I won't scare you again."

Sarah grinned. "Of course you will. Impulsiveness is in your nature. I've told you what John wanted me to say. Cullen said you're not to leave the wagon. You won't, will you?"

Kit groaned softly, letting her shoulders sag. "I'll be right here until he releases me."

Sarah chuckled on her way out. "You'd best get one of those Shakespeare books. You might be here for a while."

Kit leaned back on her bed. The last couple of hours had been strange. But she sensed that would be the way of things for the next several weeks. In the meantime, she could read Shakespeare or study class notes from the crime scene seminar she'd taken in college. A sketch formed in her mind. She grabbed her journal and her hand blitzed across the page.

The drawing depicted a woman in a jail cell with her hands gripping the bars, watching a man on the other side dangle an oversized key. Vines crept up his legs, anchoring him to the ground. The drawing was chilling.

She tossed the journal aside and stared out through the wagon's rear opening. An assemblage of men and women hustled around camp like worker bees. The scene resembled dozens of reenactments in which Kit had participated, but something was starkly different. Absent was the jovial camaraderie common among reenactors.

Her journey to South Pass was definitely *not* a reenactment.

The trip held the fragility of life and the specter of death, and the hemp rope burns across her palms spoke to that unending reality.

Chapter Twelve

CULLEN READ THE same paragraph in Homer's *Odyssey* a dozen times before slamming the book shut and tossing it on the table. After returning from nightly rounds, he'd been sitting in a rocker by the campfire. If he wanted a distraction, he would have to look elsewhere. The Camerons' music hadn't lured him away and neither had an invitation from John and Sarah to stop by for coffee. Henry had accepted, but Cullen sent his regrets. He wasn't up to socializing, especially if he might run into Kit. Even though he'd forbidden her to leave her wagon, he wasn't sure how much credence, if any, the woman gave his orders.

Henry moseyed into camp carrying a plate of cookies. "Sarah sent these. Kit made them this morning." He poked Cullen with the edge of the tin dish. "I told Sarah you were rocking and moping. She said you needed nourishment for all the thinking you were doing. You plan to mope the rest of the evening?"

Cullen ignored the mouth-watering scent of cinnamon and pushed the plate away. A cookie dropped into his lap. He glared at it, expecting it to snap at him. "I'm not moping."

"You're a lying son of a bitch."

"Mind yer own business, old man."

Henry set the cookies on top of the stack of books beside Cullen's chair. "Everything that happens on this wagon train *is* my business. You think all you need to learn you can get from a book. I'm here to tell you, if you don't have enough sense to get in out of the rain, what you learned in them books don't do no good."

Cullen glared at him. "Ye're crazy, ye know that?"

"You're the one who insisted the widow come on this trip. Remember? She saved that boy's life today, and you show gratitude by forcing her to stay in her wagon going on ten hours now. Let her out. If your mind's not set to doing what's right, I will."

Cullen let loose a long sigh. "I'll let her out in the morning."

Henry fixed a gaze that wrinkled his forehead. "The hell you will." He yanked the cookie plate out of Cullen's reach and headed off in the direction of Kit's wagon.

Cullen picked the cookie off his lap and took a bite. "Come back. Never seen ye move so fast on those saddle-bowed legs."

Henry stopped in midstride. "You get off your ass and go now, or my next step won't have a turn-around."

"I'll do it, but I want to ask ye something first."

"If you're just working up spit for your whistle, I'm not listening."

"What do ye think about what she did today? Ever seen a woman do anything like that?"

"The water part or the *after* part?"

"Both, I reckon," Cullen said.

"Seen women do men's work, but Kit's different." He wagged his finger like the tail on a hunting dog that just caught a stump-eared squirrel. "One thing's for sure. She's the prettiest, sweetest, kindest little missy I've ever met, and if I wasn't old enough to be her pa, I'd asked her to be my wife."

Cullen lurched from his chair, toppling it over. "Ye're right. Ye are too old."

Henry grabbed Cullen's arm. "You hurt that girl and you'll answer to me."

"Then ye'd best go talk to her because I'm nae sure I can keep from strangling her."

Henry dropped his grip, chuckling. "Just keep your damn hands tucked in your suspenders."

Cullen had been aroused since carrying the shivering woman in his arms. He needed to erase her from his mind. It was easy to envision Abigail Phillips sitting in her San Francisco garden, but her lovely countenance was no more a distraction than Homer's *Odyssey*.

Kit had turned his life upside down in less than a week. Bedding her would get her out of his blood, and a liaison would make the trip across the dusty prairie more enjoyable. He set off toward her wagon thinking that was exactly what he'd do.

A silver bar of moonlight and the earthy scent of the prairie tempered his mood until he heard a guitar carrying a somber and haunting tonal quality. Then Kit began to sing the ballad "The Light of Other Days," pure and beautiful and breathy. Her version of the melody held a strange, otherworldly sound. He lit a cheroot and leaned against a cottonwood, his left thumb hooked into his suspenders. The music stirred his soul. Even when she strummed the last chord, the sound, lush and bursting with flavor, continued to swirl inside his thrumming heart.

Kit stepped from the wagon, sat on the tailgate, and swung her legs.

Cullen stubbed out his cigar and walked from the shadows. "Why'd ye do it, Kit?"

Her legs stopped on an upward swing, hung in midair for a moment, then she resumed pumping them at an easy glide. "I don't know what you mean."

"Ye could have drowned."

"Saving the boy was worth the risk."

"Worth risking yer life for a person ye didna know?"

She jumped to the ground, landing only a few feet from him. "He needed saving."

"Even if it killed ye?"

She chewed on her lower lip.

"How did ye know to breathe into his mouth?"

She continued chewing on her lip. Finally, she said, "It doesn't always revive a person. If bacteria are in his lungs, he might still die."

Bacteria in his lungs? She said the damnedest things.

The breeze fluttered through silky strands of vanilla-scented hair.

Golden tendrils danced across her cheek. He barely breathed through an engulfing rush of heat. Compelled by an incomprehensible force, he closed the distance between them. His fingers burned. His muscles throbbed. He had to hold her tiny body in his arms once again.

His thumb trembled as it slid over the curve of her cheek, stopping below her mouth. With the tip of his finger, he lifted her chin and gazed into mystical eyes. He lowered his head slowly, giving her a chance to withdraw. When she didn't, he brushed his lips against hers, sipping her as if she were a glass of the finest French champagne, fruity and sweet. Still, she didn't pull away, so he deepened the kiss, feeling her firm breasts pressing against him. He wanted to touch her, feel the rise and fall of her breath against his naked skin. Would she agree to take a lover? Gently, he cupped the back of her head, and his fingers furrowed into her hair. A groan of desire slipped from her lips. *Maybe.* His arousal pulsed between them.

The kiss ended but their lips lingered only a breath apart. Should he ask her to slip away with him into the darkness where he would bury his face in her hair, his hands in her pleasing curves, and satisfy them both?

He gazed again into her eyes. This time the campfire's red glow reflected what he hadn't seen before—quiet eyes filled with sadness and pain and loss. Emotions he knew too well.

Tiny hands too small to capture the wild beat of his heart rested against his chest. Without saying a word in English or French or Latin or Greek or Gaelic or the smidgeon of Spanish he knew, she walked away. He followed as if an invisible cord connected them, but after a step or two, he realized there was no cord. She was not pulling him, but separating them.

"Damn." He had just made the biggest mistake in his life. While seducing her had been his intention, he'd been the one drawn into the flame and burned. That wasn't what he wanted. But what exactly did he want? A one-night romp in the tall grass, or a torrid affair that would last until he reached Oregon. Both sounded pleasurable, but the consequences were unacceptable.

He walked into the coolness of the evening, into a breeze blowing through the cottonwood trees growing alongside the river, carrying with him the faint scent of vanilla on his fingers and the sweet taste of Kit's lips on his tongue.

He tried to conjure a picture of Abigail, but all he saw was Kit. A distracting temptation and one he couldn't allow. There was too much at stake. Abigail's father had handpicked Cullen from a long line of suitors, and if she were agreeable, they would wed as soon as he returned to California. That's what he wanted. Wasn't it?

Chapter Thirteen

"EN GARDE!" Adam waved a cattle prod in one hand and held a volume of Shakespeare in the other.

Kit perked up. "What's my part?" Sword fighting was better than watching the muddy bottomland along the north bank of the Kansas pass by at two miles an hour while remembering Cullen's kiss. *Why'd he do it?* Everything about the kiss was wrong, and the guilt overwhelmed her. It was the wrong time, and Cullen was the wrong man. He had a life he was moving toward, and she had a life she was trying to find. They weren't for each other. Not in the past. Not in the present.

"*En garde!*" Adam yelled again.

She grabbed the extra prod and lunged, imagining her opponent was Cullen. No, he didn't deserve to be stabbed through the heart, but another body part came to mind.

"Here, you take the book and read the parts of Romeo and Mercutio. I have Tybalt's lines memorized." Adam squared his shoulders, pointed his cattle-prod sword at her, and advanced. "I am for you."

"Gentle Mercutio, put thy rapier up." Kit read Romeo's lines then lowered her voice and read Mercutio's part. "Come, sir, your passado."

Tybalt extended his sword arm and attacked Mercutio, who counterattacked with a chopping motion.

Kit held the book at arm's length, projected her voice, and read Romeo's lines. "Draw, Benvolio; beat down their weapons. Gentlemen, for shame, forbear this outrage! Tybalt, Mercutio, the prince expressly hath forbidden bandying in Verona streets: Hold, Tybalt! good Mercutio!"

Tybalt/Adam ducked and stabbed Mercutio/Kit.

"I am hurt. A plague o' both your houses! I am sped. Is he gone, and hath nothing?" Kit read her lines with dramatic flair, then fell to the ground with the book in one hand, cattle prod in the other. Folks walking alongside their wagons applauded as they passed the impromptu theatrical production.

Adam reached for her hand. "Have you seen this play on stage? A professional actor couldn't have done better."

Kit clasped his hand, and he pulled her to her feet. She took a bow. "Thank you, sir." She turned and bowed to their clapping audience. "I saw it performed in New—"

A woman's bone-chilling scream invaded the quiet prairie. The clapping stopped. Smiles froze. Kit squeezed Adam's hand. They listened in silence. The piercing sound hung in the air like the last note of an operatic performance sung in a vibrato-free voice.

Then the woman took a breath and screamed again.

There was a half-mile distance between the first wagon and the last, making it impossible for Kit, standing in the middle of the long line of wagons, to identify the voice.

"Where're your sisters?" she asked.

Adam shook his head. "I haven't seen them since y'all got out of the buckboard to walk."

"Go find them. Frances may be with Anna. I'm going up ahead."

The wagons stopped, and everyone ran in the direction of the screams. A crowd packed six-deep had gathered by the time Kit reached the wailing woman. "Excuse me. Excuse me. Let me through."

The sight of Mrs. Ingram hugging the blood-soaked body of her child shocked Kit, sending her to the edge of a mental crevasse.

The mother's wailing continued. "*Oh my God. My God.*"

A patchwork quilt hung over her husband's shaking arms. Acute pain had twisted and pressed his ghostly white face out of shape. "Martha, give me the boy." He pried her hands loose, one bloody finger at a time. Then he wrapped the child in the multicolored shroud.

Her bloody hands grasped the air in a futile attempt to reclaim the stolen life. "Please don't take him away. Don't take my baby."

The nightmarish scene stripped Kit of her paramedic-in-control façade, and she tumbled over the edge into a deep, dark hole.

I've got to get out of here.

She ran from the red-stained earth and the pungent smell of blood. But she couldn't outrun the memory of that singular moment when death stole Scott from her arms. The phantom pain remained, stinging and jabbing, not with a cattle prod but with a double-edged rapier. Her lungs burned like hot coals, pushing her to run faster until her legs simply withered beneath her and she fell to the ground. Tears rippled down her cheeks.

Footsteps sounded behind her. "Shh." Cullen's warm breath blew across her neck as he knelt at her side. "The boy jumped off the wagon and fell under the wheel."

She folded her arms in a self-embrace. "It's my fault. I should have told the children not to jump from wagons."

"All the children sing the song ye wrote. They know the rules." He pressed his strong hand against her arm's chilled flesh. "Ye knew the dangers when ye signed on for this trip. Accidents happen."

"Dangers are everywhere." Words tumbled out with her cascading sobs. "You scared me. Why'd you kiss me?"

He tensed against her. "Ye have such bravado. How could I scare ye?"

She covered her face with her apron and cried into the scratchy fabric. "There's nothing brave about me." She wanted to ask him to hold her, but she wouldn't.

Two small hands grabbed Kit's wrists. "I saw the wheel roll over him."

She looked up and gazed into Frances's eyes, red and swollen eyes that had seen much more than they needed to see. Kit's heart splintered into even more pieces. Frances needed hope and reassurance. She needed to know she was safe and protected. She needed love and compassion in the midst of trauma and grief. How could Kit give what she so desperately needed herself?

She looked into Cullen's eyes imploringly.

"Ye're not alone, lass. I'm here."

He pulled her onto his lap as Kit pulled Frances onto hers, and Kit began to sing softly, "*And the children will find their hope and the promise of peace. What they lost will be restored, in His arms and at His feet.*"

Cullen hummed along. His calming presence had a soothing effect on Kit, and Frances relaxed against her. If Kit had the power to erase only one horrible memory, it would not be one of hers. It would be the one claiming a corner of Frances's mind.

KIT WIPED SWEAT from her forehead and glared at the log fort built along the bottomland south of the Platte River. The wagon train had traveled three weeks and three hundred twenty miles and had reached the first milestone—Fort Kearny.

"Doesn't look like much, does it?" she said.

"But it's got a sutler's store," Sarah said.

Kit put her arm around her friend's thick waist. "I've never heard you say anything critical or even get angry. How do you do that?"

Sarah laughed. "Oh, I get angry. I just don't let anyone see it. John and the children don't need to worry over me."

"As my Granny Mac would say, you're going straight up when you die. You're as close to perfect as any person I've ever met."

Sarah patted Kit's hand as they approached the store. "You're sweet to say that, but I'm far from perfect. Now, Cullen," she said straight-faced, "*is* as close to perfect as any person could be."

Kit laughed so hard she got a stitch in her side.

Cullen walked out of the store. The door's squeaky hinges cried out with a groan. "Are you women laughing at me?"

Kit dabbed her eyes with the tail of her apron. "You shouldn't eavesdrop."

Sarah eased a path around Cullen, and he opened the door for her. She paused in the doorway. "You coming to dinner? Kit made an apple pie."

"I make no guarantees on how it tastes," Kit said. "It was my first Dutch-oven pie in several years."

Cullen flashed a wide grin. "I'm not one to incommode, but I canna pass up any sweets ye're offering."

His double entendres were becoming more blatant.

He slipped a letter into his vest pocket and ambled toward her, pulling his hat lower to shade his eyes from the glaring sun.

"You got mail?"

He patted his chest. "It's from my friend, Braham. He's meeting us at Fort Laramie."

"He's the friend you mentioned to General Sherman."

"That's Captain Sherman, but I'm sure he'd be pleased with the promotion. Yes, Braham is the friend I mentioned. We were close as brothers growing up. Went to the University of Edinburgh, then on to Harvard. We'll be law partners in San Francisco."

"How'd y'all decide on California?"

"We were in San Francisco last spring and made the decision."

"Is that when you met Abigail?" No one other than Sarah had ever mentioned the woman to Kit, but her curiosity needed to be fed.

He cocked an eyebrow, nodded, but didn't offer any details.

Sarah stepped out of the store. The door slammed behind her, almost knocking the packages from her arms.

Kit reached out to help. "Let me carry those."

"Don't forget dinner, Cullen. We don't want to waste Kit's pie."

His eyes crinkled at the corners, "My mouth's already watering knowing how sweet it'll taste."

Chapter Fourteen

THE WAGON TRAIN traveled across the South Platte's upper ford, arriving at Windlass Hill, five hundred miles from Independence.

Henry blasted his trumpet and the wagons pulled into a circle. While the men unyoked the teams and chained the wagons, Kit helped Sarah start the campfire and put coffee on to boil. The exhausting routine never let up. Not on rainy days. Not on dry days either when the choking dust crept into Kit's food and hair. She didn't mind being gritty. It was never getting clean that drove her crazy.

She shook dust from her apron. "Cullen's coming for supper when he finishes his meeting."

"Lordy," Sarah said, "that man has more get-togethers than a parson in springtime."

Kit made a mental note to add Sarah's colloquialism to her ever-growing list. "He's trying to figure out the best way to get down the hill."

"He doesn't need a meeting to do that. Go around the blooming thing is what I say. Told John that just a bit ago."

Frances finished arranging a handful of wild flowers in a cup of water and placed the arrangement in the center of the table. "Momma, can Mrs. MacKlenna take me to see the bad hill?"

Kit rubbed goose bumps from her arms. Every time someone called her Mrs. MacKlenna she got a creepy-crawly feeling. The name reminded her of all the lies she had told. She needed a new name. The grooms and hot walkers on the farm had always called her Miss Kit. Maybe that would work for the children?

"Since we're traveling sisters, do you think you and Elizabeth could call me Miss Kit instead of Mrs. MacKlenna?"

Frances's eyes lit up. "*Can* we, Momma? That's easy for me to say."

"I don't reckon it matters none." Sarah waved a large wooden spoon. "You two go on now. Dinner's about ready."

Kit snagged Frances's hand. "Come on. Let's hurry."

A few minutes later they stood at the top of the steep incline at the head of Ash Hollow and stared down at the jagged scar leading to the springs below. A breeze picked up and beat Kit's skirt around her legs, just as the scar and the hardship it represented hammered concern into her heart.

"We're going down *that*?" Frances's rose-tinted face pinched with worry.

"Going around the hill would take us miles out of the way."

"But is it safe?"

Kit didn't think so, but strong and resilient Frances constantly worried about others. Kit didn't want to add to the child's growing alarm. When she spotted Cullen walking in their direction, she decided to turn the question over to him. He could answer it without upsetting Frances. "Here comes Mr. Montgomery. Ask him."

Frances folded her arms and waited for Cullen to come within hearing distance. "Are we *really* going down that hill?"

He crouched to be at eye level with her and pressed his forearms against his thighs. "Hundreds of wagons have already gone that way. We'll be safe enough."

She twiddled her fingers against her elbows.

"I need ye to do something special while your pa and I get the wagons ready." He gently tapped her chin. "Stay close to Mrs. MacKlenna—"

Frances shook her head. "Momma said I could call her Miss

Kit."

Cullen cocked an eyebrow. "Then stay close to Miss Kit so she willna wander off and get hurt. Will ye do that?"

"I'll watch her, but will you take our wagon down first?"

"Why would you want to do that, honey?" Kit asked.

Frances gave an easy shrug. "If the Barretts go first, everyone will know it's safe."

"To be so trusting," Cullen said.

"Children are naturally. Then they grow up, get hurt, and forget."

"Or they're lied to," he said.

"*Mrs. MacKlenna.*" Elizabeth came to a running stop, breathing hard, with Tate at her side.

Frances lifted her chin, expressing an I-know-more-than-you attitude. "Momma said we could call her Miss Kit."

Elizabeth glared at her sister, and Tate, not wanting to be left out, planted his front paws on Kit's chest.

"Down, Tate." She pushed him away and brushed the dirty prints from her blouse.

Elizabeth tugged on Kit's arm. "Will you take us exploring?"

"Are your chores done?"

"Yes, ma'am," the girls said in unison.

"Are your lessons done?"

"Yes, ma'am," Elizabeth said, but Frances stuck out her lower lip and didn't answer.

Kit gave the child's bonnet strings a teasing pull. "What's the matter?"

Frances curled her bottom lip. "I lost my pencil."

Kit whispered in Frances's ear loud enough for everyone to hear. "I have one you can use, but it's a secret pencil."

Elizabeth planted her fists on her hips. "How can it be a secret if I know about it?"

Cullen smiled. "I've seen Miss Kit's pencils. They're magical."

Frances jumped up and down, clapping. "Will I draw like Miss Kit, too?"

"Ye might draw better. I havena seen her drawings."

"We've seen them." Elizabeth shrugged. "She makes cartoons out of you."

Cullen crossed his hands over his heart. "Cartoons? I'm crushed."

The children giggled, and Kit chuckled. "Say good-bye to Mr. Montgomery. We have to go. Supper's ready." She clasped their hands and led them back toward the wagons, walking around patches of shrubbery and over lumpy terrain covered with wind-blown sand.

Cullen's deep, contented laugh followed.

A man who understood the joy of laughter was special. A man who could take fifteen minutes to banish an eight-year-old's fear was even more so. Kit couldn't deny that he plucked at her heartstrings, creating an alluring sound. But why now when there was no possibility of a future?

"Will you finish the story about the magician and the gargoyle?" Frances asked, interrupting Kit's thoughts.

"I thought you'd like *Growing Disenchantments*. Yes, we'll finish it tonight," Kit said.

"I like the story, too." Elizabeth put a finger to her chin. "There's something I'm curious about. Do Ganfrey and Ragonnard kiss? Do you and Mr. Montgomery kiss?"

Kit gulped and dropped the children's hands. The precocious little girls had a habit of asking whatever was on their mind. She let the question hang in the air for a moment.

Frances picked up a rock and studied it. "I saw Adam and Allison kiss."

"Really? When'd you see—" Kit's foot caught on a root. She pitched forward spread eagle, tucked and rolled, and landed on her back under a bush. "*Ouch.*"

"Are you hurt?" Elizabeth's voice rose with alarm.

A distinctive rattle stopped Kit's heart in the middle of a beat. The snake struck in a moment of horror, burying its fangs into her right thigh. Blue blazing terror shoved her into the bowels of a dark, empty hole. The cold-blooded creature slithered away.

Elizabeth screamed. Frances screamed. Tate barked. They all ran away, leaving Kit alone and injured. The kind of messed-up, mixed-up, dead-in-an-instant injured. White-knuckled, heart stopping, fear-of-dying—injured. Her chest constricted. Without a weapon, she had no protection if the snake returned. She scooped up two rocks and gripped them with ice-cold hands.

Stay calm. Stay still. Moving will spread the venom faster. But sitting still amidst a possible den of snakes was a bad idea.

The bite should soon be swelling and bleeding. But how long afterward? Immediately, or a few minutes? With her dress hiked up, she could see that only a trickle of blood had seeped through the trousers she wore under her skirt, and her leg wasn't ballooning into a mass of poisoned tissue. Those were good signs.

Panic tied her up with tentacles of fear. Even if it meant spreading the venom, she had to get out from under the bush.

Don't panic. Take slow breaths, and get out. Now.

"Kit." Cullen's voice penetrated her fog of fear. His feet pounded in the sandy soil. "My God, what happened?" He pulled her out from under the bush.

"Rattler."

"Where's the bite?" The urgency in his voice did nothing to calm her.

She pointed to the bloody spot and small tear in her trousers. He drew his bowie knife. "I'll have to suck out the poison. This will hurt, but I have to do it."

"*No, you don't.*" She swatted at his arm. "Help me to my wagon."

"Damn, Kit. This is serious."

She grabbed his shirtfront and jerked him down until his face was inches from hers. "You are *not* going to cut and suck and get germs in my wound. If you don't carry me back, I swear I'll walk."

"Like hell ye will."

She shoved him aside and tried to stand.

"Hold on." He scooped her up and ran hell-bent for camp. When they reached Kit's wagon, he placed her on the bed.

"Help me. I have to take off my pants. It might be a dry bite."

"What the hell's a dry bite?" With his jaw shadowed by several days' growth of whiskers, he had a hard and angry appearance.

She clawed at her boots. "I'd be in excruciating pain by now if there was venom."

"Be still. I'm nae convinced ye're right." He removed her boots and again tried to cut her pants.

"*Stop!* I'll take them off."

If he cut her trousers, she couldn't replace them. There wasn't a corner Gap store anywhere between Ash Hollow and say…1969. She bunched up her skirt at her waist then unbuttoned the pants and pushed them down over her hips.

He yanked off the trousers and tossed them on the floor. Lodged in the wound six inches above her knee was a snake's fang. Seeing the grooved tooth poking out of her skin stretched her band of control to the point of breaking.

He pinched the fang between his fingers, but she pushed his hand away. "Wait. Get my medical box." She pointed over her shoulder. "It's by the trunk." Everything she needed and could explain would be in there. He tossed his hat onto the rocking chair, grabbed the box, and opened it.

"Hand me the vial on the back row at the end, the small forceps, and a piece of gauze." She splashed antiseptic wash from one of the unlabeled vials over the wound and then removed the fang with the forceps. The punctures barely bled. She spread antibiotic ointment she'd previously squirted into an unlabeled vial over the wound, and then wrapped her leg with gauze. He returned the vials to their slots and closed the box.

Nausea hit, and she gagged. Cullen grabbed a bowl and a towel off the table and placed the bowl under her chin, but she didn't vomit. Sweat broke out across her forehead. She waved the bowl away. "Would you mind wetting the towel?"

He filled the washbowl with water from the pitcher and soaked the cloth. After wringing it out, he knelt beside the bed and wiped her forehead.

She reached for the washcloth. "I'm not a child. I can wash my own face."

He blocked her hand with his arm. "No, ye're nae a child."

She glanced out through the open flaps in the front of the wagon. The threatened rain had moved out, leaving the clouds soft and white, framing a blue sky. Thinking about how she would sketch the scene provided a distraction she desperately needed. She didn't want to think about the snake. And she definitely didn't want to think about the man who was tenderly washing her face.

"Ye've got a scratch here." The pad of his thumb skimmed her cheek.

Breathe.

"There're twigs and dry leaves in yer braid." He pulled a leaf from her hair. "I'll get the rest." He spoke calmly against her ear, each word a gently rolling wave of cool water. His long, slim fingers worked through the braid, untwisting the strands with ease. Her scalp tingled with each little tug. "Where's yer comb?"

She was hesitant to say anything, not fully trusting her voice. "On the table."

He stood and collected her brush. She took it from him quickly before he had a chance to untangle her hair. She needed to concentrate on the snakebite, not on Cullen's breath caressing her neck with the softness of cashmere.

Watching her, he furrowed his hand through his own hair, creating creases in the lush, dark waves always hidden beneath his hat.

"Cullen," John yelled from outside the wagon. "We just heard. What can we do?"

Cullen drew back the bonnet flaps, gripping them so tightly his fingers turned white.

"How is she?" John asked.

"She says the snake didna release any venom."

"How'd she know that?"

"I dinna ken."

"Do you believe her?"

"I believe she believes it. I'll let you know if we need anything."

He dropped the flaps and turned back to her with the parched look of a man with no hope of a drink.

There was an undercurrent of steamy tension inside the wagon.

He crossed one arm over his chest, grasped his other elbow, and plucked at his chin, playing with an invisible goatee. "When ye jumped into the water to save the Springer boy, did ye believe ye could rescue him?"

"Yes."

"When ye pushed on his chest, did ye believe ye could save him?"

"Yes."

"Do ye have that belief, that confidence now?" He seemed to stare right through her, evaluating her answers.

Her hands stilled with plaits of hair twisted in her fingers. "Yes."

He sat in the rocking chair and twirled his hat. "Ye're too calm."

"What would hysteria accomplish?"

"How can ye be so *blasé*? What would ye have done if the bite had venom?"

She would have opened the brooch and never looked back, but she couldn't tell him that.

The veins in his neck pulsed, and his eyes were like hard, blue marbles.

"Can we talk later? I'd like to rest for a while." Tears clustered at the corners of her eyes. She ached to be held, but he didn't offer. *Go away, Cullen Montgomery, and let me cry.*

"Rest. I'll be back." He jumped off the tailgate, hitting the ground with a thud.

The cluster of tears now rolled down her face. She'd always lived in a community of caring people who knew when she needed hugs. Sarah and the children would hug her, but she needed more, much more. Alone and confused, she buried her face in her pillow and wept silent tears.

CULLEN RETURNED TO find Kit asleep. Her breasts lifted in rhythm with her soft breath. He peeked beneath the sheet. A small amount of blood had oozed through the gauze. Should he change the dressing? No. She'd been particular about her care and wouldn't want him touching the bandage.

Her flawless, golden-tinted skin beckoned. His fingertips burned to touch her. How did her legs and belly become bronzed? Had she lain naked in the sun with her husband? Was the lass a sybarite?

He had never found muscular legs arousing, but hers were provocative. Would they grip and fold around him? Would they squeeze and pull him deeper into her body? Had her husband encouraged her sensuality, and what kind of lover had he taught her to be? Cullen's body throbbed. He wanted her and had little doubt he would have her. What shocked him was his belief that making love once would not sate his desire for her.

The scrap of pink fabric she wore puzzled him. He'd seen his share of women in various stages of undress, but had never seen anything resembling the garment, almost like a loincloth. It wasn't Parisian, and as far as he knew, not oriental, either. What was the point of wearing such a skimpy, and he had to admit, erotic garment?

From the corner of his eye, he caught something glinting against the floor of the wagon. He looked closer and noticed the gleam came from a piece of jewelry pinned to the waistband of her trousers. He picked up the pants and inspected the pin, a Celtic-design brooch made of silver and Iona marble. Heat radiated from the blood red stone. Did she, like his Celtic ancestors, understand the power in the ruby, or could the brooch be only a family heirloom?

Another mystery surrounding the Widow MacKlenna.

Her life seemed very cryptic, and unless she chose to hand over the deciphering key, he would not easily uncover her secrets. He folded the wool trousers and placed them next to her pillow. Heirloom or mystical stone, she would want to know the jewelry was safe.

While gazing at her, he again found himself astounded by her beauty, not the current standard of beauty, but something else, something timeless. Pursed lips dared him to kiss her. Did he? No. He wouldn't steal a kiss, but he would give her one on her forehead.

Her satiny skin was warm against his lips. The arousing aroma of vanilla and white flowers brought him to his knees. What was it about this woman that ignited his fury and confounded his logic and created an inextinguishable desire, making him forget his renowned self-control?

He inhaled a deep breath and blew it out, slow and easy. Kit was an enigma—tenacious and fearless, but at her center, fragile. With time, he would strip away every layer until he uncovered the true Kit MacKlenna. The question that plagued him was did he have enough time?

WHEN SARAH SHOOK Cullen's shoulder, he woke to a dwindling light bathing Ash Hollow in an orange-yellow sunset. Confused, he shook his head, clearing it of the dream he'd had of his sister, Kristen. She'd appeared to him as an ethereal woman with liquid blue eyes, and had guided him through a starless night toward a destination he couldn't remember.

The dream disturbed him.

"I've brought dinner," Sarah whispered.

He gestured with his thumb. "Let's go outside." Before leaving the wagon, he knelt beside Kit and felt her forehead, warm but not hot. He sighed and let go of his tension, or as much of it as he could.

Once outside the wagon, he remained standing while he ate, using the tailgate as a table. The air rustled around him in the last pitch of sunlight and the fresh smell of grass. Flecks of yellow gave the horizon a shimmery appearance. Over the last few weeks, he'd watched Kit study the sunsets and had wondered what inspired her artistically. Was it color or some vague sensation?

"Kit's going to be all right, isn't she?" Sarah asked.

The question tugged at his thoughts like a chain attached to an anchor at the bottom of the sea. "I've traveled throughout the world, but I've never met anyone, man or woman, with Kit's tenacity. I'd be the last one to predict anything she might do, but I believe she'll recover."

"I was scared when she jumped into the river." Sarah fiddled with her apron, ironing it with her hands. "The snakebite terrified me. Next time, and I know there will be a next time, Kit will likely give me an apoplectic fit."

Cullen juxtaposed an image of Kit in the water and an image of the snake's fang embedded in her leg. Something inside him bent and stretched. "I thought she was going to die. My heart was beating so fast I thought I'd drop where I stood." He shoved in the last spoonful of stew and wiped his mouth with his handkerchief. "Thank ye for the food."

He leaned against the tailgate and crossed his arms. "When I started this trip, I thought I'd watch over her and protect her. Hard as hell to do when someone doesna want protection. I dinna believe Kit wants anyone to love her either, except maybe the children."

"She's been hurt, Cullen. Loving children is safe. She gives and they give back. But you're like the land we're traveling through—unknown and dangerous."

He shoved away from the wagon gate with a level of anger that made him wince. "God, Sarah, I'd never hurt her."

"That's not what I meant by dangerous." She placed the empty bowl into her basket. "Since that day in Independence when you rescued me from the overturning shelf, I've treated you like one of my boys."

He gave her a teasing grin. "Ye speak to me like one of them, too."

"Then I'm going to ask you a question same as I'd ask Adam. What are your intentions toward Abigail?"

Cullen gave her a rote answer. "She's a fine woman."

"But do you have feelings for her?"

If John or Henry had asked these questions, he'd have told them to mind their own business, but he'd never be rude to Sarah. "Marriage to Abigail will be profitable, the beginning of a political force in California. She'll give my father the grandson he's been hounding me for."

Cullen gulped hot coffee and burned his tongue. "*Damn.*" He dumped the coffee dregs and placed the empty cup into Sarah's basket. "I'd best go help Henry."

She looked as if she had something else to say but thought better of it. Instead, she picked up the basket and left him alone to sort out feelings he didn't want to deal with.

Cullen lifted the wagon flaps and gazed at Kit. Her hair was disheveled, her cheeks flushed. All she needed were swollen lips and she'd have the look of a well-loved woman. A look he intended to paint on her face. God help him.

Chapter Fifteen

CULLEN KNOCKED ON the side of Kit's wagon shortly before dawn the next morning. She didn't answer. "Kit." Still no answer. Should he go in? A chill of alarm said yes.

The predawn air inside the wagon lay heavy with the scent of dew and vanilla. Kit breathed in a slow, melodic rhythm. He relaxed. He should leave now, but the fey creature bewitched him. Even in her sleep, she cast an erotic spell.

The sheet had slipped to her waist, exposing a pink silk camisole type garment with ribbon ties. Her nipples pressed against the silk. His pulse spiked at the tempting, delectable feast spread out on a banquet table. As if he willed her to wake, her eyes opened soft with sleep. Her hair looked tousled by a lover's hands. He cleared his throat to remove the raw huskiness.

"Good morning."

She yawned and stretched, seemingly unaware each titillating move was a siren's call to come to the table. "Isn't it early for visitors, or have you been waiting all night?"

"I slept outside."

"You'll cause a scandal if folks catch you here."

"No one is up yet."

She laughed, her voice coated with morning dew. "I'm fine." Apparently unfazed over her near nakedness, she sat and ran both hands up and down her right thigh. "No swelling." She unwrapped the dressing. "No red streaks either." She eased her feet over the side of the bed and stood. "I'm starving."

"Hunger's a good sign." Tight trousers provided evidence of his. "Now that I know ye're going to recover, I have a question."

"I'll answer what I can." She gathered her hair into a tail and clipped it to the top of her head.

He made a hook with his finger and wiggled the digit suggestively. "Come here." She turned toward him. "I've never seen anything like what ye're wearing."

"Hmm." Her eyebrow arched. "You're accustomed to seeing women's undergarments?"

He cleared his throat again.

She laughed and playfully fluffed his hair. "I ordered them from a catalogue."

"What kind of catalogue has undergarments?"

"Victoria's Secret. Now, you need to go so I can dress and go help Sarah with breakfast."

"I dinna think ye should go anywhere. Rest yer leg today."

"I'm not an invalid and won't be treated like one."

He reached for her hands and held them between his own. "Are ye sure ye're well?"

"I am, and you can stop worrying about me."

He pulled her close. "I'll leave ye alone if ye'll kiss me."

"That's black—"

He pressed his lips to hers, swallowing her protest. Heated blood roared to his groin, and he held her firmly against him, skimming his hands down her back, burying his fingers in the cool silk. Her hair tumbled from its clip and vanilla-scented tresses cascaded about her shoulders. He deepened the kiss, stroking the interior of her mouth, tasting her tongue while it explored his.

"Cullen." She moaned his name. He pressed her closer to his arousal, rubbing her against him. All that separated them were his trousers and a slip of fabric. He could unbutton his pants and enter her, even if it meant ripping the silk. The way she rubbed against him in a crescendo of passion said all he needed to know. His skin tingled with expectation.

"Let me make love to ye."

She pushed back, breaking away from their kiss. "*What* are we doing? This has to stop. I can't do this with you."

His breath stalled in his lungs. "Yer husband's dead, Kit."

She rubbed the scars on her neck. "Please leave."

"Yer body needs release, lass. Let me please ye."

"*No.*"

"How long has it been since ye made love?"

Her face turned scarlet, and she dropped her chin. "I've never...made love."

He lifted her head with the crook of his finger and gazed into her eyes. The level of fear he saw there made him wince. "Never?"

She pulled her head away. "It's complicated."

The air between them grew thick and heavy. "This is not complicated. What kind of man wouldna touch a desirable woman?"

Her tongue swept her lower lip. "The problem was with me. He wanted to, but—"

"Why?"

She grabbed her trousers and slipped them on. "He died before we got engaged."

Her words swung like the trapdoor to the gallows. "Ye lied?"

"Not exactly, I mean..."

"But ye're nae a widow?" He could feel his pulse beating in his wrists.

"It's complicated."

"Ye said that already, Kitherina MacKlenna." He grabbed the back of the rocker for a foothold to keep from slipping beneath his rising anger. "Is that yer real name, or did ye steal his name, too?"

She flinched. "It's *my* name."

A rush of chilly air swept through the wagon and stirred up the scent she carried. He ignored the arousing smells.

She grabbed her blouse. "Go away. I didn't ask for your help." She gazed at him without blinking, her expression unreadable.

"Without help, ye'd be dead by now."

He'd caught her lying, just as he'd caught witnesses lying in court. She couldn't or wouldn't explain why she was passing herself off as a widow. That meant one thing. She was protecting a bigger secret. His arm and shoulder muscles knotted. He had seen innocent men hanged, and guilty men go free, all because of lies. He had no tolerance for liars.

None.

He rushed past her and jumped free of the wagon, letting go a halting laugh. "Unlike Odysseus, I willna bathe in the fullness of a siren's song."

Chapter Sixteen

ANOTHER WEEK DRAGGED by as the wagon train traveled through Nebraska's dry and sandy grassland dunes. The ever-present dust tagged along as an annoying companion that made Kit itch and scratch. But Cullen's parting words played in an off-key loop in her head. To her, listening to anything off-key was a form of mind torture.

Homer's *Odyssey* had been required reading in high school English. From what she remembered of the story and what she gathered from Cullen's words, he thought she was tempting him. Hogwash. The last thing she wanted was a relationship with a womanizing, egotistical, overbearing jerk from the nineteenth century.

Fortunately, he was rarely in camp, and when he was, he kept his distance. In weak moments, she wanted to explain why she had lied about being a widow. But an explanation would lead to more questions she couldn't answer truthfully. No point in giving him an opportunity to catch her in more lies. Besides, Homer exhausted her knowledge of Greek literature, and her repertoire of Shakespeare was sketchy at best. She wouldn't be able to interpret his outbursts.

Even though Cullen occasionally acted like a jerk, she missed him. She missed his stories, his humming, and most of all his laughter. Other men laughed. So why did his laugh speak to her soul?

Because it harmonized with her own.

To avoid the dust, she and Stormy rode ahead of the wagon

train. Soon, she could no longer hear the shouts of the men driving their oxen. She'd ridden too far ahead and needed to turn around. But as she started back, she noticed the sky, not because it was paint worthy, just the opposite. Mushroom-shaped, green-tinted clouds canopied the prairie.

"*Hail.*" Fear crawled through her belly.

The children were with Sarah and safe from the approaching storm. But what about the animals? Tate and Tabor were with the girls. Hail would be tough on the oxen, but they'd survive. Out in the open, Stormy might not.

Up ahead there appeared to be an outcropping where she and her horse might be able to wait out the storm, but first she had to let Adam know where she was going. She raced back, waving for him to stop. "I need to get a bag out of the wagon."

"Those clouds don't look good, Miss Kit. You think Henry will circle up?"

"Probably. Secure the wagon and settle in. I'm going on ahead to find cover for Stormy. I'll be back as soon as the storm passes."

"Where?"

Kit pointed toward a ridge in the distance.

"You won't make it before the storm hits. Let me tell Pa where we're going, and I'll go with you."

"I can make better time by myself."

"But—"

"Adam, I have to go." She filled a small sack with oats and grabbed her backpack with emergency supplies.

"How can I explain to Mr. Montgomery that I let you go?"

Normally, she carried guilt around like a well-traveled makeup bag, but she refused to worry about what Cullen would think or do. "He'll probably hope I don't come back."

The dramatic widening of Adam's big brown eyes told her he didn't believe that was true. "I'll be back before Cullen knows I'm gone. Don't worry."

Before Adam could raise another objection, she galloped toward the lead wagon to find Henry. He and two other men huddled together battling the wind for control of a map. "We're in for a bad one," he said to Kit. "We'll circle here." A gust of wind buffeted him. He braced himself against his horse.

The wind tugged at her hat, and Stormy danced anxious steps. She couldn't keep up with both. She let the hat go. "I've got to find cover for Stormy. I'll be back."

"Don't be a fool. You got cover here."

"I do. Stormy doesn't. This storm could kill him." MacKlenna Farm treated its stallions like horses, not pampered pets, yet although they spent most days in their paddocks, they were never outside during a storm.

"Could kill you, too, missy."

"I've got to go."

"Get back to your wagon, or I'll hog-tie you."

Arguing with Henry would take time she didn't have. She put heels to her horse and galloped off, ignoring his ultimatum to turn around.

A mile from the wagon train, she rode smack into a dark shelf of clouds hanging close to the ground and blocking out the daylight. No cover. No protection. She'd made a horrible mistake. Fear no longer crawled in her belly. It sprinted.

A streak of lightning shot through the sky and struck a tree several yards away. Stormy screamed an almost human shriek of terror, reared, and climbed the air with his forelegs. His hooves hit the ground ready to run, but Kit yanked the reins and turned him in tight circles. Her adrenaline went haywire. Her body knew what her mind couldn't wrap itself around. This was about survival. She and her horse could very well die.

She rushed into a gully with sloped sandstone walls. The rain shafts turned thick and white. Within moments, hail would fall from the sky. Thunder rumbled through the gully. Wind whipped around a patch of thick brush and thorny branches and revealed an opening in the side of the gully. A cave? She galloped toward it.

Reaching the spot, she grabbed a flashlight from her backpack and peered inside. The short hairs on her neck stood at attention as she flashed the light into a space half the size of a one-car garage. She saw no nests, droppings, or snakes.

"Come on, boy. I think it's safe."

The sandstone walls felt cool to the touch. The air held a musky, damp scent and the stale odor of burnt wood.

Stormy's ears flattened against his head, his nostrils flared, and he stomped his feet.

"You're okay, boy, you're okay." She rubbed his nose and sang a medley of Tim McGraw tunes until he cocked his rear leg and relaxed his lips. "Wish Tim's music did the same for me." If she could, she'd cower in the corner with her ears covered against the frightening tin-drum sound of the hail. But she forced herself to hover at the entrance and watch the baseball-size stones collide and explode in midair. Ice chips sailed in her direction.

A long, worried sigh slipped between her lips. She'd found cover and Stormy was safe, but there would be ramifications for running off. Her prickly skin told her so. If Cullen returned to camp before she did, he might be angry enough to kick her off the wagon train. What would she do then? Stalk him? Probably. She wasn't about to put too much distance between them. Not until June 16. Then a century and a half might not be enough.

Chapter Seventeen

CULLEN MET UP with the wagon train, rain-soaked and weary. His back hurt like hell, and he wanted nothing more than a hot meal and a dry bed. He doubted he'd find either.

Rain cascaded in streams off his hat's wide brim as he looked across the corral. From behind the veil of water, he didn't see Kit's Thoroughbred. He gritted his teeth. "I swear to God, this time I'll wring her blasted neck."

He yanked back the flaps of Henry's tent and ducked in out of the rain. An oil lamp's light cast a dark shadow of Henry dozing in his rocking chair. A book lay open in his lap, his reading glasses down on his nose, and a snuffed-out pipe dangled from his hand.

"Ye awake?"

Henry sat straight in his chair, and the book dropped to the floor. "'Bout time you made it."

"Where's Stormy?"

Henry set down his pipe and folded his glasses. "You can blame me for not stopping her."

"From what?"

"Hailstorm was coming. She headed out to find cover for that stallion she should have sold in Independence. Can't keep that gal roped in no matter how hard you—"

"How long has she been gone?" Cullen dragged his hands down his face.

"Rode out early afternoon."

Cullen checked the time on his pocket watch. "It's midnight."

"She's holed up waiting for the rain to stop. Feel it in my bones. She'll be back by morning."

"Damn. I've got to go find her."

Henry rose and squeezed Cullen's shoulder. "We didn't get hail. Doubt she did either. Get some rest. Head out in the morning."

When Cullen turned his face toward the light, Henry let out a slow whistle. "What happened to you, son?"

Cullen twisted out of his poncho. "*Merde.*" Fingers of pain shot up his back. "Met up with three vaqueros who wanted what I wasna willing to give. Eye's fine. Ribs hurt. Back hurts more."

"Let me look."

He shrugged Henry off. "I'll ask Kit to patch me up."

"She's got healing magic, that's for sure. You best try to get some shut-eye."

Between the downpour causing a ruckus and the throbbing pain in his back, Cullen never closed his eyes. At least that's what he blamed for his inability to sleep. But he hadn't slept in the past week since he'd attempted to seduce Kit, which was why he'd welcomed a fistfight. The pummeling did nothing to assuage his guilt and made his bad temper more volatile.

He finally gave up the pretense of sleep, saddled Jasper, and rode out. Each mile he rode, staying balanced in the saddle became harder. With every footfall, he felt the sting of a cat-o'-nine-tails on his sweat-covered back. His poncho did nothing to protect him from sinking into a labyrinth of self-recrimination. He had replayed his last conversation with Kit a hundred times, and each time he reached the same verdict. They were both guilty parties. While he couldn't condone lying, he couldn't condone his own behavior either. She'd tried to stop him, but he'd swallowed her protests with a kiss.

Her plaintive words *the problem was with me* haunted him, as did the scars on her neck.

KIT WOKE TO the sound of heavy rainfall. That alone didn't

frighten her. The pitch-black darkness did. The arteries in her neck pulsed to the point of exploding. Cold, clammy hands searched for the flashlight she'd been holding when she drifted off to sleep. Where was it now? She patted the ground with open palms, gulping back the knot in her throat. The tips of her fingers touched something hard. It moved, and she yanked back her hand.

It's the flashlight, silly.

A hard breath of relief whooshed out when she flipped the switch. The beam of light cut through the darkness of the musky cave. Stormy's soft, low whine loosened the knot in her throat. He walked toward her, bringing heat and his familiar smell of oats and early mornings in the barn. "Hi, boy. You okay?" He playfully nudged her shoulder. "I love you, too."

Now fully awake, there was no chance of going back to sleep. What she needed was a cup of hot chocolate. There was a package of powdered chocolate and freeze-dried marshmallows in her bag. The warm drink might ease the anxiety that had replaced her fear.

While waiting for the chocolate to heat on the miniature camping stove, she stood at the cave's entrance and stared out into the inky void. No moon or stars filled the sky. And the only sound was rain splattering on water.

Water?

The knot raced back to her throat. She shone the light into the darkness. Water was rising in the gully. Her body froze, gripped in a terrifying moment. The cave could flood if the rain continued. She flashed the light through the cave. A high water event could have left sediment on the cave's walls. She didn't notice any, but she wasn't a spelunker and could easily miss significant signs.

Should she leave before the water rose higher? Stormy would balk if she tried to get him into the water in the middle of the night. She paced. What would her father do? Weigh the risk of leaving a safe, dry place, possibly drowning, against the improbability of the water rising high enough to flood the cave. That's what he would do. And that's what she would do. Remain vigilant and stay put until daylight, unless Cullen came by and threw another lasso in her direction. As angry as he was, she put the odds of a rescue at a million to one.

CULLEN HEADED TOWARD the rocks, doubled back, then headed back toward the rocks again. He knew Kit's general direction, but she could have veered right or left. Visibility was only a few feet.

He stared at a white blur in the darkness. "Whoa, Jasper." He dismounted and picked up what looked like Kit's straw hat caked in mud. Then he sent a howling call into the night. "Kit, where are ye?" He climbed back in the saddle and let out a second howl. Not for Kit, but a howl against the pain.

The minutes turned into an hour, the hour into hours, and still he searched, desperate to find her and apologize for his behavior.

Jasper trudged on, never faltering in his step, never refusing a command.

A beam of white light penetrated the darkness. He followed the beacon to the edge of a cliff overlooking a gully filling with water. The light disappeared. He funneled his hands at his mouth and yelled, "Kit, where are ye?" His voice, however, had abandoned him, and his whispered yell went no farther than his own ears.

Cullen, help me.

Her voice lured him toward the bluff's lip. He nudged Jasper with his heels, but the horse snorted his refusal to go over the edge. Cullen dismounted, angered by Jasper's betrayal.

Kristen needed him. Kit needed him. If Jasper wouldn't carry him, he would cross the gully alone. He stepped into the darkness, slid several feet down the cliff's side, and hit his head on a rock. With his face inches from the lapping water and Kit's name on his lips, he slipped into unconsciousness.

AT FIRST LIGHT, Henry found Jasper standing guard over Cullen's body. He lay facedown in the mud with water licking the top of his head. Henry had seen his share of dying men. Fear rose in his throat; fear that he'd lost part of himself without realizing how important it was.

He touched Cullen's neck. When he felt the twin rhythms of pulse and breath, his own heart beat in quiet gratitude. The boy was alive, and although his face was a sickly white and his breathing shallow, he had a chance to see another sunrise.

Henry heaved Cullen over Jasper's back and lashed him to the saddle. He took no pleasure in Cullen's pained moans, but that didn't stop him from lambasting the pigheaded fool the entire way back to camp.

"Serves you right, you son of a bitch, heading out in the middle of the night, hunting for a whisper in the wind. Soon as you get better, you can dig out your bedroll and drift. I ain't going to watch you kill yourself over that little widow. She ain't looking to have her weeds plowed. You need to leave her be." Cullen never answered him, and Henry doubted he even heard.

When he arrived back at camp, he and John hauled Cullen into the tent, out of his muddy rain gear, and onto Henry's cot.

"Sarah's fixing some willow bark tea. Should help with the fever."

Henry poured water into a bowl and soaked a cloth. "Kit's his only hope now. Rain's stopped. Time for her to be coming back."

"She might not make it, Henry," John said.

Henry washed the mud from Cullen's face and hair. "I won't allow that kind of talk. She's coming back."

"Keep your dreams, but prepare for losing them both."

Henry pointed to the tent flaps. "Go on, get out of here."

"I'm going, but if you need anything, you holler."

"I'll tell you one thing for sure. Only the Lord knows when a person's time's up. These two got lives to live. I know it in my heart."

As soon as John left the tent, the sting of tears came into Henry's eyes. He'd played a lone hand for a long time. Never met a woman he wanted to settle down with, but if he had, Cullen would have been what he wanted in a son. Henry wouldn't give up on the boy. Not today. Not ever. "Kit will be here soon enough. I don't doubt it. No sirree. She'll be riding in here any minute now."

When Cullen fell asleep, Henry left the tent to stretch and puff on his pipe. There was a sweet smell in the air from the storm washing the prairie clean. He adjusted his hat to shade his eyes from the morning sun and noticed a horse and rider far off in the distance. He watched for several minutes until he recognized the blond-haired beauty riding a chestnut stallion with three white stockings.

"Yes sirree, she's back. Best go tell the boy help's arrived."

Chapter Eighteen

K IT SPOTTED JASPER as soon as she rode into camp. She glanced around and was surprised and thankful that there were no storm-damaged wagons or dead animals. The chewing out she expected might well be the only storm-related disaster. But what could Cullen do worse than accusing her of being a siren luring him to his death? Well, for one, he could toss her off the wagon train. If he did, would Henry come to her defense? Or John? She'd tried to plead her case to Henry before without success, so she doubted he would be any help if she were banished. She just hoped she hadn't tossed her chance of finding the South Pass wagon train in the trash like a pocketful of two-dollar losing tickets.

There was no point in going to her wagon and delaying the inevitable confrontation. She rode straight to Henry's camp and dismounted just as he exited his tent. He had tear streaks in his whiskers. "Good God, Henry. What's the matter?"

"Where you been, missy?"

Heat flushed her cheeks. "Where's Cullen? I'll tell you both at the same time."

"He's asleep."

"This late?"

"Don't reckon he knows the time."

"What're you talking about?"

"He went out looking for you. I found him facedown in the mud a few hours ago."

She shifted into paramedic mode, sensing something serious had happened. "What's wrong with him?"

"You two are dumber than crock-heads."

She breathed in and out slowly, so tempted to grab the gun out of Henry's holster and shoot him. "Where's Cullen?"

Henry pointed over his shoulder. "In there."

She threw back the flaps. Cullen's deathbed face shocked her. "Did he get shot?"

Henry massaged his brow. "Nope."

"Stabbed?"

"Nope."

Her fists clenched and unclenched. "*Henry*. Don't make me drag it out of you. Tell me what happened."

And he told her all he knew.

To treat Cullen, she needed her bag, and she needed to get him away from Henry. "Will you carry him to my wagon?"

"He's fine where he is."

"No, he's *not*. Everything I need is in my wagon." She turned on her heels and hurried to her campsite. A few minutes later, Henry and John delivered the patient.

"What else can we do?" Henry asked.

"Take off his clothes," Kit said.

Henry's eyes widened above pink-tinted cheeks. "All?"

"I want to see his cuts and bruises." She chewed on her bottom lip while she studied the bruise around Cullen's eye. "How long ago was he in a fight?"

"Four days, I reckon."

"Wonder what the other guy looks like."

"Other *guy*?" Henry said with a grunt. "There was three of 'em. Cullen's got more guts than you can hang on a fence."

She blew out a breath, hot with exasperation. "It doesn't take guts to get into a fight. It takes guts to stay out of one." On closer inspection, the bruises on his chest concerned her. He might have a rib or two broken. If so, a jagged bone could injure another organ. For now, she'd keep him quiet and control his pain, enabling him to breathe easier.

"Help me roll him over."

Henry squeezed Cullen's shoulder and tilted him forward. He moaned.

Kit drew back at the sight of a three-inch, jagged laceration just above his hips. Anger brought her blood to a quick boil. "Why didn't he do something about this?"

"Didn't want me to see to it. Said he'd wait for you."

"He's too smart to let this go untreated."

"Finding you was more important."

She held out her hands in a questioning gesture. "But he wasn't even speaking to me."

Henry spoke with quiet words. "The boy's mixed up when it comes to feelings for you."

Whatever those mixed up feelings were, she couldn't dwell on them now. "Henry, you and John go outside and wait. Let me see what I can do."

"He'll be all right, then." Henry's words formed a statement, not a question.

She didn't deserve such faith. If he could see her shaking hands knotted in her lap, he'd have doubts instead. "Let me do what I can," she said with false confidence.

Cullen groaned and tried to lift his head.

She pressed back on his shoulders. "Be still. I'm going to give you something for pain. Can you tell me where you hurt and what the pain feels like? Is it sharp, throbbing, burning? Can you swallow a pill?"

"Sharp. Hurts like hell in my back. I can swallow." His raspy voice barely sounded human.

She placed a Percocet on his tongue and gave him a drink from a canteen.

"What is it?"

"Percocet."

"Never heard…" His words slurred as if he'd had several shots of whisky.

"It's a narcotic. Give it a few minutes. It will take the edge off your pain." Between the well-stocked medicine cabinets at MacKlenna Mansion and Scott's medical bag, she'd collected a generous supply of painkillers and antibiotics. "Open your mouth and take this one, too."

"What is it?"

"Ciprofloxacin."

She pulled a stethoscope from her bag and listened to his heart. He watched her from beneath hooded lids. "What's on yer neck? What's on my arm?"

"Stethoscope." She placed the chest piece in his hand. "I can hear your heart and lungs. That's a blood pressure cuff on your arm. Your pressure is too low."

"Why'd ye go away?"

She stuck a thermometer in his mouth. "Keep this under your tongue. Don't talk. I'm back now. It doesn't matter."

In his condition, she couldn't imagine how he had stayed on a horse. And the thought of him lying in the mud made her sick to her stomach. She removed the thermometer. His fever was too high.

"I need to apologize," he said.

"Quiet." Before she could get the tourniquet around his arm to start an IV, he drifted off to asleep. She started an IV with saline to rehydrate him, then rolled him over and cleaned the laceration's jagged edge. He looked like he'd been kicked with a sharp-toed boot then raked with the spur's rowel. The cut had been open too long to stitch. She cut away small pieces of devitalized tissue and dressed the wound. Healing would have to occur from the inside out.

Henry had done a half-decent job cleaning him up, but he still had mud in his hair. The medication took the edge off his discomfort, and the tension in his arms, neck, and face seemed to ease. She pressed a light kiss on his mouth, surprised by how warm and soft his lips were.

"Get well, Cullen."

"Kiss me again," he mumbled.

And she did, convinced his memory would fade as quickly as the kiss.

KIT MADE A pallet in the back of the buckboard and with John's help, Cullen hobbled to the carriage for the day's ride across Nebraska.

He contorted his face with each step. "I'm nae a damn invalid. I can ride my horse."

Kit watched as his head wobbled on his shoulders. With his eyes so glassy, it was a wonder he could see to put one foot in front of the other. Sure, he could ride. That's what got him into this mess to begin with.

"I stayed up all night taking care of you. Either you ride in the buckboard, or John will put you back in my wagon and you can bounce across Nebraska for all I care. What do you want to do?"

"Ride with me."

She crossed her arms and tapped her fingers against her elbows. "I'm in no mood for surliness."

"I willna complain."

He probably wouldn't complain, but he'd ask questions she couldn't answer. "Okay."

The move from the wagon to the buckboard exhausted him. He was asleep within minutes. When he woke hours later, he appeared to be coming out of a fog, blinking rapidly to focus. She handed him two pills and held his head while he drank from a canteen.

"Better?"

He nodded and wiped away drops of water from his chin. "Where'd ye go?"

"I've been right here."

"During the hailstorm."

"I found a cave about a mile from the wagons. The gully filled with water, and I got trapped inside."

His eyes moved along her face. Her cheeks flushed, and she glanced away, afraid she'd reveal something about herself he didn't need to know. "I was there. At the gully. I saw a light, but I didna see a cave."

The light must have been her flashlight. Should she say something? No. Ignore it and move on. She grabbed Tabor's hairbrush and began to brush him, avoiding eye contact with Cullen. "It was a miracle I found it."

He rubbed a small bruise on his arm made by the IV needle. She sensed a question sat on his tongue ready to roll out. Tabor meowed and jumped from her lap. The brush held globs of cat hair.

"Where'd yer people come from?" Cullen asked.

She pulled hair from the brush, stalling to think. "The MacKlennas came from Scotland."

"What year?"

"The first Thomas MacKlenna left Callander and immigrated around 1763."

"A Highlander?"

"You're not the only one in America."

The corners of his mouth wrinkled with a smile that pushed into his dimples. "Aye, there are a few of us."

"Where's your family from?" she asked.

"I grew up around Callander, but my family immigrated to Richmond, Virginia. I'll mention the MacKlennas to my father. We might share common ancestors."

She swallowed a tickling of anxiety. Could he post a letter and get a response before they reached South Pass? She didn't think so, but...

"Did Thomas MacKlenna immigrate to Kentucky?"

"He got a land grant for the original four hundred acres. Stayed and farmed for a few years, then returned to Scotland where he died. His son Thomas inherited MacKlenna Farm. That's where I grew up. Three thousand acres of lush bluegrass."

"Old Thomas is yer grandfather?"

"Great." *Great-great-great-great-great-great.*

Cullen kept his eyes focused on hers for a beat or two. "Why'd ye leave? What does Oregon offer that your farm didna?"

If she tried to tell him it was complicated, he might strangle her. She scratched her nose, took a breath. "I needed to get away for a while."

"*Get away?*" Suspicion dripped from his voice. "From a farm ye love and still own?"

"Yes, but—"

"Dinna ye dare say it's complicated."

"This is where our last argument ended." She paused, took the edge off her tone, and continued. "I don't want to fight with you. I'm not going to talk about certain topics. Either you accept that, or—"

"We keep arguing?"

"I'm not going to argue."

He glanced at his arm and rubbed the small puncture wound. "If I ask ye what ye did to my arm, are ye going to say it's complicated, too?"

She gazed at his hooded eyes and sensed he already knew the answer, but that was impossible. He was asleep when she gave him the IV. She took a deep, shivery breath and said, "Yes, it's complicated."

Chapter Nineteen

T HE WAGON TRAIN reached Chimney Rock, five hundred seventy-five miles and thirty-five exhausting days from Independence and halfway to South Pass. The rock's buff-colored, sandy clay finger was visible on the horizon and had been for the past twenty-four hours. If the little girls had asked how much farther one more time, Kit would have put them on Stormy and taken them on ahead, which would have really irritated their brothers who were just as excited to see the most famous landmark on the trail.

Henry found a level spot close to the river, and they camped in the shadow of the rock.

Frances came to the supper table with two drawings. She handed one to Kit and the other to her ma. "I drew pictures of the Chimney."

Kit put down her fork and studied the drawing. "This is wonderful. When'd you do this?"

"Yesterday, when we were far, far away. How tall is it?"

Kit put her finger to her cheek. "Hmm, about three hundred and twenty-five feet."

John crinkled his brow. "How do you know that?"

Kit passed Frances's drawing around the table for everyone to see. "Somebody measured its shadow, didn't they?"

John propped the drawing up in front of him. "Well, I never heard that."

Kit shrugged. "Maybe I'm wrong." *Or maybe I just gave them the twenty-first century measurement.*

"There's plenty of room to carve our names. Can we, Pa?" Elizabeth asked, batting her eyelashes.

Where'd she learn to do that?

John looked over his shoulder toward the landmark, scratching his chin. When he turned back around he said, "Eat your dinner. Soon as you've done your chores, we'll go see it."

Frances pumped her fist like a champion. "*Yeah.*"

Kit put her hand to her forehead and lowered her head. *What have I done?*

After dinner, John hitched the buckboard and drove the family over to the rock where he chiseled their names in the sandstone. Kit sketched a picture of the family with Chimney Rock and the pine- and juniper-dotted bluffs in the background.

As an artist, she paid special attention to the dichotomy between the land's breathtaking beauty and the unrelenting hardship they faced, and she tried to show that in the drawing's coloring and shading. On another sheet of paper, she jotted random notes: Nebraska's rugged beauty, Wyoming's swales and ruts, Sweetwater River valley to South Pass, South Pass—final destination.

How in the world would she ever be able to say good-bye to the Barretts? In a short time, she had come to love them. She shook away the thought and went back to drawing. In the midst of sketching John, her fingers began to tingle, and she dropped the pencil. The man in the drawing wasn't John. It was her father. Her head started swimming, and she fell smack into the memory of the crash. She was once again riding in the backseat of the car as it careened off the road, smashed through a fence, and into an oak tree.

"Kit, what's the matter?" Sarah's voice sounded garbled and distant.

"I don't feel well…"

The next thing Kit knew she was sitting in a rocking chair back at camp with her head resting on the stenciled, wide-curved rail. John and Sarah hovered over her. "What happened?"

"You fainted." Sarah wiped Kit's forehead with a wet cloth.

John pulled his eyebrows into a frown. "I'll leave you two to sort this out." He and Sarah gazed at each for a brief moment, long enough for a conversation with their eyes. Kit glanced away feeling awkward, and if she were honest, envious.

"Tell me what happened," Sarah asked.

"I was drawing a picture of your family, but instead of sketching John's face, I drew my father's. Then I was back in the car—" She stopped before she revealed too much. After a moment, she continued. "Life is so uncertain, and there're no do-overs."

Sarah laid the washcloth aside and pulled a chair next to Kit. Their knees pressed together, and layers of cotton softened the bone-to-bone touch. Sarah's rough, work-worn hands patted Kit's callused ones. "You know what it means to be free. That's what you feel when you ride your horse or play the guitar, but I'm not sure you understand freedom. If you did, you wouldn't be stuck in pain's clutch. You're hurting. I see it in your eyes. But you'll heal. You'll be whole again." Sarah sat back in her chair with a sigh. "Your story is a tapestry with intricate detail work. Sadness is woven throughout with different shades of gray threads. It's time to open your heart and let joy weave bright colors through your masterpiece."

"But—"

Sarah held up her hand to silence Kit. "I can't promise we'll all make it to Oregon, but I promise we'll stay together and see this through to the end. You can't give up. Keep in your heart the knowledge that we walk *through* the valley of the shadow. We don't stay there. Take this journey and every journey one day at a time."

Kit wiped away her tears, overwhelmed by the depth of Sarah's wisdom.

"Cullen should be ready for supper. Wash your face now and take him dinner. We'll talk again."

KIT CARRIED A plate of food to Cullen and sat on the tailgate waiting for him to wake. A low sweep of clouds reminded her of home. Sunset on the farm was like no other, especially in early fall when the cool air whipped through the trees, sprinkling a treasure of gold over the bluegrass. While she missed home, she wasn't ready to return.

The low rumble of his voice pulled her from her thoughts. "Either I'm sicker than I thought, or something else has upset ye."

She swung around. "What makes you think something's wrong?"

"Seen ye sit there before with a straight back and square shoulders, swinging yer legs. Ye dinna look like that now."

She stood and stepped to his side. "If you can read me so well, tell me what you see."

He studied her face. "A woman full of life and love but afraid to live it. Afraid to feel it."

"Ouch. Sorry I asked."

He took the plate and set it aside, then pulled her down to sit on the bed beside him. "Ye're much more than ye appear to be." He traced the veins in her hand with his fingertips. "Ye pour gifts out on others, but ye tenaciously guard yer heart." He brought her hand to his lips and kissed the inside of her wrist. His warm breath sent tingles up her arms and across her shoulders. "No one can give ye the reassurance ye want."

Beneath a growth of whiskers, his face had thinned, but his voice held calmness and compassion that spoke from the soul of the man enshrouded in layers of a complex personality.

"I got the same lecture from Sarah. Most of the time I'm fine, but then the grief and guilt hit me, and I feel like I'm starting all over."

He caressed her hand. "Ye're nae starting over. I see healing in yer eyes, which I might add, dinna have tears at the moment. And ye're nae biting yer lip to keep them away either."

Was it true? Was she really getting better? Or was she just hanging on until the next big wind sucked her into another vortex? Another big wind was on its way. Every healed bone in her body told her so.

THREE DAYS HAD passed since Kit returned from the cave and

found Cullen seriously ill. He now walked a few steps around camp and found reasons to bark at John and Henry. He saw her approaching the buckboard. "I'm nae riding in that wagon again. I've got a horse. I'm getting on it."

Make that John, Henry, and her.

Jasper appeared as if by magic. Cullen had a co-conspirator. She glanced around and caught a flash of Adam's plaid shirt on the other side of the wagon. *Traitor.*

If Cullen thought he was well enough to ride, he could just sit his sorry ass in the saddle, and she'd see how long he could last. With his innate stubbornness, it occurred to her that he might make it until the nooning, so she packed a lunch basket.

"Mount up, Mr. Montgomery," she said. "I'll get my horse."

The weather was perfect—the kind of day that defined spring. She sketched in her journal as they rode across the prairie. The clouds formed odd shapes that drifted at a leisurely pace across the robin's-egg-blue sky. Colored pencils would be nice. Wildflowers splashed the tall grass with vivid purples and golds. In between the sky and wildflowers was a view of Scotts Bluff that added mystery to the landscape. And looming beyond the bluff was snow-capped Laramie Peak, a vivid reminder of the ascent into the Rocky Mountains.

From an artistic perspective—sublime to dangerous—it didn't get any better.

When Cullen stretched, his saddle creaked under his weight.

"You sure you're all right?"

He crossed his hands over his saddle horn. "Ye've asked twice in the past hour. My answer is the same. Fine."

She lowered her head and looked at him over the top edge of the sunglasses she wished she was wearing. "Don't get testy."

There was no pleasure in his expression when he glanced at his arm for the umpteenth time. The pinprick and discoloration had faded, but he remembered. As she'd discovered, Cullen never forgot anything, and she knew he found it irritating that he didn't understand what she'd done to him. To get his mind off the pinprick, she hummed a few measures of Bach's "Toccata and Fugue in D Minor."

"Shall we work our way through Bach?" he asked.

"You can't stump me."

"Would ye like to place a wager?"

"I would, but I know you don't bet."

He chuckled. "I'll make an exception."

"And what would you bet?"

He glared at his arm as if the appendage had betrayed him. "I'll give up an annoying habit."

She burst out laughing, startling Stormy who danced sideways. "Okay, boy." She patted his neck. "I was going to ask what annoying habits you have, but a list formed in my mind immediately."

He slapped his chest. "Ouch."

"Well, what habit did you have in mind? I'll decide if it's worth a wager."

"I had hoped if I called enough attention to this pinprick, ye'd tell me where it came from. But our donkey determination has butted heads."

"So what's the bet?"

"If I stump ye, ye'll tell me what ye put in my arm. If ye stump me, I willna mention it again."

She waved her arm in a grand gesture. "You go first."

They went through Bach's instrumentals and vocals then moved on to Mozart. Toward noon, Cullen's shoulders slumped, but she knew he'd never admit to being tired.

"I think Stormy picked up a rock. I need to stop."

"There's shade ahead. Can ye make it to that overhang?"

The real question was, could he? She pulled two Tylenol from her shirt pocket. "Take these."

He popped them into his mouth then swigged water from his canteen. "What—"

She gave an inward groan. "Swallow the pills."

He corked the canteen. "I was going to ask what the word 'Tylenol' means."

"It's taken from the chemical compound *cetylaminophenol*. And if you'd rather not take them, I won't give you any more."

"Whoa, I'm nae complaining. Two pills and my aches go away. But I think I've discovered yer secret."

"What's that?"

"Ye have a laboratory on yer farm in Kentucky where ye make mystery pills. Then ye give them to patients to test their healing potential."

She wrote in her palm with an invisible pen. "Dear laboratory assistants. The patient reports that after taking two Tylenol his pain goes away." She glanced at Cullen. "Can I report anything else?"

"Yes, I have more anecdotal evidence." He leaned out of his saddle and kissed her. "Add that to the letter to yer laboratory assistants."

She laughed until tears poured down her cheeks.

CULLEN STRETCHED OUT on a blanket and pillowed his head with folded arms. His black hat covered his forehead and eyes. "Tell me what ye see."

She glanced up and around. "A cloud-filled sky and a concentrated disturbance of vegetation."

A wisp of a smile crinkled the corners of his lips.

"What do you see?" There was a bit of touch-me-tease-me in her voice.

"A beautiful woman I want to kiss." His fingers wrapped gently around her arm, and he pulled her toward him.

"Not a good idea."

"Tsk, tsk, *not a good idea* would be wasting the time we have alone."

"You need rest." She tried to sit, but he pulled her back down.

"Rest with me."

"That's all you want?"

"Nae, not all I want." He moved with the speed of a man fully recovered.

Damn those pills.

Before she could escape, he had her beneath him, her head resting in the crook of his elbow. He traced the curve of her jaw with the back of his finger. "There is something so uniquely beautiful about ye. Worldly, yet innocent. I believe ye're from the Aegean Isle?"

"Nope, the far side of the moon." She teased her fingertips down the length of his pulsing neck.

His lips met hers in a soft, seductive dance. "I've never met anyone from the far side before." The sounds of the warm cello, the soft mellow flute, the rumbling beat of the kettledrum, the mysterious oboe, the soulful bagpipes blended in his voice and created a symphony that played to her heart.

"You have now."

Cullen nuzzled her neck, sending silky shivers whispering across her skin. His hand glided over her breasts. "No corset for Kit MacKlenna."

"Easier for you to touch me."

"And taste ye." He unbuttoned her blouse, slipped his hand inside her camisole, and cupped her breast. "Yellow silk." His voice was creamy and delicious. His thumb circled her nipple, eliciting heady sensations that rolled through her body, producing a dizzying explosion of pleasure. He lowered his head and took her nipple into his mouth.

Sizzling heat twirled her in a Viennese waltz of surrender.

Her virginity had almost been stolen on a stormy night years earlier, and because of that she held on to it tenaciously, but now beneath the Nebraska sky, she wanted to give herself to the man she had fallen in love with—a man who could never be part of her life.

She traced the tip of her tongue around the shell of his ear, and whispered. "Make love to me."

He shuddered and let out a long sigh. "Aye, lass, there's nothing I want more." He gazed into her eyes. "I willna take your maidenhead or risk getting ye with child."

"I have...condoms."

He drew back with a gasp. "Good God, woman. *Why?*" He

rolled away from her and jumped to his feet.

She took the verbal attack with a confused shudder. "They were in my backpack to use for emergency water storage—"

"Ye'd give yerself to me knowing I'm going to marry Abigail?" His voice was a deep wolf's growl. His eyes smoked with fury.

"What a jerk. You're crazy." She clamored to her feet, but in her adrenaline rage, caught her shoe in the dress's hem. She tugged on her skirt. "Thoughts of *her* didn't stop you from touching me. If you're going to marry the woman, marry her. But leave me the hell alone." White-hot anger boiled inside her gut.

His lip held a sardonic crook. "Ye've known my intentions all along."

"What are you saying? I'm a condom-toting slut?"

"That isna what—"

She spun on her heels. "Go to hell, Cullen Montgomery."

"Come back here." He grabbed her arm, but she jerked it out of his grasp.

"Leave me alone." She bunched up her skirt and mounted Stormy.

Don't cry. Not in front of him.

She galloped away, found an isolated spot by the river, and dismounted. What in the world happened? Cullen had turned on her quicker than that rattlesnake sank his fang. The venomous betrayal went deep into her bloodstream. She had trusted him and even wanted to give...*oh, God, how could I have been so stupid?*

She'd risked more than she could afford to risk, and he had violated her trust. She rubbed the scars on her neck. The memories heaved her into a Machiavellian chamber of horrors. Feeling violently sick, she threw up her lunch.

Damn him.

FROM A DISTANCE, Cullen watched Kit cry. His heart crawled into his throat and hung there, choking him. The only women he had known with condoms were the courtesans he visited in Europe. Knowing Kit had them sent his mind reeling in all sorts of deviant directions.

Was she offering herself to him for pleasure? If to him, then who else? The thought of another man holding her, touching her, kissing her filled him with the burn of jealousy and fire of rage.

Now that his heart no longer thundered, he could see clearly. And what he saw made him cower in shame. In her pain and tears, her trust in him had shattered before his eyes.

He groaned like the ground erupting. "Lord, what have I done?"

Bits and pieces of the dream he had the night of Kit's snakebite coiled in his mind. In the dream, she had left him, and he couldn't find her. He yelled, but she didn't answer. He grieved, but she didn't return to console him. Kristen appeared and led him to the path he needed to take, but he woke before the journey began.

He had a sense he'd just taken the first step on that journey.

Chapter Twenty

THE WAGON TRAIN crossed the toll bridge at the tree-fringed North Platte River, then had followed Cullen to a camping spot three miles west of Fort Laramie. The fort marked another milestone on the trail, six hundred fifty miles from Independence—less than three hundred miles from South Pass. Kit made notes in her journal, frowning as she often did when she thought of leaving her friends.

"Why are you frowning? It's a beautiful day." Sarah sat in a rocking chair, mending a pair of trousers.

Kit looked about. The dark blue sky bordered on purple and the temperature hovered in the high seventies, but the dust and an insensitive lawyer kept the day from ranking up there with the gorgeous ones. The paint-worthy ones. The ones she remembered because something extraordinary happened.

"I need to take Stormy to the fort to see the farrier."

"Take Adam with you."

"He's fixing a wheel and doesn't have time to babysit me."

Sarah tied off the thread and folded the pants. "What about Ben?"

"He and Clint are both with John."

"It's not safe for you to go alone."

Nothing in the nineteenth century was safe. Cullen wasn't safe. The trail wasn't safe. The food wasn't safe. The water wasn't safe. Why should the fort be safe? She didn't have the energy to argue.

"What if I put on my short-hair wig and wear trousers? Everyone will think I'm a boy. Will that make you feel better?"

Sarah's gasp told Kit exactly what she thought of the idea. But her eyes held a spark of interest. "Get dressed and let me see."

Kit scrunched her face in disbelief. "You sure?"

Sarah gulped. "I think. Hurry up."

A few minutes later, Kit returned with her pant legs tucked into her riding boots and a wide-brim hat covering a short, blond wig.

Sarah stood, placed her hands on Kit's shoulders, and spun her around. "Why, you're the prettiest boy I ever did see."

Kit suppressed a smile. "Can I go now?"

"Please stay out of trouble. If John finds out I encouraged you, he'll be upset with me. Keep your voice low and hurry back."

"I'll be a couple of hours. You sure you don't need anything?"

"If I do, we can get it tomorrow."

Kit pulled her hat brim close to her eyes and rode off, passing Henry's wagon. She didn't see Cullen's horse. Did that mean he was at the fort? She hoped not. In the past week, he'd made no effort to apologize. Never again would his smooth talk turn her into a fool.

No talking. No fraternizing. No way. No.

She rode into the fort with her head down, hunching her shoulders. Could she pull off the charade? Sure, as long as she didn't see Cullen.

The farrier wasn't at the stables, and there was no one around to ask when he'd return. If he didn't show up soon, she'd leave and come back later. While she waited, she decided to give Stormy a bath.

A hand slapped her shoulder and spun her around, bringing her nose-to-chest with a scraggly haired, hard-ass-looking soldier. A lieutenant, judging from his uniform.

"That's mighty fine horseflesh, boy. You interested in a race?"

A race?

He hawked up a wad of phlegm and spat into the dirt next to her toes. "Are you deaf? Do you want to race that there stallion?"

Yuk. A disgusting man with a hard-life story written in the wrinkles of his face. A tale she certainly didn't care to read. "How far?"

"A mile."

She loved to race and had been trained by some of the best jockeys in the business. A spirited one-on-one challenge was just what she needed to wipe Cullen Montgomery right out of her mind.

"You got yourself a race, mister."

He pointed toward the other side of the fort. "Track's that way."

Kit stretched her neck, looking where he was pointing. "I'll meet you over there."

After grooming Stormy, she mounted up and trotted over to the track. News of a horse race had already spread around the fort. A crowd of soldiers, civilians, and a handful of Indians had gathered to watch. A man yelled odds and was taking bets, creating a buzz of activity. The bookmaker set the odds at 20:1 that Stormy would beat the crowd favorite, a stallion whose black coat glistened in the afternoon sun.

Luck was playing nice with her. Cullen wasn't in the crowd. Relief tempered her excitement. If he had any inkling of what she was about to do, he'd make the same effort to stop her as he'd made rescuing her from the Kansas. He'd throw his lasso and pull her off the track.

Stormy swaggered toward the starting line, tilting his ears like a windmill.

Someone yelled, "Look at the boy. He's got one of them fancy pancake saddles." The crowd roared. "He'll fall and bust his ass."

She straightened, feeling as if her courage had migrated south, leaving her heart pounding faster than normal.

A pistol-toting soldier jogged to the oval-shaped track. He stood opposite the crowd and raised his gun. "Riders ready?"

An ever-swelling howl of catcalls arose from the spectators.

"Set," the soldier yelled.

Kit knew what Stormy was capable of under normal circumstances. But what had the last few weeks done to his stamina? The horse pranced and waited for the call, and she diverted distractive thoughts to her brain's trash bin, currently filled to overflowing.

The soldier fired a single shot, and the crowd burst into cheers.

Stormy broke fast, hurtled away, and ran a length ahead at the break. She balanced in midair with her weight on her toes, pressed against the stirrups' metal bases. Hunching forward, she grabbed the reins just behind Stormy's neck. The lieutenant drew his whip and laid a series of stinging blows across his horse's withers. His stallion leaped forward.

The first turn came quickly, and Kit moved Stormy toward the inside. The lieutenant bore in and bumped her horse, almost knocking her off. Someone with less experience would have fallen. She regained her balance and let the reins run through her fingers, giving Stormy his head to lengthen his stride. She positioned him right behind the lieutenant's horse, turning wide into the back-stretch. Kit moved inside and gained the lead, but the black stallion repulsed the challenge and moved ahead by a length.

At the far turn, Kit made her move. Using her entire upper body, she worked with her horse. A chorus of cheers boomed across the prairie. At the top of the stretch, a lion of a roar erupted. Stormy accelerated. His muscled neck pumped beneath her hands, and his hooves pounded the hard-packed ground. The horses hit the last furlong stake, matching stride for stride.

"Come on, boy, you can do it." And he did, pulling ahead and galloping across the finish line. Kit stood in the stirrups and craned her neck to see the other horse back three lengths. She rode to the next quarter turn before circling back.

The high-pitched twittering of a bald eagle drew her gaze to the sky. The creature soared above the plains on fully extended wings. There were similarities between the eagle's dominance and grace and Stormy's power and beauty. And there was something else, something intangible—an indomitable spirit linked with hers. Yes, she would get to South Pass and find the answers she sought. And nothing, not Cullen, not snakes, not rivers would stand in her way.

SHOUTING INTERRUPTED CULLEN'S meeting with Fort Laramie's commander.

"Sergeant," Commander Garnett hollered. "What's the ruckus?"

The sergeant appeared at the doorway of the commander's office. "A race is 'bout to start, sir."

"Who's racing?"

"A boy from the wagon train camped north of here is racing a chestnut stallion."

Cullen's hand jerked and knocked against his cup. Coffee splattered on the corner of a map spread open on the table.

"Against the lieutenant's black stallion, I assume," Garrett said.

"Yes, sir," the sergeant answered.

The commander faced Cullen. "If that horse is from your wagon train, Mr. Montgomery, I doubt it will be much of a race. The lieutenant's horse has never been beaten."

Cullen wiped up the spill with his handkerchief. "I dinna ken who's riding the stallion, but he can beat anything ye got." He gazed out the window across the parade ground. With the exception of Adam, Cullen couldn't imagine Kit letting anyone ride Stormy. And Adam was too smart to get talked into a race. If the jockey wasn't Adam, then who was he?

Garnett's slow, knowing smile segued into a chuckle. "How much you willing to wager?"

Braham McCabe walked away from the map table and joined his friend at the window. "Cullen and I have known each other since we were lads," Braham said to Garnett. "As far as I ken, he's never wagered on anything. But as for me"—he thumped his chest—"I've got a five dollar gold piece that says he's right about this horse."

Cullen felt a shiver race down his back. "Ye betting on a horse ye've never seen?"

Braham grinned. "Ye've seen him, and ye're a better judge of horseflesh than I am." He slapped Cullen on the shoulder. "Come on. Let's watch a race. If I lose, ye're buying me a drink."

"Hell, I'll need more than a drink when this is over."

A sick expression crossed Braham's face. "I've put money on yer horse. Now ye dinna sound so convincing."

"It isna the horse I doubt." A nagging uneasiness settled in his gut. Did he want to watch the race, or try to stop it? He vacillated between a slow walk and fast trot to the track. But the commander and Braham set the pace, and they arrived at the starting line as the gun fired.

"What I can see, I believe ye're right about that horse," Braham said. "But the rider willna stay on his back riding like that."

The feeling of imminent calamity punctured his armor with the heavy steel of a battle-ax. Stormy's rider wasn't one of the Barrett boys. The graceful curves of the jockey's derriere rising above the Thoroughbred's back in a delicate balancing act were obvious to him, if not to everyone else. He couldn't work up enough spit to swallow. His vision narrowed to only one horse—one rider. Mentally, he prepared to fight or rescue, whatever needed doing to save Kit's life. Again.

Cheers grew louder as the horses entered the stretch. Cullen braced for the final few seconds of the race. A riot would break out if the fan favorite went down in defeat and the soldiers discovered the winning jockey was a woman.

As long as he lived, he would never forget walking out of the freight office in Independence and seeing Stormy, recognizing immediately the strength and power born of a true champion. But it was the beautiful woman who embodied the pair's true spirit.

Cullen held his breath as the Thoroughbred's explosive kick put him across the finish line three lengths ahead of his rival. The dazzling burst sucked the breath from the spectators, leaving a momentary hushed silence echoing beneath the pounding hooves.

Relieved, he swabbed his sleeve across his sweaty brow and released a ragged sigh.

Braham took off his hat and waved it high above his head. "Yippee! I'll be damned. What a race." He shouted the only celebratory cheers amidst the rising din of disgruntled voices.

Commander Garnett, although white in the face from shock, took defeat in the gracious style of a southern gentleman. "You know your horses, but that rider has an unorthodox riding style." He flipped a gold coin to Braham. "Hope you give me an opportunity to win that back over a game of cards tonight?"

Braham caught the coin and twirled it between his fingers. "Canna say no to that offer."

The crowd dispersed, leaving Cullen and Braham to congratulate the winner.

Kit rode up beside the two men. "Did you see the race?" Her eyes were wide, her chest heaving with each deep breath.

Cullen felt an angry red flush on his face. "We'll talk about this later. What the hell have ye done to your hair?"

Braham stroked his chin, squinting in confusion. "I didna think you knew this kid, Cul." Then he added, "What's wrong with his hair?"

"I know *him*." He spit out coal-fired words. "At least, I thought I did."

Kit jumped to the ground and removed the lightweight saddle. "That was my best ride ever. You could congratulate me."

He grabbed his hat and slammed it against his thigh. "I just spent two excruciating minutes holding my breath, praying you wouldna fall off and kill yerself. And why did ye cut your hair?"

Kit stepped to him, almost belly-to-belly, glaring. "And why didn't I ignore you at hello?" She pushed past him.

Cullen stomped off in the opposite direction. It didn't matter if the path led him to the river or to hell. He was going wherever it took him. He glanced over his shoulder, catching a glimpse of the Siren's back.

Why didn't I ignore you at hello? Damn woman. What the hell is she talking about?

KIT KNOTTED HER fists at her sides and stalked away. "What a jerk." From behind her, a man chuckled, but she ignored him. *Must be the man who was with Cullen.*

"Excuse me."

She paid no attention and kept walking.

"Excuse me." He stepped in front of her and walked backward, making it impossible to ignore him. "I think my friend needs someone to apologize for him."

She dodged around him and walked faster. "I wouldn't accept one from him. I doubt I'd accept it from you."

"Do ye mind if I walk with ye?"

She glanced back at him. "Who are you?"

"Braham McCabe. That's a magnificent horse. Where'd ye get him?"

Okay, that got her attention. She stopped. "Thank you. My father."

"Never seen anyone ride off the saddle before."

What? "Damn," she said under her breath. Jockeys didn't start riding forward-seat style until the end of the nineteenth century. How many people saw her race? How many would remember the ride? A feeling that she'd royally screwed up quashed her excitement. "My father taught me."

"Bending over the horse's withers—"

"Lowers the wind resistance. Now, why don't you leave me alone?"

"If he challenges ye to a rematch, will ye race again? And if ye do, can ye beat him a second time?"

"No. Yes."

"Why—"

Enough. She wheeled around quickly to shoo the man like an annoying fly, but hit the brakes when she gazed into green eyes with specks of gold. A spinning sensation almost wiped her feet out from under her. She leaned against Stormy for support and studied Braham's face. Except for their coloring, he and Cullen looked like bookends. After a moment, she reclaimed her steadiness and said, "Cullen told me about you."

Braham gave her a raffish smile. "Ye have me at a disadvantage. He didna mention ye."

"I'm not surprised," she said, rolling her eyes. "I'm Kit MacKlenna. Come on. I need to keep Stormy moving."

"Ye calculated every move in that race, didna ye?"

"You're observant."

"Nae observant enough, *Mrs.* MacKlenna."

She fingered her mother's wedding ring. "Do you think I'm not what I appear to be?"

Amusement played out in the twitch of Braham's mouth as his eyes roamed the length of her body. Not in a suggestive way, but in a curious way that didn't offend her.

"I imagine Cul finds yer altered state distracting."

Her lip turned up, forming a semi-smile. "He can't accept the fact there are accomplished women who don't fit his traditional view. He needs to stop thinking inside the box and get out a little bit. And by the way, it's *Miss* MacKlenna."

"I have the impression ye're a reformer, *Miss* MacKlenna."

No, just a thoroughly modern Millie. "I suppose I am."

When they reached the stables, Kit called out, "Anybody here?"

"If ye're looking for the blacksmith," Braham said, "the fort commander said he went missing a few days ago."

Her shoulders sagged. *Crap.* "So much for new shoes."

"Cullen's reaction goes deeper than a horse race, doesna it?" Braham's eye dipped in a slight wink, or appeared to.

"Your friend's an intelligent man who happens to be overprotective, opinionated, and annoying. His reaction doesn't go any deeper than that."

"If ye've seen those sides, ye've seen the best and worst of him."

"I'll take the intelligent side. You can have the overprotective and annoying one."

"Where Cullen is concerned, ye have to take the good with the bad."

"Fortunately," she said, resaddling her horse, "I don't have to take either."

"Dinna worry about him," Braham said. "After he thinks about the race, he'll have more appreciation for what ye did."

Cullen exited the commander's office. A determined gait replaced his usual saunter.

"Here comes your friend, and it doesn't look like he's reached that level of appreciation."

Braham scratched the back of his neck and scrunched his face in what appeared to be a thinking expression. "He will."

Kit shot another glance at Cullen. If his eyes were six-shooters, she'd be dead. Dead-dead.

"Give him time," Braham continued.

"I don't have that kind of time, Mr. McCabe." She mounted up. Stormy immediately started his stomping, ear-pinning routine that meant he didn't want to go anywhere. He wanted to eat. Two obstinate studs were two too many. "Come on, boy, let's get out of here."

Chapter Twenty-One

CULLEN WALKED THROUGH the veil of dust kicked up by Stormy's hooves. His feelings for Kit had become too convoluted, and he didn't want to discuss her with Braham. She would become ammunition in Braham's battle to keep him from marrying Abigail.

His friend stood beyond the swirling dust, arms folded, glaring.

"What's gotten ye all riled up?" Cullen asked.

"Never seen ye act like that. What the hell is going on?"

"Not a damn thing."

One of Braham's brows rose in an ironic arch. "I beg to differ."

Cullen untied Jasper's reins from the hitching post and put his foot in the stirrup. "It's complicated." He groaned. Did he really say that?

"Complicated?"

"I've got to get back to the wagon train. Ye coming?"

Braham mounted, wearing an almost secret smile. "Ye're showing your foibles, Cul, and that's always entertaining."

"Glad to provide ye some sport." Cullen spurred Jasper into a lope.

"Mr. Montgomery." A soldier waving a handful of letters stopped him. "Mail arrived. Any of these folks traveling with you?"

Cullen flipped through the stack and removed several letters. Braham pulled up beside him, and Cullen handed him an envelope. "Looks like a letter from yer father."

Braham studied the return address, then folded the envelope and put it in the lining of his hat. "I'll read it tonight."

A twinge of longing needled its way into Cullen's gut. If he'd received a letter from his father, he'd have ripped into it immediately. He shook off thoughts of home, tucked the mail into his saddlebag, and rode out.

Braham eased his horse into a trot. "Are ye going to tell me, or not?"

Cullen knew he'd have to give in to Braham's curiosity or be badgered relentlessly. It was better if Braham heard the Kit MacKlenna story from him and not rumors from John or Henry. He turned his horse toward a grove of cottonwood trees lining the North Platte River and dismounted. He threw the reins over a branch, walked to the water, and picked up a handful of river stones.

"The secret to stone skipping is finding the perfect rock," he said. "It has to fit in yer palm, be flat but nae too flat, rounded on the ends, and heavy enough to withstand the wind, but light enough to hit its mark."

He rolled a rock in each hand, testing its weight, then held one between his right thumb and middle finger. "When ye find the perfect stone, ye're filled with expectation. This is a perfect stone for skipping, but if ye toss a perfect stone using perfect form into rough waters, the stone might sink right away."

He stood with his feet shoulder-width apart, then flicked the rock toward the water with the snap of his wrist. The stone skipped once before sinking. "Perfect stone, perfect throw, turbulent water."

He pulled two cigars from his pocket, handed one to Braham, lit the other, then sat down in the shade. "I met Kit the day before we left Independence. Most striking woman I've ever seen. She needed a family to travel with, and I knew folks who needed financial help. I introduced them and negotiated an agreement."

He remembered watching from the window after Kit left the freight office and knowing in his gut that he had to help her, and only partly because she resembled the lady in his childhood vision.

"Over the last few weeks, I've spent time with her. Beneath that sassy exterior you'll find a grieving woman."

Braham flicked his cigar's gray ash. "What do ye suppose ye'd find if ye look beneath yer exterior?"

Cullen didn't want to look and didn't want anyone else to either.

"What's happened between the two of ye since Independence?"

Cullen gave Braham a synopsis, barely mentioning what happened the morning he stormed out of her wagon.

Braham chomped down on his cigar. "Ye havena talked to her since?"

"The words we had at the fort were the first since—"

"Ye acted like an arse. What the hell's the matter with ye? She should have shot ye, or cut off yer bollocks."

"I appreciate ye seeing my side."

Braham leaned against a cottonwood tree and rolled the cigar between his thumb and fingers, not saying anything.

Cullen pressed the heels of his hands to his forehead, trying to relieve the headache that started during the hurried walk to the track. "She told me she was going to Oregon to get away for a while. Why would a woman go to Oregon and keep a farm in Kentucky?"

"Did ye ask her?"

"She didna want to talk about it."

They sat in silence for several minutes. Then Braham said, "We have the same eyes."

"Green eyes aren't that uncommon."

"She has gold flecks in her right eye. I have them. My father has them. He said his brother had them, too."

"What are ye implying?"

Braham picked up one of the stones Cullen had piled into a pyramid and tossed it into the river. It skipped twice before sinking. "Nothing, nothing a'tall."

"Yellow hair. Green eyes with gold specks. Ye're both left-handed. Her family is from Callander, too. Ye could be cousins."

"Cousins? She said ye told her about me. Did ye mention the resemblance?"

"Thought it might be my imagination."

"I'll write Father and ask him about the MacKlennas. He lost his only brother more than twenty years ago. His two sisters married Fraser brothers, and none of their families immigrated. If there's a connection, it must go back another generation. Curious, though, isna it?"

"Only a coincidence."

"Whether she's my cousin or nae has little to do with ye. What about Abigail? How does she fit into yer master plan now?"

"Nothing has changed. Kit is honeycombed with secrets. I'm intrigued, that's all."

CULLEN CLOSED KENT'S *Commentaries on American Law* and laid it on the ground beside him. He'd read the same four pages several times. After years of preparation, he stood on the cusp of his plan coming to fruition. He had a position with a San Francisco law firm and a politically connected potential bride. But doubts were boring holes in his plan. Or was it one doubt in particular?

He had declined an invitation to play cards with the post commander and refused to play the winner of a chess match between Henry and John. Now his mind was jumbled with thoughts he shouldn't have.

In a hazy dusk lit by a waning moon, he walked away from the campfire and took a thoughtful turn around the wagon train's perimeter, eventually finding himself at the river. In spite of his sister's death, bodies of water, whether an ocean or a pond, brought him solace.

He replayed the horse race in his mind. Where could Kit have learned to ride with such natural balance and fearlessness? The training must have started at a young age. But what kind of father would put an impressionable young girl on a racehorse? He wouldn't even put the son he intended to have on a racehorse.

It had been an intense race with anxious moments, but he never doubted she'd win. As he thought back over the past several weeks, he realized this time he wasn't angry. Scared, but not angry. Maybe he knew her better than he thought, or maybe he now had more faith in her ability to do extraordinary things. He couldn't let her walk out of his life. Neither could he offer to marry her until he did the honorable thing and talked to Abigail. He could ride ahead to California and explain that he'd met someone else, then meet up with the wagon train at some point in Oregon. He weighed the thought in his mind, but knew he couldn't leave. He'd made a commitment to Henry and wouldn't abandon him.

The scent of vanilla wafted through the warm night breeze, and desire flooded his body. His gaze scoured the semidarkness. He spotted a dark, gray form leaning against a nearby cottonwood tree. "I havena seen ye since ye rode out of the fort this afternoon."

"You must not have been looking," Kit's quiet voice answered.

"I stopped by the Barretts'. Ye werena there."

"You found me now."

He moved into the shadow, closer to her. "Ye knew I wouldna allow ye to race, didna ye?"

"Sometimes it's easier to ask forgiveness than permission, and we weren't exactly speaking."

The pain in her voice fed the knot in his throat.

She swept the ground beside her. "You're welcome to share my little spot of riverfront property. The ground's not particularly comfortable, but the view is to die for."

He sat cross-legged and rested his forearms across his thighs. "I owe ye an apology for acting like a cad."

"Is that for last week or this afternoon?"

"Both."

Her face turned into the moonlight, her lips slightly parted. "You hurt me."

Each softly spoken word cut a gouge in his gut. He reached for her hand, but she pulled away. "Kit—"

"We needed to stop before we went too far." The breeze stirred her hair, and she pushed flyaway strands from her face.

"Taking scalps wasna necessary."

"Would you have preferred a calm discussion over coffee?"

He flinched and felt a shiver of disquiet.

Tears filled her eyes, but she held his gaze. He held hers. Then she gathered her skirt and stood. "We have nothing more to say. Go to California and marry Abigail. I hope you'll be very happy."

Her words seemed to hang in the air, forming a canopy of guilt over him.

He watched her slender form move away, out of his life. Her tears played a mournful aria in the smooth, cool moonlight. *Go after her, you idiot.* He stood and took a step, but stopped and jabbed his boot heel into the dirt. Then he turned and walked toward the river.

BRAHAM GAVE UP trying to sleep. He wrapped a blanket around his shoulders and walked down to the river. A thin veil of clouds hid a rose-yellow moon within a deep sea of darkness, the kind of darkness that clouded his soul. In his pocket was a nine-word telegram from Mr. Phillips that Braham's father had included with his letter. He'd read it twice. The second reading punctuated the reality.

Riding with friends. Horse spooked. Abigail fell. Died instantly.

If Cullen knew about Abigail's death, he would ride to California immediately even though there was nothing he could do. If he left the wagon train now, what would happen to Kit?

An angel's voice out of the darkness startled Braham. "It appears I'm not the only one who can't sleep tonight."

He turned, tracking the musical sound he'd heard earlier in the day. His quick intake of breath sounded like a bellow in the night's stillness. Even though he'd only seen Kit in a short-haired wig and trousers, he would have known her anywhere. Thick blond hair a man could lose himself in fell loose around her shoulders. He clenched his fists at the sight of the small waist his hands would span.

"I didn't mean to surprise you," she said.

"Ye're lovely…"

Her gaze held a hypnotic intensity. "From the look on your face, you'd think you're trying to solve the problem of world hunger. I might have some ideas, if you'd like to talk."

He shook his head. "My problem isna as complicated as feeding the world." He spread his blanket on the ground, then drew his left leg back and made a deep bow with his hand pressed across his abdomen. "May I offer my lady a seat?"

She took his proffered hand. "So tell me your not-so-complicated problem."

Enchanting. "A client had a dilemma that kept him awake at night. He had a secret. He knew if he shared it, it could devastate people he loved. But if he didna share it, people he loved could find happiness, but it could cost him the love of the people he wanted to protect."

She didn't answer right away, but when she did, her voice wasn't much more than a whisper. "Secrets are dangerous, Mr. McCabe. When they concern the lives of people you love, you don't have a choice. You protect them and live with the consequences."

He wasn't expecting that answer from her, but she validated his decision. He would live with the consequences. "Cullen tells me yer family originally came from Callander."

"My adoptive parents' family is from Callander. I was abandoned as an infant."

"A changeling. That explains everything."

The soft trill of laughter floated on the night breeze. He didn't know if he was relieved or disappointed she couldn't be a cousin. Gold flakes in green eyes—a coincidence.

They talked about horse breeding and racing and life in Kentucky until the first shaft of buttery light appeared on the horizon, opening their cocoon of darkness to a new day.

"It's been a pleasure getting to know ye, Miss MacKlenna."

"Please call me Kit. After spending the night with you, I think we can call each other by first names." She gave him a bright grin.

"Ye are brazen, my lady."

"And you, sir, a perfect knight."

He helped her to her feet. "Until we meet again, ma'am."

She squeezed his arm. "I understand why Cullen cares so much for you. You reflect each other's good qualities."

"And I understand why he holds ye in such high regard. Ye're a woman of mystery and intelligence, with a sharp wit stirred into the mix."

"It's the mystery that intrigues him. But it also distances him."

He reached for her hand and brought it to his lips. "If I can ever be of service, I hope ye'll call on me."

She laughed softly. "If I have dragons to slay, I will." She studied him for a moment. "Has anyone ever said you and Cullen bookend each other?"

"How so?"

"Same height, same build, different coloring. I wonder...well, never mind. Good-bye."

Braham folded the wool blanket into a perfect rectangle while he thought about Cullen's master plan. As far as Braham could see, that plan just folded like the worst hand of poker.

Chapter Twenty-Two

KIT SAT AT the supper table looking out over LaBonte Creek and the meadow beyond. Since leaving Fort Laramie four days earlier, the wagon train had added another eighty miles to their seven hundred in seven weeks. From the beginning, she knew the trip would be tough, but the trail's hardships had been only part of the danger.

She'd just finished the last bite on her plate when Cullen and Henry walked up to the Barretts' camp.

"Still some stew left," John said. "Y'all hungry?"

"Ate at the Camerons, but thanks," Cullen said.

Sarah held up the coffeepot. "How about coffee?"

"Cain't never get enough coffee," Henry said.

John pointed toward the table. "Welcome to sit."

Cullen sat. Kit stood. "Excuse me," she said. "I'm going to help Frances with her lessons." As she left the table, Cullen's eyes settled on hers with a heated, disturbing gaze. A trickle of sweat dripped between her breasts. The breasts he had touched.

Don't go there, Kit.

Why couldn't they enjoy each other's company? Their time together would be so short. Just as well, really. This was the wrong time and the wrong place. But he *was* the right man.

She turned in early and tossed for hours, much as she did every night. Finally, she drifted off to sleep.

"Kit, we need ye." Cullen's whispering invaded her dream.

She rolled over and snuggled deeper into the feather mattress, into him, into their embrace.

"Kit," he said louder. He knocked on the side of her wagon, bringing her fully awake.

"Folks are sick. We need ye."

"I'm coming." She rolled out of bed and into her trousers and boots with the same efficiency she'd learned at the firehouse. Then she tossed a dress over her head and gathered her hair into a ponytail that she tied with a strip of rawhide.

Folks are sick. We need ye.

With her shawl pulled tightly around her shoulders to ward off the middle-of-the-night chill, she left her wagon to find Cullen and discover what new danger they faced. Halfway around the circle of wagons, she heard a buzz of voices.

"Are ye sure?" Cullen asked.

"Looks it to me," Henry said. "Seen the sickness before."

Kit found Henry, Cullen, and Braham at the Dunns' wagon. "What's wrong?"

"Henry thinks it's cholera," Cullen said.

This is not good. She glanced down at Mr. Dunn. The emaciated man lay on a pallet, his head in his wife's lap. If he had cholera, the wagon train faced a powerful enemy. She had no gloves, so she shoved her hands in her pockets so she wouldn't be tempted to touch anything as she knelt beside the ailing man. Shriveled skin, sunken eyes. He was dying. "How long has he been like this?" she asked Mrs. Dunn.

"He's been getting worse since supper."

"What time is it, Cullen?" Kit asked.

He opened his pocket watch and peered at it in the low moon-light. "Three o'clock."

Eight hours, more or less. "Do you have vomiting and diarrhea, too?"

The woman pushed damp hair off her face. "I just started feeling poorly."

"What about your children?" Kit braced for the answer she

didn't want to hear.

"The two older girls are complaining," Mrs. Dunn said.

"Has your husband had any food or water?"

"Can't keep nothing down."

"I'll fix your family something to drink that might help." Kit stood and motioned for the men to step away with her. They huddled out of earshot of the Dunns. "I agree with Henry. We have four probable cases of cholera. Anyone else sick?"

"We dinna ken," Cullen said.

"This could spread quickly," Kit said.

Cullen glanced at the dying man. "What can we do for him?"

"I'll give him water mixed with sugar and salt. That'll help."

Henry scratched his whiskered cheek. "How do we keep it from spreading?"

Safe water and sanitation. "Did you touch him or Mrs. Dunn?" She looked each man in the eye. They looked at their hands, then at each other.

"No," Cullen said.

Henry shrugged. "I might have."

"Dinna think so," Braham said.

"Scrub your hands. Don't eat, drink, or touch your mouth until you've done that. What about the Barretts? Do they know?"

Cullen shook his head. "No one else knows."

She chewed on her lower lip. In an hour, folks would be up and moving about. "I'm going to make an oral rehydration solution. You three go around camp. See if anyone else is sick."

"We should move the Dunns away from camp," Henry said.

Kit shook her head. "Wait. Let's see how many sick we've got first. If it's only them, we can contain it."

The men disbursed, and Kit hurried to her wagon. Within minutes, she had fed the campfire and put on a pot of water to boil. She added a three-finger pinch of salt and a two-finger scoop of sugar to the gently rolling water. The solution worked in third-world countries. No reason it shouldn't work in Wyoming.

When the drink was ready, she poured the mixture into a canteen and carried it to the Dunns', but she was too late. Mrs. Dunn had fallen into a stupor. Kit tried to get her to drink, but she was distraught. The oldest daughter was awake so Kit left instructions with her, then hurried back to her camp to make another batch of the solution.

Henry's tired, hunched form appeared in the fire's flickering light, throwing grotesque shadows onto the bushes behind him.

"What'd you find?" she asked.

"At least ten people have symptoms."

She took a deep breath before she asked, "What about the Barretts?"

Cullen appeared in the circle of light. "I woke John to let him know. He checked his family. None of them show any signs."

"If we have ten sick, we'll have more in a few hours. I need help making the solution."

"Sarah's on her way," Cullen said.

Henry removed his hat and finger-combed his thinning hair. "What do you want us to do?"

"For now, tell folks we're making medicine. And ask them to please wash their hands."

THE HEALTHY FOLKS didn't get much rest over the next three days. They set up hand-washing stations around camp and dug latrines in an effort to contain the disease. Kit didn't sleep, didn't eat. Eight people died, four of them children. Each death took a chunk of her soul. A large chunk.

John confined Elizabeth and Frances to their wagon, and Kit tied Tabor and Tate up with them. After two days, all four were gnawing on their restraints, but Kit refused to let them out. She stopped by the wagon to check on them. "Do you need anything?" she asked.

"Frances isn't back," Elizabeth said. Her face clouded with worried. "She went to the bushes."

"I'll check on her." Kit stomped over to the bushes not twenty feet from the wagon. Frances wasn't there. Kit moved quickly around camp asking folks if they'd seen the child. Everyone assumed she was in the wagon.

Barely able to stand from exhaustion, Kit circled camp, looking under and around the wagons. Every muscle in her body ached from the constant bending and lifting.

Circling back around, she spotted the eight freshly dug graves. A pile of calico rags littered the graves. "That's odd." She walked closer, then her step grew still.

"Dear God, no."

She fell to her knees beside the pile of rags. But it wasn't a pile of rags at all. It was Frances.

Muddy tears formed tracks down the child's puckered, silver-blue tinted face. The skin on her pudgy hands had shriveled. Her cold wrinkled fingers resembled those of an old washerwoman, and her eyes sunk deep into her sockets.

Kit didn't know she had a heart left to break, but she heard the crunch, the splinter, the blast. She hugged Frances to her breast. "We're going home. I won't let you die, but you've got to hold on." Had it only been a few months since she'd made the same plea of Scott? But she had failed him. She wouldn't fail Frances, too.

She punched her fist skyward. "You can't take her. I won't let you."

Then she bundled Frances in her arms and ran back toward camp. Home. She was going home.

"Kit." She barely heard Cullen for the blood pounding in her ears. She brushed past him, but he grabbed her arm and whipped her around to face him. "Frances?"

"I'm taking her home." She yanked from his grasp.

He locked her arm in a tighter grip. "She needs the special water."

"Look at her," Kit hissed. "The solution won't help."

"Ye're nae taking her anywhere except to yer wagon." His eyes turned icy. "Ye're the only one who can save her. Ye saved me. Ye can save Frances."

"Let me go!" She tried to jerk her arm free again, but his fingers were five fiery vises searing her with heat. "Her heart can't supply enough blood to her body. I can't save her. Going to the hospital is her only chance."

"If ye canna save her, she'll die." He spoke in the slow, emphatic tone of a man who understood consequences. "Is that what ye want?"

"The doctors can save her. I can't."

He pressed his hands against the sides of her face. "Pull yerself together. *Now*." He took Frances from her arms and dragged Kit to her wagon. He lifted her up onto the tailgate and jumped up beside her. After laying the child on the bed, he blocked Kit's retreat with the force of his will and the strength of his body.

"Get yer red bag and put medicine into her arm," he said with barely controlled fury. "Ye think I dinna know what ye did to me? Ye think I didna see the bag and the needles? Ye think I didna hear the pops and snaps of whatever ye did? I dinna ken who ye are or where ye came from. Ye could be a witch for all I know. But ye have the power to save this child, and that's what ye're going to do."

"You don't know what you're asking."

"I'm nae asking anything. I'm demanding. After ye save her life, ye can get on your damn horse and ride the hell out of here." He grabbed her arms and shook her. "Do ye hear me?"

Tired but not deaf, she pushed him aside, her heart hammering. "Move. I need room to work. You need to wait outside."

"I'm nae leaving." His face shut, hiding his anger below the surface.

Frances's pulse beat dangerously low. Kit considered the consequences of treating the child with twenty-first century medicine. The treatment would force Kit to reveal where she came from and ultimately send her home, but Frances was more important than what Kit hoped to accomplish during her trip to the past. She was in the nineteenth century because the child had pulled her there, maybe for this moment, maybe to save her life.

Kit had accessed the medical database stored on her iPhone several times in the past few days. The battery was running low. She turned it on and checked doses. When she set it aside, she noticed Cullen pick it up, but she didn't have time to deal with him.

She laid out her supplies, put on latex gloves, and started an IV to deliver 30 ml of Ringer's lactate in thirty minutes, then another 70 ml in the next two hours. In the meantime, she'd try to get her to drink some rehydration salt solution.

"That's what ye did to me."

She didn't answer.

"How'd ye learn to do that?"

"School."

For the next two hours, they sat in silence while Kit continued the IV and gave Frances sips of the ORS. Her blood pressure rose as she rehydrated. She remained very sick, but improving. It would take four to six hours to rehydrate and the vomiting to stop.

She turned to Cullen, who had hovered over her. "Will you tell John and Sarah that Frances is getting better? But ask them to give me a couple more hours with her before they come in."

"Do I have yer word ye willna run off?"

"I'm not going anywhere." *Yet.*

He left her with a hard thud in her heart, his absence now as painful as his presence had been. He would never hold her or kiss her again. She wanted not to care, but it was too late for that.

She gave Frances a bath, and while she slept, Kit cleaned up the sick bay, repacked the red bag, and put everything away. Then she stripped and bathed herself. If only she could wipe away the heartache as easily as the germs.

Frances's vital signs were all good and showing continued improvement. Kit was cautiously relieved. She closed her eyes to rest for a few minutes.

"Who are ye? Why are ye here?" Cullen startled her awake with a voice that cracked like a whip. She flinched from the verbal flogging and stared at him through dry, scratchy eyes.

He struck a match and lit the lantern sitting on a small table.

Not now, please, not now. She pressed the heels of her hands into her eye sockets and held them in place for a few seconds. Under normal conditions, the darkness had a way of revitalizing her, but she was past the point of quick fixes.

"Kit." He shook her shoulder.

"I need sleep." She studied the tight brackets at the corners of his mouth. If he insisted on a conversation now, there would be nothing to salvage later.

"We'll talk *now*." He locked her in a death stare. Her throat closed. He stepped toward her, controlling the moment with authority. As soon as she told him what he wanted to know, he would turn on her as he had done before, slashing with razor sharp words. She rubbed the scars on her neck. A heated silence hung in the air while she checked the sleeping child's vitals and summoned much needed courage.

She edged past him to the back of the wagon and threw open the flaps. Drifting clouds scuttled across the crescent-shaped moon. The air above the smoky campfires seemed thicker than usual. An eerie stillness sounded across the plains.

How did she reach this moment? In all her planning, she had never considered she would have to tell someone where she came from. He would never believe her.

"Weeks ago," she began, searching for the right words, "you told me when the light of the day joins the light of the night mystical encounters between the visible and invisible world occur." She paused and shot him a pleading glance.

"Spit it out," he said with an acerbic tone.

"My home is in the twenty-first century."

He jerked as if he'd been pierced with a poison-tipped lance.

She picked up a discarded IV bag she'd left on the table. "Look at this." She shoved it in his face and pointed to the expiration date. "What does that say? I have more evidence. Do you want to see it?" She threw the bag on the floor and collapsed on the end of the bed.

He picked up the bag and glared with a look of disdain. "What are ye?"

She placed her hand over her mouth to contain a distressed gasp. Only in horror flicks did aliens take over human bodies. She wasn't an alien or a monster.

"What are ye?" Lips that had kissed her passionately now thinned to a hard, unhesitating line.

"What do you think I am?"

His eyes narrowed into slits. "Dinna answer my question with a question. Who are ye? What are ye?"

Hold it together for a few more minutes. Just a few more minutes. "I'm a woman who knows a little bit about a lot of things, but not enough to answer your questions. I don't know who I am. That's why I'm here."

His eyebrows furrowed. His hands closed around her shoulders, squeezing muscle against bone. "No more riddles. Tell me who ye are, then take yer red bag full of magic and yer menagerie and go back to where ye belong." His words held the stinging power of a thousand wasps.

Tears pushed into her eyes. "I have a magical brooch. It opened the door to your time, and I passed through."

He laughed a dark, ominous laugh. "I saw yer brooch, even thought it was mystical, but open a door to another time—impossible."

Silence filled the wagon with an impenetrable cloud of doubt. If only she could say more to help him understand. In the face of disbelief, words proved inadequate.

He stood, sneering. They were two people standing on opposite sides of a chasm with a frayed, irreparable rope between them. Without another word, he left, and the last fiber holding the rope together snapped.

Chapter Twenty-Three

K IT WOKE TO the beat of a small hand patting the top of her head. Little brown eyes searched her face.

"Welcome back, sweetheart. How do you feel?" Kit lightly squeezed Frances's hand, relieved that the plump network of veins beneath the child's pale skin were no longer shriveled with dehydration.

"The angel told me to go home. She said you were waiting for me."

"What angel?"

"A beautiful angel. She called me lassie and told me to go back." Frances licked her lips. "Did I get the cholera?"

"You'll be fine now." Kit pushed the child's Shirley-Temple-like curls off her forehead and washed her face.

"Anna was alone, but the angel told me she'd take care of her."

"Is that why you went to the graves? To be with Anna?"

Frances nodded.

"What else did the angel say?"

Frances scrunched her face as if squeezing every thought through a memory sieve. "That's all I remember."

The slow, deliberate words gave Kit the impression there was more to the message. "We must thank the beautiful angel."

Frances mumbled, "I did." Then she closed her eyes and drifted off.

"Thank you, beautiful angel." Kit fell back to sleep, only to wake a short time later. A trace of moonlight filtered into the wagon along with the fragrant smell of wildflowers hidden for days beneath the stench of sickness and death. She heard no voices, music, or hammering. *Must be after midnight.* Then she realized the bed was empty. A swell of panic raced up Kit's spine, but faded when she remembered the child had been recovering when they both fell asleep. Sarah must have taken her.

Kit stripped and climbed into bed. Then a second wave of panic hit with heart-attack proportions. *Dear God, Cullen knows the truth.* He wouldn't tell anyone, would he? She didn't think so. He was angry, but not vindictive. Telling folks would start a riot to burn the witch. No. He needed time to process.

Thoughts of him continued to swirl in her mind, churning up dust and debris, making sleep impossible. A walk and a glass of wine would calm her spirit—a gentle rain for her soul.

She dressed in trousers, slipped on the wig, then headed toward the river carrying a small bag in one hand, a blanket in the other.

Shafts of moonlight lit the path along the water's edge. If only the moon would shine its light in her heart. Why had she fallen in love with a man from the nineteenth century? She should go home and get out of the mess she'd created. But South Pass was only two weeks away, fourteen more days to reach her goal. With just a smidgen of courage, she could make it unless Cullen did something drastic, like reconvene the Salem witch trials. Predicting what he would do was beyond her capability, except that he was predictably overreactive and overprotective, which meant he might have spotted her leaving camp. She stopped and listened. Chirps, lapping water, a snore here and a cough there, but no footsteps or snapping twigs. Relieved? Yes. Surprised? Yes. Disappointed? Yes.

Within a few minutes, she found a quiet and secluded spot. The blanket made a soft bed on the ground. She quickly dozed off with the sound of an oboe—Cullen's soft, warm voice—playing a concert in her mind.

"I SHOULD TURN ye over my knee and whale yer backside."

Cullen's voice was a lit fuse on a stick of dynamite. "Do ye know how far ye are from camp?"

Kit shot straight up, heart racing. "How'd you find me?"

"I could follow yer footprints around the world." Aggravation hissed between his teeth.

"Not unless you've got your own brooch."

He dropped to the ground beside her. "If ye're going home, why aren't ye gone?"

She scooted away from him. "I'm thinking about it."

"If ye'd been thinking, ye'd still be in yer wagon, not roaming about in the dark."

She'd had enough of his accusations and attitude. "Why are you here?"

"I thought ye were leaving."

She made a fist ready to punch him. "I wouldn't leave without my animals. You know that. So what do you want?"

"I want to know who ye are."

She bit down hard on her lip. "I told you."

"Ye said you didna *ken* who ye were."

"So you think I've figured it out since then?" She drew in a long breath and blew it out.

"Tell me who ye are deep down inside where no one goes, not even you."

She thought about his question, then thought about it some more. "You don't want to hear the ugly stuff." She pulled off the wig and finger-combed her hair.

An expression she hadn't seen before came over his features. "Nothing about ye is ugly." He picked up the wig and smoothed strands of hair. "We try on all sorts of disguises to hide who we are."

"That's profound."

He held up the hairpiece. "I dinna ken how any man could be tricked by this."

She snatched it from him. "Don't ruin the illusion of safety."

He pointed to the handgun tucked into her waistband. "Is that an illusion, too?"

She handed over the weapon. "Smith and Wesson 3913 Lady Smith pistol, nine millimeter, eight plus one rounds, made of aluminum alloy and stainless steel. Accurate. Nice shooter. Good trigger. Light recoil."

He pointed the gun into the night, then flipped it around and handed it back. "I willna let anything happen to ye."

"You'll throw me another rope?"

"Ye didna get the scars at the same time. One looks older than the other."

Her heart raced, causing a burning sensation of fear in her chest. She pointed to the scar on the left side of her neck, unable to touch the fine *S*-shaped line. "I got this one the night of the storm."

"Go on, lass. Tell me." His request was a gentle prod.

She cleared her throat. "Five years ago, a bad storm knocked out the electricity in the barn while Shadow Cat was foaling. Dad, the vet, and Scott were in the stall with her. Everything was going fine, so my godfather went to another barn to get an emergency generator. Then something happened to the mare and they needed him."

Cullen steepled his hands and pressed his index fingers against his chin. "What's a generator?"

"It makes power that lights up our homes. Our main source had gone out."

Cullen nodded as if he understood.

"When Elliott didn't come back right away, they sent me to get him. I ran over to the next barn and found him in the tack room lying on the floor in a pool of blood." A trembling hand rose to her neck as she slid further into the memory. "A man grabbed me from behind and cut me before I knew anyone else was in the room." She scratched at her neck until she drew blood.

Cullen tried to pull her hand away.

"Don't touch me." She went quiet for a moment, sharing only the sound of her shallow breathing. "He threw me on the floor, intending to rape me."

Cullen hissed between his teeth and reached for her, but she blocked him with a stiff arm.

"Scott pulled him off seconds before he could…hurt me." She tucked into an upright fetal position and tears slipped down her cheeks.

Kit jerked when Cullen touched her shoulder with a gentle press of his fingers. "Here's a handkerchief." His voice was calm, neutral, but his body trembled.

She grabbed the tail end of her composure and fought for control. After wiping her eyes, she carefully folded the fabric into a perfect square. The top fold had a monogrammed *M* exactly like the locket and the shawl. Her heart felt skewed with new emotion.

She gazed into his eyes and wondered again why he was there, why he'd haunted her for so many years, and why she was sharing something so intimate with him. Maybe she didn't have to know. Maybe it was enough that her heart knew.

"Everything that happened after Scott rescued me blurred into my nightmare, but I think he beat the man up. He never told me what happened. I never asked." She unfolded and refolded the handkerchief, this time burying the monogram within the folds. "I had bruises for days. Every time I saw them, I threw up."

"Did ye know the man?" Cullen's gaze was almost a physical touch.

"His name was Wayne. He'd worked for Elliott. I fired him months earlier when I caught him abusing a horse." She paused. "I hear his laugh sometimes in the wind, especially on cold days. It makes my teeth rattle."

"I havena treated ye much better than Wayne." There was something bleak in his voice, and her heart quickened, but she had no answer for him. "I looked at one facet of a multifaceted gem and thought that made up the entire stone." He held her gaze pointedly. "To let others see all sides of us takes a great deal of trust. I thought I'd destroyed yer trust in me."

"You came close."

They sat for several minutes beside the river covered in moonlight, motionless, without speaking, and then Cullen asked, "What happened to him?"

"An inmate killed him." The moment she had heard the news, during a phone call from her attorney, silent relief took her legs out from under her. As she sat on the floor awash in tears, she hated herself for being glad.

"Good."

For a minute, she just stared at him, thinking about what he'd said. "That's odd for you to say."

"It saves me a trip to yer century to kill him."

The thought of Cullen traveling to the twenty-first century seeking vengeance sprinkled shivers up and down Kit's spine.

"Do ye think yer father had Wayne killed?" Cullen asked.

"You're thinking of your client and his victim's family, aren't you?"

He gazed at her with deep, thoughtful eyes.

"When I heard Wayne was dead, I wondered if Dad had anything to do with it. He didn't want me to go through the ordeal of testifying at the trial. Dad could be ruthless, but I don't think he could have anyone murdered."

"If ye told a jury what happened, they'd have hung him from the nearest tree."

"American jurisprudence has changed. They don't hang people anymore. He probably would have pled guilty, taken twenty years for the felonies, and been paroled after sixteen years. He might have come looking for me when he got out."

"Ye never would have felt safe again, would ye?"

"That's why I learned to fight. I'll never be helpless again."

He patted his gut. "I've been on the receiving end of yer skills."

She gave him a tight smile. "I could have hurt you a lot worse."

"I appreciate yer restraint."

She was glad for the note of humor in his voice, then he surprised her by the tenderness with which he lifted her chin and pressed his lips against hers. A touch at first, then a burst of hunger as he sought to deepen the kiss.

I will protect you, she heard his heart say. *But will I let you?* she heard hers reply.

"Cullen."

"Hmm." His moan was a request for greater intimacy.

"Are you thirsty?"

He kissed her forehead, her eyes, her cheeks. "Yes, for ye."

She slipped her hand inside the bag and pulled out a bottle of wine.

He took the bottle from her, and chuckled. "Only ye could top off a story like that with a bottle of merlot." He twisted the bottle in the beam of moonlight and whistled.

"You probably thought me a brazen hussy drinking wine the first night we met."

"I only thought about this." He kissed her again.

Tate stuck his nose between their faces, and she pushed him away. "Where'd you come from?"

Cullen patted the dog's head. "He followed me. Ye have three animals who think they're human. Who's responsible for that?"

Kit uncorked the bottle and filled the wineglass she had brought with her. "Mom's responsible for Tate and Tabor. Stormy is all my doing."

"Yer horse was born the night of the storm, wasna he?"

She closed her eyes for a brief second. When she opened them, she whispered with a shaky voice, "Shadow Cat died. Stormy barely survived. Dad swore the horse would never race, even though he'd been bred to be a champion. I don't think Dad wanted to be reminded every time Stormy raced of what happened that night."

Cullen's finger traced the line of the scar on the other side of her neck. "How did ye get this one?"

She'd told him half the story. He deserved to hear the rest. She sipped, then handed him the glass. He put it to his lips and gazed at her over the rim of the crystal. "Ye can tell me later."

Later? She thought of their scheduled parting at South Pass, of the emptiness that would follow. "We don't have later. We only have now."

He traced a finger across her cheek to the corner of her lips. "Now will never be enough."

Nor for her either. He had irrevocably changed the melody of her life.

He took a sip and handed her back the glass. She savored the soft velvet-bodied wine with a hint of plum. "My parents, Scott, and I attended a charity ball on New Year's Eve. We were on our way home when a vehicle hit us head-on. Dad was driving. I was in the backseat with Scott. Our car plowed through a fence. A plank sheared off and smashed through my window. A chunk lodged in my neck, barely missing the carotid artery. The car stopped when we hit an oak tree."

"Car?"

"Vehicle, transportation, conveyance, carriage." She gestured, caught in a game of charades.

"Ye can explain later. Go on."

"The impact knocked me out. When I came to, my parents were dead. Scott was still alive, but a piece of fence had impaled him. I called nine-one-one."

"What's nine-one-one?"

"People with red bags. People like me."

"There was nae medicine in yer bag for him, was there?" For a moment, Cullen glanced away, grew distant, as if looking into his past.

"Scott's only hope was getting to the hospital. All I could do was hold him and tell him help was on the way. He died before the ambulance arrived. He saved my life that night in the barn, but I couldn't save him. I couldn't save my parents. I'd been trained to save lives, but I couldn't save the three people I loved most in the world."

"Yer parents were dead. Yer Scott had a piece of fence in his chest. Ye're nae God. They were in His hands, not yers."

"You don't understand. I was trained—"

"I *do* understand. Ye've set yerself against an impossible standard and perceive anything less as failure. Ye didna fail. Ye did what only ye could do. Provide comfort and hope during the last moments of his life. Ye have to let it go. His death wasna yer fault."

It *was* her fault. All of it was her fault. She was living a life she never should have had all because of a damned ruby brooch. She jumped to her feet and ran toward the river. Cullen ran after her. "Kit, stop."

"Go away."

"Without ye, we would have lost most of the folks on the wagon train. Ye saved our lives. That has to count for something."

"Every life is important. Saving one person doesn't negate the guilt of being unable to save another."

He spread his arms wide. "Ye think I dinna ken that? God knows I've been trying most of my life to make up for failing my sister, but at some point we have to move on."

"When I get home—"

He pulled her into his arms. "Dinna go."

"I don't belong here."

He kissed her, tasting of sweet wine. Her fingers combed through his thick hair, effortlessly—so easy, and so right. She heard the unsung lyrics of her heart's song.

He lifted her into his arms and carried her back to the blanket. "I have every intention of making love to ye. Stop me if ye must, but stop me right now."

If I only have one night, one night will be enough. "I couldn't live with the regret if I stopped you now."

CULLEN SNUGGED KIT into the curve of his long body and regarded her for several moments. "Are ye sure, lass?" A worried frown creased his brow.

"You are what I want."

His thumb slid over her cheek. "I dinna want to hurt ye."

She traced the shape of his prominent brow, down his nose, across high cheekbones, then down the line of his square jaw to kissable lips, putting to memory the chiseled planes of his face. "I don't want to disappoint you."

He swept a wild lock of hair away from her face. "Nae, lass, ne'er canna disappoint this Scotsman." The timbre of his voice bore the sound of the land that had informed him. "Ye're a beauty." His hand trembled as he unbuttoned her shirt and tenderly slipped the fabric off her shoulder.

Her nipples tightened beneath the camisole and pressed against the silk. *Kiss me.* She had no breath to ask.

He blew warm caresses across her skin. "I dinna want to frighten ye."

"You won't."

His thick, dark lashes lifted. "Kiss me," he whispered against her lips.

She nibbled at his mouth, then slipped her tongue inside and tasted the plum-flavored merlot, tantalizing and succulent. She breathed him in, fully expanding her lungs with the first deep breath she had taken in months, maybe years.

In his arms, she lived.

The pieces of her jumbled brain snapped into place, creating a perfect picture in warm, amber tones. Their meeting was not an engineered one of two souls, but a realignment of the stars to put lives back to the way they should have been.

Cullen unbuttoned her trousers. His hand moved lower, gliding over her abdomen, brushing her skin with his fingertips. Her stomach muscles tensed, and she squirmed to help him. "There's nae hurry, lass." His warm chuckle poured over her with tingly heat.

She understood now that her virginity was not a result of a teenage pledge, but because she had never truly been in love. Until now. Until Cullen.

Cool air breezed across her naked skin, but a flame burned inside, warming her with each touch of his hand, his tongue, his lips, creating an aching need. She tugged on his shirt, desperately wanting his skin next to hers. "Take off your clothes." Her voice was demanding and unrecognizable.

His shirt came up and over his broad shoulders. His trousers slipped from his solid form. And then he was naked. She'd seen other men undressed, but there was something uniquely beautiful about Cullen. His beauty went far deeper than rippling muscles, or patches of thick black hair, or long legs, or the pulsing arousal resting against his abdomen. His beauty came from beneath the skin, from his very soul.

He possessed her lips, feasting on her. He nuzzled her neck and ran his hands through her hair, teasing every strand with his sensuous touch. She melded into him until it was impossible to know where she ended and he began.

His arms and shoulder muscles rippled as he lowered himself between her legs. A tiny, high-pitched sound slipped from her lips. "Cullen—"

There was a hitch in his breath. "I'm here."

Frantic need drew her to a bridge she'd yet to cross to a place she'd never been. She writhed beneath him as she stepped onto the bridge. Her muscles tightened as she ran toward the other end and the release she desperately sought and willingly embraced.

"Let go, lass. Let go." His husky voice was a sliver of light in the darkness.

A wave of immense pleasure washed over her and fulfilled her deepest longing. *I love you.*

He kissed her, capturing her lips with voracious hunger. He slipped into the cradle of her thighs and welcomed her hot moisture that drenched him as he nudged inside her tight opening. When he reached her maidenhead, he paused, and held himself to a level of unnatural restraint, giving Kit a moment to prepare. "Only a wee bit of pain, lass."

He took her mouth, thrusting his tongue deep within her as he thrust through the thin barrier, splitting it in two. Swallowing her scream, he stilled until her trembling ceased. Then he watched her intently, holding his breath until her tightly drawn lips relaxed and a slow smile spread across her face. Joy reflected in her eyes, and her silky skin vibrated against him. With panting gasps, she wrapped him in her legs and convulsed. Within the sound of her pleasure, he found the only woman he had ever loved, and he heard a new melody.

A melody written for his heart alone.

Awed by the vividness of her release, he arched his back and in a state of euphoria plunged at a fevered pitch until he erupted, sending his seed deep into her body.

My God, he loved her, and he would never let her go.

SLEEP CAME QUICKLY for Kit, but it didn't last long. An hour before dawn she woke entwined in Cullen's arms, her palm resting on his chest, feeling his heart thump. She loved him, but he would never be hers. One night was all she could have. The wagon train was two weeks from South Pass. She didn't know what she would find there, but she knew it would end her time in the nineteenth century.

She gazed at him with a touch of tears in her eyes. *You are an extraordinary man, Cullen Montgomery, and it will break my heart to leave you.*

Her teeth clamped down on her lower lip swollen from his kisses. He stirred and pulled her closer to him. His musky scent mixed with the earthy smells of early morning. She wanted to make love again. But she couldn't. Even now, walking away would be hell, although survivable. If she stayed in his arms, spent the next two weeks where she truly wanted to be, she'd never be able to leave. She should go now, eliminate the temptation.

Quietly, she lifted his arm and rolled away.

He reached for her. "Where're ye going?"

"I have to go."

"Hurry back."

"I'm not coming back."

He sat up and brushed his hair off his face. "What do ye mean?"

She slipped on her shirt. "I'm going home." She reached over him for her trousers, but he grabbed them out of her hand.

"Don't do this."

She moistened her lips with a flick of her tongue. "I don't belong here. This is not where I'm supposed to be. This is your life, not mine. You have a woman waiting in San Francisco and an office with your name on the door. The life you've planned is waiting." She reached for her trousers. "Let me have my pants."

"Give me time to work this out, Kit." His voice shook. Maybe it was the early hour. Maybe it was doubt that he could. She couldn't tell and wasn't sure it mattered.

"There's nothing to work out. I'm staying until we reach South Pass. Then I'm going home." She paused and swallowed a giant knot in her throat, a knot that squeezed her breath. "What happened last night can never happen again."

"Why canna ye stay until we reach Oregon?"

She tried to grab her pants. "Please give them to me. It's almost daylight. I have to go."

"Why not Oregon?" A puzzled expression knitted his brow. "Ye're lying again."

"Give me my pants." Good God, she couldn't tell him about the wagon train at South Pass. What if he found it too soon? The murderers could kill him, too. Fear crunched in her gut like ice in a melting lake. "Don't accuse me of lying when you're the one who's marrying one woman and screwing another."

Shock scrawled across his face. He handed the trousers to her. "I thought ye trusted me. I thought ye finally punched through the wall guarding yer heart. Maybe ye did and it sealed back up in yer sleep."

She wrenched her gaze from his soul-deep eyes.

"Go on home, lass." He stood and dressed in a hurry, foregoing the shirt's buttons. His jaw tensed, and she saw pain in his eyes, but she couldn't help him.

He slipped his foot inside his boot and hopped away, putting on the other.

I didn't just punch a hole in the wall. I knocked it down and let you in.

Chapter Twenty-Four

THE WAGON TRAIN was camped in the meadow at Three Crossings when Braham reached a new level of suspicion that something had happened between Cullen and Kit. In fifteen years, his friend had never been private or reluctant to share his thoughts. Until now. *Did I do the right thing not telling Cul about Abigail?* If he told him now, Braham would land smack in the teeth of a gale. He'd battled worse storms before. The time had come to batten down the hatches and confess.

He rounded the circle of wagons and spotted Cullen sitting at their campsite reading by the light of a lamp perched on the small table at his elbow. *This might be my best opportunity.* He pulled up a chair next to his friend, sat, and threw one leg over the other. "Sarah invited us for a slice of Kit's apple pie."

Cullen's chair creaked as he shifted his weight. "I'm nae hungry."

"How could ye nae be hungry for pie?"

Cullen puffed on his cigar, sending the rich tobacco's fragrance into the air between them. He turned the page, much too quickly to be reading. "Leave it alone, Braham."

Cullen removed his spectacles and pressed his fingers against the bridge of his nose. A look of pain traveled across his face, and Braham almost regretted intruding. Almost. Gathering his thoughts he said, "I could help."

Cullen closed the book, caressing the cover. "I told ye. Leave it alone."

Braham let go a philosophical sigh, an unlit cheroot poking from the corner of his mouth. "I'll ask again tomorrow. I'm nae going to quit."

"I'm heading out in the morning."

Braham swallowed back an uneasy sense of guilt that had formed a fist around his throat. "Then I'm going, too."

Cullen gave Braham a speculative look. "Suit yerself. I'm leaving before sunup."

That went well.

BRAHAM AND CULLEN camped at Rocky Ridge, a stony formation flanking both sides of the Sweetwater River. Braham couldn't sleep. Instead of tossing about, he sat by the river and skipped rocks, pondering the predicament he'd put himself in with all the best of intentions.

It's time.

He stomped back to his bedroll, rubbing the nasty ache in his arm. "Cullen, ye asleep?"

"Yep." Cullen's black hat covered his face, and his fingers lay knitted on his chest.

"Ye got something weighing on yer mind, and I got something to tell ye," Braham said.

Cullen unlaced his fingers and tossed his hat aside. "Sounds like we need some of that good old Pennsylvania rye whisky. If ye're wanting to talk, then I'm sure ye've got a bottle to share." He emptied the coffee dregs from his cup. "Fill it up and tell me what needs telling."

Braham shook his head. "The rule's always been that the one with the whisky gets his choice—first or last." He took a bottle from his saddlebag and poured the liquor into their empty coffee cups. "Ye go first."

"What do ye want to know?"

"What happened with Kit?"

A line of pain lanced across Cullen's face, and Braham felt sorry for his friend.

"Not sure ye've got enough in that bottle to hear it all," Cullen said.

"I brought two."

Cullen scrubbed his face, letting out a long sigh. Then he pulled something out of his saddlebag and handed it to Braham. "I picked that up off the floor in Kit's wagon. There's a date on the bottom corner."

Braham moved closer to the fire and studied the writing on the clear rubberlike material. "*Expires seven slash two thousand twelve.* What's it mean?"

"Just what it says."

Braham flicked his hat back with a snap of his finger and let out a long whistle. "I dinna understand."

Cullen sipped from his cup. "When the Barrett girl got sick, Kit started talking crazy, saying she was taking the child to the hospital. I told Kit she was the only one who could save Frances and that she had to put medicine in the child's arm just like she did to me."

"Ye didna tell me that."

"Ye wouldna have believed me."

"That's no reason—"

"Kit attached a needle to that bag ye're holding," Cullen interrupted. "It was full of medicine. Then she put the needle into the child's arm. I asked her who she was and where she came from."

"And…"

"She said she didna ken who she was, but that she came from the twenty-first century."

Braham turned up his cup and drank until it was empty. "I dinna believe it."

"I didna believe it either. Then she told me she'd discovered a letter from her dead father telling her she'd been found on his doorstep as an infant—"

Braham smirked. "I called her a changeling."

"Ye knew? Why didna ye tell me?"

"It meant she wasna my cousin."

"Ye should have told me."

"Probably." Braham clamped his mouth shut and looked away.

"Her father found her with a ruby brooch pinned to her dress. Kit says it has magic, and allows a person to pass through a door to another time."

Braham tossed the rubber bag to Cullen. "With a horse and a dog and a cat. How?"

"She didna say."

"Why's she here?" Braham refilled his cup. He checked the amount of alcohol left in the bottle. There wasn't enough for this story.

"She's looking for her family."

"If she finds what she's looking for, will she go back to her century?"

Cullen sat still for an unmeasured time. Finally he said, "I canna stop her."

"She canna leave."

He shook his head, sighing. "If I've learned one thing about the woman, she can do damn near anything she wants."

"Ye have to convince her to stay."

Cullen looked regretful. "Until I settle things with Abigail…"

Braham hung his head. "I've got something to tell ye, Cul."

Cullen stared, holding his cup inches from his mouth, waiting.

"She's dead."

"Who's dead?"

"Abigail"—Braham gulped—"died this past spring. She fell off her horse." He braced for the punch he expected Cullen to throw. A punch he well deserved.

Cullen jumped to his feet, spilling his whisky. "How do ye know?"

"I got a letter."

"From whom?"

"There was a telegram from Mr. Phillips with the letter from my father."

"The letter ye got at Fort Laramie?" Cullen balled his hands into fists and stepped toward Braham. "Ye've known since then, and ye didna tell me." His voice grated past his throat. He punched the air. "How could ye keep that from me?"

Being hit with a two-handed broadsword wouldn't have hurt Braham any more than the pain he saw in his friend's face. "I was wrong."

"If I hadna taken the wagon train job, I'd have been in California. She wouldna have died."

"Ye couldna have saved your sister or Abigail. Kristen hit her head. But ye forget that part so ye can blame yerself. Abigail hit her head, too. If ye'd been in San Francisco, ye couldna have changed the outcome."

"Ye dinna ken that, and ye were wrong for not telling me." He kicked dirt at the flames that nipped at his toes. "Ye were damn wrong." Cullen turned away from Braham and walked to the river, where he threw off his clothes and dived into the water.

Braham started to go after his friend, but instead he sat and watched to make sure Cullen didn't drown.

I dinna know how I can make this up to ye, but I will. Somehow, someway, someday.

AT DAYLIGHT, CULLEN walked into camp as Braham was pulling on his boots. "Ye're up early."

"Tell Henry I'm going to California to see Mr. Phillips and pay my respects. I'll meet ye in San Francisco by year's end," Cullen said.

Braham jumped up and stabbed the air with his finger. "Ye leave, I'm leaving, too."

"Ye shouldna have lied to me, Braham."

He dragged his hands down his face covered with whiskers and lined with sleep. "I didna lie to ye."

Cullen pumped his fist at him. "Withholding the truth isna as bad as lying because yer motives werena malicious. Is that it?"

"We dinna need to debate the criminalization of acts of omission."

Cullen saddled Jasper. "I'd appreciate it if ye'd help Henry."

"Damn it." Braham picked up his saddle. "Ye're doing exactly what I thought ye'd do. That's why I didna tell ye. Ye dinna need to be running off to California. Ye need to be making things right with Kit. She's the first woman Ye've ever respected. First woman ye've ever loved. I know ye bedded her. I'm nae an imbecile. That's why ye're eaten up with guilt. God, Cul, she could be carrying yer child. Marry her."

Cullen wondered if there was any whisky left. "She willna marry me. She's going home."

"Well then, go with her."

He sucked in a shuddering breath.

Braham squeezed his shoulder. "I'm leaving the wagon train soon, heading to San Francisco. I'll see Phillips. I'll tell him how ye're feeling. He's a good man. He'll understand."

Cullen's gut twisted with grief. Although he hadn't loved Abigail, he was fond of her. She would have been a good wife and mother. His father still grieved the death of his sister, and he prayed Mr. Phillips would find a way to cope with his loss. Braham was right, though. Phillips was a gracious man and would understand.

The morning air smelled of sweet wildflowers. It reminded Cullen of a simpler time when he and Braham were lads and the consequences of their actions weren't as life-changing.

Cullen gazed at the sunrise that never failed to humble him, then looked into his friend's strained face. The truth hit him hard. His life would never be what he wanted without Kit by his side. The last vestiges of his life's plan gave way to his heart's desire.

But even his heart's desire needed a plan. He would propose to Kit. If she said no, he'd steal the brooch and hold it ransom until she changed her mind. Not much of a plan, but until he came up with something better, it was the only one he had.

Chapter Twenty-Five

C ULLEN AND BRAHAM topped Pacific Butte at South Pass in the late afternoon. They looked out over the expansive valley filled with sand dunes and bluffs that formed a gate through the Rocky Mountains. Cullen whistled, letting his shoulders slacken a little under his red striped shirt. "Do ye ken what the Shoshone say about the pass?"

Braham tipped back his hat and gazed out over the Continental Divide toward Oregon Territory. "Probably something about God running out of mountains."

Cullen nodded as he glanced to the north, where the snow-topped Wind River Range loomed, then looked southeast toward the sage-covered Antelope Hills that bordered the valley on the side. To the right was the Sweetwater River. To the west, the Pacific Creek. "We're looking at the land of promise."

Braham laughed. "Some promise. Looks rather bleak to me."

Cullen had crossed through the pass twice before and had a camping site for the wagon train in mind. It would be the perfect place to either propose to Kit and marry her, or propose and become a thief in the night. The longer he thought about his alternate plan, the sourer it turned. No, he wouldn't hold her against her will. Should she want to leave, he'd tell her he loved her and let her go. But it would be another loss from which he'd never recover.

Braham pointed ahead. "Look at that. What do ye think it is?"

Cullen looked through his binoculars. The hairs on the back of his neck bristled. He handed the glasses to Braham. "Buffalo. Must be hundreds. If they get spooked, they could run right through the wagon train."

"I thought there were only small bands around here."

"I did, too."

"Somebody forgot to tell the damn buffalo."

CULLEN AND BRAHAM rode into the valley and met up with the wagon train.

"Look-see who blew in with the tumbleweeds," Henry said. "Glad to have you boys back. See anything?"

Cullen eyed the train, spread three wagons abreast, and nodded to the west. "Hundreds of buffalo a couple of miles north of here. We need to tighten our line and stay south while we cross the pass."

Henry turned to Braham. "You get the Preston boys. They're salty riders. Y'all watch those critters. Anything spooks 'em, make sure they're heading west, not east."

"Those boys got guts enough for all of us," Braham said. "We'll stay between the wagons and the herd. Pass the word to keep the noise down."

"If they get spooked, it'll be easier to scratch your ear with your elbow than stop 'em," Henry said.

Thunder rolled through the valley. The horses pricked their ears and sidestepped.

Henry grimaced. "Clear day. Can't be thunder."

Cullen clamped his cigar between his teeth. "Not thunder. Stampede. Not enough time to move the wagons."

"Give me your bring-'em-close glasses," Henry said. "Want to see what we're dealing with." He focused the binoculars at the dust cloud. "Damn." He lowered the glasses and pointed them offhandedly at Braham. "Get those boys to help you. If y'all can't turn them, I'll damn well put windows in those skulls and make a breastwork of carcasses."

Henry tossed Cullen the binoculars, spurred his horse into a lope, and yelled over his shoulder. "Come on. Get the women and children into the wagons. Tell the men to load their rifles. If the boys can't turn them, we'll shoot the ones in the middle and hope they'll pass on either side. If not, they'll run right through us. I'll ride the far outside of the wagons. You ride inside."

Cullen had heard of men facing down stampedes, heard of the fear, and its crippling panic. He hoped to God he wouldn't fail the people who depended on him. He checked his holstered .44 Colt revolver, then wiped his palms dry on his trousers.

He and Henry trotted down parallel lines. "Pack the wagons together and form a shield wall," Cullen yelled. When he saw Adam, he stopped. "Get everybody inside the wagon, then load yer rifle and stand ready." Cullen drew his carbine. As he rode back down the line, he shouted, "Make every shot count."

The ground groaned and heaved beneath the crazed animals. Pots and pans swinging from hooks inside the wagons clanged like cymbals.

Cullen dismounted in the center of the front line. He noticed a slender backside, then wisps of blond hair tucked under a hat. He yanked the woman up by the back of her collar and pulled a strange-looking rifle from her hands.

"Holy hell, Kit. What are ye doing? Get in the wagon with Sarah and the children."

"Give me my rifle." She grabbed the weapon and depressed the bolt release. The bolt sprang forward, chambering a round. "I've got thirty bullets in the magazine and five magazines in my bag. If I hit what I'm aiming at, I can down those critters pretty fast. Faster than you."

His body tensed with the red rage of fear.

"You need my rifle. You need me. People I love are in these wagons, and I'll shoot every bullet I have before I let one of them get hurt."

He didn't have time to fight with her while buffaloes waged war on them. "Show me how to use the gun. Then get out of my way."

She shook her head. "I'll reload for you, but I'm not leaving."

He shouldered the weapon and aimed. "What's the range?"

"Two hundred yards."

"How fast?"

"As fast as you can fire."

"When this is over, we have some talking to do."

"Then let's shoot some buffalo."

He pointed to the magazine box under the rifle's barrel. "Ye have five of these?"

"I'll refill them as you empty them."

He looked through the scope and placed the crosshairs on a target. If the weapon performed to Kit's expectations, he could damn well shoot a third of the herd before anyone else got off a second shot. "Where's yer handgun?"

"It's only accurate to twenty-five feet. Not much good here."

"Keep it close."

"If the buffalo get that close, we won't be here."

"It'll be too late to run."

"We're not running. The brooch will take us out of here if those buffalo get close enough we can smell their breath."

"They willna get that close."

But they sure as hell were getting closer, packed in a dense mass and running toward the wagons in a panic. At any moment, Kit expected the pulverized ground to open into fissures and gobble up everything in one dry, dusty gulp.

As she slipped a clip into her pistol and racked the slide, she heard the oxen and mules struggling against their hobbles to flee from the roll of thunder and choking dust.

Cullen looked up from his own weapon and turned to her. "Ye sure about this rifle?"

"Yes."

"Look—ride the line and tell the men to hold their fire until the herd gets within range. Make sure they understand we're shooting the buffalo in the center."

She squeezed his arm. His muscles tensed, and his face creased with concern.

"Come straight back."

Kit rode the line and shouted instructions to the men. By the time she returned to Cullen, he was firing into the herd. An empty magazine and a pile of shells had collected at his feet. Dead buffalo littered the pass.

"Start reloading." Sweat poured off his brow and ran into hard, focused eyes.

She placed a round between the empty magazine's feed lips and followed with another, and another, loading bullets as fast as her clammy fingers could shove them into place. A bullet dropped, but she didn't pick it up. Another dropped.

Concentrate, damn it.

Why hadn't Frances's journal mentioned the stampede? *Oh.* Below the entry mentioning the Murrays' missing baby were three words: *buffalo scared me.* Frances did write about it, and there was one other identifiable word farther down on the page—*miracle.*

The chamber clicked. Empty. Cullen yelled with a chilly demand. "Need another—"

She had a replacement mag ready before he ejected the used one. With surgical precision, he pushed the magazine up into the well and slapped upward on the bottom to seat it. He aimed and let go a round of bullets, killing dozens of buffalo.

He paused, surveying the scene before him. He'd fired more than three hundred rounds. A layer of dust covered him. The muscles in his arm, visible beneath his sweat-soaked shirt, rippled under the strain of shooter fatigue.

"Fire yer pistol. The herd's splitting." His commanding voice was barely a ripple over the roar.

She planted her feet shoulder-width apart and extended her left arm, its elbow slightly bent and the weapon at shoulder level. Gripping the shaking gun hand with her other hand, she fired. The gun discharged and something inside Kit snapped. She found herself lost in the taste of blood and the fog of memories—of fear and anger.

Bang. Bang. Bang. Over and over and over.

Somewhere in the madness, Cullen yelled, "Cease firing."

Her eyes cut a glance to the empty shell box at her side. Fear rose up her spine, caught on the calluses of her mended bones, and threatened to rebreak each one. "We're out of bullets." She didn't recognize the cold steel tone in her voice.

He grasped her pistol and wiggled it from her frozen grip. "Ye dinna need more."

"What if they come back?"

He lifted her chin with his finger and turned her face toward where the herd had been. She blinked and the blurriness cleared. A pile of carcasses stood twenty yards from the wagons.

Slowly, she slid to the ground, her clothes damp with sweat, her pulse racing more erratically than before. Reality broke through, and she emerged from the swamps of her festering soul, shivering. Words came slowly. "I wasn't shooting the buffalo."

He pulled her into his arms. His body shook against hers. "I know. It's over now. Ye shot them all."

AS SOON AS the dust settled, Cullen and Henry formed work crews to skin as many of the buffalo as possible. Henry sent riders to wagon trains trailing behind them to let folks know what happened and invited others to take what they needed.

Kit put her guns away and picked up every spent shell. She tried to defuse the questions, saying the gun had been an experimental weapon belonging to her husband, and that she and Cullen were relieved it didn't explode in their faces.

Just as things were quieting down, Braham's galloping horse came to a sudden stop only a few feet from where she and Cullen were standing, stirring up the dust again.

Braham pointed off into the distance. "See those circling buzzards?"

Cullen raised a dirt-covered eyebrow. "Did ye check it out?"

"Yep. Better get yer horse. Ye, too, Kit."

Chapter Twenty-Six

KIT KNEW BEFORE she left MacKlenna Farm that she'd find dead people in South Pass. The same quiet tension she'd experienced as a paramedic racing through Lexington's streets en route to an accident infused her with a concentrated focus. She always expected the worst. This time was no different.

The miasma of death hit her nostrils mere seconds before she saw ten bullet-ridden human corpses. Eight men, two women, no children. The site was a bloody crime scene. The victims had been gathered and massacred together. The savagery was incomprehensible. Kit's stomach roiled at the huge pools of congealed blood. Her mind tried to compartmentalize. She needed to see the scene through her professional lens, only peripherally through a personal one. But that would take a minute or two or five or maybe not at all.

Was her birth mother one of the bloodied women? Her birth father one of the bloodied men? She inched her fingers inside her blouse and fondled the locket around her neck. Why had some demented person stolen their dreams and robbed them of their hopes? She tried to piece the puzzle together, to get a clear picture in her mind, but the effort manifested in a whirl of confusion.

Cullen dismounted amidst a roar of flies. A blue vein pulsed in his temple. His hand caressed the handle of his holstered Colt canting over his hip. Eyes alert, searching. He looped Jasper's reins through the spokes of a wheel on one of the six wagons chained together. The smashed grass indicated animals had been in the corral, but they were gone now.

Kit untied her neck scarf and wrapped it around her nose and mouth, filtering the omnipresent dust sticking to every surface, even her sweat-covered body.

Look at their faces.

She swallowed hard, unsure of herself. There was an awkward tumble of her heartbeat as she dismounted and stepped toward *the dead people.* Until this moment, they were only words on a page she'd found in Frances's journal. Now the scene unfolded, frame by frame, in a grotesque silent movie.

She smelled them. Saw them. Heard their phantom screams.

Then, one by one, she approached each male corpse and looked into the rictus of horror on his face and the pain in his terror-filled eyes.

No. No. No. No. No. No. No. No.

The man in the portrait miniature was not among them. Relief swarmed through her, stinging every nerve with pinpoint precision. Why was she relieved? Now she'd never identify the man. But that seemed easier to accept than the fact he'd been rounded up and butchered like an animal.

A storm grew in her mind of hurricane proportions. She needed to go to work and let the hurricane stall out over the desert until later, until she got home and mixed the pain and trauma in with all the rest.

She gazed at Cullen. He caressed her briefly with eyes so blue they bordered on purple. She nodded, answering his unspoken question. *I'm okay.*

Kit swung her arms in an encompassing gesture. "Please don't touch anything until I can get pictures. I want to document what happened here."

"We dinna have time for ye to sketch." Cullen spoke without looking at her, his eyes intense with thought.

"I'm not." She grabbed a digital camera from her saddlebag. "You told Braham about me, didn't you?"

He swept his gloved hand across her cheek. "He knows."

She stood frozen a moment, then shrugged.

Cullen pointed at her camera. "What's that?"

"I'll explain later." She took a discriminating turn around the crime scene, snapping pictures of scattered clothing and bedding, opened burlap bags, overturned furniture, flour dumped into white piles. The murderers had thoroughly searched the wagons, but for what? Pouches of gold nuggets? She tried to make sense of the senselessness.

"What do ye suppose they were looking for?" Braham asked.

Cullen removed his hat and swiped his arm across his forehead. "The question is did they find it?"

"Let me get pictures inside the wagons, then you can gather up Bibles, letters, journals, anything that might help identify them. Then we'll bury them."

The wagons were easy to photograph. But later, as each face came into the frame, the shock weighed her down. The camera became too heavy to hold, and the air too thick to breathe.

Kit closed her eyes, blocking out the scene, but she saw it all through closed lids. Ten weeks she'd spent in the nineteenth century and traveled a thousand miles to take one picture. She had dozens now. But not the *one* she had framed in her mind. Not the *one* she had set out to take.

Cullen and Braham proceeded through the crime scene, climbing in and out of the wagons and searching pockets. When they finished, she went back to each wagon and took more photographs. That's when she spotted a cradle. Every muscle in her body fibrillated. She crossed her arms, held them close, and waited for the rapid twitching to stop.

After a few moments, her body relaxed but the mingled apprehension and bafflement remained. She poked her head around the corner of the wagon. "Cullen." He shifted his gaze from the buzzards flying lazy circles in the sky. "There's a cradle in this wagon but there's no sign of a baby. Have you seen a grave?" She heard the waffle in her voice.

Cullen wore an expression of intense concentration. "No."

"Where's Braham? Maybe he found one."

"He left a while ago to water the horses and put on some coffee. He thought we'd want to talk before we told the others what we found here."

She glanced back at the cradle. It didn't make sense. Both women had multiple chest wounds, as did the men. All ten would have died instantly. None of them could have wrapped a baby in a bloody shawl and sent the infant through time. So what did that mean?

"I'm through here. Are ye?" Cullen asked.

"I've seen enough," she said.

He offered his arm. Maybe he noticed her trembling. Maybe he sensed it, but she knew she couldn't walk without support. If he said anything else to her, she didn't hear him. She heard only the sweep of their boots through the tall grass as they walked the short distance to Braham's campfire and a cup of strong, black coffee.

The earth was quiet now. It no longer rumbled, but she imagined it did way down deep below the surface. She removed her scarf, eased to the ground, and sipped the coffee Braham handed her.

Cullen sat and placed a burlap sack of the items he and Braham had collected on the grass between them. Kit emptied it onto the ground and spread the contents out. There were four Bibles, three journals, and two stacks of letters tied with black ribbons. She took a shivery breath, opened a Bible, and read aloud from the dedication page. "Kenneth and Jean Murray married in Springfield, Illinois, February 16, 1851. Heather Marie Murray, born May 1, 1852."

Kit closed the Bible, her hands cold and shaky. "Where is Heather now?"

Cullen removed his gloves and dusted his hands, then picked up a stack of letters and untied the ribbon. "Probably didna survive."

"Why didn't they enter her date of death?"

"Maybe the baby died yesterday. Maybe last week. We dinna ken. Probably never will."

Braham turned to them. "Why would someone murder these folks?"

Maybe they were looking for gold. Kit had the sensation of scrambling for purchase on a rocky ledge, battered, bruised, and bloodied.

Hold on for a little while longer.

Cullen squeezed her hand. "I'm here, lass." He gazed at her, but she avoided his eyes. After a moment, he tilted her chin, forcing her to look at him. "I've seen this look before. Ye ken something about this, don't ye?"

She didn't reply for a long moment. Then, she said, "It's why I'm here."

"Who'd ye come to see?"

"The Murrays."

"I'm sorry they're dead, lass."

She hooded her eyes. "I knew they would be."

"Ye came here to find dead people?"

When she opened her mouth to answer, Cullen placed two fingers against her lips. "Tell me anything, but dinna tell me it's complicated."

She licked her lips and caught his finger in the sweep of her tongue. He dropped his hand. *What will he say when he finds out I came looking for him?* "A journal written by Frances Barrett—"

"John's little girl?" Braham asked.

"Yes." She followed her answer with a thin smile. "Frances's journal was or will be discovered in Portland, Oregon. Most of it unreadable. But an entry dated June 16, 1852—"

"That's today," Cullen said.

She squeezed his hand. "The entry says—" Kit stopped and took a breath. "—June 16, 1852 South Pass. Mr. Montgomery found a bloody mess. All murdered on Murray wagon train. Murray baby girl missing.'"

Cullen's jaw dropped. "Ye knew of me before we met? Why didna ye tell me?"

"Tell you what? That I came back in time to meet you so you'd take me to South Pass to find a wagon train full of dead people? What would you have done?"

"I might have been able to stop what happened."

"No, you would've gotten yourself killed."

"I dinna understand what this has to do with ye?"

"I thought the Murrays might be my birth parents." The idea suddenly seemed ludicrous. Had she put two and two together, come up with ten, and convinced herself it was four? She toyed with the portrait miniature hanging around her neck from a gilt chain.

Cullen sat motionless except for a stress tic in his jaw. His eventual response was chilly. "Explain, please."

"Based on the journal and other information I had, I believed there was a good possibility I was their baby."

Braham stepped up to them. "I dinna need to be hornin' in here—"

"Then dinna," Cullen said, glaring at him. He turned to Kit. "What's yer evidence?"

"The letter from my father said that when he found me I had the brooch, a blood-splattered lace shawl with a monogrammed *M*, and a portrait miniature. At first, I thought the *M* stood for MacKlenna. After I read about the Murrays' missing baby, I thought it might stand for Murray. Since the Murrays were murdered, I assumed that's how blood got on the shawl."

"What else do ye have?" Cullen asked.

"I made three assumptions. The bloody shawl belonged to my mother. My last name started with an *M*, and the man in the miniature portrait was my father."

"What portrait?" Cullen asked.

She pulled the miniature from under her blouse.

"It's a huge leap for ye to assume ye're the Murrays' missing baby," Cullen said.

"I agree."

"Ye do?"

"That's why I decided to be here on June 16. If I could see the bodies, I would know if Mr. Murray and the man in the portrait were one and the same. I now know they aren't, but I still don't know who he is. Finding the bodies didn't answer the question I needed answered."

Cullen pointed to the portrait miniature. "May I see it?"

Kit unclasped the chain and placed the jewelry in his palm. He studied the portrait with no visible change in expression. Then he handed the portrait to Braham.

Braham looked at the miniature. His face drained of color. "I've seen this man."

"Where?" Cullen and Kit asked simultaneously.

"He was at the Phillipses' party." Braham gave Cullen a thinking stare. "He came into the ballroom and spoke to Mr. Phillips, ten maybe fifteen minutes. Phillips welcomed him in a friendly manner, then he left. I wasna introduced, so I dinna ken his name. Didna ye meet him?"

Cullen cleared his throat. "I met Abigail that night."

Braham tugged on his lips. "I know this is the same man. He's older now, probably approaching fifty, distinguished, impeccably dressed, carefully groomed. I assumed he was Phillips's client, or a partner in one of his business ventures." He handed the portrait back to Kit. "He's alive. At least he was nine months ago. We'll find him in San Francisco."

"We?" She felt herself sliding down the side of the slippery ridge. "I can't go to San Francisco. I have to go home. People are worried about me."

"Send them a letter. Tell them ye'll be home in a few months," Braham said, giving her a wisp of a smile.

"We dinna have to decide on our next steps right now. But we do need to bury the dead. We'll talk about this later," Cullen said.

"There's nothing to talk about. You're going to San Francisco to marry Abigail. I'm going home."

A charged silence passed among them.

"Abigail died in the spring before I met ye. Braham told me yesterday." The muscles tightened around his eyes. "He was afraid if he told me I'd run off to California."

"Because he'd feel responsible," Braham added.

She fixed Cullen with a serious gaze. "You feel responsible for everybody. That's probably why you've haunted me since I was ten years old."

His face turned more shades of gray than she could draw. "I'm nae sure I want to hear this."

"Well, I do." Braham stretched out his legs and laced his hands behind his head as if expecting the reading of a massive tome. "Just out of curiosity, how many years has that been?"

"Fifteen years this November."

"Ye were twelve, Cul. That was the year yer sister died. How many times have ye seen him as a ghost?"

"Dozens. But some I remember more than others because of what happened to me the same day. Like the sighting five years ago."

Braham dropped his arms and leaned forward. "That's when we decided to go to California. When was the next time ye remember?"

"Six months ago."

Braham removed a cigar from his pocket and pointed it at Cullen. "That's when ye and Mr. Phillips had the conversation about Abigail."

"And the next?"

"Two months later," Kit said.

"That's when ye decided not to go back to San Francisco, but stay and help Henry with the wagon train."

"Are there any others ye recall?" Cullen frowned, and his gaze turned inward.

"The day I left my century and met you in Independence," she said.

"I wasna supposed to be in town. Henry and I planned to ride over to the Blue River, but decided against it early that morning." His frown grew deeper.

"We ken what Cullen was doing. What were ye doing, Kit?"

The events unnerved her. "The first time I ever saw you was on my tenth birthday. I fell off my horse and broke my back. The doctors said I'd never walk again."

"Next," Cullen asked.

Her heart rate escalated with each memory, the significance of the timing more astounding. "You appeared at dawn on the day

Wayne attacked me, and I remember seeing you the night my family died, and again the day I found the letter from my father."

"And then again before ye left yer century," Cullen said.

"That vision was different, though. It was of you and Sean MacKlenna selecting Thomas's gravesite on MacKlenna Farm. But Thomas doesn't die until January 25, 1853. I don't think you'll be in Kentucky in six months, do you?"

"Canna see how that's likely to happen."

"That vision doesna fit the pattern at all," Braham said.

"Do ye want to meet Thomas MacKlenna before he dies?" Cullen asked.

"I'm not a MacKlenna. There's no reason."

"Then why did ye see me there?"

The question hung in the air for a moment, and then she said, "We'll probably never know."

Chapter Twenty-Seven

"**I**T'S ALMOST MIDNIGHT," Cullen said, snapping closed his pocket watch.

She shivered. One of the longest days in her life was ending. "Will you walk me back to the wagon? I think I can sleep now." The breeze had cleared away the dust and perfumed the air with the sweet scent of prairie flowers, and Pacific Springs gurgled in the background. "I don't want to think about buffalo and dead people and an empty cradle."

He opened his watch and checked the time again before stroking the sides of her face with trembling fingers. "So much was left unsaid the night we were together." His breath was but a wisp against her lips.

Nothing felt more natural than to slip into his arms and share a kiss. She belonged there. His mouth came down on hers, tentatively at first, then deeper with more insistence.

"I'm sorry for lying to you," she mumbled against his lips. "But I couldn't tell you why I was here."

"I know." Moonlight illuminated the understanding in his expression. "I want to ask ye…" He opened his watch and checked the time again.

She'd never seen him so nervous.

"It's now June seventeenth." His voice sounded melodic, softer, like a string quartet. His body, however, conveyed a different message, tense and high-strung.

Was something on his mind?

He stood shrouded in the sky's pale light as he took her hands and dropped to one knee.

Ohmygod. Now, she began to tremble.

His hands felt moist in hers. "Kitherina MacKlenna…"

A tingling sensation raced up her spine.

"Let me love ye for the rest of yer life." Then he added without taking a breath, "Marry me."

She dropped to her knees, literally swept off her feet by his declaration. "You're asking me to—"

"Ye told me before we made love ye couldna live with the regret if ye said no. I hope ye feel the same about marriage."

"Where will we live?" The question came out fast and jumbled as one long word.

"My job's in San Francisco."

"Mine's in Kentucky."

He sat on the ground and pulled her into his lap. "I ken ye're nae asking about cities."

"I can't disappear permanently."

"I wouldna have asked ye to marry me without a feasible plan."

"I have to go back."

"Until ye ken the identity of the man in the portrait and how he fits into yer life, ye canna go home."

"But—"

He pressed a finger to her lips. "After ye discover his identity, if ye still want to leave, I'll go with ye."

"But you have a law practice and a family."

"If I have to choose between my family and ye, I choose ye."

She pulled away from him and sat up straight. "I have to go home. If only to settle my affairs, I have to go."

"Marry me at noon."

She gasped. "That's just twelve hours."

"I'm afraid of losing ye."

She closed her eyes and tried to gain a sense of what was happening. Cullen had haunted her since she was ten, which was probably when she fell in love with him. Now he wanted to marry her, and he even agreed to live in her time. How could she say no?

"I'll do anything for ye." His finger drew a line from her lips, over her chin, down her neck to the cup at her throat. "Just give me a chance." He kissed her, whispering against her lips, "How sweet is yer love, my treasure, my bride? Let's go to the field and spend the night among the wildflowers."

"You're quoting Shakespeare again."

"A liberal interpretation of King Solomon. A man who appreciated his bonnie bride, as do I."

The sound of his heartbeat increased from a rumble to a deep roar, matching hers. Enrapt, she moved closer to his heat, rubbing against him.

He let out a deep-throated chuckle. "The lassie is ready for her wedding night."

She raised her chin a fraction, only a fraction, but enough to sass him. "You're incorrigible."

His eyes twinkled. "I have another question—"

"The answer is no. I'm not making love again until you put a ring on my finger."

"That wasna my question, but it will do for now." He slipped his thumb and forefinger into his vest pocket and pulled out a triangular shaped fancy vivid blue diamond mounted on a silver band with baguette-cut diamonds.

"Oh my," she gasped. "Seventeen-eighties. It's absolutely exquisite. You can't find a piece of jewelry like this in my time. They didn't survive in their original settings."

A look of delight blossomed across his face. "It belonged to my late grandmother, Aquila Montgomery. I was going to wait until the wedding, but..."

Kit shook her head and pushed his hand away. "I'd be honored to wear her ring, but I won't dishonor her memory by wearing it just so we can make love."

He frowned, unable to hide his disappointment, then slipped the ring back into his pocket.

They sat quietly for several minutes. Finally, Cullen asked, "Ye dinna have any more secrets, do ye?"

Her mouth crawled into a tight, upside-down smile. "There's a little matter of money we need to talk about."

A short chuckle rumbled through his chest. "I may not look like a man of means, but I am verra wealthy. My grandparents left me a sizable estate, and I'll eventually inherit from my father."

"You're educated and well-traveled. I assumed your family had money."

"Och. The lass agreed to marry me with the expectation of wealth."

She gave him an I'm-offended glare. "I happen to be an heiress. Maybe you're marrying me for mine."

"We're nae in yer century."

"I have pouches of gold nuggets and diamonds with me."

His jaw dropped. "In yer red bag?"

"In the trunk *with* the red bag."

"But ye ken ye werena going to stay here."

"My father didn't mention the gold in his journal. When I found out about the Murrays, I thought the treasure might belong to them. If it did, I wanted their families to have it. Now we know from reading the Murrays' letters they had their own gold."

"Which probably got them killed. If Mr. Murray was on his way to South Pass from California to meet up with his family, then the killers could have followed him from his claim."

"But why kill ten people?

"With everyone dead, there was no one to identify them."

Heat crept up her neck. In a quiet voice she said, "The killers are still out there."

He held her close. "Dinna mention yer gold. If the killers hear of it, they could come after us next."

Chapter Twenty-Eight

CULLEN FOUND KIT at her wagon, pacing, not in a normal back and forth pattern but in random circles. He watched from a distance. When she started mumbling, he decided to make his presence known. He'd spent the past hour working out details of his plan, a plan that needed Kit's agreement. Her bleak expression and bloodshot eyes made the prospect doubtful. He quashed the uneasy feeling and approached her with levity. "If ye're having second thoughts, I'm prepared to kidnap ye. I had ancestors who did that successfully, by the way."

Kit quit pacing. "I'm this close," she said pinching her thumb and forefinger together, "to throwing up my hands, stomping my feet, and screaming hysterically."

Levity isn't going to work.

"My stomach's upset, and I can't stop thinking about the baby. Where is she?"

"Maybe she's standing right here all grown up."

"It's the not knowing," she said, ignoring him, "that's gnawing at me like a coyote chewing off a leg to escape from a trap."

"Ye're nae trapped. And if there's going to be any gnawing on limbs, I'll be the one doing the gnawing."

"I'm serious."

"So am I." He picked her up and set her on the tailgate. "Once we find yer mystery man in San Francisco, ye'll have answers."

"You don't know that."

He paused to consider a response. Since meeting Kit, there had been times he thought he'd lost all power of logical reasoning. This, however, was not one of those times. He didn't believe farmers from Illinois would have had a twelfth century Celtic brooch, but a wealthy gentleman from San Francisco? That, he could believe. "Are there details ye havena told me that led ye to believe ye might be the Murrays' baby?"

Kit tented her fingers and appeared to contemplate his question. "You need to read Dad's letter." She reached inside the wagon and grabbed her journal off the bed. When she opened the book, the page flipped to the first caricature she had drawn of Cullen.

"That's what ye were drawing at the Noland House. I caught a peek before ye closed the journal. What does it say underneath?"

She turned the book around so he could read the caption.

"Rescued by a tall glass of sweet tea, swaying in a hammock under a large shade tree." The allegorical cartoon represented him as a glass of tea in a hammock under an oak tree. Interesting that Kit sensed he offered her both protection and pleasure.

With mounting interest, he turned the pages. The children had been right. His pictures were the only cartoons. He discovered in her drawings a gifted artist. Her sketches revealed depth and emotion.

She pulled a piece of paper from the journal and dangled it in front of his face. "Read."

The creased letter had scorch marks around the edges. "Did ye set it on fire?"

A rose-colored flush tinged her face. "It's a long story."

He steeled his features and remained impassive while he read. When he finished, he slipped the letter back inside the journal. "Sean MacKlenna should nae have kept this from ye." He considered the letter for a moment longer before he spoke again. "Ye've taken a bloody shawl and a journal entry and formed a hypothesis ye canna prove unless we find Heather's body."

"Either Baby Heather died and was buried somewhere along the nine-hundred-mile trail from Independence to South Pass, or she was sent into the future," Kit said.

"There's another possibility."

Kit jumped to the ground. "What?"

"The murderers took the baby."

She splayed her fingers and shook them like jazz hands. "Then…then we have to find them."

He picked her up and set her back on the tailgate. "Whoa."

"But don't you see? We have to."

"There're nae clues. Nae names to put on wanted posters. Nae descriptions to give the authorities."

She sucked in an exasperated breath.

He rubbed up and down on her arms, trying to relax her tense muscles, but it was only tensing her more. "Don't go getting yer bloomers in a wad."

"You're giving me that mischievous blue-eyed look, Cullen. Can't you see I'm having an identity crisis? Find a hot spring where I can take a long bath. Then you might get lucky in South Pass."

He smiled. "Ye up for a ride?"

Kit quickly backpedaled. "I can't ride off to a hot spring with you."

"Marry me at noon and ye can."

Her shoulders sagged. "I don't even know who I am."

"Ye're Heather Murray."

"No, I'm not." She smacked her hand on the tailgate.

His lip twitched at her unusual display of surliness. "I love ye. Yer name doesna matter to me. 'A rose by any other name would smell as sweet.'"

"Damn those books. I wish you'd give them all away." She slid off the tailgate and resumed pacing, then stopped, and planted her hands on her hips. "I might be Heather, but I'll never know for sure. So absent proof, I think I'll just keep my name."

His face split into a huge grin. "It's a beautiful and unusual name."

"It was my granny's name, and her granny's, and her granny's granny. I don't know who had it first."

"Marry me this afternoon?"

Sarah peeked around the corner of Kit's wagon. "Am I interrupting? I just heard the news. Congratulations. But why the gloomy look?"

A sudden babel of noise descended upon the encampment. "What's going on?" All the women on the wagon train were walking toward her carrying flowers and an assortment of calico dresses. "Everybody knows. Not just the Barretts? How'd that happen?" Kit asked.

Cullen tried to hide a self-satisfied smile behind his hand and a fake cough. "I might have told Braham."

"*Might have?* And who else?"

"I think I told Henry, too," Cullen said.

"*You think.* And who else?"

"Probably John."

Kit tapped her foot. Not a good sign when there wasn't any music playing. "And John sent Sarah to find out what I thought of your plan."

Sarah's cheeks flushed.

"*Cullen.*" Kit huffed.

"I was afraid ye might want to wait until we reached San Francisco. I needed help persuading ye to marry me today."

"I'll marry you this afternoon because I can't think of anything I'd rather do than soak in a hot spring." She turned with a flourish and hooked arms with Sarah. "Let's go see what the ladies have planned for an afternoon wedding." Kit gave him an over-the-shoulder toodle-oo wave. But before she strode out of sight, she turned and flashed the most breathtaking smile he had ever seen. His body sizzled. He cupped his hands around his mouth and yelled, "I'll be waiting for ye at noon."

"Two o'clock, Cullen. Not a minute earlier."

AFTER KIT SOAKED in a tub of lukewarm water, Sarah helped her into a rose-colored calico gown trimmed in ruffle lace with a cotton underskirt, another one of her mother's creations.

Sarah fluffed Kit's dress. "You're a beautiful bride, and your groom is a handsome man."

"He is, isn't he? I hope he'll shave for the occasion." Kit twirled in her crowded quarters. "Everything in place?"

"Until he gets his hands on you." Sarah patted her cheeks in mock embarrassment.

Kit wiggled her eyebrows. "He's not too subtle about his needs."

"At least you're a widow and know what to expect."

Her face heated and grew hotter as the blush approached her hairline and beyond. Yes, she was aware of what to expect and not because she was a widow.

"It's almost two o'clock," Henry announced, knocking on the side of her wagon.

"Give me five minutes." Pre-wedding jitters now had her wrapped in cold tentacles. How in the world could she remain so calm in death-defying situations yet panic at the thought of making a public profession of her love?

"Will you check on your daughters? They've been holding their bouquets so long the flowers are probably squashed."

"Or Tate and Tabor ate them," Sarah said.

"That wouldn't surprise me. They consider everything consumable."

Sarah swiped at the corners of her eyes. "I can't tell you how happy this wedding makes me."

Kit took a deep breath. Tears threatened to ruin the glow of her freshly scrubbed skin and pinched-pink cheeks. She swished Sarah away. "Go before I start crying."

Sarah hugged her. "I hope Frances doesn't embarrass you this afternoon. She said this morning that she was going to be a big sister when you have a baby. Lordy, I don't know where that child gets her ideas." Sarah punctuated the statement with a combination eye roll and tsk-tsk. "I'll see you outside."

Many of the ideas came directly from Kit. She'd been subtly turning both girls into suffragettes. And if she had to guess, she'd say Sarah secretly encouraged the indoctrination.

Kit had one last thing to do before she presented herself. Pin the ruby brooch to her dress. Whoever her birth mother was, she sensed the woman would be pleased. She patted the jewelry and smiled. "I hope you don't whisk me away."

Henry knocked again. "It's time, missy. The boy will cut a big gut if he don't lay eyes on you right away."

Kit had no idea what that meant, but it didn't sound healthy for Cullen. She peeked in the mirror again, pinched her cheeks, and patted the brooch. *Let's go get married.* She opened the wagon flaps and gazed into Henry's face, a face she had once thought of as old and leathery. Now she saw only a loveable, no-nonsense man.

"You look like a princess." He held up rough, callused hands and lifted her off the tailgate. Skirt and petticoats swished through the air. When he set her velvet-shoed feet on the ground, he pulled her into his arms for a fatherly hug. "I'm mighty proud to step in for your pa." His keen eyes captured hers. "You ready to marry my boy?"

"I'm ready." She kissed his cheek, then stood back and looked him over. "You're quite dashing in your Sunday finery."

A blush rushed to his face. "I clean up nice, don't I?"

She laced her hand into the crook of his arm. "Real nice."

Henry signaled Mr. Cameron, who began to play Bach's "Minuet Number Two" on his fiddle. Kit's heart warmed with delight. Cullen must have spent hours with the musician perfecting the arrangement. Although Mr. Cameron was talented, his repertoire did not include classical music. Until now.

Henry and Kit walked toward the river. The crowd had assembled on both sides of a four-foot-wide path sprinkled with red Indian paintbrush. Cullen stood at the end of the path between Reverend Hamilton and Braham, facing the gathering with hands clasped behind his back, gazing only at her. Rarely was he without his black hat. His hair lay in easy waves combed off his face. Her legs trembled at the breathtaking sight of her groom. Her step faltered, but Henry kept her upright. Her misstep probably went unnoticed by all except Cullen. When she regained her footing, an easy grin split his face.

Henry escorted her to the front of the assembly. Cullen extended his hand and whispered, "The yellow gold of morning sun shimmers in yer hair. Come with me, lass, and ride to Loch Lomond." Once again, her step faltered. He had her hand, though, and he would never let her fall. Since she was ten, he had been reaching out to her. Now she understood why she'd survived the crash. She was meant to love him and have his children.

And on this day, she was marrying him.

The wedding location wasn't a church with the sun shining through stained glass windows, creating rainbows on the walls. It was commencing on the prairie under a canopy of cotton ball clouds, swimming with a gentle breath of a June breeze cooling the hot afternoon air.

Perfect. Absolutely perfect.

The reverend dabbed at sweat trickling down his temples. "Dearly beloved, we are assembled here in the presence of God, to join this man and this woman in holy marriage, instituted of God, regulated by His commandments, blessed by our Lord Jesus Christ. Forasmuch as these two people have come together, if there is any person who knows why they may not be joined in marriage, that person is required to make it known, or ever after to hold his peace."

The minister paused. She heard the rustle of the crowd, a cough, a murmur, and then silence. She inhaled, noticing for the first time she'd been holding her breath. No one objected to the marriage, and the brooch didn't hustle her off to the amber light.

"Do you, William Cullen Montgomery, declare in the presence of God that you know of no reason that you may not be lawfully married to this woman?"

"I do not."

"Do you, Kitherina Mary MacKlenna, declare in the presence of God that you know of no reason that you may not be lawfully married to this man?"

"I do not." She spoke in a clear, soft voice that sounded unfamiliar.

The minister prayed over their guidance and protection, and then he said, "Do you, William, take this woman to be your lawful and married wife?"

"I do."

"Do you, Kitherina, take this man to be your lawful and married husband?"

"I do."

"Who gives this woman to be married?"

Henry took Kit's other hand and placed it in the minister's soft, comforting palm. "I do." The minister joined Cullen's hand with hers.

"Repeat after me," Reverend Hamilton said to Cullen. "I, William Cullen Montgomery, take thee, Kitherina Mary MacKlenna, to be my wedded wife. And I promise to be loving and faithful, in plenty and in want, as long as we both shall live." Cullen repeated the words, his voice low, almost a whisper. But she felt the words vibrating as if he wanted her to not only hear the promise, but also sense its true meaning.

Her legs wobbled, and Cullen squeezed her hands harder, infusing her with his strength and his promises.

The minister turned toward Kit. The ceremony was happening too fast, going by in an anxious blur.

"Repeat after me," he said. And she did, saying, "I, Kitherina Mary MacKlenna, take thee, William Cullen Montgomery, to be my wedded husband." She fell silent, shaking. The minister cleared his throat, encouraging her to continue. After a moment, she took a breath. "I promise to be loving and faithful, in plenty and in want, as long as we both shall live." Her tongue felt thick, unnatural, and she barely delivered the words.

The rest of the ceremony fell into a foggy world where she participated but was not fully cognizant of what was happening.

"I pronounce you husband and wife, according to the ordinance of God; whom therefore God hath joined together, let no man put asunder."

Mr. Cameron began to play his fiddle. The music infiltrated the fog and the mist lifted from Kit's mind. "Mozart?" she asked.

Cullen smiled. "'Allegro.' Now, kiss me, Mrs. Montgomery."

And she did.

Braham cleared his throat. "Step aside." He brushed Cullen out of the way. "The best man deserves a kiss." He kissed her on the lips. "Ye are a beautiful bride, Mrs. Montgomery."

"And you are the most handsome best man I've ever seen."

Henry stepped in, nudging Braham aside. "My turn." He kissed Kit's cheek, then hugged Cullen. "Mighty proud of you, son." He sniffed a time or two before moving to make room for John and Sarah.

"Thank ye, John," Cullen said, "for asking me to join ye on this venture. If not for ye, I never would have met her."

Kit heard Cullen's comment, but she knew in her heart the brooch would have taken her to wherever he had been— Independence, San Francisco, London, Paris.

John patted Cullen's shoulder. "I'm happy it worked out."

Elizabeth and Frances tugged on Kit's sleeve. "Will you still be our teacher?"

"Of course."

"But Mr. Montgomery's going to California," Frances said.

Sarah stepped forward and placed her hands on top of the children's heads. "Come along, now. I'm sure Mr. and Mrs. Montgomery will tell us as soon as they've decided where they'll live."

A myriad of emotions churned Kit's already overactive stomach. The Barretts and Henry had become her family. How could she leave them? Cullen lost his smile for a moment. He leaned in and whispered, "There's plenty of time to decide."

For the first time in her memory, she didn't own a well-thought-out plan. But Cullen had one. And she trusted him with her heart and her life.

Chapter Twenty-Nine

KIT'S EARS PERKED up at the sound of a purling waterfall hidden amidst a magical twilight. Cullen reined Jasper to a stop and pointed ahead. "We'll camp between that sandstone outcropping and those pine trees."

After a two-hour ride across the hot, grassy prairie and sage-covered hills, she gazed at the honeymoon suite with eager expectation, and not only for her promised soak in a hot spring.

How had the day come to this?

At sunrise she'd paced and stomped and fretted over who she was and where she'd come from. Now the sun was setting and although the answers she sought were still unknown, her identity somehow didn't seem as important. All that mattered now was who she had become during the days and weeks leading up to this whirlwind day. A day that even in her most creative and inspirational moments was unimaginable.

Instead of Second Presbyterian Church, the Lexington Philharmonic, and an outrageously expensive wedding gown, she'd had an open-air wedding on the plains of what would become Wyoming with buffalo roasting on a spit and Mozart and Bach played on a fiddle. On reflection, the day was spectacular for the singular reason that people she loved, people who had inserted themselves into her life, had celebrated with her.

From the razzing Cullen received from Henry, John, and especially Braham, one would have thought that Cullen had never bedded a woman. She had caught him watching her with eyes so hot she was afraid she would combust. His eyes weren't as hot now. Then her glance drifted lower and she licked her lips in anticipation. Other parts of him were steaming.

Kit dismounted. After she watered, fed, and brushed Stormy, she stripped, not to entice her husband with a stripper's slow tease, but simply to get her clothes out of the way. The rip 'em off, throw 'em down kind of peel enticed Cullen nonetheless.

He watched with his head cocked to the side, arms folded. "Never seen anyone in such a hurry for a soak." He threw her a crooked grin.

Tension knotted inside her, almost distracting her from a bath. She tore her gaze from him and dug through her carpetbag for a bar of soap, shampoo, and a razor.

"What's the pink thing in yer hand?"

"A razor."

"Do ye need my shaving mirror?"

"Oh?" She scratched her chin and with a deadpan, neutral voice said, "I thought it might be broken."

Cullen's quizzical look furrowed his brow.

For someone with a trenchant sense of humor, he often seemed stymied by her sarcasm and jokes. She smiled. "You need a modern perspective on sarcasm and the panoply of jokes that keep twenty-first century audiences laughing until the wee hours of the morning."

"Aye, many things from yer time arena clear to me, but lingerie is nae one of them." He brushed his hand across her bra. "What do ye call this little piece of lacy fabric?"

"A demi-bra."

He caressed her breasts. "I like yer little bra." His voice, raw and sexy, teased as much as his fingertips.

She clasped her arms around his neck and settled contentedly against him, feathering his hair through her fingers. "Join me in the water."

He moaned. "I need to make camp before it gets dark. I'll join you shortly."

She kissed him, her lips slightly parted. "Don't make me wait too long." He unhooked the bra's front closure. *How'd he do that?* Before she could figure it out, he lowered his head and swirled his tongue around a nipple. Whatever thoughts had been roaming through her brain gave in to the incredible heat. His palm pressed against her lower back, bringing her closer to his erection. Their rasping breaths mingled. She reclined her head, giving him full access to her neck. "Come with me," she moaned.

"I have every intention of coming with ye." Her pulse leaped at the expectation that he would fulfill his promise. "Go now, or I willna get camp set up." He unclasped her hands from around his neck and set her away from him. The straps slipped off her shoulders and the bra fell to the ground. Before she moved out of his reach, he slid his fingers into her bikini panties and caressed her bottom. "Fifteen minutes, lass."

She leaned into his hand and mewed.

"Vixen. Ye're set on torturing me." He picked her up and carried her to the water, his eyes dancing with happiness.

"Don't throw me in."

He laughed. "The thought occurred to me, but I wouldna dare risk harming my bride." He pulled off her panties and eased her into the bubbling foam as if he were laying a baby down for a nap. "Fifteen minutes." He walked away, whistling. "Beethoven's 'Symphony No. 6,'" she yelled.

"Och, my bonnie bride knows Beethoven."

"I know Haydn, too. You can't stump me." She sank into the mineral water and reveled in the way it laved her with its wizardly powers. Since meeting him at the freight office, how often had she listened to him whistle? Every time they were together. He rarely whistled around other people, though. Why? She'd have to ask him. She ducked under the gurgling waterfall and washed away the shampoo. Sore muscles also disappeared, but others tensed in wanton anticipation.

When she broke through the curtain of foamy water and wiped her eyes, she spotted Cullen silhouetted against the rising moon and the shadow of rugged land—a Greek statue perfectly sculpted—six feet, two inches of corded muscles and long, lean legs. Black hair trailed a path down his chest, past his navel, to the thick patch at his groin. His arousal jutted back up the path.

Goodness, he's certainly endowed with a lot more than inalienable rights.

The moment was a breath-stopping memory to savor, a vivid memory to paint, a sensate memory never to place on her shelf of collectibles, but to hold close and cherish—forever.

A deep red glow, a reflection or a trick of the dying light, slashed across Cullen's chest and held there until he slipped into the water. Although the light disappeared when he moved, its presence notched an eerie premonition in Kit's heart.

"Mmm." He sniffed, nuzzling her neck. His stubble brushed her wet skin. "Succulent enough to eat, *ma chérie.*"

"Nibble away, I'm all yours." She floated into his arms and into the realm of heightened sensuality. The water became warmer, the dying sun brighter, the cool air smoldering, his kisses liquid. A cry came from low in her throat as their tongues danced to the rhythm of lovers written at the beginning of time. Their limbs entwined like soft-tipped tendrils of fragrant wisteria. His scent was an intoxicating blend of sun and pine, redolent of musk.

Cullen entered her in a single powerful thrust, stretching, filling her with sensations that moved like an enveloping groundswell of energy from deep within her pelvic core, pulsing outward along her body's sensuous pathways.

"I've thought of little else since the last time I held ye in my arms."

Kit had everything she ever wanted, everything she needed to be complete. She shivered against him.

"Are ye cold?" He wrapped her tighter in his embrace.

"I'm burning." She gazed into his eyes, dark and intense. "Don't ever leave me."

"I'll never leave ye."

Her fingers raked through his hair, down the length of his neck, and along broad shoulders. She indulged herself in the velvet smooth texture of his skin. Without inhibition, her hands glided down hard, muscular arms and across his chest and became entangled with patches of black hair.

"Ouch."

She ignored his gentle complaint as heat and tension roared through her, igniting an uncontrollable fire. Tremors washed over her like the perfect storm engulfing everything in its path. His subtle stroking became a maelstrom of dazzling sensations as powerful as the final movement of a symphony pulling the listener toward the ultimate climax and reward.

She inhaled without exhaling, and with each inhalation, her muscles tensed to a new and higher level until they contracted in orgasmic spasms. The tempo of Cullen's strokes increased, moving within her toward his own release. Upon reaching his destination, he shouted his ecstasy. His hot breath blew across her neck. "I love ye, lass."

With her legs still wrapped around him, he climbed out of the water, and grabbed a towel that he wrapped around her. Tension in his face had softened, and his smile warmed her in places already overheated.

He dropped to his knees, keeping them joined together, and he laid her on the bed he had prepared for them with warm blankets and a soft cushion of pine needles. He had even packed her pillow. When her head touched the cotton ticking covering the goose down, tears of joy streamed down her cheeks. Then she noticed the picnic dinner with a bottle of wine and lighted candles.

"Cullen," she sighed his name.

"I took the liberty of searching yer trunk. I'm afraid this is the last bottle."

"Whatever is mine is yours." The tears fell faster now.

"Dinna cry." He wiped her tears with his fingertips and then licked away the droplets he'd collected. "There'll be nae more tears."

"I want to crawl inside you. Feel what you feel, taste what you taste, see life from your eyes."

"Ye're already inside. Hear the beat of my heart? The rhythm is yers."

"Keep me inside forever," she whispered.

"As I am inside ye, so ye shall always be inside me."

He thrust in short rhythmic strokes once again, pressing his body against her pubic mound, sending powerful sensations rippling through her. She reached for his hand and squeezed as another orgasmic cry broke from her lips. He kissed her, pulling her breath of pleasure into his mouth.

Within moments, he followed with his own explosive release. "*Je t'aime.*"

She fell asleep with her head on his chest listening to the beat of his heart, replete.

Twice he tried to wake her, but she rolled over saying she needed sleep more than food. She had no idea what time it was when her eyes finally popped open, but the big round moon lighting up the sky welcomed her, and so did Cullen, pulling her gently into his embrace. "Are ye hungry?"

"What's on your mind?" she asked, stretching overused muscles.

He had an almost hypnotic intensity in his eyes. "Ye need to eat to keep up yer strength." He pulled her to him so her head rested on his chest. Her leg crisscrossed his body. The evidence of his hunger poked her leg.

"I think you're still hungry." She wiggled her hips.

"Nae, lass. I dinna want to make ye sore. We can wait until morning."

"*You* can wait?" she said, sticking out her bottom lip. "Ooookay."

"Aye, even a Montgomery thinks about his lassie's comfort."

"If you're going to make a noble sacrifice, I'll give you a surprise." She dug into her carpetbag until she found her iPod she kept charged with a solar charger. "Are you ready?"

"Aye, I'm never *ready* for yer surprises, but I'm always intrigued by them."

As soon as she'd discovered his musical passion, she'd imagined exposing him to the sound quality of twenty-first century music. Now she wondered what recording he should listen to first. What would be most compelling for him? He was familiar with all the

Baroque composers from Monteverdi to Handel and Bach, and all the classical composers from Haydn to Beethoven. He'd listened to early opera but hadn't experienced the golden age with Wagner, Verdi, Puccini. He'd never heard blues and jazz and rock and roll, or Loretta Lynn or Bob Dylan or Bruce Springsteen. What would take his breath, capture his imagination?

"I'm going to put these buds into your ears."

"What are they?"

"You'll find out." She scrolled through her playlist and clicked on Vivaldi's "Lute Concerto in D Major," one of her favorites. Vivaldi's concertos and arias deeply influenced his contemporary, Bach, and the recording she had on her iPod featured the brilliant John Williams on guitar. His musical artistry informed her. She took a deep breath and hit the play button.

Cullen shot up off the blanket with his hands pressed firmly against his ears. "*Crivens!*" His rapid breathing and pounding heart disquieted the still night. His eyes grew wide as he listened, enthralled by the violins and harpsichord and guitar.

Within moments, his hands moved in concert with the music, and he conducted the orchestra to its lingering conclusion. Several seconds after the last note faded, he gazed up into the solid darkness of the starry sky. He didn't say anything for several minutes. Finally, he said, "Yesterday I heard the sound of hell. Tonight I heard the sound of heaven. Ye gave me the gift of yerself, the most beautiful gift I've ever been given. This is the second." His voice quivered. "How is it possible for this little box to hold the sound of God's own orchestra?"

Her heart slammed against her ribs. Although he'd asked a hypothetical, he deserved an answer. "Because men like you and John and Braham, and women like Sarah, and children like Adam and Frances never stopped dreaming their dreams."

He fell back onto the blanket and pulled her on top of him. The heavy beat of his heart thrummed against her. "I can never give ye anything that would compare to the wonders of yer time."

She shook her head. "You've already given me much more. I was fortunate to experience the future, but I don't belong there permanently. I belong with you in your world." Even after her affirmation, his eyes held the glaze of doubt.

Determined to waylay both his doubts and fears before they took hold of his mind, she positioned herself over his erection and slid down his shaft, embedding him deep inside her.

AS THE SUN rose on their first full day of marriage, Kit woke nestled in the crook of her husband's arm. Her hand rested on his chest, gently moving with the rise and fall of his breathing. His smile was enough to melt her heart.

She did her best imitation of a cat, stretching from her fingertips down through her big toes. "Have you been listening to music all night?" she asked between yawns.

He removed the ear buds and rolled over onto his side. "How many songs are in this box? It will take days to listen to all of them."

"Fourteen thousand."

"I canna begin to comprehend this miracle."

"What did you listen to?"

"Not only did I listen, I *watched* something called *Meet the Press*. The men at the table discussed the president's agenda, and they showed him. He's a colored man."

"And he graduated from Harvard Law School," she said.

"Yer world is verra different."

"But the people are the same. Hardworking folks doing the best they can for their families."

"Yer pa did well for his. I saw pictures of yer farm and the mansion."

"MacKlenna Farm doesn't belong to me. I'm not a MacKlenna."

His fingertips brushed her face as if they were pencils drawing intricate lines and shapes. "Ye say that, but there's a voice behind yer eyes that screams it isna true."

"The MacKlenna tradition informed the person I am."

"And ye'll teach that tradition to our children."

One day she would birth his son, and the child would grow up to be like his father whom she knew very little about. "How many women have you been with?"

"What kind of question is that?" His tone was brusque, his eyes glaring.

"A reasonable one. You might have a disease."

"I've always been careful."

"Are you going to answer my question?"

"It's none of yer concern." His handsome face appeared troubled, the corners of his eyes strained.

"I have a right to know."

"Nae." He rolled on top of her and nuzzled her neck, scratching her with his whiskers.

She pushed him away. "This is important."

"Ye dinna need to worry yerself with this matter, Kitherina."

She swallowed back tears. "I'm getting in the spring." Grabbing their top blanket, she threw it around her shoulders and rushed off to the water.

The soaking did wonders for her body, but nothing for her hurt feelings.

She had been in the water for only a few minutes when Cullen appeared at her side and tenderly stroked her arm. "I've had no one to answer to for several years. I considered yer question intrusive, but I dinna think ye were asking for a number. I believe ye were asking me to share who I am."

He paused and sighed with a heavy breath. "There have been more women than I can count, more than I can remember. None of them meant anything, and I'm nae proud of that." He moved his hands up her arms and gently kneaded her shoulders.

"I never met a woman I cared to be with more than once until I met ye. I've had feelings with ye I havena ever had before. I wish I could give ye an answer that would satisfy ye. I canna. I've been more discreet as I've aged. Please understand that my life began the moment I met ye."

As had hers. She slipped into his arms and their honeymoon ended the way it began. But Kit could not dislodge the memory of the deep red glow across Cullen's chest and the fear notched on her heart.

Chapter Thirty

"IT'S TOO QUIET." A tingling sensation ran up and down Kit's spine as she and Cullen approached the wagon train camped at the Dry Sandy Ford. Campfires and strong coffee infused twilight with familiar smells, but the absence of Mr. Cameron's fiddle sent a hot spasm to the back of her throat and visions of murdered people to the forefront of her mind.

Those damn killers could be anywhere at any time.

Cullen shifted in his saddle and eased his hand closer to his hip, to his gun. His eyes swept the camp right to left, then slowly back again. "Mr. Cameron's fingers must be sore tonight."

She pulled her gun from her saddlebag and tucked it between the folds of her bunched-up skirt. Her trouser-covered legs twitched slightly from the long horseback ride. "I hope he's not sick."

They fell silent as they drew near Kit's wagon on the north side of the circle.

Adam spotted them and sprang to his feet, holding a book with a two-fisted grip. "Glad you're back." A sigh of relief relaxed his shoulders.

Cullen dismounted and stretched his long frame. "Anything we should know?"

"Quiet as a hog's tit." Adam tucked the book under one arm and held Stormy's bridle while Kit dismounted. The pistol went back into her saddlebag.

"Where's Mr. Cameron?"

"Said he was taking the night off. I suspect his fingers are tired. He kept playing long after you rode off yesterday."

"Bless his fiddle-fingered heart," Kit said.

"I'll tend to the horses. Pa wanted to know as soon as you got back, Mr. Montgomery."

"I'd best head over there." Cullen whispered into Kit's ear, "Thank you, Mrs. Montgomery, for a night I'll long remember." He put his hands to her cheeks, eased her head back, and kissed her soundly.

Adam coughed.

She smiled a bittersweet smile. Now that they were back in camp, she had to share her husband with everyone else. "I'll go with you."

A few minutes later, they walked into the Barretts' camp.

"About time you two showed up," John said.

Henry chuckled. "I thought we'd have to send out a search party."

"Looks to me like ye were relaxing, not rounding up volunteers."

Braham handed Cullen a cigar. "How was the hot spring?"

He winked at Kit. "Well worth the ride."

He waved his double entendre like a red flag in front of a bull. Her face heated. Thankfully, Frances, with her impeccable timing, plowed into Kit's legs, nearly bowling her over.

"*You're back.* We thought Mr. Montgomery would keep you *forever.*"

"We'll have school tomorrow. Are your lessons done?"

"Mama helped us."

"Frances, run along. Mrs. Montgomery is tired," Sarah said.

Frances whispered in Kit's ear loud enough for everyone to hear. "Did you get a baby while you were gone?"

"There's no baby, Frances. It's time for bed," Sarah said.

Frances bobbed her mane of leonine curls. "Maybe next time you go away you'll get a boy."

Kit vacillated between bursting out laughing or throwing cold water on her heated face. The child defined precociousness.

"*Frances.*" Sarah's tone was uncharacteristically sharp.

The little girl skipped away, unfazed by her mother's censure. Sarah seemed either worried or ill. Kit poured a cup of coffee and hugged her friend.

Sarah eased back in her chair at the table, her eyes unreadable in the firelight. "The girl's too sassy."

Kit settled into a chair next to Sarah and patted her hand. "I think she's tired of being the youngest, but I'm not ready to be a mother."

Sarah traced the grooves in the wood tabletop with a chipped fingernail, following its deep lines as they splintered off into different directions. "Life has a way of tempting us with the easier path when the harder one is often more rewarding."

Kit shook her head. Another pithy *Sarahism*. "You don't feel well, do you?"

Sarah stood, rubbing her chest. "Supper didn't sit right. I'm turning in. I'll be better by morning."

A flurry of goose bumps flew up Kit's arms. "Send John if you need me during the night."

"I'll see you in the morning." Sarah waddled away, her hand pressed against her lower back. Abrupt, short tempered, shallow breathing, flushed face. Kit's paramedic antenna inched out of her scalp.

The men were huddled over a map spread out on the table. John pointed his pipe at Cullen. "Folks are talking about the Sublette Cut-off to the Green River."

Cullen removed his glasses and rubbed his eyes. He'd had very little sleep in the past two days. "I took the cut-off last time out. Four days of dry camp. Hell on the people. Worse on the animals. Canna recommend the route. The trail through Fort Bridger adds three days, but at least ye've got water and grass."

John tapped his pipe against his bottom teeth. "It takes us in the wrong direction."

"Temporarily," Henry said.

"You'll get opposition, but if that's what you recommend, I'm with you." John paused then turned to Braham. "What about you? You still leaving?"

Braham puffed on his cigar. "When we reach the Hudspeth Cut-Off."

"Hate to lose you. You're the best hunter we got," Henry said.

"If I didna have a job waiting, I'd be tempted to head to Oregon."

"And you, Cullen?"

He tugged on his lips. "Like Braham, I have a job waiting in San Francisco."

"Surely lawyers are needed in the Willamette Valley same as California," John said. "Why don't you both open an office there?"

Cullen slapped Braham's shoulder. "I believe he'll find more opportunities in San—"

"Where's Sarah?" John asked, narrowing his eyes.

"She went to bed. Said she didn't feel well," Kit said.

He pushed away from the table. "Did she say what was wrong?"

"Not specifically."

"I need to go to her." In the ten weeks they'd been traveling together, Kit had never seen intense, methodical John rush off to do anything.

"She was quiet at dinner. Didna eat much," Braham said.

"Then that's not why she's sick." Kit mulled over possible illnesses.

Henry tapped the burnt tobacco from his pipe bowl. "Is she breeding?"

Kit shook her head slowly. "Surely not." With a husband, five children, and more than nine hundred miles to travel before they'd reach Oregon, she hoped Sarah wasn't pregnant. Although from comments she'd made, Kit was certain her friend wanted another baby.

John stuck his head through the tent flaps. "Kit, Sarah's asking for you."

Kit's mouth went dry as she hurried over to the Barretts' tent. Inside she found Sarah on her cot, curled in the fetal position. Her deep low moans sounded like a woman in labor. "Sarah, are you pregnant?"

Sweat trickled down John's face. "Baby's due in October. She didn't want anyone to know."

Kit did a quick calculation. The baby was only about twenty-four weeks. There was no chance of survival. She squatted next to Sarah's cot and dabbed at the perspiration on her face. "I'm going to my wagon for supplies. I'll be right back."

Kit motioned to John to meet her outside. Mr. Cameron had finally picked up his fiddle and was playing a piece Kit didn't recognize, slow and mournful.

John leaned over and kissed his wife. "I'll return directly."

Kit and John walked out together. Once out of Sarah's earshot, she turned to him. "I need a few things from my wagon. Sarah will probably deliver the baby tonight. You understand what that means, don't you?"

He sweated copiously now. A sheen of tears welled in his eyes.

Cullen stepped close, calmly threading his hat's brim through his fingers. "How can I help, lass?" His voice whispered over her like a cool breeze, bringing his strength and reassurance.

"Sarah's going to lose the baby," John said, his Adam's apple bobbing. "Please don't let anything happen to her. She's my life." He buried his face in his hands. Cullen squeezed John's shoulder in a tender expression of sympathy that reflected in Cullen's liquid eyes. The shared moment passed quickly. John dried his eyes and went back to his wife.

"I didn't even know she was pregnant," Kit said. "If I had known, I would have done more of her work, taken more responsibility. Now she's losing her baby. I could have made a difference."

Cullen hooked her elbow and turned her to face him. "Dinna take this on yerself. What ye did or didna do has no bearing on Sarah's baby. If anything, ye've made her trip easier. This is not yer fault, and I willna have ye blaming yerself."

She sighed, her shoulders sagging under the weight of all that had happened during the past three days. "Walk with me to get my red bag."

"Ye have medicine that will help, dinna ye?" His question came with the expectation she had an unlimited supply of miracle cures. She didn't.

She gave him a sad smile. "I can't save the baby."

"Have ye ever delivered one?"

"Four. All healthy and full term. They arrived before the moms could get to the hospital. This will be the first…little one."

"Should we get Mrs. Cameron to help?"

"It would be best if no one else was in there. Just in case…"

Cullen climbed into their wagon and came back out with the red bag wrapped in a blanket. "Do ye need yer medical box, too?"

"This has everything I need."

"Could yer hospital save Sarah's baby?" There was a curious emphasis in his question.

She leaned against the wagon and scrubbed her face with her hands. "Are you asking me if I'd consider taking Sarah to my time to save her baby? If you are, the answer is no. There have been incredible medical advances over the past century and a half, but saving a baby that size is rare. Those who survive usually have serious health problems."

His face creased with a mixture of sadness and relief.

"There's another reason I wouldn't take her back." She lowered her voice to almost a whisper. "I don't think the brooch is a revolving door. I could be wrong. But I believe the stone comes with a purpose. If I'm not pursuing that purpose, it might not work. I don't know that for sure, but neither do I want to test it."

He managed a thin-lipped smile. "The time might come, lass, when ye'll need to test its magic. But ye're right. The stone will do what it's meant to do. Nae more. Nae less." His quiet eyes held some emotion he tightly guarded.

She stood on tiptoes and kissed him. "Thank you for loving me."

He returned her kiss, pulling her against his body. The muscled planes of his chest were familiar to her now. "Take care of Sarah. I'll take care of ye."

Kit entered the Barretts' stuffy tent carrying her paramedic bag rolled up in a wool blanket.

John squeezed his wife's hand. "I'll wait outside. But when the time comes, I want to be with you." He turned to leave.

"John," Sarah called after him. "Don't tell the girls."

He shoved both hands through his hair. "They went with Mrs. Cameron. They know you're feeling poorly. That's all they're to know."

Kit's throat thickened at the thought of how heartsick Frances would be, but Sarah's heart must be on the verge of breaking, too. What emotions had Kit's birth mother experienced when she'd sent her spiraling through the amber light, scared and alone? Twenty-five years later, the sense of aloneness had never left her—until now. Until Cullen pierced the veil.

After John left, Kit said, "Let's get you into something more comfortable."

Sarah lifted her arms, and Kit undressed her and slipped on a nightgown. The woman stared with large eyes. "If my baby comes now, he'll be too little to live."

Kit swallowed her reply. Being powerless to change the birth's outcome wasn't easy to accept. She slipped on a watch, opened a notebook, and started taking notes, concentrating on what she could do, not what she couldn't. "When did your labor start?"

"Early afternoon. I'd hoped the pains would stop but they kept—" Sarah gasped with a contraction. From that point on, the labor pains continued—longer, stronger, closer together.

An hour later, Cullen stood outside the tent and called softly, "Kit, do ye need anything?" His voice seeped into her skin and overlaid a soothing ointment.

"I'll be right back." Outside, she took a deep breath of cool, fresh air. The breeze took hold of her hair that had fallen free of her braid and swept the flyaway strands about her face.

He tucked the wild locks behind her ears. "Ye're so tired. What can I do?"

She pointed to the center of her shoulder blades. "Rub that spot, please." His fingers kneaded the tight muscle. She moaned and stretched her neck. "Sweet."

"How is she?"

"Tired. This will take a few hours. Why don't you get some rest?"

John walked up with a cup of coffee, which Kit gladly accepted. "Will my Sarah be"—he paused to gather his composure—"safe?" The fear in his voice increased Kit's apprehension.

"Every birth has risk, John. Has she had any problems before?"

He glanced longingly toward the tent as if his laboring wife was visible through the canvas. "No problems, not with any of them. Always got right back up on her feet. Never a fear of having another. Not like some women I hear tell of."

"Do you want to sit with her?"

"She'd rather me wait out here." He looked at his hands. His big, callused fingers seemed to be questioning why they were idle, or why Sarah's hand wasn't close by to grasp. He held out a small blanket. "I just got this out of her trunk. It's for…you know…for later."

A sharp tug pulled at Kit's emotions and a band constricted her heart. "I need to go back. The waiting is hard, John. Poke your head inside the tent if you want to check on her."

Tears rimmed his eyes, but he seemed unashamed of his emotional display. He glanced once more at the tent, then sat in his chair and bowed his head.

Kit rolled her neck. "Much better. Please get some rest."

"I'll be here waiting for you."

Deep shadows lined Sarah's puffy eyes. Patches of flushed skin dotted her cheeks and pain pulled her lips tight. Ringlets of damp hair lay plastered to her forehead. But even in the darkest of moments, Sarah radiated inner strength.

Another hour passed during which the contractions came every two to three minutes. Finally, she looked up, panting. "I think it's time."

"Do you want John with you?"

"If there's a chance the baby is alive, he needs to be here."

Kit lifted the tent flaps and found him sitting motionless in his chair staring straight ahead, his face ashen. "Sarah needs you."

He hurried to reach his wife.

Cullen rose from his rocking chair by the fire. "Is it time?"

"It's close."

"Are ye holding up?" He stroked her face and wiped away the perspiration. "Can I do anything?" Written in the depths of his blue eyes and in the creases in his face was his love for her. She loved him completely. She also loved the woman suffering inside the tent.

Kit leaned in to him and breathed deeply of pine and leather and earth, replenishing her soul with his strength. By replenishing her, she could now give back to the woman who had given her so much.

Well onto midnight, amid deep, muffled groans, Sarah pushed her tiny baby out into the world. Kit cleaned his nose and face. His heart was beating, but it wouldn't beat for long. She clamped and cut the cord, and then wrapped the baby in a blanket and placed him in Sarah's arms. "It's a boy." Sorrow swelled in Kit's throat as she gazed into Sarah's face, the face of a woman filled with unfathomable love and inconsolable grief. Her tears dropped onto the baby's forehead, sprinkling him with liquid love.

"I think we should name him Gabriel." A stream of tears slid down John's cheeks.

Sarah kissed the babe on the top of his head. "Gabriel is a good name."

Kit left the parents alone to sing their child into heaven. She found Cullen rocking in a chair by the fire, elbows resting on the rocker's arms, fingers tented beneath his chin, eyes half-lidded. "How are they?"

"Gabriel's still alive." She spoke softly, but her voice carried an edge. "I held him…" She glanced at her hands and rubbed one over the other as if trying to wake up his little body and make him breathe. "He's so small, Cullen. Just barely reached the tip of my fingers."

"How long will he live?"

"Not much longer." She remembered Scott's last few breaths and how inadequate she felt.

"Probably brings up memories of their boy, David. They lost him a few years back," Cullen said.

"I wondered why they skipped the letter *D*."

"What do you mean?"

"Adam, Ben, Clint, Elizabeth, Frances, and now Gabriel. They're private people. I'm surprised John told you."

"He needed to talk while you women were going about the birthing. The boy was three. A cold settled in his chest. He died on his birthday."

Kit dropped to the ground and laid her head on Cullen's thigh. "Why did this happen? Sarah is such a dear, dear person. It breaks my heart." Kit was unable to resist the pressure from tears building in her eyes. She cried for baby Gabriel, for Sarah, for Scott, for her parents, and because she damn well just needed to cry.

Cullen caressed her head, running his fingers through her hair. His strong hand had a barely discernible tremble. "Sarah wouldna want ye to cry on her account."

"I love her. She's so much like my mom."

He handed Kit his handkerchief. "What was her name, lass?"

"Mary Spencer." The handkerchief smelled of lye soap, clean and fresh. "Dad met her in Independence."

Cullen's hand stilled. "I knew her."

Kit dabbed at her eyes. "I'm not surprised."

"She'd planned to travel on this wagon train. Henry has worried over her for months. That's why he wouldna let ye go by yerself. He agreed to let yer ma sign on, then she disappeared. He'll be glad to know—"

"What? That she's dead now?"

Cullen shifted in his chair. "I reckon she had a good life with yer pa."

Her mother did have a good life. They all did. Kit felt the stirring of a smile tinged with sadness. "The paths to our ultimate destination intersected long before we met."

He continued his caresses. "Ye sound like a Calvinist."

She laid her head on his thigh. "Are you one?"

"Ye married a man without knowing his religious convictions?"

"You married a woman without knowing hers."

"Ye've never appeared to be particularly spiritual."

She swallowed, unsure of herself. "God and I had a disagreement awhile back." Her voice was soft now.

His fingers massaged her neck at the base of her skull. "Mayhap it's time the two of ye worked things out."

"How can I when He takes precious children like Gabriel?"

Cullen's fingertips worked their way down her neck to the middle of her back, kneading tight muscles. "He didna take Frances."

"He took your Kristen." Her words came out on a long sigh.

"I never turned my back on Him."

Kit didn't say anything for several minutes while she reflected on the past few days. "If we get to Oregon without anyone else dying, I'll think about it."

SHORTLY BEFORE THE sun rose, Kit and Cullen and John and Sarah found a secluded spot on the Dry Sandy Ford's sagebrush-covered bank. John dug a grave deep enough so the animals wouldn't dig it up, then he placed Baby Gabriel in the ground while they all sang "Amazing Grace." Kit knew no one would ever visit the baby's gravesite, one of over twenty thousand along the trail. No one would cry over the grave after today. But Gabriel's short life would be forever marked on his parents' hearts and on her heart, too. She prayed for the babies yet to be born.

Would one of them be hers?

Chapter Thirty-One

A WEEK LATER, the wagon train arrived at Fort Bridger built on Blacks Fork of the Green River. In three months, they had traveled more than a thousand miles and were only halfway to the Willamette Valley. The trip wore on everyone, fraying nerves and exhausting even the young and physically fit.

Kit didn't need a reason to cry. Tears spilled over burned biscuits or a splinter in her finger or a cheerful *good morning* from one of the children. For someone with a penchant for leaving clothes, art supplies, and shoes lying about on the floor, she became a shrew, nagging Cullen for unpacking his books and stacking them in piles inside their new tent.

John received the brunt of her churlishness, though. "He won't listen to me," she said to Cullen. "I've tried to tell him he needs to buy a new team, but he won't." She poured a cup of coffee then absentmindedly set the pot on the table instead of returning it to the campfire grate.

Cullen closed his legal treatise and put it aside along with his glasses. "He doesna want to be any more beholden to ye than he already is."

"He's being stubborn. Why doesn't he think more about his family and less about his pride?" She picked up her sewing basket and sat in the chair beside him.

"I'll talk to him." Cullen leaned over, kissed her, and trailed the backs of his long fingers over the curve of her breasts.

Kit jumped. "Ouch."

He drew back his hand.

She hunched her shoulders, protecting her chest. "My breasts are sore."

"They werena sore last night."

"That's why they're sore tonight. Don't you have reading to do? A map to study? A meeting to go to?"

"Kitherina, what's wrong?"

"Kitherina? Do you know how many different names you call me?" She counted them off on her fingers. "Kitherina, lass, sweetling, Kit. And Henry calls me missy. I don't know why I answer either of you."

"Ye always answer when I call ye sweetling, and it's usually with a breathy sigh."

"If you're trying to get on my good side, you're not." She set her basket on the table next to the misplaced coffeepot.

What's wrong with me?

She carried the pot back to the campfire, paced for a couple of minutes, then went inside the tent to get something but couldn't remember what.

Cullen followed, hands clasped behind his back, his head slightly lowered as if he were in deep thought. "What's on yer mind?"

The timbre of his voice found a warm place in her heart. "My boobs hurt, my stomach's queasy, and I'm in a bad mood."

"Boobs?"

She waved him off. "My breasts."

"Come here and tell me what's bothering ye."

She drew in a deep, ragged breath. "We made love for the first time over a month ago."

A tiny tic leaped at the corner of his jaw. "A wonderful, memorable night."

"A night with consequences."

"Consequences?" He paused. The silence seemed to take on weight. He threw her a crooked grin. "Are ye expecting?"

"I think so. And if I am, that means I got pregnant *before* we got married."

"When was yer last…" Cullen's cheeks turned red.

Kit pinched the bridge of her nose, thinking. "I've never had regular periods, and I haven't had one at all since I've been in your time."

"Do ye want to ask Sarah what she thinks?"

Kit shook her head. "Not right now." She tapped her fingernail on her bottom teeth. "There's a way to find out."

He fixed her with a serious gaze, wrinkling his brow.

"I packed a pregnancy test in my red bag."

He gave her a heart-splitting smile. "What kind of questions are on the test? When was the last time ye made love?"

She swatted him with the tail of her apron. "Not that kind of test."

"How many tests did ye bring with ye?"

"One test, one time."

He grinned. "I suggest ye take it now unless ye have to study beforehand."

"Why?"

He shrugged. "Then ye willna have to worry about it."

She narrowed her eyes at him. "Okay. You wait outside?"

"I'm nae leaving."

She put her hands on her hips and growled. "I love you to death, Cullen Montgomery, but you're not going to watch me pee on a pregnancy strip."

"What does peeing have to do with taking the test?"

She threw up her hands. "Go away. Come back in five minutes." She pushed him through the tent flaps then dug through her paramedic bag for the pregnancy test. It was one of the things she'd tossed into her bag without thinking during the raid on the farm's clinic the night before she left. She'd grabbed one or two of everything whether she needed it or not.

Cullen reentered the tent, pulled the box from her hands, and read the directions. "Hold the stick under yer stream of urine for five seconds." He then removed the foil wrapper and handed her the stick.

She didn't budge.

"Pee on the stick, Kit. I willna watch." He turned his back.

She blew out an exasperated breath, pulled up her dress, squatted over the chamber pot, and held the stick in the correct position for five seconds.

They sat side by side on the bed and stared at the small flashing hourglass in the plastic window.

At three minutes, she wrung her hands.

At two minutes, she gnawed on her lower lip.

At one minute, she broke out in a sweat.

At thirty seconds, she held her breath.

The answer flashed. The stick shook in her hand.

Cullen's eyes grew wide, the blue—bluer. "It says ye're pregnant."

She let out the breath she was holding. "Looks that way."

Visibly shaking, he asked, "I'm going to be a father?"

Kit nodded, slowly processing. *I'm going to be a mother.* She'd had two mothers and lost both. Tears streaked her face.

He pulled her onto his lap, pressing her head against his chest. "I'm going to be a father."

"I'm scared." She imagined herself hanging by a frayed rope on the rotted board side of a bridge, swinging precipitously over a dangerous ravine.

"Women birth babies every day."

"I'm not afraid of birthing. I'm afraid of the next thousand miles. I'm afraid of the decisions we have to make. I'm afraid I'll not be strong enough to carry the baby and will miscarry like Sarah. I'm afraid I'll be forced to make a decision like my birth mother."

"Ye're nae alone in this venture. I canna guarantee everything will be as ye want, but I will give my life to see that ye and our son arrive safely in San Francisco."

Our son?

Time stopped for a moment. A baby, a brooch, and now another baby. She felt like she'd been cast in a play without a script. She wasn't even sure which role she was supposed to play.

Chapter Thirty-Two

BRAHAM WALKED ALONG the bank of the Bear River at the Hudspeth Cutoff at a slow, uneasy pace. The wind sighed through the trees and underbrush carrying the scent of pine. Dark thoughts swirled in his mind and mirrored the gloomy, overcast evening that limited visibility to shadowy outlines of the opposite bank and the rugged land beyond. A damp chill cooled the air. By morning, the weight of icy dewdrops would bend the grass—but not his decision. He would be gone by then, following the gossamer stillness across the desert to California.

His farewell supper had lasted through two desserts while Kit sang his favorite songs: "Meet Me by Moonlight" and "Do You Think I Can Forget." Her voice, tuned to musical perfection, whispered over his skin like a sultry breeze, and he had squirmed in his chair like a sinner in church.

He tossed his last rock into the river, and it skipped twice before it sank. *Plop.* Nothing he did assuaged his guilt or silenced its incessant chatter.

Do not leave your friends. Do not.

He let out a long, deflated breath. Who would protect them once he was gone? Cullen would protect Kit, but who would protect Cullen? The killers posed a threat to everyone on the trail. If the wagon train met up with them, Cullen and Henry would need his gun.

An irritating tingle stole over him. Maybe he should stay with the wagon train until it reached Oregon. Damn. For someone who prided himself on his decision-making skills, he'd done a lousy job on this trip.

He considered his commitments. A conflict grew inside him like an intense and powerful heat. He had promised Mr. Phillips he would be in San Francisco by mid-July, and he had promised Cullen he would offer condolences to Phillips. Braham didn't want to leave. He pounded his fist into his palm. Should an injury befall either Kit or Cullen, or God forbid, one of them be killed, he would never forgive himself.

Braham's preternatural hearing picked up sounds of nocturnal animals rustling in the foliage and footsteps passing gingerly through the grass. He pivoted toward the approaching sound. His hand hovered over his holster, and his eyes grew wide and alert. At the sight of golden hair glimmering in a tiny sliver of moonlight, his trigger finger relaxed.

Kit paused in the near darkness. "Only a few weeks ago you were trying to solve the problem of world hunger. You must have found a solution and moved on to the next problem on your list."

"Ye're wandering about rather late, Mrs. Montgomery."

"I've lost Cullen. Have you seen him?"

"Not since dinner, but I'll help ye find him."

She pulled her shawl tightly around her shoulders and looped the fringed ends through her apron strings. "I brought you a gift."

"I dinna need a gift."

"I want to give you one anyway. But you have to choose."

"What are my choices?"

"Whether you want to look far into the present or far into the future."

He rested his thumb under his chin and poked at his upper lip with his index finger. "Michael Abraham McCabe doesna need to glance into the future. However, seeing far in the present would be an advantage."

"You've made a wise decision, Major McCabe."

"Major?"

She sucked in a long breath between her teeth. "I...I didn't mean to say that."

"What'd ye intend to say?"

She handed him a pair of binoculars.

He lifted them to his eyes. "To see far into the present?" His tone was a mixture of appreciation and curiosity. "What's the gift for the future?"

"A book."

Braham noted a flash of nervousness in her hesitation.

"*American History From 1776 Through the Inauguration of the Forty-fourth President.*"

"Does it mention a Major McCabe?"

She shrugged.

"Why'd ye call me a major?"

"You said you didn't want to see into the future."

"I've reconsidered." While inspecting the binoculars he watched her from the corner of his eye. She wore a puzzled expression that reminded him of his grandmother McCabe.

"Did Cullen tell you I'm pregnant?"

Twigs snapped to the left. "Not yet," Cullen said, striding down the path toward them. "John said ye were looking for me."

She brought her forearm up in front of her face as if reading the time on the special watch Braham had seen on her wrist before. "Um...an hour ago."

Cullen kissed her. "Adam and I were discussing—"

"Let me guess." She tapped her toe. "He's into the comedies this week. *Tempest?* No. *Twelfth Night?* No, that's not it. *Much Ado about Nothing.*"

Cullen chuckled. "Ye, my lass, have become a Shakespeare devotee. I'd say ye know exactly what he's reading because ye finished *Much Ado about Nothing* last week and encouraged him to read it next."

"Do you know all my secrets?"

Cullen whispered into her ear. There wasn't enough light for Braham to see well, but he believed she blushed. He felt a lump rise in his throat. His friend was a lucky man. He had an intelligent, beautiful woman to love and a baby on the way. He didn't want to begrudge Cullen's blessings, but down deep, he did.

"If ye're through jabbering about Shakespeare, I believe ye mentioned something about a baby. I'll accept the role of cousin, uncle, or godfather."

"Uncle Braham?" Cullen laughed with an ease Braham hadn't heard in his friend's voice for a very long time. "Consider yerself asked." He retrieved the book from Kit's hand. "Braham didna want this?"

He snatched the book from Cullen. "If this mentions me, I do want it."

"I didn't say you were in the book." Kit tried to grab it, but Braham held the book over his head. She jumped, laughing, caught in a game of keep-away.

Cullen placed his hands around her waist. "Settle down, lass, and tell me why he believes he's in yer history book."

She grabbed Braham's arm and tugged on it. "I called him Major McCabe."

Cullen grabbed the book and gave it to Kit. "Who's Major McCabe?"

"Secret agent to President Abraham Lincoln."

"The lawyer from Illinois? What's he president of?"

"The country."

Braham pulled two cigars out of his pocket and offered one to Cullen. He declined. "Will I be a major in the cavalry?"

"Does it matter?" she asked.

"Of course it matters. Who wants to be in the infantry?"

"You really want me to tell you?"

Braham thought a moment. What harm could it do? "Yes."

"According to historical resources, Major Michael Abraham McCabe served in the United States Cavalry on special assignment to President Lincoln from 1863 to 1865."

"Why will the president need a special agent?" Cullen asked.

Braham lit his cigar. "That sounds like a fair question."

Kit fanned the smoke. "I've already told you more than you wanted to know."

"I changed my mind."

"If Braham wants the information, tell him," Cullen said.

"If I give you a picture of the man in the portrait, will you try to find him?" she asked.

"If ye'll tell me why I'm assigned to the president."

"That's not fair."

Cullen chuckled again.

She elbowed him in the gut.

"Ouch."

Her fingers flittered against her chin, and her eyes glanced upward. "A war starts in 1861, and no one knows for sure how or why you become involved. You live in California when it starts. Historians say it's because of an old relationship with General Sherman. Others say it's your northern sympathies."

He'd never met Sherman, although Cullen had mentioned him, and Braham didn't think he had particularly northern or southern sympathies. "How do ye ken?"

"The MacKlennas have a chess set that was made in the late 1860s. All the pieces are Civil War generals, except for one black knight—Major Michael Abraham McCabe. The chest set is one of a kind. There's no legend, no story, no family history, no information as to why the black knight is included."

"Why didna ye mention this before?" Cullen asked.

"I never knew Braham's full name until now, and the black knight has a beard. I didn't make the connection. But I'll tell you this—there's something special about the chest set, and there's something special about the black knight."

Chapter Thirty-Three

THE WAGON TRAIN followed a difficult stretch of trail over a rocky road and seven miles of deep sand before arriving at Fort Hall on the Snake River. The trip had worn Kit out, as well as everyone else. Dust covered her hair and clothes and left a gritty, disgusting taste in her mouth.

July 12, 1852. Nothing special about the date other than it marked the seventh week of pregnancy and her first serious bout of morning sickness—at six o'clock in the afternoon. She wanted to be home in her own bed with her own toilet to throw up in, and her own shower to wash off the filth, and her own sink to brush her teeth.

"How can I help ye?" Cullen's furrowed brow conveyed his empathy, which she didn't want.

"Leave me alone. Don't touch me. This is your fault. Go away." She collapsed on her bed as if someone had pushed her. After twelve hundred miles, her reserves were empty. Time to wave the white flag.

"Walk to the fort with me?" he said.

"It's a misnomer to call that collection of adobe buildings a fort."

Cullen squeezed his lips between his thumb and the crook of his index finger in an attempt to downgrade a laugh to a mere chuckle.

She huffed. "You're laughing at me. I can tell. Your shoulders are shaking."

He stilled himself, posture erect. "I'll work on my acting skills." His lulling voice was both calming and reassuring.

"Adam is developing into quite a thespian. I'm sure he'll be glad to help you." The sarcastic bite in her tone of voice distressed her and gave her another reason to refer to herself as a shrew.

"I'm sorry ye're sick. Do ye have any medicine?" Cullen sat next to her, his bright eyes teasing and mischievous.

She sank her elbow into his rib cage.

"Ouch."

"Stop laughing at me." She'd take a sprained wrist, a broken bone, anything but a queasy stomach and huge, swollen boobs. The misery shaved off a layer of her resolve to stay in the nineteenth century. "Tums will help my stomach, but not these," she said, cupping her breasts. "They're so sore."

"Tylenol will make ye feel better." He sounded like a damned commercial. Johnson & Johnson would probably hire him on the spot to pitch their product. He kissed her cleavage. His warm breath tickled, and she shivered, not because she was cold. She tilted her head, peeked at him through lowered lashes, and found him gazing not at her, but inwardly as if watching and listening to a silent voice. He leaned back on the bed and pulled her into his arms. "Ye want to go home, dinna ye, lass?"

There was a moment of utter stillness. She bowed her head, feeling defeated. "In weak moments, yes."

He pulled pins from her hair and massaged her scalp. "This is a weak moment. Yer eyes are filled with doubt." The circular pressure relieved tension in her head and shoulders but increased it in her breasts and between her legs.

She rolled her head in circles matching the movement of his fingers. With each rotation, her respiration increased. "You know what your massages do to me."

"I thought ye needed relief." His voice was a sexy rumble. He slid her dress up over her thighs. "Yer stomach may feel poorly, but the rest of ye..." He flashed his dimples as he unbuttoned his trousers. His erection jutted from a mass of dark, wiry hair.

Trembling with anticipation and too anxious to delay, she strad-
dled his legs, slid down the length of him, and pulled him deep into
her body. She forgot about her stomach and the dust and dirt. His
arousing scent hypnotized her. She lost herself in her need for him
and in the blue eyes that gazed up at her, saying *I love you.*

Frantically, she tossed off her blouse and jerked down her che-
mise. The fabric crumpled into a thin ring around her waist. She
leaned over, letting her breasts sway inches from his face. He swirled
the tip of his tongue around her right nipple.

A hiss slipped between her lips as she dissolved into the pleasure
he gave her.

His rapid breath mingled with hers. She moistened her lips with
a flick of her tongue as each nibble took her another step in her
search for completion. She wanted him, needed him; her life would
stop without him.

He teased her to the edge of climax, mumbling erotic words in a
language she couldn't understand. A gripping sensation began at her
core and spread outward like a ferocious wave, pulling everything in
its wake, unstoppable, unquenchable, and unfathomable.

They clung together in a pulsing rhythm of release, tied by an
invisible cord binding them in their love, together for all time.

If anything happened to him, she'd fade away to the dark side
and there'd be no pulling her back.

THREE HOURS LATER, with supper over and dishes put away,
Kit left the Barretts' and strolled back to her campsite singing
"When the Dew is on the Grass." Tate and Tabor pitter-pattered
behind her for a short distance, then circled back to play with the
children.

Guess I'm not as much fun anymore.

Maybe the animals didn't think so, but Cullen had a different
opinion. Whatever had ailed her earlier, he'd healed with a kiss and a
touch and, well…other things.

Guilt, however, wagged its sticky little finger at her for acting so
snarky. He didn't deserve to bear the brunt of her foul moods. Their

time together was too precious.

The sound of his voice drifting from the far side of her wagon stopped her midstride.

"…throwing gold around like they'd found the mother lode. Bragged about panning for gold at Dutch Flat. The Hudson Bay Company employees said their story didna add up."

"Why'd they think that?" Kit smelled John's tobacco and imagined him pointing both his pipe and his question at Cullen.

"Didna seem the type to do a day's lick of work," Cullen said.

She tiptoed toward the end of the wagon, censuring herself for spying but too intrigued to walk away.

"Do you think they're the wagon train killers?" Henry asked.

She gasped, quickly covering her mouth.

"Hard to say," Cullen said.

"Which way they'd go?"

Each slingshot question drew her closer to unwittingly revealing her presence.

"West toward Fort Boise," Cullen said.

"Are you going to tell Kit?"

She waited through his pause, expecting him to say *of course*.

"Nae. I'll tell her I'm going scouting and will be gone overnight."

Her mouth opened, shocked by his planned subterfuge. She stomped from her place of concealment, fists to hips. "Like hell you will."

Cullen dropped his foot that he'd been resting on the wheel spoke and walked toward her, sparks flying from the tip of his cheroot.

She rethought her rash decision to intrude. He wasn't wearing the soft face of her satisfied lover. But she refused to be…what? Bullied? She crossed her arms. "I can't believe you'd lie to me."

"Why?" The question was a crossbreed of demand and curiosity. "Is that purview limited to ye?" She raised her hand to slap him, but he wrapped his fingers around her wrist. "Ye'd slap me?"

She reclaimed her hand, staring at it as if it had acted on its own. "Never." Tears trickled from the corners of her eyes. What in the world was wrong with her? Her emotions swung from one side of the trail to the other. Adam had even asked her if Mr. Montgomery had turned into a snapping turtle.

A *snapping turtle,* for Pete's sake.

He wiped away her tears with his thumbs. "If I told ye what I planned, ye'd worry."

"Did they say anything about the Murrays' baby?"

He shook his head.

"What does that mean? The killers didn't have a baby in their arms, or tied to their horses, or what?"

"We dinna ken they're the killers. The fort employees I talked to said three men rode in, rode out, and werena carrying a baby."

She took a steadying breath to calm her wildly beating heart. "I want to talk to them."

Cullen's eyes widened in surprise. "I'll tell ye what I know."

"Did you get descriptions?"

"General ones."

"Like what—brown hair and stands this tall?" She held her hand at eye level. "I can get better descriptions. Please take me to the fort. If you don't—"

"What? Ye'll go by yerself?" He finished her threat, adding a challenging gaze.

"If I have to, I will." She gathered her skirt and hurried away, but got only a few feet before Cullen scooped her into his arms.

Henry chuckled, but the laugh died on his lips when Kit and Cullen both glared at him. "'Pears you've got this under control, son," Henry said, backing away. "We'll be at John's if'n you got anything more to say."

"Put me down. I can walk." At least he didn't throw her over his shoulder like a sack of spoiled-rotten…something.

The corners of his lips curled. "I ken ye can walk. I'm just nae sure where ye've a mind to walk to."

"Take me to the fort."

"Tomorrow."

"Memories fade. People disappear. It has to be now."

He let out a long, exasperated sigh and set her on her feet. "Get yer pencils."

Thirty minutes later, Kit sat across the table from the two men Cullen had spoken with earlier. For the next hour, they answered her questions about the shape of the suspected killers' faces, their eyes, and hair coloring. She sketched, erased, sketched again, until the witnesses agreed the drawings were a reasonable facsimile of the men they had seen.

They refused payment for their time but asked for drawings of their sweethearts. It was almost midnight by the time Kit finished sketching.

"Let's head back to camp," Cullen said. "Ye need sleep." He had sat at her side the entire time watching her and humming Beethoven.

As they left the fort, Kit walked close to him, snuggled underneath his arm. "Do you think their sweethearts exist?"

"Did ye look at yer drawings?"

"I usually don't *see* a sketch until long after it's done. Why?"

"Both men described the set of yer eyes, yer high cheekbones, and yer willful chin." He gave her a playful tap below her mouth.

"I think you're imagining it."

"Ye draw like ye sing. Yer range is extraordinary." His tone was full of veneration.

"There's nothing spectacular about my talent." As a student of the arts, she knew her drawings hung from the bottom rung of the artistic ladder, regardless of the century.

"Ye, my sweet, have never watched yerself draw. Ye sketch fine lines as if ye're plucking stringed instruments. Broader lines have the rumble of percussion. The full orchestra plays between the chin and brow. Ye're both composer and conductor. It's brilliant."

While there had been synchronicity between his humming and the movement of her drawing hand, she thought it accidental, not intentional. She swallowed a thick lump. "You're the only person who's ever *heard* me draw."

"Aye, lass. Others see what ye create. Not how ye create it."

Cullen sighed, his breath easing out and flowing into her. They were intertwining circles, soul mates. How did the brooch weave those circles? Did it start them? Or did the stone complete them? She trembled, every muscle tensed.

What-if questions bombarded her. The latest: If she were born in 1852, she and Cullen never would have met. And if they were soul mates, that didn't make sense. Therefore, she must have been born earlier, much earlier, maybe 1824. If that was the case, she could discard the possibility of being Heather Murray. If not Heather, then who was she?

As they neared the wagons, Cullen said, "I want to take the drawings to Fort Boise. I might catch up with those men."

"We'll leave drawings there when we pass through. You don't need to ride ahead and risk running into them." A maternal tone voiced her growing sense of panic. "They're dangerous men. Especially the one called Jess. There's evil in his eyes."

"I dinna intend to tangle with them, only inform the authorities."

Her fear morphed into terror. "Don't chase after them, please."

"I thought ye wanted to find the baby."

"I'm not the Murrays' child." Her denial sounded stronger than she intended. "The man in San Francisco will identify me. Let this go, Cullen."

Clouds whipped across the face of the moon, and she could no longer distinguish his features in the inky void. A breeze spanked the bottom of her skirt and bound her legs, preventing her from moving closer to him, to the safety of his arms. An eerie quietness settled over the plains as if a hand covered the mouth of every creature, preventing even a whisper from escaping. In the stillness of the night, she sensed a malefic force.

"I'm afraid."

As he'd done earlier, he scooped her up into his arms and carried her away. "There's nothing to fear. We are joined in spirit as we are in body, and nothing—not time, not death—will ever separate us."

Chapter Thirty-Four

KIT CLEANED UP after supper at their camp on the Snake River at Three Island Crossing, and put the utensils away. Cullen sat at the table studying maps and notes in preparation for the meeting the men would have later. They'd left Fort Hall ten days earlier, and had a decision to make. Would they ford the river, the most treacherous crossing on the entire trail, or would they take the dry southern route that wound around sand dunes and canyons?

She packed her drawing implements and found a quiet place to draw. She sketched the sagebrush-covered hill they had descended earlier that day. When she finished, she placed her sketchpad and pencils on the ground beside her. What decisions had previous travelers made? Had they had a heated debate over which was the best route? She hoped for Cullen's sake there would be a unanimous decision. Splitting the wagon train wouldn't benefit anyone. The river was formidable, but so was the alternate route. She picked up a pencil and tapped it against her palm. If anyone could lead the group to a consensus, Cullen would.

She gazed out over the water. Surely they would select the course Cullen recommended. Three prairie-grass-covered islands, resembling stepping stones, lay in the middle of the river. She began to draw them, concentrating on the southernmost and middle islands.

"Last time I was here, we lost an entire family on the island ye're drawing."

Her body jerked, and her arms flew up in the air. "Damn, Cullen." She whacked him on the head with her pad and accidentally jabbed his face with the blunt end of her pencil. "Why do you scare me?"

"Ouch. Ye hurt my chin."

She looked at the small red dot below his lip. "Serves you right."

"I'm sorry. I forget ye go into a—what do ye call it?—a zone?"

"I could have poked you in the eye."

He grimaced. "I willna scare ye again."

"Do you know how many times you've promised that?"

He raised his brows theatrically.

"Isn't it time for your meeting to start?"

"Almost, but I needed a kiss first." After he gave a lingering kiss, he studied her drawing. "Yer sketch doesna even hint at the dangerous current hiding below the surface."

"I don't want to draw the danger. I want to appreciate the beauty. After we cross, if that's the vote, I'll consider adding shading and intensity to the water."

He handed her the sketchpad. "Promise me ye willna jump into this river." His voice was soft, but she caught an edge of fear in his eyes.

She squeezed his hand. The trip west had turned out much more dangerous than she had imagined. Her naiveté had convinced her that knowledge, a gun, and karate would protect her. But these skills had only made her overconfident. Her risk-taking days were over. "You needn't worry."

"Pretend I just gasped," he said, returning her smile. "Worrying is part and parcel of loving ye."

Her mouth opened to level a retort announcing the same was true in reverse, but Henry shouted, gesturing Cullen to join him at John's wagon.

He checked his timepiece. "Time for the meeting."

"What do you think the vote will be?"

"Folks are staying tight-lipped, even opinionated Mr. Cameron. If the wagon train splits, I'm committed to go with the largest group."

"What does John want?"

"He kens I'll recommend the crossing. I have his support."

"Ask Reverend Hamilton to say a prayer that the crossing leads straight to green pastures."

Cullen chuckled. "I'll suggest that." He lifted her hand and kissed the inside of her wrist, a kiss guaranteed to leave her wanting more. "I'll be late to bed. If we're to make the crossing, we'll caulk the wagons tonight."

"You can try to wake me, but I don't promise you'll be successful."

"I've ne'er yet to wake ye when ye havena been sweetness in my arms."

Her face heated. Cullen still had a way of making her blush.

BY TEN O'CLOCK, she had completed the weekly inventory of her red bag and repacked the backpack, adding a pair of Cullen's trousers. Then, exhausted, she went to sleep. Sometime later, he woke her, nuzzling her ear.

"What happened at the meeting?" She rolled over and wrapped her arms around his neck.

"We're fording in the morning."

"It'll be dangerous."

He kissed her. "Yes, and I expect ye to stay where I put ye."

She kissed him back, whispering against his lips, "Do you ever not get your way?"

He lifted the hem of her gown. "Ye tell me, sweetling."

SHORTLY BEFORE MIDMORNING, the dark clouds broke free and scattered, taking away fear of an impending storm. The men finished stringing rope from one side to the other, bridging the thousand-foot-wide river.

Everything was ready now.

The oxen pulled the first wagon into the three-foot-deep water. The next wagon followed, then the next as the animals forged ahead, finally touching the tip of the first island. When the wagons reached the second island, the men unhitched the teams to swim the remaining distance without their heavy loads. The caulked wagons became boats and floated to the north bank using the ropes as guides. Cullen and Henry rode along as outriders helping to keep the boat-wagons in line.

By late afternoon, two thirds of the wagons were on the north bank.

Kit and Sarah sat in the shade of the Barretts' open-sided dining tent, facing the river, their sewing baskets and a pile of clothes to mend sitting on the table between them. Kit couldn't concentrate on anything other than watching their men in the water, and she knew that was also true with Sarah. The crossing had gone smoothly so far, but she couldn't relax until everyone was across.

The afternoon sun slanted across the river, obscuring details that might distinguish one dirty, worn wagon from another. Kit frowned as a wagon entered the water. "Whose wagon? Can you tell? Looks like it's tipping."

Sarah knitted her hands and held them under her chin. "That's the Abbots'. They might have a broken wheel."

Kit stood and walked from under the tent. "They're unhitching the team." Her pulse quickened. "Looks like they're going to float the wagon all the way across."

Suddenly, men jumped out of other wagons and swarmed the disabled one.

Kit cupped her hands at her forehead to shade her eyes. "Somebody's hurt."

"Maybe they're just afraid the wagon will tip and they'll lose control."

"Where's Cullen?" Dread wrapped Kit's chest in tight rubber bands.

"I don't see John or the boys either."

Minutes ticked by. Kit paced, gazing at the disabled wagon. "I can't wait any longer. I've got to find out what's happening."

Sarah squeezed Kit's arm. "Cullen wouldn't want you back in the water."

She considered her promise. But since she wouldn't actually be jumping into the river, she wasn't technically breaking her word, right? "I won't be long." She mounted Stormy and raced into the water. The current was stronger now, but her horse was a confident swimmer and easily reached the middle island. Voices grew louder but words were unintelligible.

The men had pulled the wagon's nose onto the first island. The left front wheel had fallen off, and the wagon sat lopsided. Where was Cullen? Where were the Barrett men? Cullen's voice rose above the commotion. "Go back."

She funneled her hands around her mouth. "Where are you?"

He poked his head from behind the wagon. "Adam's hurt. Go back."

Adam was hurt, but Cullen wanted her to go back. Why? Ignoring his command, she entered the water, then stopped, turned around, and headed back toward shore. In her century, she was a first responder, but in the nineteenth century, she was much more. She needed to hurry back and get ready.

Sarah ran to meet her. "Is anybody hurt?"

Kit dismounted and hobbled Stormy. "It's Adam."

Sarah slapped her hand against her chest. "How bad?"

"Cullen didn't say. They're bringing him in now."

Each minute carried the weight of an hour. Finally, Cullen and the wagon reached the north shore. He dismounted.

"What happened?" Kit's throat held her heart.

"Axle broke. The boy fell."

Tears rimmed Sarah's eyes, and she wrung her hands. "Is John with him?"

"They're both in the wagon." Cullen's face showed more concern than his voice reflected.

Sarah ran toward the wagon, calling for her husband.

"How bad is he hurt?" Kit asked, watching Sarah.

"A chunk of the wheel sheared off, rammed into his groin."

Blood drained from her body. Visions of Scott swarmed inside her brain. She'd been unable to help him. What could she possibly do for Adam?

Cullen grabbed her, held her steady. "We need to get ready. I told John to bring him to our tent."

She gazed into Cullen's eyes and drew strength from him. Whatever else happened, he was with her. She didn't have to face this or anything else alone, ever again.

"This way. Careful with the leg," Henry said.

Adam moaned. The sound of his pain climbed into Kit's heart, shocking her like a jolt of electricity. She ducked inside the tent. "Get my bag and the rubber sheet out of the trunk." Cullen helped her cover the bed with the sheet, then Henry and John laid Adam down.

A six-inch sheared-off piece of the spoke, a half inch in diameter, protruded from his body.

"Can't we pull it out?" John asked.

A few beats of silence followed.

"No," Kit said, finding her voice. "The femoral artery might be punctured." She took a shaky breath.

"Tell me what to do," Cullen said.

She rummaged in the bag and withdrew a bottle of Percocet. "This'll cut the pain. Hand me a canteen."

Adam jerked. His eyes were wide and wild. Kit shoved two pills into his mouth and placed the canteen against his trembling lips. "Swallow," she ordered.

The men stood back while Kit cut away Adam's pants leg. "His wet shirt and boots need to come off, too." She squatted beside the bed and studied the stake's point of entry in the crease between the torso and right leg. It was impossible to tell how deeply it was embedded. Blood oozed from the wound, and his foot and ankle had turned pale and cold. She compared the pulses in his feet. The injured leg was much weaker. The stake had probably hit a blood vessel. Which one and how extensive the damage she couldn't tell until she extended the wound and removed the piece of wood.

She ushered Sarah and the three men out of the tent. "I think the stake is embedded in a blood vessel and is decreasing the blood flow to his foot. I can open him up and see what's going on, but I'm not a surgeon. I can't repair a vessel."

"Will he lose the leg?" Cullen asked.

"It's possible. But I couldn't..." Her stomached roiled.

"Wait just a damned minute. Nobody's cutting my boy's leg off," John said.

Sarah's work-worn fingers curled into fists at her side. Tears streaked down her face. "Don't let him die, Kit. You do whatever you have to do. I *won't* lose another child. I won't."

"They're not going to take his leg, Sarah." John embraced his wife. "He's going to be fine."

"Let's get the spoke out," Kit said. "I'll repair what I can, and then we'll watch him. We might have to take the leg later, but not right now."

How in the world did this happen? She wasn't trained to open someone and tie off blood vessels. Sure, she'd seen vets do it at the equine center and had seen videos of vascular repair on people. But actually performing the surgery... She hugged Sarah. "Why don't you and John wait out here? I'll call you if I need you."

Sarah shook her head. "Adam needs his ma. I want to be with him."

They all reentered the tent. Kit looked into the tensed faces of the people she had come to love. This was not how she wanted to reveal her identity to them. Not in a moment of crisis. Not like this. But she had no choice. Their lives would change now. They would treat her differently. They would know she wasn't one of them. No matter how much she longed to be a member of the flock, they wouldn't accept her. Even Cullen, coming from a Celtic, mystical background, had a difficult time accepting her identity. John, Sarah, and Henry were simple folk—not simple-minded, but grounded in what they could see and feel and taste. Yet they had their faith and they believed in dreams. If they didn't, they wouldn't be more than halfway to Oregon. What would she do if they wouldn't let her teach Frances and Elizabeth? She swallowed, trying to conceal the ache and flutter of fear.

Was there any place she truly belonged? Now was not the time to worry about herself. She turned to the spectators. "I'm going to use instruments and procedures you haven't seen before. Please be patient. I'll explain everything later." Her friends were probably too worried about Adam to care about instruments and procedures. She took a deep, steadying breath.

"John. Henry. You hold Adam's legs. I don't think he'll move, but if he does, try to hold him still. Sarah, you stand on the other side and hold his hand." They shuffled into position, wearing pinched expressions.

Cullen cleared the table, and Kit opened a suture set. "I'll need you to hold the spoke while I cut around it."

He nodded.

Adam attempted his usual cockeyed grin. "Is it bad, Miss Kit?"

"I don't know yet. How's your pain?"

"Not bad." His eyes told her the pain was less severe, but still palpable.

"No one will think less of you if you vocalize your discomfort." She whispered in his ear. "Scream if you have to."

"Do they scream in Mr. Shakespeare's plays?"

"I'm sure if they had a sword stuck in their side, they'd let someone know."

He squeezed his ma's hand until her knuckles turned white.

"I'm going to put a needle in your arm. Don't be alarmed." Henry and John whispered to each other as Kit started an IV. "You'll have to ask Cullen to tell you the story about when I did this to him."

Cullen patted Adam's shoulder. "It'll be all right, son."

"I'm going to cut around the spoke. Cullen will hold it steady until I'm ready to take it out. How's the pain?"

"Don't feel much." His face shone with nervous perspiration. As she'd discovered with Cullen, modern pain medication seemed to take effect more quickly in nineteenth-century patients.

"I'm going to put a tourniquet around your upper thigh to slow the bleeding so I can see what happened to you."

Cullen donned gloves and stood at her side to assist. "Will you hand me the surgical knife?" she asked.

He held up the scalpel. "This?"

Kit nodded, and he placed the instrument in her hand. She took a deep breath and checked the tourniquet. "Hold the tip of the spoke, easy." She cut through Adam's skin, extending the edges of the wound. "Sponge." Cullen placed the gauze in Kit's hand. "Now pull, slowly." The spoke came out. It had embedded deeper than an inch into his groin and severed a vessel. Not the femoral artery. She breathed a sigh of relief. "Will you wipe my forehead, please?"

"With the gauze?"

"Yes."

She needed to tie off both ends of the vessel. She tightened the tourniquet. "Catgut and needle." Cullen's hand shook as he handed Kit what she requested.

"Can ye fix it?" he asked.

"No," she said, with calm deliberateness. "But I can tie it off. He'll lose the vessel but he's got others to carry blood to his leg."

"Adam, do ye need anything?" Cullen asked.

Adam's fingers tapped against the sheet to a cadence only he could hear.

"Do you want Cullen to read to you?" Kit asked.

"If'n he'll read *Midsummer Night's Dream*." Adam's voice was low, trembling.

In his sonorous voice, Cullen began to recite, "Act 1, Scene 1. Athens. The palace of Theseus."

She glanced at her husband and a throb of affection raced through her.

An hour later, Kit finished stitching and dressing the wound. Color slowly returned to Adam's foot and ankle, and the pulse grew stronger. Exhausted by the ordeal, he drifted off to sleep, his face no longer taut from fighting pain.

The inside of the tent resembled an operating room. Bloody sponges were tossed haphazardly on the table, along with the instruments Kit had used to put Adam back together.

Sarah's soft sobs filled the air with a mother's quiet relief. John and Henry lit their pipes.

"As long as his pulse stays strong," Kit said, "we can hope for the best."

Adam's brothers, Ben and Clint, slipped into the tent. "How is he?"

"We'll know more in a few hours," Kit said.

"We made coffee," Ben said.

John turned to him. "Thanks, son. Bring in some chairs, too. We need to sit a spell."

Five tense people sat on the edge of their chairs, drinking coffee, watching Adam breathe, and all waiting for something to happen. Henry leaned forward, elbows on his knees, wearing a no-nonsense expression. "I believe you owe us an explanation, missy."

Cullen gave her a silent nod of encouragement. She cleared her throat and crossed her hands in her lap. He tented his hands, which she noticed shook slightly.

"What Kit is about to tell ye may be more than ye're wanting to hear. Listen to her with yer heart. If ye try to listen with yer mind, ye willna understand." He paused and laid his hand over hers, warm and reassuring. "Go on, lass. Tell them who ye are."

She cleared her throat again, and laced her fingers with his. "I was raised believing my name was Kitherina Mary MacKlenna. I discovered that wasn't my real name only weeks before I left my home in the twenty-first century—"

They gasped, then her friends fell silent and still. For the next thirty minutes, they listened. Occasionally, they asked questions. Cullen interjected his own disbelief and confusion, and he explained how he finally came to accept Kit's identity.

"If Kit had told this story weeks ago, we would have set her on the side of the road," John said. "I'm not sure we wouldn't have done the same this morning, even with you speaking on her behalf, Cullen. But after watching her work on the boy, I have no doubt she is who she says she is." John glanced at Henry, then at his wife.

There seemed to be silent agreement among them.

John continued. "It's best if we put your other life behind us. Once we leave this tent, we'll never mention the subject again. We'll never ask you about your home. Not that we aren't curious, but the future is not meant for us to know."

"I respect that, John," she said.

"You've been teaching the little ones about voting for women. I won't object to you teaching subjects they need to learn. I will object if you teach subjects they don't have a right to know." He paused. "Do we have an understanding?"

She took a deep breath, nodded, then relaxed against Cullen.

John turned to the rest. "Do you have anything to say, Sarah? Henry?"

Henry tapped the bowl of his pipe against his palm. "I said all that needs saying the day I walked you down the aisle."

Sarah stood and laid hands on Kit. Heat seeped into her skin, her soul, her heart. "You were misplaced for some reason, but Frances called you home for just such a time as this."

Kit buried her face in Cullen's shirt and sobbed. How could they still love her and forgive her after all she'd done to deceive them?

He wrapped her in the warmth of his arms. "Shh. We're yer family now."

She wasn't sure that was such a good thing. In her lifetime, she'd already lost two.

WHILE CULLEN MADE rounds, Kit walked along the quiet shore reflecting on all that had happened. The memory of Cullen reciting *Midsummer Night's Dream* would remain embedded in her heart for a lifetime. His powerful voice brought the poetry to life, but it also brought calmness to her spirit and enabled her to do abundantly more than she ever imagined she could.

"I've been searching for ye," he said.

She laced her arm with his. "Did you look in on Adam?"

"I stopped at the Barretts' first."

"Both color and pulses are improving," she said.

He patted her hand. "Ye're a miracle worker."

"I couldn't have done the procedure without you."

"Ye're stronger than ye think."

They walked without speaking, welcoming the calm of the late-night hour.

"I'm so relieved John and Sarah and Henry know the truth. I hated deceiving them."

A grin pulled at the corners of Cullen's mouth. "Ye had nae such compunction with me."

"You'll never forgive me, will you?"

He kissed the top of her head. "I forgave ye before I asked ye to marry me."

In her heart, she had experienced the warmth of his forgiveness. If he could forgive her, if Henry, Sarah, and John could forgive her, then she should forgive her parents and Elliott. She no longer had the nagging ache in her gut and the emptiness in her soul. Soon she would be a mother, and like her parents, she would do whatever she had to do to protect her child.

The time had come to forgive them. And while she was in a forgiving mood, she might as well forgive herself, too.

THE WAGON TRAIN approached the base of Flagstaff Hill, heading toward the Lone Tree and the Powder River. Kit and Cullen rode to the summit and dismounted. She peered out toward the horizon, relieved to have survived the monotonous trip from the Snake River through shoulder-high sagebrush.

"They say the optimist sees the magnificent lush green Baker Valley."

"And what does the pessimist see?" Cullen asked.

"Those," she said, pointing toward the snow-capped Blue Mountains etched against the dusk. She entwined an arm around his waist, and they watched the wagons roll westward across the valley. "I found a quote by Yeats in my dad's notes. 'I have spread my dreams under your feet. Tread softly because you tread on my dreams.'"

He kissed her. "I wouldna ever tread on yer dreams. I want to be one of them."

"A ghost and now a dream? You certainly have high expectations."

"I have only one expectation at the moment—fulfillment of a promise ye made." His murmur trailed down her neck.

She gave him a saucy smile. "And I intend to deliver." She pulled him to the ground, wanting him with an incomprehensible madness. As the flaming sun drifted below the horizon, he entered her in a smoky haze of heat.

Chapter Thirty-Five

"**D**O YE WANT to stretch yer legs before we head back?" Cullen asked.

"Yes." Kit dismounted, feeling stiff and achy. She stepped to the cliff's edge that overlooked the Deschutes River to get a broader view of the falls and rapids. A low timber growth spread out before her, and the air smelled of river water, dead leaves, and rain-soaked earth.

Travel had been hard since leaving Baker Valley. The trail had led through heavily forested mountains then a narrow pass, which ended the climb out of the Grand Ronde and the last stretch of the Blue Mountains. From there, they'd descended the Umatilla Hill to the valley, crossed the Umatilla River, and headed into a forty-mile stretch of sandy land until they had reached the John Day River the day before. Now Cullen was scouting the Deschutes crossing.

Looking out over the expanse, Kit experienced an unsettling flutter in her stomach. Was it the baby? Cullen appeared somber and reflective. The sun caught in his eyes, and for a second, she saw him as he had first appeared to her when she was ten. An isolated cloud cast his face in shadow. Her stomach fluttered again, and sweat trickled between her swollen breasts. Then the cloud moved away and the sun returned.

"I need to go to the bushes," she said.

Cullen gave her a pensive smile. "Give me the backpack. I'll wear it."

She slipped the pack off her shoulders and handed it to him, then walked down the trail. Why was she being so secretive? Because of the flutter? She wanted to see if it would happen again before she told him. He'd want to know everything about it, and she'd be embarrassed if it was just gas or something else. It didn't happen again, and a few minutes later, she walked out of the bushes, cinching her belt. "I'm ready—"

The words stuck in her throat. She stopped cold. A few feet away, two men held guns aimed at Cullen's chest. The air was wrapped in an odor of rot, decay, and death. Adrenaline rushed through her. She needed to distract the men and give Cullen a chance to draw against them. But how? Call attention to herself? She licked her lips, prepared to—

A powerful arm covered with thick red scars grabbed her in a headlock. "Here's the other one, Jess. Gussied up like a boy." His rancid breath blew hot on her neck.

Thick red scars. One of the witnesses at the fort had used that description the night she sketched the faces of the ghost train killers. Hard angles, skin stretched tight across their bones, ruddy complexions, and scars. But her sketches had not captured the depth of evil in their soulless eyes, burning like a raging fire.

"Looks like you caught us a sage hen, Billy. Pretty 'nough to eat fer sure." Jess's scaly skin and rigid snout somehow matched the sinister rattle in his throat.

Billy squeezed her breast, letting out a long, slow whistle. "Handful's what I got. I caught her. I get her first. We'll chock up nice." His icy laugh slithered over her.

She had to do something fast. Her lips formed a tight seam, holding back fear for Cullen and her unborn child. She would kill for both of them. First, she had to disarm the man holding her.

Cullen's nostrils flared. His eyes narrowed into two slits of blue ice. He lurched forward. Jess pressed his gun against Cullen's ribs.

"You looking to die?"

Kit pinned him with a frozen stare, and he eased back.

"Didn't think so." Jess smashed his elbow into Cullen's gut. He doubled over, letting out a low groan.

Kit's stomach muscles clenched.

Billy ripped her shirt open with his callused hand. "Think he wants to watch me poke you?" He kissed her neck. Vomit raced up her throat, but she swallowed it back. "We're going to the bushes. Let him listen to you scream and wonder what hole I'm poking ya in." He humped her from behind.

That did it.

Another dose of adrenaline swelled through her veins. Whatever she did needed to be quick and deadly. She prepared to fight to the end if necessary. She searched Cullen's eyes for a sign that he expected her to act. His gaze flicked, almost imperceptibly.

Silence swamped her as she moved beyond herself. She no longer heard the tumbling rapids behind her, Billy's vulgar threats, or the bass drumbeat of her heart.

Silence. Deadly silence.

With their faces only inches apart and Billy's sickening spittle on her neck, she grabbed his arm with both hands and dropped into a straddle-leg stance. The sudden move pulled him off-balance and unable to maintain his hold. She threw a quick elbow punch to his right side followed immediately by one to his left. She stomped on his instep, feeling the soft, worn leather of his boot give way.

Without losing momentum, she turned, brought up her knee, and broke his arm, the crack loud and violent. Warm blood sprayed on her face from the compound fracture. Quickly, she snapped another kick behind his knee. He dropped.

A swift kick to the groin produced a gut-hollowing scream of agony. His eyes grew wide with pain and disbelief. She jammed her forearm into his Adam's apple. A slow wet stain covered his trousers as he crumpled into a lifeless heap.

You'll never touch me again, asshole.

She tried to steady the frantic rise and fall of her chest.

From the corner of her eye, she saw Cullen land an elbow to Jess's face, breaking his nose, and follow up with a rib-cracking punch.

The third man's neck veins bulged. He pointed his gun at Cullen but Jess stood in the line of fire, so he waved the gun toward Kit. Her pulse thundered in her ears. She dropped and rolled, swung her legs and swept the man's feet from under him. He dropped the gun as he went down on one knee, but immediately scrambled to his feet. He grabbed the front of her shirt with a meaty fist, tangling his fingers in the cloth. The force was enough to steal her breath, but she stepped back and dipped underneath his shoulder, just as she'd been trained. The move twisted his hand, which freed her to whack down on his right arm. Splintering bone gave her silent satisfaction. He screamed.

His pockmarked face glowed with an angry red sheen. He released her shirt but grabbed her hair with his uninjured hand and yanked her head back. Kit gagged on the pungent whisky odor on his breath. She pinned his hand, regaining control of her hair, then torqued her body until he let her go, but he smacked her face. She bit back the pain, and with a whipping action of her shoulder and arm, threw a hand strike to his temple. His head whipped back. He was unconscious before he hit the ground.

Cullen connected with another punch to Jess's stomach and wrestled for the gun. Then an explosion—a whip-crack sound of a bullet.

Kit, swimming in a sharp current of fear, swiveled toward the pistol shot and the caustic smell of spent gunfire. She watched with horror as Cullen grabbed his shoulder, blood oozing between his fingers.

Jess plunged his beefy fist into Cullen's chest, forcing him backward toward the cliff's edge. Caught off-balance, Cullen struggled to right himself. But there was nothing to grab. His eyes met hers, embracing her with love for one long, indefinable moment. "I love ye." His mouth moved soundlessly. And then he was gone.

Jess turned the gun toward her, blood dripping from his nose and the corners of his mouth. Her adrenaline went haywire while the seconds of her life ticked toward zero. No time to think. She reacted, spinning counterclockwise. She kicked him and smashed his arm. Another kick shoved his testicles into his abdomen. More blood spewed from his mouth.

Her world turned blood red.

She threw one final jab with her hand directly into his windpipe. His eye grew wide with shock and disbelief. He gurgled, trying to speak and deny what he obviously knew to be true. He was a dead man standing. And with his thoughts telegraphing across his face, he toppled over and crushed his head on the corner of a large rock.

Frantically, with her heart in her mouth, Kit dropped to all fours and crawled, following blood spores to the cliff's edge. She leaned over into the emptiness and screamed.

"*Cullen!*"

Chapter Thirty-Six

K IT RODE ALONG the riverbank, leaning from the saddle, searching the ground for any sign Cullen had come ashore. After repeated dismounts to study broken branches and dark stains on the dry ground, she gave up riding and walked. Fear clung to her ankles and each weighted step dragged her further into a rising pit of despair.

She found nothing. No blood, no footprints, no trampled underbrush. But she wasn't an experienced tracker. She needed help. She needed Henry. That meant delaying the search and racing back to camp.

I have to go, Cullen, but I'll be back. We'll find you. I promise. Don't give up. Don't ever give up.

She gathered Cullen's and the dead men's horses, put heels to Stormy, and galloped toward the wagon train. She passed landmarks Cullen had pointed out earlier in the day. Two of them she missed because her eyes were too blurry with tears to watch where she was going. Backtracking wasted precious time. Jasper and the other three horses slowed her down, but she couldn't have left them behind. She knew bringing them along wasn't logical, but somehow worrying over the horses helped her construct a wall of denial, and she snugged in behind it.

Cullen was missing. *Only* missing.

Her denial grew even stronger while watching the sun struggle to show itself from behind fast-scudding rain clouds. It won't rain. Not yet. Not until she found her husband.

KIT SPOTTED THE red cross she'd painted on her wagon's canvas. She needed more than medical help right now. She needed Henry. An inkling of hope crawled up her brick wall of denial. Grab Henry and hurry back to the river. There'd be no time for discussion or debate.

Kit jerked on the reins and stopped at the Barretts' campsite, the horses lathered up and blowing, their hooves swirling dirt and dust up around her. She spotted Henry and John right away and waved frantically. They dropped the map they were studying and raced toward her, alarm written on their creased faces.

Henry reached her first and grasped Stormy's bridle to settle him. "What's wrong?"

"Where's Cullen?" John asked, taking the lead rope attached to the other horses.

"We got jumped." She was breathing too fast, making speech difficult. "Cullen fell into the Deschutes. I need…I need you to come back with me. Now."

"Who jumped you?" Henry asked.

Kit was overbreathing, and the faster she breathed the more panicky she became. She covered her mouth with clammy hands and breathed in and out, trying to get CO_2 back into her system. Too late. Her arms and legs went numb, and she tumbled out of the saddle.

KIT MOANED AND snuggled into Cullen's chest. No, it wasn't Cullen's scent. Who was carrying her, taking her farther from her husband? She wrestled her arms free and pushed.

"I got you, missy. No one's going to hurt you." Henry's soothing voice gave her a moment's reprieve. Her eyes fluttered, then opened. She stared up into his weathered face.

"Oh God." She wiggled to get free. "We need to hurry. Cullen needs us."

"Tell me what happened." He carried her to the Barretts' dining tent and set her on the bench next to the table.

Sarah hurried in behind Henry, wringing her hands. A contingent of men followed, bringing a buzz of low-voiced conversations. One man's voice raised above the others, asking, "What happened? Where's Cullen?"

Henry held up his hand, demanding silence from the gathering. "Step back and give her room to breathe." He squatted in front of Kit and took her hand in his. "Now, start at the beginning."

A malignant odor lingered in the air. Pregnancy made her olfactory sense more acute, but even if she hadn't been pregnant, she'd have recognized the smell of unadulterated fear—blood and decay. She reeked of it.

"We rode to the top of a cliff." Her voice wobbled. "The cliff overlooked the Deschutes." She touched her throat, remembering the chokehold. She gagged. "Three men jumped us. You know those men...those men in my pictures."

The crowd gasped and started murmuring. Henry held up his hand again, silencing them.

"We fought." The memories came back in a rush, and her hands flittered in front of her face, trying to push them away. "They shot Cullen." She pressed her shaking fingers against the muscle burning in her arm as if she could staunch the blood flowing from Cullen's wound.

"Go on." Blue veins pulsed on the sides of Henry's head.

Kit ran her tongue over her lips. Her mouth was dry, thick with trail dust. Sarah handed her a cup, and she turned it up and gulped. Water dribbled down her chin. She moved in slow motion, wiping her face and speaking at the same sluggish speed.

"Cullen lost his balance." Her voice sounded distant as if she stood outside herself, an observer, not a participant. "The man they called Jess pushed Cullen, and he fell off the cliff."

She covered her eyes with her forearm. Reliving the horror stopped her heart as it had originally. After a pause, her heart restarted with the shock of a defibrillator, instantly reminding her of the urgency. "I searched the riverbank for several miles, but I couldn't find him. I came back to get you, Henry. We have to go *now*." She stood, but Henry drew her back onto the bench.

"You just fell off your horse. You're not going anywhere." His eyes were dark and intense.

"I have to go." She tried again to stand, but he pressed on her shoulders.

"John and I will go, but you're staying put."

She sucked in a shuddering breath and steadied herself for a battle with Henry. Sarah scooted him aside. "Let me bandage that cut on your cheek." Kit grabbed Sarah's arm and dug her fingers into the woman's soft flesh. "Don't let them leave without me. They don't know where to go."

"What happened to the men who attacked you?" John asked.

"They're dead."

Questions scribbled across his chiseled face. How could she admit she'd killed three men when she couldn't reconcile it in her own mind?

"Draw us a map. We'll find him," Henry said.

"You either take me with you, or I'll follow you. I'm not staying behind."

Henry frowned. "You're beat up and you've had a hard ride. Think about your baby."

"The baby's fine, and other than getting smacked in the face, I'm not hurt. Please, don't leave me behind."

Henry glanced at the sky. "Near impossible to track him at night, especially if it rains."

"We should wait until first light," John said.

Another wave of panic swamped her. "Are you crazy? He'll be dead by morning." She shook Henry's arm. "You can find him. You did before. I know he's still alive."

"Not even Henry can track in the dark," John said.

Her gaze shot upward. The edges of another storm cloud churned the sky into an ugly gray. Her heart raced, thudding in her ears. She heard what John *wasn't* saying. "You don't believe he's alive, do you?"

"Never lied to you before. Won't start now. Cullen would have made it to shore if he'd survived."

Kit whipped around to face Henry. "Is that what you believe, too?"

Henry shoved a shaking hand through graying hair. Their eyes met for a moment and she saw worry, but also something much deeper, and that scared her. Henry was afraid.

She stiffened. "I'm packing medical supplies, and then I'm leaving again."

This can't be happening.

She shambled away, her legs wobbly from the fight and hard ride. She was going back to search, and neither shaking legs nor disingenuous friends were going to stop her.

Sarah hurried after her. "Kit, don't go. Think about your baby. The men will find Cullen."

"I don't have a choice. My husband needs medical care. I have to go." Her stomach fluttered like it had earlier. A moment of indecision hit her hard. She fell silent. Then the answer came. This was not a time for second-guessing. "Ask Adam to wipe Stormy down and give him some food and water. I need to leave as soon as I pack."

In the dwindling light, she saw Sarah's worried face. The expression caused something to corkscrew in her heart and Kit imagined the look mirrored hers. "You have faith that can move mountains. Move the one standing in my way so I can find Cullen."

Sarah closed her eyes and her lips moved in silent prayer, and Kit felt a twinge of hope.

Henry stopped her before she reached her wagon and wrapped his burly arm around her shoulders. Her throat constricted, and she waited without breathing for him to speak.

"I'll be ready in ten minutes. Get your rain gear."

A sudden breeze, smelling of pine, stirred the damp hair on her forehead, and in that singular moment, facing the unknown and a possible rainstorm, Kit realized she was profoundly afraid. More afraid than she had ever been in her life. What if she couldn't find him?

She shook her head, refusing to believe she had lost him, too.

Chapter Thirty-Seven

KIT AND HENRY returned to camp twenty-four hours later. She sat in her saddle in a catatonic stupor. *We need to search the other side of the river,* she had begged Henry, but he had said it was pointless. How could searching for Cullen ever be pointless?

Sarah offered her food. Knowing she needed nourishment, Kit grudgingly accepted child-sized portions. Her hands trembled so badly she couldn't hold a fork, so she ate with her fingers, one small bite at a time. Cullen probably wasn't eating, so why should she? Food made her sick anyway.

Another flutter. Too early in her pregnancy to feel the baby, the women said, but she knew Cullen's son was also grieving. He wanted to hear his father's laughter. He wanted to feel the tickle of his kisses on her belly. He wanted to hear the roar of his huge heart beating with love.

Sounds she would never hear again and neither would their child.

Physical torture could hurt no worse than the pain of losing her life's breath. *Please take me instead. Give me back my husband, and I will take his place.* But as she begged for release from the agony of living, she realized her child's life depended on her own. How could she surrender when someone so small, so fragile depended on her?

She couldn't.

Tears clogged her throat, choking her. She grew weaker in her despair. Sleep was her enemy, or maybe the enemy was sleep's companion—waking up. That was the true enemy, wasn't it? The moment of full consciousness held the weight of a crushing stone placed on her chest to torture her with life's reality—Cullen was gone. Knowing that god-awful pain would assault her, Kit feared sleep, avoiding it until she dropped from exhaustion.

Come back to me.

If she had not traveled back in time for her own selfish needs, Cullen would still be alive. If not for her, he wouldn't have gone to the top of the cliff to see the view.

A day passed, then another, and another. And although the wagon train had traveled sixty or more miles from where she had seen him last, she wandered off into the woods, searching the ground for his footsteps or a piece of his plaid shirt. Cullen's vine had so intricately intertwined with hers. Severed, they shriveled and died.

Henry found her curled under a tree a mile from camp, sobbing in a bed of pine needles. He picked her up, brushed the needles from her hair. "You can't wander off, missy. You'll get hurt."

"Cullen's hurt. Doesn't matter what happens to me." Grief gripped with such tenacity she could barely speak.

Tenderly, he carried her back to her camp, crooning, "Come back to us, little missy, come back to us." He sat her in her rocker and patiently watched over her.

Mr. Cameron's fiddle came alive, and she squeezed her hands against her ears. "Make him turn it off."

"What?" Henry asked.

She wagged a pointed finger toward the music. "*Make him turn it off.*"

He lowered his head, and his eyes lifted over the rim of the wire glasses riding low on his nose, but he said nothing.

"Don't you hear it?" She slammed her palms on the rocker's arms and jumped up. "Don't you *hear it*?" If Henry wouldn't end it, she would. She stormed into her tent, grabbed her guitar, and ran out swinging the instrument by the neck. "I want the music to stop *now*." Henry moved faster than a gunfighter on a draw, catching her arm midswing before she bashed the guitar against a tree.

He rescued the instrument and held it over his head. Kit danced around, trying to take it back, but he held the guitar much too high for her to reach. "Don't destroy the music."

"Music died when Cullen fell off that cliff. I never want to listen to it again. *Give* it to me." She pounded her fists against his barrel chest, her voice a dark, keening wail. "Bring him back, Henry. *Bring him back.*"

"Shh…" He put the guitar in his chair and cuddled her, his body shaking.

She laid her cheek against his chest, and her tears soaked his shirt. "Why did God take him, too? Weren't my parents and Scott enough? Why Cullen? Why?" Her loss and failure and heartache were eating her alive. She would not survive the cannibalism this time. "Nothing is left for me." She slid out of his arms and fell to her knees, into an abyss of abandoned hope. "Nothing. No husband, no family, no name, nothing."

Henry knelt beside her, tears streaming down his cheeks. "John, Sarah, the children, me. We're your family now."

"Don't you understand?" She shoved him away. "Everybody who loves me dies. I don't want anybody to love me ever again."

"I'm not afraid to love you."

"But I don't deserve—"

"Your pa wouldn't abandon you now, and neither will this old soldier."

SEVERAL HOURS LATER, she woke, confused. Then she shuddered as memory and consciousness collided. She buried her face in her pillow. Her tears mingled with Cullen's scent, and she cried harder knowing she was washing away his musky smell. The scent, once gone, would never come again.

She didn't even remember how she got to her bed. Did Henry carry her?

Thank goodness the music had stopped. The only sound now was her breathing, irregular, agitated. She rolled out of bed, feeling a sharp cramp in her abdomen and muscle spasms in her calves. Cramps and spasms? A result of the fight? She'd probably be sore for a few days.

She took tentative steps over to Cullen's desk and lit the lamp. Her sketchpad lay open next to the book of poems by his favorite poet, Robert Burns—*The Parting Kiss: Sorrowing joy, Adieu's last action, Lingering lips must now disjoin.*

She swallowed a throat full of tears, and noticed the sketch she'd drawn of him only a few hours before he disappeared. *Every now and again*, as an unknown poet had written, *God makes a giant of a man*, and he had made Cullen Montgomery an irreplaceable giant.

How would she ever live without him?

In deep despair, she sat in his chair. Her father's chair had never fit her, but Cullen's embraced her just as she was. With a heavy heart, she crossed her arms on the desk and lowered her head. She'd never again allow the joy of music to filter into her soul, but she would draw the ugliness, the evil that invaded her life and destroyed the best part of her.

I'll draw pictures of hell and the devils who live there.

By the time the sun peeked above the horizon, dozens of sketches littered the floor, some ripped in half, a few crushed into wads and thrown across the tent, several folded into airplanes and intentionally crashed into the ground. Her emotions were still ripe and the cramps were worse. What was going on with her stomach? Sarah had made sure she drank plenty of water so she wasn't dehydrated. She'd eaten most of her dinner the night before only because Henry stood guard, treating her like a child who couldn't leave the table until her plate was cleaned. She was probably still hungry. Sarah should be awake, and she'd fix something light that wouldn't make the cramps worse.

She pushed the chair away from the desk and stood, but immediately doubled over, letting out a sharp scream.

Adam ducked his head inside the tent. "What's wrong?"

Kit dropped to the floor, her hands clutching her belly. "Get your ma."

A few minutes later, Sarah wrapped her arms around Kit's shoulders. "What's wrong?"

"I'm bleeding."

Sarah's sharp intake of breath added shudders of fear to Kit's growing anxiety. "Let's get you to bed."

"I haven't taken care of my body, and now I'm bleeding."

"That doesn't mean you'll lose the baby."

"I can't let that happen. I've lost Cullen. I can't lose his baby, too."

They walked to the bed, and Kit sat. "Lie down and rest. Stay off your feet. I'll fix some tea."

"I don't want tea. I want my doctor."

"We don't have a doctor," Sarah said.

I have a doctor. A solution unfolded in her mind. "I'm going home."

Sarah fluffed her pillow and smoothed the sheets, ignoring Kit's pronouncement. "The baby will be fine, but you have to eat more and sleep."

"I won't risk anything else. This entire trip has been nothing but risks, and I'm through. I'm going home."

Sarah stopped what she was doing. "When?"

"Now."

"But how—"

"I'll take Stormy, Tate, and Tabor."

"Don't do this."

Kit's heart rate accelerated.

Sarah sat beside her with white-knuckled hands clasped in her lap. "Will you come back?"

The brooch is probably not a revolving door. Maybe she couldn't even go home, but her dad had a round-trip ticket, so surely she did, too. She shuddered and a fresh trickle of blood seeped from her body. The clock was ticking. She turned to Sarah and said, "You've been my source of strength since the day we met. I won't be able to leave if you don't help me."

Sarah bowed her head and closed her eyes. After a minute, she opened them and said calmly with conviction, "As sure as you leave, you'll return." She then placed warm hands on Kit's belly. "You're doing what you're meant to do."

You'll return. No. This time, her friend was wrong.

Sarah called to her son, "Adam."

He opened the flaps and peeked inside, his face white with concern.

"Get the girls, Pa, and Henry."

Kit stood, and although she continued to cramp, a calmness that hadn't existed before washed over her. She noticed the mess on the floor. "Will you help me gather my sketches? Even the crumpled ones. I need my journal and camera, too, I guess."

Henry barged in. "What happened?" His voice was rough with restrained emotion.

Fear of losing her baby and leaving her friends crawled through Kit's stomach, piggybacking on her cramps. "I'm going home." *God, this hurts.* She bit her lip in an unsuccessful attempt to keep from crying. She loved these people. They were truly her family. A family she thought she'd never have again, and now she had to say good-bye.

She took a steadying breath and pointed at her trunk. "I'm leaving everything behind. There's no time to pack or worry with the wagon. Henry, there's gold in there for you and John to set up your homesteads. There's also plenty for the children's education."

Kit ignored their simultaneous refusals. She didn't have time to listen to what they didn't want. "Remove the gold and take the trunk to San Francisco," she said to Henry. "Explain to Braham what happened, and ask him to take care of the contents. He'll know what to do."

Adam returned with the girls. "What's wrong, Mama?" Elizabeth asked.

Sarah dabbed at her eyes. "Miss Kit is going away, and she wanted to tell you good-bye."

Kit massaged her belly as another cramp gripped her abdomen. *Not much time.*

"Where?" Frances asked.

"Home." Kit bit her lip harder. "To see my doctor." She pulled the girls into her arms.

"Does this mean the angel was wrong?" Frances asked.

"About what?" Kit asked.

"When I got the cholera, the angel told me to go back and help care for Baby Thomas."

"Who's baby Thomas?"

Frances gave a palms-up, dramatic shrug. "He's your boy."

My boy? "Even if you take him away," Frances continued, "I'll *still* be his big sister."

"You'll always be his big sister, and he'll grow up loving you just as I do. Be sweet to each other." Kit kissed the tops of their heads, and their baby-fine hair tickled her lips.

"Do we have to be sweet to the boys, too?" Elizabeth asked.

"What do you think?" Kit tensed, preparing to watch the children walk out of her life.

Both girls gave exaggerated sighs.

"Run along now. I need to talk to your ma."

Another cramp.

Tate entered the tent and sat, guarding the entrance.

"I have to go." Another cramp, harder this time. "Adam, will you get Stormy and Tabor?"

Kit and Sarah walked outside together. How many times over the past months had they looped arms and giggled like schoolgirls? How many times had they shared sweet moments that made their hearts blossom like lilac bushes in the spring? How many?

Whatever the count, it wasn't high enough.

Adam handed her Stormy's reins.

"Will you get leashes for Tate and Tabor?" Kit asked.

"You said the trip to our time made you sick," Sarah said.

A wave of nausea hit her, remembering the rollercoaster ride. "I'll get through it."

Another cramp. "Give me a hug." She and Sarah embraced one last time. A friendship born of necessity had grown into something so much more. Sisters, friends, lifelong confidants.

"You'll always be a member of my family," John said.

Henry gave her a rib-breaking hug. "I love you, missy." He walked away, head down, shoulders bowed and shaking.

"Good-bye, Miss Kit." Adam removed his hat and resettled it on his head, exactly the way Cullen had done.

A thin streak of light danced across the twilight sky. *A shooting star.* "I'm leaving money for you to go to a university. My wish is that I read about you in the history books. I don't care where you make your mark, as long as you contribute in an honorable way. Make me proud."

"Yes, ma'am." He handed over the leashes, and without another word, Kit walked away into the woods, leading her animals, her granny's prophetic words on her mind:

The day will come, Kitherina, when you believe everything is lost, but in fact, it will be a new beginning.

With tears in her eyes, Kit opened the brooch, and repeated the magical words.

The date was August 10, 1852, and she was ten weeks' pregnant.

Chapter Thirty-Eight

MacKlenna Farm, May 15

K IT GRIPPED THE leashes with white-knuckled fingers in a death-defying backward spin. Gravity pulled her up into interweaving turns and twists toward flickering amber light.

The inbound trip turned out to be identical to the outbound. As soon as the spinning stopped, she leaned over and threw up in the flowerbed in front of MacKlenna Mansion's west portico. Her memory was fuzzy. She rubbed her arms, feeling as if she'd just scrambled through a nightmare.

Tate barked, Tabor meowed, and both pulled against their leashes. She untied them and they ran off looking like an animal version of Butch and Sundance. Elliott would be furious at how ragged they were.

She untied Stormy's shank. "Go on. Get to the barn." He was dirty and thinner, but he was back in his bluegrass looking magnificent, a rippling mass of muscle, sinew, and bone glistening in the afternoon sun. He swerved his massive head toward her and whinnied softly through flaring nostrils.

"Go on." Kit waved.

He reared, climbing the air with his front legs, something he rarely did.

You're glad to be home, aren't you? What about her? Was she glad to be home? Before pondering the question deeper, her belly cramped, reminding her exactly why she had returned. She couldn't begin to understand the power and purpose of the blood-red stone, but it no longer mattered. Her time-traveling days were over.

The brooch had deposited her near the large oak door. She opened it and crossed the threshold. The scent of lemon polish rolled over her, and she inhaled deeply. The smell of time embedded in the furniture, the walls, and in the cherry and beech parquet floor grounded her.

I'm home.

She went in search of her back-up cell phone and found it on her father's desk, plugged into the charger. *Elliott, you're the best.*

The phone listed a hundred unread emails and fifty missed calls. The numbers didn't surprise her. The date did. She'd only been gone six weeks. How could so much happen in such a short time?

She scrolled through the contact list and punched in Dr. Olson's number. Following a brief explanation of her symptoms, the nurse scheduled an immediate appointment.

Not the way I smell.

Ten minutes later, the steam from her shower dissipated, and Kit caught her reflection in the mirror. She grabbed the towel bar for support. Purple bruises covered her right cheek, neck, and both arms. Her face had burned and peeled, and stress had worn fine lines around her mouth. Callused hands and chipped nails needed a major overhaul. She clipped wet hair to the top of her head. The dull strands could air dry in the car.

For sixteen weeks, she had covered herself from bonnet to boots. Now, slipping into a black cotton sundress, she seemed almost naked. Pain and grief joined forces and grabbed her in a choke hold, pushing her down into an ocean of memories where silence screamed the loudest and the pressure was unbearable.

Cullen.

Her body ached for him. His face would light with joy if he could see her now, fresh from the shower, wearing next to nothing. His desire would be demanding her attention.

The covers on the cherry four-poster bed held a freshly laundered lavender smell. He always kicked the covers off their cot and languidly stretched out wearing only a sated smile. The blood drained from her legs, and she grabbed the end post for support, envisioning him asleep in her bed, linens piled on the floor.

Get out of the house now. If I start crying, I'll never make it to the doctor.

Her hair dried during the convertible ride, but she pretty much looked like crap. The office staff smiled sympathetically and escorted her to the examining room. A few minutes later, Dr. Olson, her father's dear friend, walked in with his nose buried in her chart.

"Well, Kit, what brings you in this afternoon?" He closed the folder and glanced up. The usually unflappable ob-gyn swallowed noisily. He dropped the chart on the exam table and wrapped her in a hug. "What happened, child?"

"Everything." The word came out on a sob. She took a moment to gather her composure and, at his quiet urging, told her first twenty-first century lie. "I went on an Oregon Trail reenactment, fell in love, and ended up pregnant. My baby's father was killed five days ago."

Dr. O gasped.

Kit bit her quivering lip, but the pain didn't stop her tears. "I've been cramping and spotting for over an hour."

He lifted her chin and turned her head to the side "These are handprints on you. Now, why don't you tell me what really happened?"

The years slipped away, and she was once again the brutally attacked college student. She pushed aside the violent memory. "It's different this time. I loved this man, and I want his baby. They killed him. Don't let them kill his child, too."

Dr. O handed her a tissue. "Let's do an ultrasound, take a look, and run a few tests. See what's going on. I'll do everything I can to help you."

In the middle of the ultrasound, he said, "There're two embryos, but only one's viable. It's too early to tell if the other will survive—"

One survived.

"I want you to go home," he continued, "limit your activity, and rest. There aren't any twins in the family that I can remember."

"Did I cause this to happen?" She didn't want to know, but she had to know.

"It's not your fault."

She wasn't quite sure she believed that. All she knew was that people who loved her died, and she couldn't let that happen to her baby.

Armed with vitamins, instructions, and a return appointment, Kit drove home in a daze.

She called Elliott.

"What took ye so long?" he asked.

"I had to go to the doctor."

"Ye okay?"

She scrunched her face. "Yep. I have a lot to tell you, but can we wait until breakfast? I'm exhausted."

There was silence on the other end of the phone. Finally, he said, "I'll meet ye in the kitchen at seven. If ye wake in the middle of the night and want to talk, call me."

She went straight to bed and, except for waking twice to go the bathroom, slept until six the next morning. Nightmares invaded her sleep, and she wrestled with faceless demons. In one nightmare, someone ripped off her arms and legs. She was fitted with prosthetics, but no matter how hard she tried to use them, they wouldn't work.

Elliott was pouring coffee when she walked into the kitchen. "I saw the sketches ye left on the desk. Did ye kill those men?"

"Yes."

He handed her a cup. "I cleared my calendar for the day."

She rested her forearms on the table and intertwined her callused fingers. "I'll skip the long story and go straight to the short version." She took a deep breath. "I fell in love, got married, fought the men in those pictures, watched my husband die, and I'm pregnant."

"Damn." Elliott pulled her into his arms.

"I love him so much." Deep wrenching sobs poured out as grief rolled off her in tsunami-sized waves. Elliott said nothing. He just hugged her until the shivering stopped and her tears turned to sniffles.

He reached for a nearby box of tissues. "Here, blow yer nose, then start at the beginning—the day ye went off and left me behind."

It was well on noon when Kit finished her story. Her throat was raw, and the tissue box was empty. Elliott's gray hair spiked from raking his fingers through it repeatedly. They sat in silence just as they had done at the funeral home.

He finally broke the silence. "Want a sandwich? I picked up some egg salad from Whole Foods yesterday."

She gave him a hungry smile. "It's the best in town."

He fixed sandwiches then poured himself a cup of coffee and Kit a glass of milk. He settled back into his chair at the table. "What do ye suppose happened to the Murrays' baby?"

"She must have died shortly after birth and her parents never wrote the date of her death in their Bible. Now that I have their full names, I might be able to find something through the BYU Family History Archives. If she'd been alive when her family was murdered, those men would've killed her, too. They were evil."

"Ye dinna ken if yer baby will survive or what happened to yer husband. And ye'll never learn the identity of the man in the portrait. Can ye live with that?"

"Dr. Olson asked if there were twins in the family. I couldn't answer, and I realize I'll never be able to." She blew her nose, then collected the handful of tissues and threw them into the trash.

"The first Sean MacKlenna and his sister were twins. Her picture's hanging in the hallway," Elliott said.

Kit gave a so-what shrug.

Several moments of silence passed between them while she picked at her ragged nails. "Cullen was an incredible man. If anyone could have survived the shot, the fall, and the rapids, he could, but there were no signs he came ashore. Can I live with that? I don't have any other choice. I can't go back."

"Why not?"

"In my heart, I believe I went back in time to be with him. The brooch was the vehicle to meet him, love him, and have his child. Maybe this child, if he survives, will go back one day and finish the search."

"So what do ye do now? Are ye going to sell yer condo in town and live here permanently?"

"I'm not ready to sell, but I don't want to live there right now. There's a gaping hole in my heart, and if it's ever going to heal, it'll happen here."

"MacKlenna Farm is yer child's legacy, too. And ye both deserve to be happy," Elliott said.

"Sarah Barrett was a remarkable woman. One of the many things she taught me was that life isn't just about being happy. It's about being joyful in spite of your circumstances. Cullen's child deserves a joy-filled life."

"If someone hadna left me behind, I would have met yer friend." Elliott's tongue pushed against his cheek.

"I've apologized a half dozen times already."

"At least if I had gone, the animals wouldna have come back in such rough shape."

Kit looked down at the empty food bowls in the corner. "Where are they? I haven't seen either of them since we got back."

"Tate and Tabor are at the vet's. They'll stay a few days to get checked out and prettied up." Elliott put on his cap and walked to the door. "Ye ken what ye should do?"

"Besides put my feet up and wait?"

"Go to that fancy spa in California. Get yer skin and hair looking pretty, then go see yer psychiatrist. Ye have a few issues to work on before yer baby arrives."

"Well, tell me how you really feel." She looked around for something to throw at him that wouldn't break and settled on the empty tissue box.

He caught it and tossed it in the trash. "Call yer travel agent. The pampering will do ye good."

"Sounds tempting."

"Take the corporate jet." He grabbed an apple off the counter and left her sitting at the table, thinking of ten reasons why she shouldn't leave town again. None of them seemed that important. She scrolled through her phone's contact list and called her travel agent, who booked a reservation at the Meadowood in Napa Valley, and then she called the farm's pilot.

Chapter Thirty-Nine

ELLIOTT MET KIT at the airport following her four-week stint at the spa. She spotted his parked vehicle on the tarmac, then she saw him walking out of the executive terminal. *Why do men get more distinguished as they age?*

He was dressed in his usual uniform: pressed khakis, light green polo shirt with the MacKlenna Farm logo, Italian loafers, and perfectly styled thick gray hair. He was as handsome as she'd ever seen him.

He gobbled her up in a monster hug. "Ye look gorgeous."

"You look rather handsome yourself."

He smiled, showing perfect white teeth. "Stress lines are gone. For once in my life, I wasna worrying about ye." He grabbed her bags. "Just these two?"

"I have a crate, too."

"Paintings?"

She nodded. "The spa manager wanted to buy one of my Chimney Rock paintings, but I couldn't sell it. Not even for a free week."

"Ye passed up several thousand dollars."

"I'll never sell any of my Oregon Trail paintings." She looped her arm into his. "I've been buffed and polished, and had several appointments with the ob-gyn Dr. Olson recommended. The baby is fine. Now tell me what's been going on. How are my animals?"

"Stormy's recovered most of his weight. But I had to send the damn dog to obedience school and thought about sending the cat, too. Ye turned them into wild animals."

She climbed into the truck and buckled up. "It wasn't all my doing. I had two little helpers."

"Don't get maudlin on me." He walked around the front and climbed in the driver's seat. "Ye look good—rested and more relaxed than I've seen ye in a long time." He turned on the blinker and eased into airport traffic. "Matter of fact, ye look really good. Pregnancy becomes ye."

"I think that's part of the deal. You get fat and feel ugly but you have a radiant glow that makes you look beautiful. Go figure. But I'm back now and ready to go to work."

"Not on that damned fire truck."

She patted her belly. "No more fire trucks. I think I'm giving up on the idea of med school, too, at least for now. I don't want to do anything that will take time away from this little guy. I'll help out on the farm and paint. I might not know where my roots are, but I know where I'm rooted."

AFTER A MONTH, Kit's expanding waistline demanded she shop for maternity clothes. She'd been born without a shopping gene and hated going to the mall. Now loaded down with packages, she walked through the front door, and without thinking, tossed her keys on the side cabinet, then cringed when they slid across the marble top and fell off the back.

She dumped her packages on the staircase and pulled the table away from the wall. There were enough dust bunnies to fill an Easter egg basket. There was also an envelope from the Bank of San Francisco.

"Yikes. I hope the bank followed up by now." With the envelope in one hand, keys and cell phone in the other, she walked into the office, plopped down on the sofa, and kicked off her strappy sandals before scrolling through the fifteen emails on her phone.

While reading an email from the CFO, she dug a letter opener under the envelope flap and pulled out a sheet of paper. Her eyes did a back-and-forth dance between the email and the letter.

She dropped the phone and sat transfixed, unable to breathe.
Oh my God.

Clipped to the letter was a brittle yellow envelope, addressed in an ornate script to:

Kitherina MacKlenna Montgomery

MacKlenna Farm

Lexington, Fayette County, Kentucky

Chapter Forty

Deschutes River Crossing, August 6, 1852

T HE BULLET SLICED through the fleshy part of Cullen's upper arm, igniting a searing pain that spread through his chest. He grasped his arm and hot, sticky blood oozed between his fingers. He weaved as a belly spasm threatened to double him over. Sweat streamed from his forehead and dripped into his eyes. Jess's fist plowed into his chest, cracking his ribs and sending him tumbling backward. He teetered on the cliff's edge. His hands flailed for a branch, a ledge, anything to grab, but only air slipped through his fingers. He flipped end over end, hitting the water on his upper back. The impact drove the breath from his body.

Death held him in its embrace.

Thousands of images flashed like shooting stars in a monolithic review of his existence. His life compressed into seconds. All went dark. A single point of light flickered then turned brilliant. A light not of this world.

Cullen, take my hand. Swim to me, brother. I will help ye.

Kristen? I'm caught in the vines.

Take my hand.

Cullen pulled himself from the river and collapsed facedown on the bank. He rolled over, wincing with pain, and knew no more.

THE SUN HAD dimmed to an eerie glow in the western sky by the time Cullen groaned into consciousness. Had his head and a sledgehammer collided? His stomach reared and spilled its contents in violent spasms. What the hell happened? Where was Kit? Jumbled thoughts couldn't push past the pain in his head, and trying to sort out the situation only increased the pounding.

He surrendered and sank back into blackness.

Hours later, he opened his eyes. Smooth moonlight formed a canopy over his hideaway in the bushes. He heard lapping water nearby. Wherever he was, he was cold, damp, and bleeding.

He tried to sit, but the slightest movement drove spikes of agony deeper into his brain. Somewhere in his broken memory he recalled Kit's Tylenol. She always used the round, white tablets to ease pain. He rummaged in the backpack he'd slipped off his shoulders when he climbed ashore, brushing aside waterproof bags of bandages and creams until he found the small bag with a bottle of pain medication. He took two pills, bandaged his arm, and closed his eyes.

Consciousness arrived with the sun. The head pain remained. Even though he didn't want food, he knew he had to eat. He also had to clear his head so he could remember what happened. He sat and leaned against a tree while he ate an MRE labeled *beef stew*. It was the worst tasting food he'd ever put in his mouth, but Kit had said it would give him the nutrients he needed. Five minutes after he finished, he vomited again. The pain in his head intensified. He swallowed two more Tylenol and fell asleep.

The sun rose, set, and rose again and maybe it rose for a third day or even a fourth. He lost track of time. Lost track of everything except pasty food and little white pills.

And then the dreams started. Kit was manhandled. He was shot.

Panic and fear squeezed his mind with large deadly hands. Heat rushed through him in surges of liquid fire. Kit was in danger. Her terror-filled eyes flashed before him. He had to find her. With excruciating effort, he pulled himself to his feet, but his legs wouldn't support his weight. He fell to his knees, jarring his head. Agonizing screams scared the birds and squirrels. Exhausted, he fell into unconsciousness until the sun rose again.

How long had he floated between two worlds? He remembered the cliff, but not much more. He sensed Kit was in danger and that he had to find his way back. He scratched the whiskers on his face—probably three days of growth.

Where are you, lass?

If he had to crawl back to the cliff, he would. He packed up his few supplies and rose to his knees. He put one foot on the ground, grabbed the tree, and pushed to his feet, swaying. Dizziness made him nauseous. He'd never been this sick or in as much pain.

The bright sunlight stabbed into his eyes with knifelike precision. He had no hat and tried to shield his eyes with his hand while he studied the surrounding terrain. How in the hell did he get on the opposite side of the river? He had no memory of crossing. Finding his way back would take time. Time he didn't have. He took his first step, unsure of where it would lead or what he would find. A quote by Lao-tzu, the Chinese philosopher, came to mind: *A journey of a thousand miles begins with a single step.*

WEARY AND CAUTIOUS, Cullen approached the cliff where he had last seen Kit. The smell of rotting flesh roiled his stomach. He steeled himself and prepared to find a scene worse than South Pass. As he stepped free of the trees, the stink of decomposing bodies hit him with redoubled force. On the ground lay three blood-soaked, maggot-covered men.

What happened here?

Although he didn't remember, relief swept through him like a hard, swirling wind. Kit wasn't there. Tears welled in his eyes, and he wept unashamedly. Her face flashed before him and he heard her scream his name. Although he was far away, he heard anguish in her voice.

He searched the ground for tracks and found several, mostly trampled over each other, but there was one clear set—Henry's horse, Charley.

If Henry came looking for them he would have found Kit and carried her off. Cullen studied the ground again looking for signs she had fallen or been dragged, but found nothing. He stood at the cliff's edge for an unmeasured time, squeezing his temples to relieve the pressure in his head. The breeze rippled through the pine, whispering a single word, *hurry*. He'd delayed too long. The confrontation had occurred three, maybe four days ago. That would put Kit at least two days ahead of him, assuming she and Henry spent time looking for him. With the way he felt, he wouldn't be able to walk fast enough to catch them. His only hope was to find a fellow traveler willing to sell him a horse.

If Kit believed he was dead, she would go to San Francisco as soon as she arrived in Oregon City. No matter where she went, he would find her. He didn't believe she would go back to her time, not before talking to Braham. She would take a stagecoach from Oregon City. Astride a good horse, he could catch her en route.

With a cold sweat streaming between his shoulder blades, he set out to find his bride.

FIVE DAYS LATER, as the afternoon sun filtered through the grand firs towering overhead, Cullen caught up with his wagon train camped at Laurel Hill. He could have purchased an entire herd for what he had paid for the sorry-looking horse he bought off a family he'd met on the trail, but without the nag, he wouldn't have caught up with his friends for another week.

He found John and Henry at the top of Laurel Hill's first drop, a two-hundred-forty-foot vertical descent. Leaning against a tree trunk, arms folded, the sole of his boot flat against the bark, Cullen watched the two men study the deeply eroded trail.

John stared down the hill's scree-covered chute. "Don't care what you say, Henry. Damn near impossible to do this."

"We'll lock the wheels and anchor the wagons with ropes. Plenty of folks have done it before us." Henry pointed to several trees lining the chute. "Look at the rope burns."

Cullen cleared his throat. "How'd ye get anything done without me?"

John and Henry spun around, flashing raised brushy brows.

Henry lunged forward with open arms. "Where the hell have you been?"

Cullen eased back, his good arm extended, protectively. "Dinna give me one of yer bear hugs."

Henry stopped midstride.

"I'm pretty beat up," Cullen said.

Henry settled for a handshake.

"Where's Kit?" Cullen asked.

"Come on. Let's head back to camp. You can tell us what happened to you," Henry said.

"As soon as I kiss my wife, I'll tell ye." Neither John or Henry spoke, but color slipped from their faces. "Ye got something to say. Spit it out."

John shuffled his feet.

Fear struck Cullen square in the solar plexus. "Tell me she's alive."

Henry nodded but avoided eye contact. "Alive and unharmed."

Alive and unharmed. Henry wouldn't lie, but he would withhold information. Cullen had no doubt he was doing exactly that.

"Let's walk over to camp. Get a cup of coffee. We'll talk." Henry said.

Had those damned bastards killed his baby? Was that what Henry hesitated to tell him? Whatever had happened, he and Kit would recover from the tragedy together.

Cullen spotted Sarah the moment the men arrived in camp. She stood at the cookstove stirring a steamy pot just as he had seen her do a hundred times before. Where was Kit? He looked around the circle. Another shot of fear coursed through him, burning hot as the bullet that had pierced his skin.

"Where is she, Sarah?"

She dropped her spoon, her eyes unnaturally wide. "*Cullen.*"

"By God, somebody better tell me where she is before I rip this camp apart."

Tears welled in Henry's eyes. "No need for that."

"Tell me where she is. *Now.*"

Sarah squeezed his arm. "She started bleeding and cramping—"

"We followed the river for miles. Couldn't find any sign you came ashore," Henry said.

"I dinna have any memory of being shot or of falling. There were three dead men on the cliff. Who killed them?"

"The one who shot you fell and hit his head. The other two bled out."

A small hand tugged Cullen's shirtsleeve. He glanced down at Frances and saw wide, faith-filled eyes. "Miss Kit went home. Can you bring her back?"

Went home? He raised his eyebrows in a silent question.

A sob broke from Sarah's lips. "Kit had symptoms, same as me. She didn't want to lose the baby. She went home five days ago. Back to where she came from."

Cullen slumped against a chair; his heart lurched in his chest. "She lost faith in me," he said in a tormented whisper.

Henry shook his head. "Kit wanted to believe you were alive, but she needed a doctor to save the babe."

Cullen walked away from his friends and headed into the forest, carrying his silent screams. He breathed deeply of the scented pine, drawing air into his lungs, holding it while he listened to the sounds in the conifer woods. Even the trees seemed to know Kit's name. He took another breath. This time the scent he breathed in wasn't pine, but vanilla. And the magical sound echoing through the trees wasn't chipmunks and songbirds, it was her laughter living in the music of the forest. It was the beauty of her smile held in the glint of the afternoon sun. It was the tender touch of her hand gliding through the whispering wind.

He stumbled over twisted roots and fell into dark shadows, upon a wall of pine needles and heavy underbrush. He had no reason to get up and begged for unconsciousness to rescue him once again. But sleep wouldn't come. He rode a plunging angry wave, approaching the beach with tremendous velocity.

And he broke.

A guttural sob forced its way up from deep inside his gut and hung in the back of his throat for one long, tormented moment before bursting through his lips. The sobs kept coming, each more ferocious than the last, until he had no voice left, and his heart beat without purpose against the pine-covered forest floor.

CULLEN WOKE SEVERAL hours later, heartsick over his failure to keep Kit safe. If he added in his four failed attempts as a ghost, he had quite a history. Then he remembered Kit's ghost sighting the day she left her time. Why did she have a vision of him at Thomas MacKlenna's gravesite? That never made any sense, now even less so.

Or did it?

Cullen tensed for a moment, then sat straight up. What was today's date? He wasn't sure. The second week in August, possibly. He rubbed his temples, hoping to assuage the pain in his head. Thomas MacKlenna would die in five months—January 25, 1853. Cullen thought through possibilities. What connection could he have with MacKlenna? None that he could think of, but Kit *did* have a vision of him. Suddenly, he had a real sense that he would find the answer to Kit's return at MacKlenna Farm, but only if he arrived before Thomas died.

If he was going cross-country again, he had no time to waste.

His plan sent a shiver of anticipation coursing through him. Now filled with purpose, he rushed back to the Barretts' campsite.

"Coffee's hot," John said.

Cullen poured a cup and sat at the table.

"'Bout to go look for you," Henry said.

Cullen sipped his coffee. "Had some thinking to do."

Henry puffed on his pipe. "You going to San Francisco?"

"Going there first, then on to the MacKlenna Farm."

"Must have a pretty good reason for making your fourth crossing in two years."

Cullen shrugged. "All I ken is that I have to go."

"A man knowing what to do is enough reason for me. I'll go with you."

The moon offered faint shafts of illumination in the forest, enough to cast a pale light across Henry's determined face. His salt-and-pepper hair had turned mostly salt during the journey.

"Appreciate the offer, but there's nae need. I'm sailing east this time. Soon as we get the wagons down the hill, I'm going to San Francisco to talk to Braham. Then I'll sail on the first ship leaving port."

Henry didn't say anything. He just calmly knocked the dottle from his pipe with a single hard tap.

"Can you get her back?" John asked.

"Probably not in this lifetime." Cullen's voice sounded oddly out of place to him, as if perhaps he already was the ghost of MacKlenna Farm.

Chapter Forty-One

TWO WEEKS LATER, Cullen arrived in California amidst the salty air and the rumble of wagons rolling over the plank streets. He had traveled all over the Far East and Europe, and while his Highland home surpassed every place he'd ever been, the sparkling bay and the seven surrounding hills made San Francisco one of the most beautiful landscapes in the world.

With some impatience, he dodged the men thronging the streets wearing their plaid shirts and miners' boots. Although he had visited the emerging city only a few months ago, in his absence buildings had sprung up and new businesses had opened. San Francisco had grown and changed like all living creatures. And he had, too.

He pressed his fingers against his throbbing temples. Almost three weeks after the attack, headaches, blurred vision, and nausea still plagued him, and his memory remained hazy. All four ailments probably resulted from hitting his head when he fell. Other than taking Tylenol when the pain became unbearable, the only cure was time.

Time was also his enemy.

He rode past the docks and theaters and churches toward the Adams & Company building on Montgomery Street. Upon reaching his destination, he tied his horse and pack mule to the hitching post, and glanced up toward the stylish second-story law offices of Matthews & Phillips. Cullen would never forget his and Braham's excitement during their first visit to Phillips' office. They were determined not to leave until they had offers of employment. Not only did they get lucrative offers, but they also received an invitation to a soirée to meet the firm's clients.

Cullen paused at the first landing to steady his legs, then slowly made his way to the top floor. Underneath the Matthews & Phillips Counselors at Law sign was Braham's full name. Cullen winced, not at the sight of Braham's name, but at the absence of his own.

His hand shook as he opened the door and walked into the well-appointed office filled with John and Thomas Seymour chairs and sofas and straight-legged Hepplewhite tables. On previous visits, he had reveled in the accoutrements of wealth and power, but after weeks of listening to Kit extol the creative genius of eighteenth- and nineteenth-century furniture makers, he had a new appreciation for objects he'd once viewed and used for their utility alone.

The heady fragrance of China roses filled the room. The fragile petals of a yellow bloom reminded him of Phillips' garden where he'd stolen a kiss from Abigail. He felt ashamed of the way he had used women. He'd even set out to seduce Kit simply for the pleasure of enjoying her body, only to discover the true pleasure was her mind and her heart—fragile petals of a blooming rose.

The firm's secretary stopped in midstride halfway across the room. Wide-set, intelligent eyes discreetly perused Cullen's dusty trousers and muddy boots. Then he said, "Mr. Montgomery, I wasn't expecting you today."

Cullen scratched his whiskers. "I'm not here to see clients. In fact, if there are any in the office, dinna introduce me."

The secretary gave a nervous laugh. "May I show you to your office?"

Culled waved him away. "I ken where it is." Instead of opening the door bearing a brass plaque with his name, he knocked and entered Braham's office.

His friend looked up from reading a large volume spread open on his desk. His jaw dropped in surprise. "Hell, didna expect to see ye so soon."

Cullen met him as he rounded the desk. They embraced, slapping each other's back. Some of Cullen's tension drained away.

Braham stepped back and searched Cullen's face. "What's wrong?"

"It's a long story."

"Where's Kit?"

Cullen headed for the sideboard. "I need a whisky."

Braham blocked his path. "Tell me where she is and ye can drink all ye want."

"She's gone."

Braham clenched and unclenched his fists.

Cullen pushed against Braham's arm. "Nae need to beat it out of me, I'm going to tell ye everything. Just give me a damned drink."

Braham splashed generous amounts of single-malt scotch from a decanter on the mahogany sideboard into two crystal goblets. They toasted and emptied their glasses in a single swallow. Cullen held out his glass for a refill. Braham raised an eyebrow, then poured more of the golden liquid. After downing the second drink, Cullen sat in a straight-back chair in front of the desk and helped himself to a cigar from the oak-and-brass humidor.

Braham handed him a match. "I thought ye quit."

"I thought ye did, too."

Braham set the whisky bottle on the table as he took a seat. "Tell me she's nae dead."

"She's not."

"Where is she?"

"Home."

"That's a relief."

Cullen sighed. "Her home. Her time."

Braham sank deep into his chair. "Why?"

"She thought I was dead."

Braham picked up the bottle of whisky, frowning as he swirled the liquid. "We dinna have enough to drink, do we?"

Cullen shook his head.

"Ye probably havena eaten either. Come on." Braham grabbed Cullen's arm as he rose to his feet. "I bought a house on Rincon Hill off a banker heading back east. It came furnished with plenty of whisky and a decent Chinese cook. Plus, I have a right of first refusal on his brother's identically furnished house, if ye're interested."

"Not now, but if it's a good investment, hold on to it." Cullen allowed Braham to drag him upright. Blood rushed from his head. He staggered and dropped his glass.

"Ye can hold yer whisky better than that," Braham said.

"It isna the whisky."

"Then ye need to see a doctor."

Cullen leaned against the edge of the desk. "There's nothing a doctor can do."

"Let's get ye some food, a bath, and a good night's sleep. See how ye feel tomorrow."

"Doesna matter how I feel. If there's a ship leaving for Panama, I canna miss it."

LIGHT FROM THE gas streetlamps and a full moon filtered through the windows and added to the warm yellow glow cast by the brass chandelier's fourteen tiered candles. Braham and Cullen pushed away from the drop-leaf dining table and carried cigars and brandy to the library where bookshelves lined two walls and overflowed with richly bound volumes. Cullen perused the titles and authors.

"This is an impressive collection—Defoe, Pope, Swift, the entire works of Robert Burns, a complete set of Shakespeare, plus the Greek philosophers. The previous owner was verra well read."

Braham smirked. "Or wanted to be."

Cullen took in the rest of the room with an eye toward what Kit would notice. The tall case clock had a deep, two-inch scratch at the bottom, but was otherwise exquisite. The Brazilian rosewood grand piano had a cracked leg, needing extensive repair. The Victorian reading table snuggled in the small space before the window faced south, limiting the afternoon sun. The Persian carpet, although beautiful, hid the wide-plank oak floor, and she'd much prefer a patterned fabric upholstery on the leather sofas and winged chairs.

God, when and how did he come to know her so well?

He imagined her in the room, though, reading and listening to music. Regardless of what Henry had said, she would listen to Bach and play the guitar again. Music was enmeshed with her soul.

"This is a beautiful house." *Kit could be happy here with the music and the stables and gardens he'd seen earlier.*

Braham sat in a wing chair next to the fire and crossed one leg over the other, straightening his trouser leg. "There has to be a way to get her back."

"What do ye suggest? That we write her a letter? Dear Kit, I'm alive. Come back. Should we mail the letter to MacKlenna—"

"Stop it. Ye're acting like an arse. Self-pity doesna become ye."

Cullen's face heated. He tipped back his brandy and set the empty glass on the mantel. A red-gold fire danced in the hearth. "Do ye remember Kit's vision of me selecting Thomas MacKlenna's gravesite?"

"The ghostly appearance that didna make sense."

"I'm going to Kentucky."

"Ye think that will bring her back?"

"I believe there's more to the vision than picking out a gravesite." He poured another drink from the bottle of brandy Braham had set on the table next to his chair.

Neither man spoke for several minutes, then Cullen asked, "Have ye identified the man in the portrait?"

"His name is Donald Shelly. He owns a fleet of ships, and he's rarely in town. Phillips went to Boston following Abigail's funeral. Until he comes back, we're nae likely to learn anything more."

"I'll send him a telegram when I get to Kentucky."

"I'm going with ye. In yer condition—"

Cullen touched his friend's shoulder. "If ye leave town while Phillips is gone, the business will fail. This has been our dream since our early Harvard days. Ye're the one who said, 'People who dream small dreams, live small lives.' Dinna let our dream die."

CULLEN DIDN'T SLEEP well. He rolled over in the large four-poster cherry bed in Braham's guest room and reached for Kit. Her taste, her scent were forever embedded in his memory, but she might never be beside him again. Not in this world.

His splintered heart cracked wide open, and he wept into the pillow where her head should have rested. When the tears subsided, he reached for the half-full bottle of painkillers. He needed to ration the Tylenol. After today, he'd only take them at night.

He sneaked out of Braham's house before the sun rose, before he had to face his friend and another round of arguments he might not have the will to win. The pain in his head made logical thinking damned near impossible, and he needed all his wits to focus on what lay ahead—a sixty-day trip to MacKlenna Farm. The difficult journey would take him across the Isthmus of Panama during the rainy season, into the Caribbean Sea to the Gulf of Mexico, and up the Mississippi River. Not an easy journey for a man physically fit, but if he waited until he was well enough to travel, he wouldn't reach the farm before Thomas MacKlenna died in January.

He arrived at Long Wharf and discovered the *Golden Gate* was scheduled to depart for Panama with the morning tide. He booked the last stateroom. As he trudged up the gangplank, fighting a bout of dizziness, he wondered if he had set himself on a fool's mission, and a very dangerous one. Someone tapped his shoulder and he turned aside to make room on the gangplank. When he looked behind him, his heart pounded with surprise.

Cullen was too emotional to speak, and Henry, too, was silent. Finally, he said, "It's my fault we didn't find you. Kit begged me to cross the river and search the other side. I didn't think…" His eyes glistened, and he cleared his throat. "You're weak. You need help, and I don't give a damn what you say. I'm going with you."

At one time Cullen would have sent Henry back to Oregon, but that was before his ordinary life became extraordinary. That was before the tightness in his chest immobilized him, before waves of grief consumed him, and before headaches temporarily blinded him.

He leaned on his friend for support. "We'd better board. Dinna want this ship to sail without us."

And they trudged up the gangplank together.

Chapter Forty-Two

TWO DAYS FROM Panama, the ship ran into gale-force winds that tossed Cullen and Henry about their stateroom. White-capped waves swamped the ship, and it groaned as timbers torqued almost beyond endurance. The main mast snapped, sending shudders through the heart of the vessel.

The ship's rain-soaked captain burst through the cabin doorway with a four-sided glass lantern. A sliver of light washed over them. "The ship's holding her own. We should pass through this in a few hours." He stormed out as quickly as he had burst in.

Henry took Cullen's arm. "Get in your berth. I'm strapping you down."

Cullen knew he couldn't huddle on the water-soaked floor, but standing triggered nausea. "Leave me alone."

"Next time you hit the wall you might just kill yourself. Come on, I'll help you."

Cullen didn't have the strength to resist.

High waves battered the ship throughout the long night, but the ropes kept his body immobile and the pain tolerable.

The ship arrived in Panama on the seventeenth day. Cullen sat on deck and waited with Henry for a smaller vessel to pick them up. Cullen paid the transportation company to arrange his and Henry's travel across the isthmus to the harbor in Chagres.

As they waited to disembark, they watched the sunrise peek out of gray mist. Cullen rubbed his arms, tingling with memory of the beautiful sunrise following his wedding night. That was a magical morning, not only because Kit lay naked in his arms, but also because it had been the first full day of their life together.

A life cut much too short.

"You two found each other before. You'll find each other again," Henry said.

"If ye can read my mind, then we've been traveling together too long."

"Not hard to tell what you're thinking when you get that misty-eyed look."

Cullen cleared his throat. "I couldna have made it through the storm alone. Thanks for tagging along."

His old friend puffed on his pipe. "It's during storms we need friends the most."

As they disembarked, a messenger met them with their overland itinerary.

"Let me see that," Henry said.

With his blurry vision, Cullen couldn't read anyway. He passed the envelope over.

Henry read the piece of paper then huffed. "A five-day trip across the jungle, and two of those days we're riding damned mules. If we survive those willful beasts, there's a flat-bottom boat ride down the river, then a train ride to Chagres. If we survive that ordeal, we're booked on the *Philadelphia* to New Orleans." He turned the paper over. "Looks like we're on our own from there."

"We'll catch a paddleboat to Louisville."

The overland trip was a dreadful week of fighting mosquitoes, eating bad food, and sloshing along muddy roads. Without being robbed or dumped in the jungle, Henry's biggest fears, they arrived in Chagres, and after a four-day layover, boarded the steamer *Philadelphia* for the ten-day voyage to New Orleans.

Henry and Cullen were sitting on deck when the ship sailed into the Gulf of Mexico. "Have you thought about what you're going to say to the MacKlennas?" Henry asked.

"I've thought of nothing else," Cullen said.

"Are you going to tell them about Kit?"

"I dinna ken." Cullen closed his eyes and let the sea breeze drift over him. The headache had lessened since leaving Chagres, and he was resting better. The dizziness still bothered him, but he could walk without squeezing the blood from Henry's arm, and his appetite had improved. The water was his healing place, and he felt it at work now. Although he had no memory of falling from the cliff into the river, he sensed Kristen's presence. Maybe she'd been there. Maybe she had rescued him, just like in his dream. Maybe.

Henry lit his pipe. "Never been to New Orleans."

"Braham and I were there four years ago." Cullen remembered very little about the visit other than bottles of bourbon and several faceless, nameless French women. He winced at the memory.

At New Orleans, Cullen booked passage on the *A.L. Shotwell,* and although Henry wanted to spend a couple of days in the city, Cullen was pleased the paddle wheeler was scheduled to depart for the upriver trip the next morning.

Six days later, as they neared Louisville's port, Cullen was standing on deck, humming.

"What's that music?" Henry asked.

"One of Kit's songs. *I can feel you all around me, sweetening the air I breathe.* I feel her, Henry—in here." Cullen tapped his chest. "I will see her again."

Henry's jaw stiffened. "Come on, let's go ashore. We've a train to catch."

Cullen took a deep breath. *I will see you again.*

The train stopped in Midway, Kentucky, and they disembarked.

"Quaint little town," Henry said.

"I hope this quaint little town has a livery to hire a horse or carriage."

Henry glanced down the street. "Wait here." A few minutes later, a carriage stopped in front of the depot. Henry opened the door and leaned out. "We have a ride."

Cullen climbed aboard, glad for the bit of warmth inside the carriage. The weather was brisk. Autumn had shoved summer aside, leaving the day dressed in a glorious, red-golden coat.

"Where to, suh?" the driver asked.

"MacKlenna Farm. Do ye know it?" Cullen asked.

"Yes, suh. Everybody know they MacKlennas. Law, they rich folk. Old Mister Thomas, he look like he having the finest time now his granddaughter come a home. You'n go there now, not a speck a interest in dying no more. He gone be a great-grandaddy fore spring."

Cullen let the driver talk while he settled into the seat and made a notation in his journal: *November 11, 1852, noon, arrived Midway, Kentucky. What will I find?*

Chapter Forty-Three

BRAHAM'S WORK, LIFE, and even his house sagged under the heavy weight of guilt. Leaving the wagon train became the mistake he had feared, and allowing Cullen to sail alone compounded one mistake with another. What kind of man abandons his brother not once, but twice, then has the audacity to call himself a friend, an *anam cara*?

Braham shook his head with disgust.

His ability to analyze problems and make decisions made him a good lawyer, but those abilities failed him now. Cullen's dilemma had him stymied. His current predicament would puzzle even his philosophy professor at the University of Edinburgh. Braham visualized the old scholar standing before the classroom, wagging both his finger and tongue. *Knowing what the dilemma is not, what the wrong answers are, is the first step toward knowing what the answer may be.*

Groaning at the thought of the irritating little man, Braham tossed the treatise he was reading to the bedside table and sat on the edge of the bed.

What is the dilemma not?

Wearily, he dragged his hands down his face. "Damnation." It was not about his inability to sleep for five days. He knew that much.

He stomped off to his library, where he lit a cigar and paced.

How can you search for something, if you think you know?

Pacing didn't calm his restlessness or remove the professor's voice from his head, so he tried a shot of brandy. Then another. He stepped to the bookshelf and pulled out Volume 1 of *The Republic*. If the professor intended to haunt him, Braham might as well read Plato and try to free his mind of preconceived impossibilities.

No answer is an answer if it doesn't come from within yourself.

He sat in the wing chair with the book and poured another shot.

Risk being ridiculed to change your way of thinking.

Thoughts tumbled through his head. He threw out questions, argued with himself, even allowed the professor to interject comments before finally closing his eyes and dozing.

The sound of the grandfather clock's descending bells woke him at two o'clock. He rolled his head, relieving the neck strain from sleeping in the chair with his head cocked. His eyes shot open.

"That's it."

He stepped to his desk, and after tapping his pen against the glass inkwell, began his missive. His words scratched across the fine writing paper. He felt calm. No, that was a damnable lie. He felt himself sinking into anticipatory angst.

His hand shook as he licked the teardrop-shaped flap on the envelope's back, and then wrote the addressee's name.

BRAHAM WOKE TO a gorgeous fall day in San Francisco. Warm, sunny, and the fog had cleared. He was not one to give credence to omens, but today he did. After a leisurely breakfast while reading his daily newspaper, he slipped the letter into his jacket pocket and left the house.

An institution was the logical place to hold the letter for one hundred sixty years, and the institutions most likely to be operating in the twenty-first century were banks and universities. He intended to start with local banks with eastern connections. His most pressing problem was convincing someone he was serious, but negotiating was his forte. Besides, Kit had given him the one piece of information that would leverage his position, at least with one particular banker.

He headed down the sidewalk with a solid and determined

stride, hands clasped behind him, lips pursed. He knew where he was headed and didn't need to watch the ground to see his way. Shortly, he entered the lobby of Lucas, Turner & Company.

His eyes adjusted to the darkened room as he glanced around. The lobby's fixtures and furnishings appeared perfunctory, but miners didn't care about a well-dressed bank. They wanted safety and convenience. He agreed with that, but would add longevity to the list of requirements.

William T. Sherman met him at the door. "Good morning, Mr. McCabe."

"Good morning." Braham removed his hat. "If ye have a moment, I have a business proposition to discuss." *You'd think the lean, grizzled man would give some thought to his appearance.*

Sherman ushered Braham into his office and closed the door. "What can I do for you?"

Braham took a seat, throwing one leg over the other. "Ye'll find this to be a strange request."

"Not much I haven't heard."

"This might be a new one." He cleared his throat as he pulled the letter from his pocket and tapped it against his fingertips. "I'd like ye to put this in yer vault with a note that the bank and its successors and assigns hold it until such time as it is to be delivered to the addressee."

Sherman appeared fully attentive, eyes wide. "And when will that be?"

Braham willed his heart to hold a steady beat. "The twenty-first century. The specific year and address are on the envelope."

The banker sat back in his chair, crossed his arms, and looked down his long, slim nose. His face turned as red as the hair. "A very strange request indeed. Are you going to tell me what this is about?"

Braham shook his head. "I hope ye will understand my need for confidentiality." He uncrossed his legs, leaned forward, and tugged on the cuffs peeking out below his jacket sleeves. "I believe, possibly a decade from now, ye'll need a man with my credentials. I'll be prepared to repay ye for honoring this request."

Sherman scratched the back of his neck. "You sure about this?"

"Yes, sir."

He took the envelope and studied the addressee. "Kitherina MacKlenna Montgomery? I believe I met this woman in Independence having dinner with Cullen." Sherman looked Braham in the eye. "I'm mighty fond of the man. If this will help him, I'll do it. But I can't guarantee this letter will survive fifty years, much less a hundred and sixty. I'll put it in the vault with your instructions, and we'll never speak of it again, unless the day comes when I need a man of your experience."

"Fair enough." Braham stood and offered his hand.

They walked out to the lobby, discussing Mr. Phillips' trip to Boston following Abigail's death. A tall blond-haired man entered the bank, waving to Sherman. Braham recognized him as the man who had attended the Phillipses' party.

The man in Kit's miniature portrait.

The letter. Should Braham retrieve it and include information about the man? No, he couldn't afford the appearance of indecisiveness. That would destroy his credibility. He would include whatever information he learned in other letters he intended to place strategically around the country.

Sherman shook hands with the man. "When'd you get back to town?"

"Last night."

Sherman dropped the handshake and gestured in Braham's direction. "Mr. McCabe is a new lawyer in town."

The man turned to Braham and introduced himself. "I'm Captain Shelly. Pleased to meet you…"

Sweet Jesus.

Braham looked into Shelly's green eyes and knew the accumulated patina of almost thirty years was about to be scraped away.

Chapter Forty-Four

MacKlenna Farm, July

K IT OPENED THE letter from the Bank of San Francisco and
began to read:

Dear Ms. MacKlenna,

*The Bank of San Francisco has been holding the attached letter for
Kitherina MacKlenna Montgomery since September 1852. There were
no instructions other than to deliver the letter to this address this year.*

*Although we have no information about its origination, we will be
glad to discuss its discovery with you at your convenience.*

Sincerely,
Philip Nelson
President, Bank of San Francisco

She jumped to her feet and paced. A letter had survived all these
years in a bank vault. Sarah would call its survival a miracle. Kit
patted her baby bump. *Miracles do happen.*

Using a letter opener she picked up off the coffee table, she
eased the blade through the sealed envelope's seam and carefully
removed two sheets of folded paper. She prayed the missive
wouldn't be as transforming as her father's letter had been months
earlier.

September 5, 1852

My Dearest Kitherina,

Five days ago, a special courier delivered your traveling trunk containing a most unusual collection. Rest well knowing I will protect your supplies until we next meet, for I am certain we will.

The courier also delivered the news of your departure and Cullen's disappearance. I, of course, feel personally responsible for both. I deeply regret abandoning the wagon train and allowing you and Cullen to come to such great harm. The discovery that Cullen survived his near-death experience does partially assuage my guilt.

Tears rushed to her eyes. *My God. He's alive.* She wrapped her arms around her belly and wept. "Your father's alive." Tears turned to sobs as the pain of losing her husband collided with the pain of not being there when he returned. The sobs turned to sniffles, bringing a hunger for the rest of Braham's news.

For you see, he was the courier who delivered your possessions into my safekeeping as you directed. I was delighted to see him, unaware that he carried such dreadful news.

You are probably wondering what transpired during his absence. He was unable to explain, as he has no memory of what occurred on the cliff or how he survived a fall from such a great height. He only remembers climbing out of the water and drifting between two worlds for three excruciating days before later arriving at the wagon train after your departure.

He suffers from severe headaches, dizziness, and blurred vision, most likely from hitting his head when he fell.

She wanted to shoot Cullen for his stupidity, then hug him for his tenacity. Lord, her emotions were scattered shotgun pellets. With an exasperated sigh, she continued reading.

Fortunately, these ailments are not totally incapacitating, but he has ventured upon a quest detrimental to his full recovery. Reasoning with him, as you well know, is utterly impossible once he sets his mind on a particular course. I write that piece of tittle-tattle in confidence, my dear, as he would profess to reasonableness at all times.

It came to him in a moment of absolute despair that while in his ghostly form he assisted in the selection of Thomas MacKlenna's final resting place. Cullen has always taken his obligations quite seriously and has placed himself upon a monumental task, believing there is more to your vision than simply marking snow-covered ground with a shovel. It is his belief he will discover a way to communicate with you once he arrives at MacKlenna Farm.

Kit walked back to the sofa and sat, rubbing her belly. "Cullen, don't. You're not well, for God's sake." How in the world could he travel cross-country in his condition? Had he lost his ever-loving mind? Maybe Braham talked him out of traveling. Anxious for the rest of the story, she continued reading.

I, on the other hand, have chosen letter writing as my form of communication, as there have been no reported appearances of my doppelganger. The capricious hand of fate will ultimately decide which of us has set himself upon a fool's mission.

So, my dear Kitherina, it is our deepest desire to see you once again. Please, with haste, return to us.

Your loyal and devoted friend,
Michael Abraham McCabe

Return? Of course she'd return. But to where? And what did this mean a century and a half later? What had happened to Cullen? Had he made it to the farm? Yes, he had made it, and that's why he'd been haunting her for all these years.

"Kit? Where are ye?" Elliott called from the hallway.

"In here."

He stopped in the doorway, bracing his hands on either side of the frame. "I know it's a cliché, but ye look like ye've seen a ghost."

"I have, and now I know why." She patted the sofa cushion

beside her. "You'd better sit."

"Dinna keep me in suspense. Spit it out."

She handed him the letter. "Cullen's alive."

He took the yellowed paper. "Unless he found a way to jump through that frigging time warp, I'd say that's highly unlikely."

"Why do you have to be so pragmatic?"

"My nature, I reckon." He read the letter and then walked to the wet bar. "It's five o'clock somewhere, right?" He poured a double.

"I shouldn't have come home."

"Ye did what ye had to do." He knocked back his drink.

She said nothing, gazing at her feet propped up on the table. Her index finger gently tapped her chin.

"Ye're going back, aren't ye?"

"How could I not? Every breath I take has a catch in it as if Cullen has hold of my heart."

Elliott dropped the letter on the coffee table and crossed the room to the built-in bookcase. "Several years ago, Sean asked me to give ye something." He pulled a handful of books from the second shelf and pressed a lever. A small door in the back wall slid open. He removed an envelope and handed it to her. "He wanted ye to have this if ye ever decided to leave the farm."

"I knew you were keeping something else from me."

"Did ye have an itch about it?"

"Yes, and I've been scratching it so long I've drawn blood." She pointed toward the bookcase. "I never knew that compartment was there."

"Sean discovered it when the roof leaked and the workers emptied the bookcase to make repairs."

She ran the envelope back and forth between her fingers. "Do you know what this is about? I'm not sure I can handle any more surprises today."

"Sean didna tell me."

Her eyebrow arched. "And you didn't ask?"

Elliott returned to the sofa. "Let's just say I intuited he didna need me to know."

She ripped open the envelope and read aloud.

Dear Kitherina,

Elliott's instructions are to give you this letter if you ever decide to leave the farm permanently. There is only one reason for you to do that. You have decided to return to the past. Either you have found your birth family, or you have found someone to share your life and that person prefers not to live in your time.

I wholeheartedly support your decision, and I have laid the groundwork for you to "vanish" to the MacKlenna estate in the Highlands. The estate, as you know, is very remote, and you can announce that you intend to live in seclusion. No one will ever know you're not in residence.

At your direction, our attorneys have instructions to create a revocable trust. In the event you decide to return at some point in the future, you can sign a revocation and the farm will once again revert to your control. If you never revoke the trust, then the trust becomes irrevocable twenty-one years after your "death or disappearance" and ownership of the farm passes to your heirs. In the event you have no heirs, ownership will pass to the University of Kentucky.

Your mother and I wish you a long and happy life wherever you choose to live. We love you,

Dad

She crumpled into Elliott's warm embrace, sobbing. "He had my life all figured out and never once thought he needed to discuss arrangements with me." Her tears soaked his green polo shirt. "Why?"

Elliott pressed her head closer to his chest. "He didna want to lose ye forever and neither do I."

"My son deserves to have his father."

Elliott tensed against her. "How soon will ye leave?"

"I'd leave today if I wasn't at the mercy of attorneys and CPAs." She wiped her eyes. "I have the baby to consider, too. It'll take a few weeks to get everything worked out."

He snatched a tissue and blew his nose. "I'll go with ye."

She shook her head. "Does that sound practical?"

He walked to the bar and poured another drink. "Do ye think ye'll land in Independence again?"

She scrunched her face, thinking. "That seems to be the landing spot. I can take a steamboat from there to Kentucky."

"What ye're planning is dangerous."

"Living is dangerous, Elliott, regardless of the century."

Chapter Forty-Five

A MONTH LATER, after meetings with lawyers and account-
ants, Kit crammed trunks so full she had to stand on top of
them to close the lids. There would be no formal good-byes. After
she left, Sandy would announce Kit had moved to the MacKlenna
Estate in the Highlands and was not expected to return. Then she
would handle inquiries discreetly and discourage friends from
contacting Kit.

She was ready to go.

Saying good-bye to Stormy was heart-wrenching. The stallion
stomped and swished his tail. "I can't take you," Kit said. "You'd get
a mare in foal and we'd be in big trouble. Stay here. Sire a few stakes
winners." He pinned his ears. "I love you." She kissed his broad, flat
forehead and walked away. He ran the length of the white-planked
paddock, his hooves thundering across the soft turf, taking the
corners at high speed. Kit kept walking, tears filling her eyes.

Sobbing, she returned to the mansion and hurried to her bedroom to change. She caught her reflection in the floor-length mirror.
At twenty weeks, she only had a little pooch, but her flushed cheeks
gave her away.

Her skirt swished as she turned a slow circle, looking at her
room for the last time. After all the fantasies she'd had about making
love with her husband in her big cherry bed, it would never happen
now.

Time to go.

She closed and buckled the carpetbag stuffed with her most important belongings. If she got separated from her trunks, she'd have her journal, iPod, childbirth books, medications for Cullen's headaches and nausea, and the gold coins Elliott purchased from a rare coin dealer. He discovered when talking with the dealer that Kit's father had also purchased coins and gold nuggets from his coin shop. Kit was relieved to know the treasure in the leather pouches belonged to her father, solving one of the many mysteries.

She took one final look around, turned out the light, then closed the door.

Elliott waited at the bottom of the stairs with red eyes and trembling shoulders. "I'll never see ye again, will I?"

She paused on the second landing. "I don't think so."

"I'll never know about the baby."

She took the steps slowly, thinking with each footfall. "If I can get into Mr. MacKlenna's office, I'll leave my journal in the secret compartment in the bookcase and find a way to seal it so no one will find it."

"Ye promise to stay in Kentucky until after the baby is born, right? No traveling. It isna safe."

"I promise. When we head to San Francisco, I'll do my best to leave a breadcrumb trail for you to follow."

"I'm nae finding any humor in this, Kit." He pressed the heels of his palms into his eyes to wipe away his tears. "Are ye sure ye want to go?"

She reached the bottom step. "I've never been more certain about anything in my life."

He took her bag. "Ye'll have to take care of yerself. I willna be around to watch out for ye."

Tate's howl echoed through the silent house.

"I locked both critters in the mudroom, but they saw yer trunks."

"Tate just wants to go. He doesn't care where." She put her hands on her hips and tapped her toes. The dog howled again, and this time Tabor's trill joined in, creating a discordant duet. "Damnation." She stomped off toward the mudroom. "I hope they know what they're getting themselves in for."

Tate bounded down the hallway, barking a path for Tabor to follow. Elliott held open the front door. They ran out and jumped on top of the four trunks he'd lashed together with an old hemp rope. "Looks like ye've got everything ye need now."

She looked at her pets, shaking her head.

"They'd be miserable here without ye." As if to prove Elliott right, Stormy rounded the corner of the house at a trot, stopped when he saw her, and walked up the porch steps as if he did it every day.

"You jumped the fence?" She rubbed her hand through his mane and breathed into his nostrils, showing him how much she loved him.

"Ye're stuck with them all." Elliott laughed. "Look, his ears are forward. Can ye hear what he's saying? 'Where to now, Kemosabe?'" When Elliott produced a shank from his back pocket, Kit knew Stormy's gate had been unlatched.

Elliott tied the horse to a trunk's end strap, stepped back, and took a farewell picture with his cell phone. As he stared at the small screen, more tears rolled down his face. "Dinna go." His soft plaintive words ripped through her heart.

Elliott had taught her to ride. He'd bandaged her knees and wiped her tears. He'd found her in the pasture with a broken back and held her hand as they stood over the graves of her parents. He'd changed her diapers and picked out her prom dresses. And he'd lain helpless and bleeding while Wayne attempted to rape her.

She and Elliott had danced and laughed and drank whisky together, and in the late-night hours he'd picked her off the floor where she'd dropped exhausted from her grief. He'd been her support for her entire life, loving and protecting her, and now, much as a bride is given away by her father, it was time for him to let her go.

Time for her to let go of him.

She kissed his wet, salty cheek, picking up a whiff of his signature scent that always made her think of a big leather chair in a field of cloves. "My soul is telling me I'm making the right decision. My destiny lies somewhere behind, not forward. Let's be joyful in the midst of our loss because we choose to be." She gazed into his eyes. "I love you, Elliott."

He pulled her into his arms and rested his chin on the top of her head. "I love ye, too, my wee lassie." After a few shuddering moments, he climbed into his Suburban and drove away.

Look back, Elliott. He stopped at the end of the tree-lined drive. *Please wave. Let me know you're okay.* He stuck his arm out the window and gave her a thumbs-up. Then he was gone. She released the breath she was holding.

Tate barked.

"What? Are you ready to go?" The sight on the porch was laughable—four trunks, a cat, a dog, and a horse. The scene reminded her of landing in Independence the first time. Cullen had been there, but he wouldn't be there now. Her knees knocked beneath her green brocade dress. She fluffed out the skirt, whisked away a bead of sweat trickling down her cheek, and plopped down on the trunks. Tabor squatted in her lap.

"Everybody ready?" She squirmed to get comfortable, but couldn't. Something was haywire about her plan. What was it?

Take a gut check.

She did, and knew the answer. Not only did she have to say good-bye to Elliott, but she had to let go of the animals, too. A knot formed in her throat.

She kissed Tate's and Tabor's heads. "Y'all can't go this time." Tate tucked his tail and turned his head away. Tabor curled into a ball. Stormy neighed, and she laid her cheek against his nose. Memories of their rides across MacKlenna Farm's rolling hills flooded her mind—no saddle, no bridle, just the two of them racing into the wind. "We've been through a lot together, but it's time to let go of you, too." She blew into his nostrils again. "Sire those stakes winners. Make me proud."

Elliott would circle the farm and come back. He'd understand why she left them behind.

She stepped *away* from them—from the cat and dog her mom had loved and spoiled, and from the horse who had grown into a magnificent, powerful animal.

She stepped away from the trunks packed with trappings of her century.

She stepped away from MacKlenna Farm because she had the strength to do it.

With the carpetbag in one hand and the ruby brooch in the other, she repeated the magic words and stepped into the rest of her life.

Chapter Forty-Six

MacKlenna Farm, November 5, 1852

K IT REALIZED SOMETHING had gone terribly wrong.

She had repeated the magic words and traveled the interweaving turns and twists toward flickering amber light, but she was still standing on the east portico of MacKlenna Mansion. Had she used up her quota? Were there no more trips through the turnstile of time? She leaned against the railing, and her anguish flowed like water from a pierced vessel.

A strange quietness she'd never noticed before hung over the farm. She glanced out across the bluegrass-covered pastures. What happened to the concrete drive, the cars, and utility poles on Old Frankfort Pike? Stormy was gone. Tate and Tabor were gone. The trunks were gone.

Adrenaline raced through her bloodstream, heightening all her senses.

She sniffed back her tears and inhaled the crisp scent of fall. What happened to the lazy-day heat of summer? She was on MacKlenna Farm all right. But what year? She closed the brooch and pinned it to her collar.

Her gaze swept left to right, taking in as much of the landscape as possible. If there were no cars or trucks, it had to be before 1920, probably much earlier. How would she ever find Cullen? Find him? Crap. If she found him now, he'd be an old man. Her heart crawled up her throat, and she struggled to breathe. Wasn't she supposed to be in Independence? Why was she here? And who was living in the house? Whoever was in residence had to be one of six Sean MacKlennas. Her father was born in 1950—that ruled him out. His father was born in 1926—that ruled him out. There was only one thing left to do. Knock and see which one answered.

Before she could put knuckles to wood, she noticed there weren't any bullet holes in the oak door. The Civil War hadn't happened yet. That meant the year had to be earlier than 1861. Cullen would still be a young man. As she processed that, a servant dressed in a white shirt and black tie opened the door. "Can a help you, miss?"

"Is Mister MacKlenna home?"

"They both a home. Spec you want a see Mister Sean?"

He opened the door wider, and she stepped across the threshold, handing over her carpetbag. She breathed in the scent of the house—old as time and lemon polish. The side cabinet stood in the same location in the hallway. Upholstery woven in golden stripes covered the straight-leg Hepplewhite chairs stationed on either side. She loved both the color and the fabric. "You'n wait in the parlor."

Kit entered the large front room and stopped, taken aback by the change in color scheme. The green stripe and small floral fabrics were gone. The settee's upholstery bore a large blue floral design, and the walls painted in natural earth tones gave the room a golden tint. Floor to ceiling sapphire-blue silk draperies covered the two windows. She ran her hands up and down the luxurious panels and checked the underside to find silk stitches and a lighter blue lining. *Nice detail work.*

The sound of boots clicking across the hardwood floor pulled her attention from the drapery. A handsome man, his chin clean-shaven and pink, entered the room and halted when he saw her. "I didna know such a bonnie lass was here. I'm Sean MacKlenna." He stepped toward her, captured her hand, and bowed.

Kit needed no introduction. She'd studied the brush strokes the artist used to paint the first Sean's portrait so often she recognized him immediately. "I'm Mrs. Montgomery."

"What can I dae for ye, lass?"

Immaculately dressed in a loose-cut, dark brown suit that matched the color of his hair and eyes, a starched cravat, and a horizontal bow with a high collar, the first Sean made a striking figure of a man. Her breath caught when she noticed the gold watch-chain dangling from his vest pocket.

"What time is it?"

He pulled out the watch engraved with the initials STM on the case's cover. She shivered with a tactile memory. The paramedics had removed that watch from her father's pocket the night of the crash and slipped it into her hand in the emergency room. Except to take a bath, she hadn't let it go for weeks.

"Eleven fifteen." He snapped the case shut, tucked the watch back into his vest pocket, and gestured toward the settee. "Won't ye sit down?"

Kit sat on the cushion's edge, and he sat in a wing chair opposite her, crossing one elegant leg over the other. "Now, tell me. Whatna brings ye to MacKlenna Farm, Mrs. Montgomery?"

She glanced at her hands, the bric-a-brac on the tables, the paintings on the wall, anything to avoid eye contact. "I didn't know I was coming. I guess you could say I was dropped here accidentally."

"*Who* would leave a bonnie lass alane?"

She fingered the brooch at her neck. "This is a beautiful room. I love what you've done with the place."

"That's a lovely piece o' jewelry." He leaned back in his chair and interlaced his fingers. Kit saw a glitter of intensity she hadn't noticed before. "Where'd ye get it?"

She had to get out of the house and wait for Cullen somewhere else. These people were going to think she was crazy. "From my mother."

The servant walked into the room. "Mister Thomas come downstairs."

"Did ye tell him we had a guest?"

"No, suh. Nobody tell him. He already know she here."

"My father's not well and usually doesna leave his room."

"This might sound like an odd question but…what's the date?"

"First the time, then the date." Sean raised an eyebrow. "It's the fifth day of November, 1852. Why?"

"How did your father know I was here?"

"Father has…shall we say, a gift."

Gift?

"Ye said yer mother gave ye the brooch. Tell me about her."

"I think she died when I was a baby."

A pained look crossed his face.

"Is something wrong?"

"Here comes Father now. He'll sort this out."

Thomas MacKlenna shuffled into the room, his weight bent on his walking cane. A head full of white hair and well-defined wrinkles on his face spoke to his age, but they could not obscure his powerful presence the artist had captured in his portrait. Thomas's warm brown eyes were clear and focused, expressing the depth of intelligence and passion that informed his reputation and business acumen.

Kit jumped to her feet and rushed to his side. "May I help?" She took his other arm, guided him to the sofa, and sat beside him. "It's an honor to meet you, sir." She couldn't believe she was sitting with the family patriarch—a legend in Thoroughbred racing. She had a thousand questions for him. Where would she start?

Before she could ask even one, his cool hand patted hers. "I've waited twenty-five years for ye to come home, Kitherina."

Did he just call me Kitherina? No. I misheard him. The amber light messed with my hearing.

His warm hand squeezed hers. "Are ye wondering how I knew yer name? Ye're my granddaughter."

Time stopped as if from the press of a thumb on a stopwatch. She sat motionless for several moments until a flutter in her belly restarted the clock. She heard her father saying, "I found you on my doorstep. I searched for your identity. I don't know who you are. You may not have been born a MacKlenna, but you are one. The ninth generation…"

She shook her head. "I don't know who I am, but I'm not your granddaughter."

Sean's keen eyes challenged her. "Yer wearing my sister's brooch. A one-of-a kind stone with the proclivity to whisk ye off into the unknown. Where'd ye get it?"

Sensing accusation in his tone, she clutched the brooch, hiding it from him. Her heart beat in double time. "I arrived with it." She turned to Thomas. "When I was a baby. It was pinned to my dress."

Thomas and Sean looked at each other. Then Thomas's eyes glistened with tears. "I gave yer mother the brooch on her wedding day."

Kit's mouth went dry. *Brooch. Mother. Wedding day. Impossible.* She needed to pace and think, but Thomas gripped her hand.

Think. There had to be an explanation. Okay. What did she know for sure? Only that she had the brooch as a baby. She just assumed it belonged to her birth mother. Could her birth mother be Thomas MacKlenna's daughter?

None of this made sense.

"When I gave ye mother the stone, I told her the secret my grandmother had told me. 'The stone will take ye to a world unknown, through amber light to a time not yer own, to the one of yer heart, and the truth ye'll be shown.'"

"Was your daughter's fiancé not the one of her heart?" Kit asked.

"Aye, your mother was verra much in love," Thomas said. "Sometimes the one who holds the brooch is not the one intended to receive the gift. Tell me, lass, hae ye met the one of yer heart, the one ye couldna have found without the help of the stone?"

"My father, the sixth Sean MacKlenna, also found the one of his heart."

Sean's eyes widened with surprise. "The *sixth*? Then ye went to the wrong time so he could use the stone, and now ye have come home."

"Home? Wait a minute." Now she really needed to pace.

"You're telling me—I'm a real MacKlenna?"

"We'd be happy to claim all of ye, but we must share ye with the McCabes."

"*McCabe?*" She grabbed the seat cushion with her free hand and bounced her legs.

"Donald McCabe was yer father, lass," Thomas said.

She let go of the cushion and pulled the portrait miniature from her pocket. When she had dressed an hour ago, her hands shook so badly she couldn't clasp the chain's hook. She wouldn't be able to do it now either. Handing the portrait to Thomas, she said, "I had this with me as a baby."

He let go of her hand. "Aye. It's a good likeness of Donald."

Thomas gave the portrait back, and she returned it to her pocket. "I don't understand any of this."

Sean leaned forward in his chair. "Father asked Donald and Jamilyn—"

"*Jamilyn?*" Kit's fingers wagged in the direction of the portraits in the hallway. "A painting of her is hanging on the wall." She looked back at Sean. "I was told she was your twin sister." Her legs bounced faster. The sofa had to be shaking. If she didn't get up and pace, she'd shoot off like a rocket in about ten seconds.

"Aye. She was born first."

"You mean…you mean to tell me I've been looking at my mother's portrait all my life?" A hot flash soaked her in sweat. She fanned herself with her hand.

"Are ye ill, child?" Sean said.

She fanned faster.

The servant appeared with a tea service and cookies. "Sukey fixed tea. She bubbling up like hot cakes. She say she have a baby gone care for. I say phhh, how you know? She say fore spring she gone have a baby to rock. Say Mister Thomas he be a great-granddaddy. Sukey just smile real big like the preacher gone preach a extra service." He left the room, chuckling to himself. "Yes, suh, we gone have a baby."

Thomas's face glowed.

"How do they know about me?"

Sean clamped his teeth over his lower lip to keep from laughing. "Sukey's not only our cook but the local midwife. Everybody in three counties will ken there'll be a wean come spring."

For a private person, that prospect made Kit even more nervous.

He poured tea and handed her a cup. It rattled in her hands. She sipped from it and nibbled on a cookie. "How did I get separated from my mother?"

"We'll ne'er know," Thomas said. "Father asked Donald and Jamilyn to come here to live. Your mother was ill and couldn't travel when Donald immigrated."

"Was she pregnant with me?"

"No, child," Thomas said. "My daughter was ne'er well. She had a spell after ye were born and couldna travel. She booked passage months later. We were told the ship was caught in a storm and sank. There were nae survivors."

"I was wrapped in a white Chantilly lace shawl with a monogrammed *M*. It had blood on it."

"I gave her the shawl for a wedding present," Sean said.

"My daughter thought her illness was a burden to others. If she were injured during the storm, the lass would have stayed behind." Thomas sighed heavily. "I need to rest now." He took Kit's hand again and kissed her fingers. "Sit with me tomorrow. We have much to talk about."

"I've wanted to talk to you since I was old enough to know who you were."

Thomas shuffled from the room, leaning on the servant's arm.

"Your father is a legend," she said to Sean.

"He's yer grandfather, Kitherina."

She leaned back against the sofa and closed her eyes.

"I can see my sister in yer face."

"Tell me about her."

"She had a smile that brought light to the darkness. But it was her voice I remember. When she sang, all God's creatures sang with her. And she could paint. Her paintings are all over the house."

Kit's eyes popped open. "What happened to them?"

"What dae ye mean? They're on every wall."

Kit stepped to the fireplace and studied the painting above the mantel. "Where is this castle?"

"Eilean Donan, close to Dornie."

"It's been restored now—The Castle of Dreams. Some say it's the most beautiful castle in all of Scotland." Kit glanced around the room. "I grew up in this house. Every piece of furniture has been preserved. Fabrics are different, colors are different, but every piece is still there. So why didn't any of my mother's paintings survive?"

Sean shook his head.

"Why do you think the stone took me to the wrong time?"

"Didna ye say Sean VI found the one of his heart? Maybe ye were to take the stone to him."

"Maybe," Kit said.

"Do ye paint, Kitherina?"

"Not as well as my mother. But I'm okay, I guess. Why?"

"Do ye sing?"

"I love music."

Sean was silent for several moments then asked, "Do ye ride astride with the wind in yer hair?"

He finally asked the one question that broke her, and she buried her face in her hands and wept. Sean sat beside her, pulling her into her arms. "'Twill be all right, lass. 'Twill be all right. I'll tell ye everything about Jamilyn and ye will come to love her as I do."

AFTER SUPPER, KIT retired to her room—her real room with her cherry four-poster bed. The bed she and Cullen would share. The thought was like biting into something hot, sweet, and delicious, leaving her all warm and tingly.

Sukey had sent someone to turn down the covers and heat the bed with the copper bed warmer. Kit slipped between the sheets and pulled the comforter to her chin.

Her head and heart were turning in opposite directions from all she'd discovered in the past few hours, mixing up her emotions in a huge black cauldron. She needed to let down her hair and race across the pasture. Give her heart a chance to pound her thoughts into proper perspective.

After months of searching for her identity, the truth had been hanging on the wall all along—a portrait of her mother. She had appreciated the woman as only her ancestor. Kit shivered and scooted farther down into the warmth of the bed.

How different would her life have been if she'd grown up in Kentucky in the early 1800s? Would she even have been educated? Not a common occurrence until midcentury. Thomas didn't have a formal education. Her mother and father had some schooling but probably wouldn't have encouraged her learning. What would she have had to offer a worldly, educated man like Cullen? What could she have given him that he hadn't already gotten from scores of other women? Thankfully, she didn't have to worry about it, but the question would be fun to banter back and forth with him. He would say he would have loved her even if she couldn't read or write, but she knew in her heart that wasn't true. His mind needed stimulation as much as...well, as much as the rest of him. Was that why the magic stone sent her on a detour?

Chapter Forty-Seven

S EAN ESCORTED KIT to Thomas's room. She found him in
bed with pillows propping him up and a food tray on his lap. A
trail of gravy made it obvious he had only moved the meat and
potatoes from one side of the plate to the other. Even with Kit's
encouragement, he only took a bite before pushing the tray aside.
The valet had shaved him and brushed his hair, but he appeared
pale, and when he spoke, his weak voice didn't carry further than a
few feet. His eyes, however, gleamed with excitement.

He pointed to a straight-backed chair next to his bed. "Sit here,
lassie."

"Kitherina would be more comfortable sitting on the *chaise longue*
under the window," Sean said.

Thomas appeared crestfallen.

Kit winked at her uncle. "I'll be fine." She sat in the chair beside
the bed. "Do you have questions for me?"

"Tell me about the farm."

Sean quietly left the room, and for the next three hours, Kit
talked about the farm's breeding successes and victories on the
racetrack. She told him about the Kentucky Derby and that the
farm's stallions had won the prestigious race five times. When he
yawned, she left him and went searching for Sean, finding him in the
office.

She stood in the doorway, her eyes sweeping the interior. As she
had discovered, the only differences in the mansion of the twenty-

first century and the mansion of the nineteenth century, besides electricity, heat, and bathrooms, were colors and fabrics and her mother's paintings hanging on the walls. "This is my favorite room in the entire house."

He glanced up from a stack of papers on the desk. "Come in, lass." He rose and walked toward her. "Shall we sit o'er here?" He pointed toward the wing chairs in front of a fire crackling beneath newly added logs. They settled into the chairs. Kit kicked off her shoes and tucked her feet under her folded legs.

"I ken ye have questions," Sean said.

She fingered the locket hanging from a chain around her neck. "I want to know about my father."

"Aye. Donald and I grew up together. Yer mother loved him. He left here to meet the ship in Norfolk. When he heard it sank, he didna take the news well. Drank too much, got into a fight, and killed a man by accident. He got scared and ran. We ne'er found him. He might well be dead by now."

"He's in San Francisco. At least he was last year."

Sean sat forward in his chair. "How do ye know?"

"A friend of my husband's, Braham McCabe—"

"Peter McCabe's son?"

"Who's Peter?"

"Peter is Donald McCabe's brother."

She drew invisible lines in the air with her index fingers connecting one name to another. "So, if Peter and Donald are brothers and Peter is Braham's father, that makes Braham—"

"Your first cousin."

She stared in open-mouth shock and disbelief. Then she mentally traveled back to the day she met Braham at Fort Laramie. His green eyes seemed so familiar.

"If ye met Braham, then ye probably met his friend Cullen." Sean cocked his head and looked curiously at her wedding ring. "Yes, of course. Ye introduced yerself as Montgomery. In all the excitement, I forgot."

"Cullen is my husband."

Sean smiled, showing a dimple in his left cheek she hadn't noticed before. It mirrored her single dimple. "If my memory serves me right, ye and Cullen were pledged as bairns."

She gulped. "How's that possible?"

"Yer mother and Mary Margaret McKenzie were childhood friends. Mary Margaret married William Montgomery, Cullen's father."

She couldn't take her eyes off her uncle, finding it all so hard to believe. "How come neither Cullen nor Braham knew me?"

"Yer mother left Scotland during yer first year. Cullen's mother died, I believe, a few months later."

"He told me about losing his sister, but not his mother."

"William married again verra soon and they had a bairn right away. Would hae eased the pain for the lad."

Kit stood, shook off some of the tension the shocking news had caused, and walked over to the window. There was no garden or pergola, but there was a golden view of the rolling hills. "Uncle Sean, where does the magic come from?"

Sean joined her at the window. "That's a mystery, lass. Family legend says there were once three brooches: a ruby, emerald, and sapphire given to the MacKlenna brothers for rescuing a laird's kidnapped wife."

"How long has the brooch been in the family?"

"Four hundred years."

She gasped. "Have others gone back and forth?"

"Aye, ye be not the first. But tell me lass, where is yer Cullen now?"

"Do you want the short story or the long story?"

He laughed. "Ye are yer mother's daughter. We have all the time we need. I want the verra long one."

THOMAS SAT UP in bed and coughed. Blood trickled from the corners of his mouth. Kit wiped his face, remembering doing the same for her granny who died of lung cancer. From what Sean had told her about Thomas's condition, she suspected his chest pain, shortness of breath, and difficulty breathing were symptomatic of the same disease.

When he fell asleep, she slipped out of his room. Sukey had promised egg salad for lunch, and Kit's stomach was rumbling.

Sean strode through the front door as she neared the bottom of the stairs. He took her arm and guided her down the remaining stairs. All her life she'd taken them two at a time without a thought for her safety. Now, wearing the long gowns that Sean had a local seamstress make for her, she realized a misstep could send her tumbling to the hardwood floor and harm her and her child.

"How is Father this morning? I had an early meeting and didna visit him 'fore I left."

"He's been busy working on his journal of MacKlenna traditions. I wish I could do more for him. He's in so much pain. The laudanum helps, but he delays taking it so he can think clearly while he writes and we talk."

"That's his decision to make."

"I want him to be comfortable during the time he has left."

"How long does he hae?" Sean asked in a curious yet uncertain voice.

Her grandfather would die on January 25, but she couldn't tell her uncle. She could justify telling him about the Civil War in order to protect the family and the farm, but telling him the date his father would die seemed beyond the pale.

When she didn't answer right away or drop her gaze, he said, "I shouldna have asked."

She leaned in to him and patted his arm affectionately. Thomas would never meet her child and possibly not even her husband. She tried not to worry about Cullen's journey, but the trip was difficult for healthy people. For him—all alone—it had to be hell.

Sean escorted Kit into the dining room. "Let's eat. Ye have that look 'bout ye."

"What look is that?"

"That ye would kill for food."

She shuddered. Kill for food? No. Kill for her family? Yes. Sean must have sensed she was remembering things best left forgotten because he pulled her closer.

"Ye hae to let gae of it, Kitherina."

"The nightmares won't let me."

"When ye have yer husband back, the bad dreams will gae awa'."

Sean pulled her chair away from the table, and she sat. At the sound of footsteps at the doorway, she glanced up to see the butler entering the room.

"Mr. Sean, you have visitors," Joe said.

Sean sighed impatiently. The number of people he dealt with every day surprised Kit. In the twenty-first century, the farm had a staff person to handle every situation, especially drop-ins.

"Go on," she said.

"Are ye sure?"

She spread honey on a slice of apple. "Please go. I'm fine."

He kissed the top of her head. "I'll be back in a wee bit."

She bit into the apple, watching the rainbow of reflections created by the chandelier's crystal prisms. Multicolored light danced across the tabletop, inspiring her to paint. If her uncle were called away for the afternoon, she'd set up her easel and work on her grandfather's portrait.

The sun seemed unusually bright, pouring into the room from the unshuttered windows. Only by squinting into the light could she see the yearlings in the paddock. She rubbed her baby bump. *Where will we be this time next year?* She'd lost so much. Did she dare dream the dreams of her heart?

Chapter Forty-Eight

T HE DRIVER OF Cullen's coach turned the carriage onto a tree-lined drive ablaze with burnt-orange leaves spiraling upward before falling silently to the ground and skittering across the well-groomed lawn. Wood smoke and cider teased him with the scent of late autumn. Beyond the immediate grounds, white-fenced pastures and a meandering stream crisscrossed rolling hills.

Henry gave Cullen a slight elbow nudge in the side. "Look up ahead."

Visible through the tree line stood a stately, three-story, red brick mansion. The portico's four Doric columns guarded the residence like venerable soldiers, reminding Cullen of the quote by Horace: *Carpe diem! Rejoice while you are alive; enjoy the day; live life to the fullest; make the most of what you have.*

The thought simmered while he turned to Henry and said, "The fall from the cliff nearly killed me. This trip damned near buried me. But seeing where Kit lives, even in another time, coats my soul with a soothing balm."

Henry shoved a twitching hand through his hair. "I damn well believe she hears you, son."

Cullen coughed away the knot of emotion in his throat. "If the MacKlennas would let me, I'd live in a cabin next to the creek we just crossed. I'd always have her nearby." He lifted his hand, caught a fistful of air, brought it to his nose, and inhaled deeply. "Kit is here, if only in my heart." The driver stopped at the mansion's front steps. Cullen and Henry disembarked and ascended the bricked stairs.

Henry gripped Cullen's arm and restrained him for a moment. "Do you know what you're going to say?"

Cullen knocked on the door. "I'm praying for divine inspiration."

The door opened, and a servant stood in the doorway. "May I help you?"

Cullen steeled himself. "I'd like to see Mister MacKlenna."

The man stepped aside. "It's gone be a fine day. Yes, suh. A fine day."

Cullen entered the house, smelling roasting turkey and something else that made him stiffen not in fear but in anticipation.

"What is it?" Henry asked, crossing the threshold behind him.

Cullen quickly took in the details of the room, matching what he saw with what Kit had told him about the house. He didn't smell lemon polish. He smelled roses. "I'm nae sure."

The servant motioned to a nearby room. "You'n wait in a parlor. I'll let Mister Sean know he's got visitors."

Above the parlor's fireplace hung a painting of the Eilean Donan castle. Cullen walked straight toward it. A mere touch of his fingertips to the painted castle's crumbled stone walls evoked memories of home—breaking waves pounding the sea wall and the smell of heather growing in the fields. "Kit is part of this creation. It has her soul in every brush stroke."

A man in his midforties, dressed in a dark frock coat over lighter trousers, a linen shirt with an upstanding collar, and low-heeled shoes entered the room, smiling. "I'm Sean MacKlenna. May I help ye?"

Cullen gave him a closed-lipped smile. The man seemed pleasant enough. He extended his hand, trying hard to keep it steady. "I'm Cullen Montgomery, and this is my friend and traveling companion, Henry Peters."

Sean shook Cullen's hand and at the same time gripped his arm with his other hand as if the handshake wasn't enough to express his welcome. Cullen did the same. He then turned his attention back to the painting. "Who's the artist?"

Sean stepped over to the fireplace. "My sister painted it shortly before my niece was born. It was her last painting."

"She's quite talented."

"Aye, she was..." Sean cleared his throat. "I knew yer mother, Mr. Montgomery. Mary Margaret was a bonnie lass."

A dizzy spell hit Cullen, and he leaned against the wing chair. "How did you..."

Sean steadied him, wrapping long fingers around Cullen's upper arm. "Come with me. I have something to show ye."

Henry started to follow.

"I'll return shortly, Mr. Peters, and we'll talk."

"Cullen?" Henry's brow bunched into a puzzled frown.

Cullen patted his friend's shoulder. "I'll be fine." Although he said he would, he wasn't sure he believed it. How could this man have known his mother? A woman his father never spoke of, a woman Cullen longed to know.

Sean led Cullen down the wide entrance hall lined with dozens of paintings, all Highland scenes. In each painting, Cullen smelled the odor of the peat fires' blue-gray smoke and felt the sun's heat on his face. They reached the end of the hallway, where two small paintings hung on the wall next to a closed door. One was a portrait of a young woman. The other, a landscape with canary yellow gorse in full bloom covering the banks of a blue loch peppered with wooded islands. A bracken-clad ridge rose in the background.

Cullen's entire body shook.

"Are ye ill, lad?" Sean asked.

"The painting..." Cullen stood mere inches from the canvas, breathing it in. "'Tis Loch Lomond and the Glen Russ Hills."

"Aye, it is. The painting is one of my sister's earlier works."

"Did she paint herself on the chestnut stallion? The horse looks exactly like...I've seen a very similar horse."

"I've often wondered if it was a self-portrait, but Jamilyn's hair was dark brown, not golden like the woman in this painting."

Cullen's heart rose and clogged his throat. "She resembles a vision I had in my childhood."

"My sister had several gifts, Mr. Montgomery. Maybe she plucked it from yer mind."

Or put it there.

Sean opened the door next to the painting. "If ye'll step in here, I'll go get yer friend."

Cullen stepped into a sea-colored dining room, warmed by a crackling fire that eased the chill from his bones. A labyrinth of light from two floor-to-ceiling windows reflected off prisms suspended from the chandelier, throwing a rainbow of color across a table laden with ripe peaches and buttery pastries, creating an aurora around a golden-haired vision.

Her green eyes widened in surprise. A soft pink blush colored her cheeks. She stood and moved away from the table.

Cullen stepped closer, his heart pounding against his injured ribs. Floorboards creaked beneath his impassioned steps. His breath stilled in fear that the vision bathed in sunlight would vanish. "Are ye my dream bringing hope I've found only in my sleep?"

"Are you the dream I dared not dream?" the vision asked in a familiar dulcet voice.

He inched closer, his fists clenching and unclenching, veins pumping blood into his hands as he prepared to capture her, knowing that if he scared her away, he would surely die. "I am nae a dream, but a man who has lost his life's breath."

"Then come to me and I will breathe new life into you." She walked toward him with her palms up, lifting him from the abyss into which he had fallen.

He joined her in a circle of light. His gaze drew to her parted lips, full and lush. "Ah, lass, are ye real or a figment of my mind?" He stroked his thumbs over her tear-washed cheeks, but not until he touched her scars did he know with certainty that she was real, and she was his.

He tugged her to him. Her new rose flavored scent was more evocative than her usual vanilla. That was what he had smelled when he entered the house. His senses knew what his mind did not. "I thought I'd never see ye again this side of heaven. How is it that ye are here?"

"Braham told me you were on your way."

"I dinna understand—"

"Shh," she said. "We'll talk about it later."

He kissed her with the hunger of a starving man. "I'm sorry about the babe."

She placed his hand on her swollen abdomen. "I was pregnant with twins. One of them vanished, but our son will be born in the spring."

He was a man of many words, but they all forsook him now, even his beloved Shakespeare. Losing everything that had given his life meaning had been excruciatingly painful. Restored to all that he loved was humbling.

Kit entwined her soft fingers with his. "I have so much to tell you. Come with me." She led him through the servants' door, up the back staircase, down the hall, and into a bedroom.

"The MacKlennas have opened their home to ye," he said.

"Sean has been expecting you for several days. The servants prepared a dressing room through that door." She pointed to the corner. "You'll find everything you need." She stood on tiptoes, wrapped her arms around his neck, and kissed him deeply, sending him a passionate promise. "I'll tell you everything else *after* you make love to me."

He stroked her arms that circled his neck. Desire licked through him, and he swept his tongue against hers. "Then it will be a while before I hear yer news." He kicked the door closed, picked her up, and carried her to the cherry bed.

WHEN KIT TOUCHED the long, jagged pink scar below his shoulder, she remembered every god-awful detail of his fall from the cliff, and she remembered her fear. "I couldn't find you, Cullen. I looked but I couldn't..." Her tears splattered on his skin, not like a gentle rain, but a storm peaking in intensity. He held her head against his chest, his heartbeat supplying the rhythm for the words he whispered, calming the tempest.

"Ye've been through so much, lost so much, but yer family has been restored, and ye ken yer name. Ye're a real MacKlenna."

"Half MacKlenna. Half McCabe. Now a Montgomery."

He kissed her tender breasts. "When Frances told me ye were gone—"

"Oh, Cullen, was she crying?"

"She had faith I'd bring ye back." He paused for a moment and took a deep breath. "Sarah told me ye were bleeding and thought ye would lose the babe. I ken ye would do everything ye could to save our child, even if it meant never seeing me again." He lowered his head and kissed her belly. Silent tears dampened her skin. "I was lost without ye."

She knew his cries were not those of a man worried about the sanctity of his masculinity but of a man baring his soul.

"I was lost without you, too." She stroked his face with her fingertips. Each tip a pencil and each pencil a different shade of joy. "My granny told me that we live in an uncertain world, and the past is unchangeable—"

"And the present willna last," he said.

"But we have tomorrow to shape."

He lifted her hand and kissed her ring finger. "Ye're the love of my life."

"I love you, too, and I'll never leave you again."

She pulled him into her arms. In a moment of extraordinary poignancy, as he thrust within her, a ray of sunlight spilled through the window. Its warmth burrowed deep and melted her grief that had held her captive for almost a year. She rolled on top of him and rubbed against the sprinkling of black hair covering his chest and abdomen, savoring the sensation of his body pulsing beneath her.

Their eyes met, and they spoke in the silent language of lovers, words of healing and everlasting love. Cullen trembled, issued a guttural groan, and shuddered in surrender.

Chapter Forty-Nine

C ULLEN OPENED THE windows, letting the crisp November air into the room. The scent of roasting turkey and apple
pie wafted around them. They made love again, then spent time
laughing about wine and sunsets and how much they enjoyed Kit's
big bed.

He reclined on his side, his hand propping up his head as he
talked to his babe sleeping in Kit's womb, his voice raw with
emotion. "We'll sail around the world, laddie, and I'll make love to
yer mother under the moon and the stars in every country we visit."

She smiled through a yawn, warmed by the thought of traveling
with her two men.

"Ah, I think yer mother is tired." He ran his fingers in a languid
caress across her chin. Her lips parted, and he kissed her. "Rest now,
lass."

She yawned again, drifted off to sleep, and dreamed of sailing on
a three-masted ship. When she woke, she shivered with excitement.
Cullen's suggestion of a world tour must have unfurled her imagination like a spinnaker.

Sukey had filled the tub in Kit's dressing room to the brim with
hot, steamy water. She slipped into the bath and sighed with delight.
An hour later, she sat at her dressing table, teasing the hair at her
crown, working the strands into an elegant chignon that framed her
face. It wasn't a period hairstyle, but she liked the way it made her
feel.

When she heard the door to Cullen's dressing room open, she asked, "What time is it?" Before he could answer, she saw his reflection in the mirror and gasped with delight. He was wearing a Montgomery purple, green, and red tartan kilt and a smile that showed his dimples. "You look gorgeous. Turn around."

His kilt caught in the breeze flowing through the open window and lifted, revealing what he wasn't wearing underneath.

"Ah. A true Scotsman tonight."

"I'm glad my plaid excites ye." He attached his dress sporran below his belt buckle. "I believe ye asked me the time? 'Tis seven o'clock."

Who cared about the time? She glanced at the bed. Pregnancy hormones had infused her with an insatiable appetite, but her Highlander wasn't complaining. She tapped her fingernails on the dressing table. Seven o'clock? Darn. Sean expected them for dinner.

Cullen picked up her granny's pearls and the portrait miniature. She inhaled his scent, a heady meld of musk and a splash of bay rum and whisky. Maybe they did have time. He kissed her, chuckling against her lips. "I ken what ye're thinking, lass. I can throw up yer skirt, pull ye wee panties aside, and please ye with my tongue, or strip ye naked and have my way with ye."

She moaned and patted her chest, calming her racing heart. "Don't tempt me, please. I think I can wait."

"Hmm. Can I?" He kissed her neck, lingering at a spot behind her ear while he dangled the pearls and portrait miniature above the décolletage of her emerald brocade satin gown. "If ye're undecided about which to wear, I'd wear the miniature portrait. The gold chain looks lovely with yer dress. Yer father should be part of tonight's celebration in spirit if not in person. Even Thomas is coming down for dinner."

"I'm glad you spent time with him this afternoon."

His hot breath blew against her cheek. "He wanted to warn me about ye."

"He should have warned *me* about *you*."

The strain was gone from Cullen's face, and he laughed with

easy contentment. "Shall we go?"

She stood and straightened his tailored black wool Prince Charlie jacket. "Nice." Her hands trailed down his sides to his narrow waist. "You men can keep your secrets, but I have ways to discover what's important." She gazed up at him from beneath lowered lashes, and reached underneath his silver-decorated fur sporran, gently squeezing him.

"Ye can touch my bollocks any time, lass." His fingertips teased her ample bosom. "If ye keep that up, I'll lift yer petticoats for sure and have ye one more time before dinner." His tongue swept against hers, stroking in an erotic rhythm.

Tingling desire burned through her, hot and wet and delicious. "Cullen, if you do, we won't even make it to breakfast."

His throaty laughed wrapped around her. "We'd be forgiven." A mischievous gleam brightened his eyes.

She flicked her tongue along the seam of his lips. "How's your dizziness?"

"Whatever ye did cured me." He nibbled at the corners of her mouth.

She broke away from him, panting. "Stop. We have to go." She glanced in the mirror and reapplied clear lip gloss, smacked her swollen lips, and pinched her cheeks. "Did Sean tell you we were pledged as children?"

"Aye. If I had known, I would have saved myself for ye."

Kit burst out laughing. "If you expect me to believe—"

He kissed her again and smacked his lips as she had done. "Henry's room is across the hall, and he was about to charge in here earlier. If we delay any longer, I expect he'll break down the door."

"I should have spoken to him this afternoon before we disappeared."

"Nae, he and Sean drank whisky in the parlor until I came downstairs."

Kit felt her cheeks heat. "But we were up here for hours."

"Aye, lass. You dinna need to worry 'bout what others think. I will protect ye with my sword."

She squeezed him again. "I think I need protection now."

He reached for her dress buttons, but she stepped back and headed toward the door.

"Nae?"

"If my grandfather is joining us for dinner, I don't want to disappoint him."

"Yer grandfather and I got along well."

"After a few hours with him and Sean, you sound even more like them."

He chuckled. "What took Harvard years to pull out, the MacKlennas put back in an afternoon."

"You're incorrigible."

"Mayhap, but the lass encourages my incorrigibility." He opened the bedroom door. "I'm ready to eat that turkey that's had my mouth watering all afternoon."

"And I thought I was the reason you were drooling."

He flashed a wide grin.

As she walked out the door, she glanced back at the bed. The sheets lay twisted in a tangled heap. The image of her husband sprawled naked in her bed far surpassed her fantasies. Now she would paint the reality, lost in the feel of him, rippling with pleasure and smelling of autumn.

WHEN KIT REACHED the first landing, she spotted Henry on the bottom step. "*Henry.*"

He held out his arms. "You're prettier than you were on your wedding day."

She reached the bottom step and hugged the robust old soldier with character lines seemingly etched into his face. "I'm so glad you're here. Thank you for taking care of Cullen. If I'd known you were traveling with him, I wouldn't have worried as much."

Henry pulled a handkerchief from his pocket and wiped away a few tears. "Somebody had to watch over him. The boy don't do a good job on his own." He shook his head, wearing a wide-eyed look of disbelief. "I never thought—"

"I know." She dabbed at her eyes with her fingers until Cullen handed her his handkerchief. "I'm back now and we're all together."

As she slipped the handkerchief into her dress sleeve, she noticed the monogrammed *M*. Her initial. The only one she'd ever have.

Sean escorted Thomas into the hallway. Both men looked dashing in their MacKlenna blue and red tartan kilts. Eighty-two-year-old Thomas had a *sgian dubh* tucked into the right leg of his knitted hose with the MacKlenna crest visible on the knife's black hardwood handle.

"Shall we go to dinner? Kitherina has promised to play her mother's guitar and sing for us later," Sean said.

Cullen whispered in her ear. "If ye're going to sing, lass, ye'll have to return my handkerchief."

She gave him a smile. "If grandfather requests 'Auld Lang Syne,' I'll have to have it back."

If she knew anything about sentimental Scotsmen, the men would sing every Robert Burns' song they knew while they drank whisky and smoked cigars. The revelry would go on long into the night without her. She glanced up the stairs toward her bedroom. Her last chance for her husband's attention was slowly slipping away, at least until morning.

Henry put his arm around her shoulder. "I'm glad music found its way back into your heart."

"I never thanked you for saving my—"

"No need, missy." He kissed her cheek.

Cullen lifted Henry's fingers off her. "If ye're through manhandling my wife, I'll escort her to dinner."

She glanced at Henry and caught the twinkle in his eyes. A rapid knock on the front door captured their attention. Thomas pointed his walking stick at Joe. "Open it, 'fore whoever's pounding knocks the damned thing down."

Sean glanced up and down the hall. "Who's missing?"

Kit laughed, letting the musical rhythm of her happiness flow into the foyer. "John didn't follow you cross country, did he?"

"If he did," Cullen said, "Sarah and the children are with him. He sure as hell wouldna go off without them."

Thomas tugged on Sean's arm. "Invite them in, son. The MacKlennas are celebrating tonight."

Chapter Fifty

"**A**RE YE SURE they're here?" Braham asked the driver he'd hired at the Midway Depot.

"Yes, suh. Sukey say she gone fix a big supper tonight for all they company."

Donald McCabe tapped his fingers against the sides of his kilt. "Maybe we should wait until morning instead of barging in on their gathering."

Braham barked out a laugh. "Uncle Donald, ye broke two sailing records to get here. We're nae turning back now. I dinna care how frightened ye are. And besides, we're dressed for this. I havena worn a kilt in years. I'm glad ye insisted we bring them."

Donald stared at his nephew. Damned right he was scared. His moorings were coming loose from the dock, setting him adrift in shark-infested waters. He'd run out on his father-in-law years ago, and the old man probably thought he was dead and glad of it.

The driver turned onto the torchlit, tree-lined drive. The sugar maples, which dressed the lane in an exquisite red-orange color, had grown since Donald help plant them—a lifetime ago.

The carriage neared the house. He gazed at the Doric columns and long, arched windows guarding the door. The old soldiers presented a formidable foe. "Stop here. I'll walk the rest of the way." He buckled his cutlass around his waist and stepped to the ground, inhaling the cool air, carrying the scent of what? Pumpkin pie? The old goat always did eat well. "Let's go to the barns first. I'd like to see the horses."

Braham left the carriage, stepping quickly into his uncle's path. "Ye can delay this longer, but dinna ye think a quarter of a century is long enough?"

Donald let his gaze linger on the paddocks. His jaw clenched tight.

Braham put his hands on his hips and twitched his fingers. "Ye've been shipwrecked, stabbed and shot, fought pirates, and sailed through hurricanes. What do ye think this man is going to do to ye?"

Donald's heart pinched in an old familiar way. He'd never been afraid of anything or anybody except facing the old man. "I walked out on him. You dinna do that to Thomas MacKlenna."

"Ye didna walk out. Ye just didna come back," Braham said.

Donald gave a low, self-deprecating laugh. "I dinna ken why I let ye talk me into this."

"This was yer idea, but as drunk as ye were, ye probably dinna remember."

"I was content without sobriety."

"Who the hell are ye trying to kid? I talked to men who've sailed around the world with ye, and nae one of them ever saw ye take a drink."

"Just because nobody saw me—"

"Blow smoke in another direction, uncle. I'm nae listening. My friends are waiting, and I'm going in." Braham marched up the steps to the portico.

"He could tell me to go away."

"Perhaps, but Kit told me Thomas MacKlenna will die in January. It's time ye reconciled."

Donald forced out a deep breath. "Knock on the damned door, but dinna be surprised when they throw me out."

Braham knocked, and a servant answered. "May I help you, suh?"

"I'd like to see Mister MacKlenna," Braham said.

Donald broke out in a cold sweat at the sound of merriment.

Was a cannon firing? Or was that boom his heart? He heard Thomas invite whoever was at the door to join their celebration. If he knew who stood at the entrance to his home, he'd change his mind faster than wind could change direction in a storm. Donald moved aside so he couldn't be seen, but he could see through the front door's sidelights directly into the candlelit entrance hall.

Braham stepped into the hallway. "I hope I'm nae too late for the party."

"*Braham.*" A woman ran into his nephew's arms.

"*Kitherina?* What are ye doing here?" He swung her around, swishing her satin skirt. "We're cousins, can ye believe it?"

"You're making me dizzy. Put me down." She laughed with girlish excitement.

Donald stared, enrapt. Was this lovely creature his daughter? She had Jamilyn's high cheekbones, full rosebud lips, and long neck. Her hair was the color of his before it turned gray, and her eyes were the same green shade he saw every morning in his shaving mirror. Yes, Braham described both her countenance and her voice perfectly. But he had failed to mention her pink-tinged cheeks and the soft, warm womanly glow that radiated from her. He had never seen such an angelic appearance in any woman except his wife when she was with child.

My God, she's exquisite.

Braham kissed her cheek. "How did ye get here?"

"I got your letter."

"Ye did?"

"The bank sent it."

Donald felt separate and apart, as if he remained in his ship's crow's nest while his crew disembarked for a short swim to a tropical island.

A tall man with black hair and blue eyes slapped Braham's back. From his nephew's description, Donald assumed the man was Cullen Montgomery. "Ye can put my wife down now."

"She's *my* cousin, and I'll hold her as long as I want."

Montgomery laughed. "It's good to see ye. Yer appearance has topped off a perfect day."

Braham set Kit's feet on the ground, and her husband slipped a protective arm around her waist. "I'm nae the topping, but I brought the topping with me."

Braham was ready to spout a secret that would detonate an explosion and drastically alter lives, a secret no one in the hall was prepared to hear. He grabbed Donald's arm and pulled him into the hallway. His breath thundered in his ears louder than any hurricane he'd ever heard.

"Is that Donald McCabe?"

Donald turned toward Thomas MacKlenna's roaring voice just in time to see him throw down his cane. Color drained from the old man's gaunt face. His brown eyes looked hard and unforgiving. Donald gave him a perfunctory nod in preparation of being tossed from the house as he'd been tossed from Virginia pubs so long ago. He hoped the big man guarding the door would throw him to the soft grass instead of the brick walk. Every muscle tensed. He wouldn't fight, not in front of his daughter.

"It is ye, Donald." Thomas's voice thundered again through the room.

Donald glanced quickly at Kitherina, took a breath, and then relaxed. He would try to roll with the fall in order to keep from breaking a bone. He glanced at the servant. *I'm ready. Give me your best shot.*

"Welcome home, laddie."

Welcome home? Donald grew numb with shock. Thomas wasn't sending him away. Instead, he wrapped him in a fervent embrace. But Thomas's arms were no longer strong enough to chop down a tree in a half dozen swings of an ax. They belonged to a frail, ailing man carrying the scent of death.

"It's time ye came home, son." His eyes glistened with tears.

Donald's chest tightened. He'd never asked forgiveness from anyone, and no one had ever asked it of him, but he knew if he ever wanted peace in his soul, he had to ask the old man to forgive him. His heart raced, his fingers grew cold. "I'm sorry, sir, for leaving ye when ye needed me most."

Thomas gripped his arm with a gnarled hand. "Ye had yer reasons after killing that man, I suppose, but none that mattered to me. I forgave ye when ye did it. Ye just didna give me a chance to tell ye." Thomas stepped back and grabbed his son's hand, too. "Welcome yer brother home, Sean."

Sean's warm hands wrapped Donald's in a two-handed shake then pulled him into a hug, slapping his back. "Welcome home, brother."

Cullen handed Thomas his cane. The MacKlenna family patriarch leaned heavily on the walking stick's elephant ivory handle with one arm while still embracing Donald with the other. Thomas's face glowed. "Bring the whisky, Joe. We've toasts to make."

When Joe left the hall, Sean said, "I have someone for ye to meet." He clasped Donald's shoulder with one hand. "Kitherina, this is yer father." He clasped her shoulder, too. "I stand in the place of my sister, who loved ye both. Share all of yer tomorrows, remembering her."

Donald gazed at his daughter. Her eyes flickered and filled with tears.

For more than two dozen years he had walked his ship's deck with the stars shining overhead, wondering what kind of woman his wee lassie would have grown up to be. Now, gazing at her, he knew. "Ye are as beautiful as yer mother. I loved her so, and I love ye."

MY FATHER?

Kit had thought she'd find his broken, bloodied body at South Pass. Then Braham told her she'd find him in San Francisco. Then she had gone home and given up all hope of ever knowing his name. He had been only a picture she had sought to identify, a man with whom she had no emotional attachment, a man who had never been part of her life, a man she would probably never grow to love. Now he stood a breath away, and she saw the depth of the pain in his eyes, smelled the sea in his hair, heard his humble request for forgiveness, and felt his physical presence as viscerally powerful as his portrait.

He was a handsome man standing proud in his clan's yellow and black kilt.

Tears streamed down her face, and her heart reached out to him.

This man was her father—Donald Shelly McCabe. And she loved him, because she was born to do just that.

She kissed his cheek. "You are indeed the topping to an extraordinary day." She reached for Cullen's hand. "This is my husband, Cullen Montgomery. I married the man to whom I was promised as a child. And I want you to forget everything Braham said about him and form your own opinion."

Braham held up his hands in surrender. "I didna tell him everything, Cul."

Cullen glared at Braham. "He's my father-in-law, for God's sake."

Sean laughed.

Cullen shook Donald's hand. "'Tis a pleasure to meet ye, sir. I'm sorry I didna get the opportunity to ask ye for yer daughter's hand in marriage. I hope ye will forgive me."

Donald looked very stern, and then he smiled. "I've been forgiven, son. How could I ever withhold forgiveness from anyone?"

Joe entered the room carrying a violin and handed it to Sean, who settled the instrument under his chin and began to play. Kit recognized the Shaker hymn "Simple Gifts," and with an encouraging nod from Sean, she sang.

> *'Tis the gift to be simple, 'tis the gift to be free,*
> *'Tis the gift to come down where we ought to be,*
> *And when we find ourselves in the place just right,*
> *'Twill be in the valley of love and delight.*
> *When true simplicity is gain'd,*
> *To bow and to bend we shan't be asham'd,*
> *To turn, turn will be our delight,*
> *Till by turning, turning we come round right.*

Chapter Fifty-One

A LIGHT KNOCK on Kit's bedroom door woke her before dawn, groggy and confused. Winter's moon filtered through the naked oak outside her window, and its skeletal branches splashed eerie shadows onto her bedroom walls. The wind moaned about the mansion, worrying a shutter that rattled against the brick.

Another tap, this time louder.

She snuggled against the heat of Cullen's body, ignoring the intrusion into her warm cocoon filled with the slow, melodic beat of his heart.

The tap became a heavy knock.

"Who's there?" she asked in a croaking voice.

"Father's taken a turn. Hurry." Sean sounded unusually abrupt.

Fully awake now, a cold chill washed over her, and she rolled from Cullen's embrace.

"What's the matter, lass?"

"Is today the twenty-fifth?" She eased her pregnant body out of bed.

"Yes." Cullen swept to his feet and helped her with her robe, planting a soft kiss on her neck.

She looped the fringed belt, tying it snuggly above the swell of her child. "If I had remembered, I would have prepared."

He stood at her back and folded his arms around her, pulling her into him. "Death isna something ye can prepare for in order to minimize the pain."

"I would've liked to have known."

"Nae, it would have worried ye."

She leaned her head against his shoulder, and he kissed the sensitive spot below her ear. She shivered as a tingle raced through her. "I couldn't do this without you."

"Ye dinna have to do anything alone ever again."

She smiled. "I don't think you can birth this baby."

"Well, maybe not, but I'll be there with ye. Just like the daddies do in yer time."

"*This* is my time now."

"I'm just teasing ye, lass. Go on now and see to yer grandfather. I'll dress and join ye in his room."

She took a deep breath, slung open the bedroom door, and waddled down the hallway.

The door to Thomas's room stood ajar. The smell of incontinence permeated the air. A smell that reminded her of her granny's last few days.

Donald huddled next to the bed. His hair stood disheveled from running his fingers through its thick waves so many times. He rose when he saw her, kissed her cheek, and helped her to his chair. "He's been asking for ye."

Kit leaned over the bed. Despite a roaring fire, a chill pervaded the room. Thomas's thrashing about had crumpled the bed covers. "I'm here, Granddaddy." She straightened his blanket and threaded her fingers with his. The blue veins had stopped pumping blood through his wrinkled, arthritic hands, leaving them curled and cold. She tried to straighten them, but the frozen joints refused to move. Damn the infirmity, and damn the cancer.

Time had passed much too fast.

Not that long ago, Elliott had let her loose to ride her palomino alone, but she'd ridden farther than the boundaries he had set. She couldn't resist trotting the pony to the cemetery. That corner of the farm had always fascinated her. A two-hundred-year-old sycamore stood at the edge of Cemetery Hill's wrought-iron fence. Thomas Sean MacKlenna's granite monolith rose from the middle of the plot like a sentinel from the mist. She knew his epitaph by heart.

THOMAS SEAN MACKLENNA II
HE SAW WHAT OTHERS DID NOT.
HE LIVED WHAT OTHERS COULD NOT.
HE DREAMED WHAT OTHERS DARED NOT.
JANUARY 25, 1770—JANUARY 25, 1853

From that day on, she rode to the cemetery, circled the fence, then continued her morning ride. And that was where the ghost scared her off Stormy the day she found her father's letter, and that's where she saw the ghost for the last time.

"Sing." Thomas's whisper pulled her from her memories. His eyes held a glassy, fixed stare, and his lips wore a pasty gray. His jaw opened, and he breathed rapidly through his mouth.

Her baby kicked, and she squirmed in the chair. Her child grew stronger every day in her womb's protection, while her grandfather's life ebbed. The circle of life could not be broken, she understood that, but understanding and accepting were polar opposites.

Oh God, I'm so tired of people dying.

Tears flowed down Kit's cheeks. Cullen leaned over her shoulder and handed her his handkerchief. She wiped her eyes and rubbed her thumb over the monogrammed *M*'s smooth stitching. Sing? Yes, she would sing him into heaven, just as Sarah and John had done with baby Gabriel. She took a breath and in her cool, intimate contralto voice began to sing. "*Should auld acquaintance be forgot, and never brought to mind? Should auld acquaintance be forgot, And auld lang syne?*"

Sean, Donald, and Cullen stood at the end of the bed and picked up the chorus. The voices of three Scottish tenors resounded through the master suite. Even though no bagpipes played, she heard the Caledonian Pipes & Drums in her mind. "*For auld lang syne, my jo, for auld lang syne, We'll take a cup o' kindness yet, for auld lang syne.*"

Braham and Henry slipped quietly into the bedroom and gathered behind Kit. Braham squeezed her shoulder and joined in the singing. While they sang their final good-bye, Thomas took his last breath.

Kit bowed her head and wept for the man she'd respected all her life, but not until she met him had she come to love him, too. His last breath was not the loudest sound she'd ever heard, but a gentle rush of air exhaled from a life well lived.

They all remained by his side, lost in their own thoughts and prayers. "I didn't have enough time with him." Kit caressed his cold hand. The heat of life drifted away like the last wisps of smoke from a dying fire.

"I'm nae sure any of us did. He was a remarkable man, and I was proud to call him…to call him Father." Sean's words spilled out through a deep, racking sob.

"He forgave me," Donald said. "How can a man's heart be that big?" He buried his face in his hands and wept.

"Because he was once forgiven, and he never forgot the power of grace," Sean said.

Cullen knelt beside Kit and laid his head against her belly. "Thank ye, for dreaming me here, lass." He sighed heavily and tears spilled from his eyes, dampening her robe.

Sukey and Joe entered the room. "We'll take care of Mister Thomas," Joe said.

"Thank ye, Joe," Sean said. "Ye let us know when ye're done." The family shuffled out of the room, leaving the servants to wash and dress the old man's body. "I'm going for a walk." Sean addressed Cullen and Donald. "If ye want to go with me, we'll look about the farm for a burial site."

"I'd rather stay here and do what I can to get him ready," Donald said.

Cullen fetched a deep breath and then another, letting each out slowly. "Give me a few minutes." He and Kit held hands and returned to her bedroom. She climbed into bed, and he spooned with her while her body heaved with grief.

She fell asleep dreaming of stallions racing across rolling hills of frost-tipped Kentucky bluegrass toward a black granite monolith.

THE MACKLENNAS COVERED the furniture and paintings with black shrouds and held a wake that evening. Sean told Kit that his father had requested the shrouds remain until the birth of Kit's baby.

They buried Thomas the next morning.

The day was unusually warm for January. The bright sun sprinkled the snow-covered ground with what looked like glistening pieces of Swarovski crystals. The young sycamore's naked branches swayed in the easy wind. Reverend Breckinridge from First Presbyterian Church in Lexington delivered the eulogy to the small family gathering.

Kit had cried most of the night, and now her eyes were scratchy and strained. A pair of sunglasses would be nice. She'd worn them a year ago when she buried her parents. The pain from losing them was no longer raw. The rawness had been replaced with bittersweet memories.

A wrought-iron fence surrounded the cemetery then. Neither the fence nor the monolith existed yet. The gravesite was exactly where it should be, though, right smack in the middle of what would become known as Cemetery Hill.

The ghost of MacKlenna Farm had performed his final duty.

Chapter Fifty-Two

CULLEN LACED HIS fingers with Kit's as she waddled down the stairs. She was a week overdue, and while she didn't complain, he knew pregnancy had aggravated her prior injuries, especially her back. She tossed around the bed at night, unable to find a comfortable position. He'd gathered every pillow in the house, stuffing them under her head, shoulders, arms, knees, and feet to give her some relief. Even now, watching her take tentative steps down the stairs, while balancing what seemed like an enormous pumpkin on her belly, his heart ached for her.

Rarely did he leave her side. When he did, it was to retrieve a book, fetch a cup of tea, or conjure up some delectable treat guaranteed to put a smile on her face. She was especially fond of molasses cookies, and he made sure Sukey kept the jar full for her midnight sorties to the kitchen. His bride was his delectable treat, and he fell in love with Kit anew each morning when he woke and felt her warm breath beside him. Their painful separation of months earlier was still a constant reminder of the fragility of life. And because of that, he carried the ruby brooch in his pocket, keeping the magic stone close by. If Kit needed medical care beyond what a midwife could provide, he was prepared to send her back to her modern hospital. He often wondered if living in a time of medical and technological advances would be more enlightening, but he always circled back to his own reality. He lived when he lived. Not in the past, and not in the future.

"I can't find my toes. Someone snuck in our room, stole my feet, and left these." She lifted her foot from beneath her dressing gown. "There're bigger than a Clydesdale's."

"Yer not fat, yer voluptuous."

"I didn't say I was fat. I said my feet were."

Pure joy dwelt within, but he stifled his laugh. Kit was sensitive about her size, and in fact, had cried to the point of exhaustion the previous night, believing she no longer aroused him. He reassured her, crooning that he only thought of making love to her once a day, but the thought lasted twenty-four hours. He found his own singing amusing, but for some reason it made her weep even louder. He'd given up trying to find logic in her actions and reactions. Instead, he nodded and smiled and asked how he could make her more comfortable.

"Don't laugh at me."

Cullen raised his hand, surrendering. "I'm not, lass."

"Well, tell that to your body because it's shaking like Jell-O." He was unfamiliar with that word. He would add it to his growing list of questions. When she couldn't sleep, she kept him awake by answering them.

They reached the bottom landing, and she gingerly stepped to the floor. He pulled her wrist to his lips, touching his tongue to her pulse, her fingertips pink as seashells. "I love ye, regardless of yer size."

She rolled her bottom lip downward into a pout. Too enticing to ignore, he kissed her, nibbling on her pouty mouth.

"You're not supposed to tell me I'm big. You're *supposed* to tell me you've never seen me more beautiful."

"Aye, ye are a bonnie lass." He gave her a cheeky smile, eliciting a little slip of a laugh from her.

Donald emerged from the library, leafing through a book on horse breeding. He leaned over and kissed his daughter's cheek. "I think ye're the most gorgeous woman in the world."

"You're prejudiced, Dad, but thanks." All of a sudden, she stiffened and gasped.

"What's the matter?" Cullen asked.

"Something popped." Her eyes were wide with concern.

Alarm burned straight through him, but he knew, if he did nothing else, he had to be a calming influence. He blew a cool breath over the hot coals smoldering in his gut.

"*Oh my.*" She looked down. His gaze followed hers. Between her feet was a small puddle on the hardwood floor.

He leaned in close and whispered, "Did ye wet yourself, lass?"

She shook her head. "I think my water broke."

The rush of panic returned. Cullen swiveled to face Donald. "Page 242 explains the bag of waters. I need the manual."

Donald slammed shut the book on horse breeding. "I dinna have it."

Cullen didn't trust his memory, especially now, not with his heart reverberating inside his ears like the stampeding herd of buffalo at South Pass. "Ye had it last."

Donald pointed at Braham, who had just appeared at the top of the stairs. "He took it and said he would give it to ye."

"What?" Braham clutched his chest and slumped against the railing. "I swear, I dinna have it. I've been deemed untrustworthy."

Cullen plucked at the skin under his chin with his thumb and index finger. "I must have put it back inside Kit's armoire."

Kit stopped taking a measure of the size of the puddle. "What book are you talking about?"

"Yer birthing manual, *The Complete Book of Pregnancy and Child-birth.*"

"You've read it?"

"We've all read it," Braham said, walking down the stairs. "But Cullen's the expert. He taught us everything we need to know in case of an emergency."

"What does Cullen know about birthing babies? He's a lawyer, not a doctor."

Cullen glanced at her sideways. "Ye can ask me. I'm standing beside ye, lass."

Donald slapped Cullen between his shoulder blades. "We even

watched a birthing on itube on the uPod contraption."

"What?" Kit rubbed her temples. "Did somebody drop me into a really bad sit-com?"

"Enough of this." Cullen scooped her into his arms. "Braham, find Sukey. I'll take Kit to bed. I mean…I'll take her to our room."

Braham vaulted the newel post and ran toward the kitchen. "*Sukey!*"

Cullen took the stairs two at a time.

"What can I do?" Donald asked.

Cullen yelled over his shoulder. "Get the list and find that book."

Kit wiggled in his arms. "What list?"

"Important reminders. Get flowers, chill the champagne, and make sure yer iPod is charged."

"If you know what's on the list, why tell Dad to get it?"

"So he'll have an assignment."

She laughed, but her beautiful green eyes held a tense, focused look.

Cullen carried her to their room. "I've ne'er carried ye across a threshold."

"We could use some good luck. Take me out, and let's do it again."

Donald charged up the back stairs. His boots clicked on the wood treads. He followed them into the bedroom, huffing. "I brought Kit a cup of raspberry tea and set the champagne in the ice bucket."

"One bottle or two?"

"Four," Donald said.

Cullen laid Kit on the bed, and she hugged her belly "I get tea while y'all drink champagne?"

"It's for afterward, and ye can have a wee sip."

Sukey barged in, carrying a stack of towels. "I knew that babe gone a come today." She dropped the towels on the washstand and turned to leave. "Men don't belong in a birthing room. If you gone a come in here, stay out of my way, and don't hold your breath, cause

I ain't got time to pick you up off the floor."

"What a dear lady." Kit massaged her temples. "Sit down, both of you." She patted the blue counterpane on both sides of her. Cullen sat on one side, her father on the other. "I'm so glad you're here with us, Dad."

Donald squeezed her hand. "When ye were born, yer mother didna want me anywhere near, not even inside the house. She didna think I could handle her pain, but I could. I'd seen her sick most of her life." He gave a world-weary sigh. "I've never told anyone, but I spent eighteen hours on the roof over her room that day. I didna eat. I didna sleep. I listened to every moan, grunt, and scream. I even tried to dig through the thatch to look at her face, but it was too thick, and I didna dare leave to get a digging tool. Then I heard yer first cry, and I wept. I imagined I was holding ye and holding her. Except for yer mother's voice, yer cry was the most beautiful sound in the world."

"I wish I had known her."

"From what ye've told me about Mary Spencer and yer friend, Sarah, there is a similar generous spirit and sustaining faith. I've never loved another woman, Kit, and I've never held another baby."

"Cullen and I would like you to help bring Baby Thomas into the world."

"Stay in here with ye?" Cullen offered him a nod. The corners of Donald's eyes tightened around a shimmer of tears. He gazed at Kit, a slight smile curling his lips. "I'm pleased ye asked, but this is Cullen's time, not mine. I'll be right outside the door."

CULLEN CHECKED HIS watch—six o'clock. Kit had been laboring for ten hours. His heart swelled with pride for his wife's stamina to persevere through hours of painful contractions. He'd watched the agony etch across her face and would have done anything to make it stop. He would never ask her to go through this again, even if it meant never making love with her again. Why did pain come with something so extraordinary?

He'd heard birthing stories before. And his opinion had always been that birthing was women's work and that's what God made them to do. Now, watching the process, he became fully aware of the sacrifice, and more particularly, Kit's sacrifice.

At the Kansas River, he'd asked her why she'd risked her life for a child she didn't know. She'd said it was worth it. Now he understood. Was it possible to love her more than he did at that moment?

Kit swatted at his hand when he tried to wash her face. She yelled, "*Get out.*"

He jumped out of the way, his heart racing. Dear God, what had he done wrong?

"Don't pay no mind to what a birthing woman say, Mister Cullen. She just want that baby out. Not you."

"Ye sure, Sukey?"

"Miss Kit would a done the same to me. She don't mean it." Kit groaned with another contraction. She grabbed his wrist and dug in her nails, drawing blood. "I'll *never* do this again."

"That's the birthing talking, too, Mister Cullen. She'll want you in her bed soon enough."

Maybe, but he wasn't willing to risk her life again.

AT EIGHT THIRTY, Kit pushed one last time and Thomas Cullen Montgomery slipped into the world. Cullen held his breath until his son drew his first. "We have a son, lass." The declaration was the most powerful statement he'd ever made in his life, except for his profession of love to Kit. When Thomas cried, shivers of joy coursed through Cullen's body. He'd thought Kit's iPod held the angelic vocals of heaven, but he was wrong. His son's cry was the purest sound he'd ever heard.

Kit's head dropped on the pillow, and she let out a long sigh of relief. "Hold him up. Let me see him."

Cullen clasped the scissors, his chest tightening with the magnitude of his responsibility. "I'm cutting the cord. He's a wee babe and so perfectly made." He'd often thought while looking at Kit naked beneath him that his love was complete. He had no comprehension of how expansive love could be, until now. A wave of throbbing heat filled him. His hands shook as he placed the babe in his wife's arms.

Kit cried when she wrapped her hands around their baby. "Ah. He's so beautiful. He looks just like you."

"Nae. He has his mother's eyes. But I'll claim the rest of him."

Donald stuck his head inside the room. "I heard him cry."

"Come in and see yer grandson," Cullen said.

Donald stepped over to the bed and gazed at the child. "He is beautiful."

"Here, Daddy, you can hold him."

Donald took the babe from her. "Ye've given me more than the gift of a grandson." His voice hitched. "Ye've brought meaning and purpose back to my life." He returned the baby, kissed Kit on the top of her head, then left to share the news.

Sukey followed Donald from the room. Kit put Thomas to her breast, and he latched on as if he'd been nursing for months.

Cullen stroked his son's cheek and felt his face muscles sucking his mother's nipple. "How does he ken how to do that already?"

Kit moaned softly. "Most babies have trouble at the beginning."

"I guess he's been watching me." His fingers meandered across the landscape of her breasts. "I suppose I'll have to share ye for a while."

Humor crinkled the corners of her eyes. "Can you handle that?"

"I dinna ken. I'm rather possessive about ye."

"I've noticed, but you don't mind sharing me with Daddy. Why's that?"

Cullen looked out the window. Clouds swam across the moon's surface, blocking the light in the chilly March evening. For some reason, he remembered how cold the water had been when he fell into the Deschutes. He remembered the darkness and hearing Kristen's voice. *His sister was there.* He shook away the pain and tucked the memory into his heart.

"I know the anguish of losing ye. Yer father and I have that in common. Creates a bond between us, stronger than what Braham and I have. I'll never deny Donald McCabe his rightful share of yer love."

Threading his fingers underneath her hair to cradle her head, he gave her a long, lingering kiss on her lips, showering her with his complete and absolute devotion. Her warm mouth was inviting, and he knew he'd want to have her as soon as she healed. He just hoped she'd want him too. "What can I ever give ye that could mean as much as this wee one?"

She gazed at her suckling baby, and then presented Cullen with a gorgeous smile, her lips slightly puckered. "A daughter."

Chapter Fifty-Three

KIT FORGED A path around the packed trunks stacked in her bedroom. Her pink-cheeked son was lying peacefully on his back asleep in his cradle. She laid a gentle hand on his tummy. The rise and fall of his chest satisfied her constant worry that he had stopped breathing. He squirmed and made funny gurgling sounds.

Where had three months gone? Someone had held him twenty-four hours a day for the first two weeks. Usually his father or grandfather, but his great-uncle, second-cousin, and godfather, Henry, took their turns. By the third week, Braham and Henry demanded the majority of the time. They were heading back to California and wouldn't get to hold him for several months. After they departed for San Francisco, Baby Thomas spent every waking moment, unless he was eating, with either Cullen or Donald.

Cullen walked into the bedroom. "I think Thomas is awake. I'm going to the barn and thought he'd like to go. Sean's having a new stallion delivered." He picked up the baby, wrapped him in a blanket, kissed Kit, then they were gone.

She glanced at her watch. *I'll give you fifteen minutes.*

The sun broke out from behind a rain cloud and a stream of light flickered into her bedroom. The room where she'd stacked her trophies, tossed her schoolbooks, and spent rainy days on the window seat playing her guitar. After this visit, she might not ever return to the mansion and sleep in her bedroom. Of all the things she'd once imagined doing in her bed, none of them involved birthing a baby.

Cullen had promised he'd build her a house exactly like MacKlenna Mansion, but she was ready for something new. Something built for them to start their own tradition. Montgomery Winery Villa had a nice ring about it.

Although Sean had begged them to stay, the Montgomerys and Donald planned to leave for San Francisco in the morning. The farm was her uncle's inheritance, not hers, and that was as it should be. Her grandfather provided for her in his will. With her own gold and diamonds, Cullen's wealth, her father's fortune, and now her inheritance, she had more than enough to start her vineyard and couldn't wait to hear about Henry's scouting adventure to the Napa Valley, and whether he'd convinced the Barretts to join them in the venture.

Sean knocked on her open door.

"Come in."

He glanced at the empty cradle, scrunching his face.

Kit chuckled. "Cullen took him to the barn. He said you had a new stallion being delivered."

"Oh well. Do ye have everything ye need?"

"More than we need. If we weren't sailing on one of Daddy's ships, I don't think I'd be allowed to carry this much on board."

"Good, because there is more for ye to take."

Kit glanced around the room. "More?"

"I'm having all of yer mother's paintings crated. Jamilyn would want ye to take them."

Kit shook her head. "I can't—"

"The decision's made. Besides, didna ye tell me none of the paintings were in the house when ye were growing up?"

"You should keep the Eilean Donan."

He glanced away, and she sensed he was reconsidering. "That painting was inspired by yer mother's love for ye. If ye took only one painting, that would be the one." He kissed her. "I'm off to the barn."

"Hey, wait a minute. You didn't tell me about your new stallion.

Where'd you get him? How old is he?"

A frown line appeared between his eyebrows. "Lexington, I think." He cleared his throat. "Or Versailles or Paris, I dinna remember. I have to go." Her stuttering, red-faced uncle hurried from the room.

She followed him into the hallway. "Uncle Sean, what's going on?"

He turned, but his gaze didn't meet hers. "Nothing a'tall. I'm late."

Why wouldn't he tell her about his new stallion? She knew every horse in his stable. Then she gasped with delight. "Cullen bought me a horse, didn't he?"

Sean wore the dejected face of man who lost a bet. "Dinna ask me to ruin his surprise."

Kit folded her arms. "Well, since he doesn't think I should ride a spirited horse, he probably found me a blind twenty-year-old that someone had to beg him to take off their hands."

Sean laughed, shaking his head. "Nae, lass. Yer husband is too proud of ye to put ye on anything but the finest horse he could find."

Her face split into a huge grin. "How old is he?"

"I'll tell ye, but ye must act surprised. He's a yearling."

"What color?"

"Ah, he's a beauty. Just wait 'til ye set yer eyes on him. Yer husband knows horses. He rejected several I would have taken."

"But what color?"

"Ye'll have to wait."

"He's a chestnut, isn't he?"

Sean's eyebrows flashed slightly, enough to give away the final piece of the secret.

She hugged him. "Don't worry. I'll act surprised."

"Cullen's been searching for a horse for ye since the day Thomas was born. He said after the race at Fort Laramie he never wanted ye to ride like that again, but watching ye suffer through childbirth, he said he'd never deny ye anything he had the power to give ye."

"Thank you for telling me." Kit's voice shook with emotion. "Now, when I see the horse, I can focus on the love and the sacrifice behind the gift instead of the gift." Sean nodded and walked down the stairs. "Uncle Sean." He stopped and turned at the first landing. "What kind of horse did Cullen get Thomas?"

Sean's eyes settled on Kit and a smile played at his lips. "A pretty little Shetland pony, standing about thirty-two inches at his shoulder. But ye didna hear that from me either."

She didn't know whether to laugh or cry or both.

As soon as Sean left the house, she went downstairs, searching for Joe.

"Can I get something for you, Miss Kit?"

"The painting over the fireplace—"

"I'm crating it now."

"Would you put it in my bedroom? As soon as I'm gone, you can rehang it over the mantel."

Joe lifted the crate, smiling. "Yes, ma'am. Mister Sean loves that painting. He be happy to keep it."

She then headed to Sean's office. Donald had told her he'd left their itinerary on the desk. She found the piece of paper and sat in the chair to read.

Midway to Frankfort to Louisville by train. Paddleboat to New Orleans. Donald's ship to Chagres. Boat and mules to Panama. Donald's ship to San Francisco, all in sixty days. A hell of a trip.

The front door slammed. "*Kit.*"

She glanced at the grandfather clock. Fifteen minutes exactly. "In here, Cullen."

"Thomas is hungry." He walked into the office and, flashing his dimples, handed over his son. "After he eats, I wonder if ye might be up for a ride."

Chapter Fifty-Four

KIT NURSED THOMAS, put him in the bassinet, and slipped from her bedroom without disturbing her husband, who was sprawled naked on the bed. The night sky held a brilliant display of stars that, along with the full moon shining through the open windows, lit the hallways of MacKlenna Mansion. A warm breeze rippled the drawn-back drapes, giving the air unbridled access to the shadowed house.

She tiptoed down the stairs to perform one last task.

Even without the moonlight, Kit would not have needed a candle to light the way. She knew the house and its sounds. How odd that the mansion, even in its early days, had the same creaky floorboards she'd grown accustomed to in the twenty-first century.

As soon as she entered the office, she lit candles. She didn't need them either, but she wanted the warm glow. Hundreds of memories inhabited the room. She wanted to hear them, smell them, and wear them as a cloak one last time.

It seemed a lifetime ago that she had sat on the sofa researching the Oregon Trail and talking with Elliott about a seemingly impossible trip. Her eyes filled with tears thinking about him, her adoptive father, and Scott—three men she had loved dearly. She would never forget them.

She opened the desk's center drawer and pushed the button, releasing the door to the secret compartment. The first time she opened it, a virtual string of dominos was set in place. They'd all fallen now, and a life had unfolded more joyous, more complete than she ever thought or imagined.

"Kit, where are ye?"

If possible, Cullen's voice had become more musical and more sensual while living in MacKlenna Mansion. The sound sprinkled over her with the scent of rose petals. "In here."

He leaned against the doorway with his son in one arm, the other arm behind his back. "Thomas was crying."

She folded her arms across her middle. "I just nursed him to sleep."

"We missed ye."

"What are you going to do when our daughter is born? Carry them both around?"

His eyebrows arched. "Are ye pregnant again?"

"With your insatiable appetite, it won't take long."

His quiet laugh slid over her like a warm, sweet kiss. "If I re-member, *ye* woke *me* last night demanding my attention."

A flame sizzled through her, and she shivered at the delicious memory. "And you gave me all you had."

He bowed his head, slightly. "Yer putting the brooch away?"

"Yes, but I decided not to tell Sean."

"Why?"

She tapped her fingers against the box in her hand. "He doesn't need it. He'll meet Lyle Ann Poe next year in Charleston, and they'll have Sean II and three daughters within a few years. The brooch will be in the desk when my adoptive father needs it."

"Yer sure ye want to give it away?"

She opened the box and gazed at the stone. "I remember the first time I saw this. I was afraid to touch it." She snapped the lid closed, placed it in the compartment, and shut the door. "I've received every gift I was meant to receive, and now it's time to send it on to the next person." She stepped away from the desk. "There're two others out there somewhere—an emerald and a sapphire."

"How do ye know?"

"Sean told me. Something magical is supposed to happen when

they're all together again. I'd just as soon be as far away as possible when that occurs."

She opened the secret door in the bookcase.

"Ye included drawings of Thomas, didn't ye?"

She patted the journal in her hand. "And you, me, Sean, Braham, Henry, and some wonderful sketches of Grandfather. I'm also sending him the one Sean drew of the three of us."

"Kit?" He paused a moment. "We can go to yer time, if ye want. I know ye miss Elliott."

"There is no more *my time*. There is only *our* time." His open nightshirt gave her a view of the pulse beating in his neck. Living in the future was not his first choice, but she knew he would make the sacrifice if she asked.

She placed the notebook in the compartment, closed the door, and sealed it with wood glue she'd snatched from the laundry room when she'd rescued Tate and Tabor. "Hmm, all done." She brushed her hands together. "Let's go to bed." She waggled her eyebrows.

He cleared his throat. "I have something for ye."

"You've given me everything I could possibly want."

"I dinna have diamonds to give ye. Ye have plenty of your own. I dinna have gold. Ye have that, too. But I have this." He handed her a red rose he'd been holding behind his back. "I removed all the thorns."

He had taken her breath more than once, but this was the *pièce de résistance*. When she could breathe again, she kissed him, sweeping her tongue against his lips. "Thank you for loving me. Thank you for believing in me. Thank you for giving me my dreams."

She sniffed the sweet flower. He had indeed removed every one of her thorns, and she knew in her heart, she had truly bloomed in the power of his love.

Chapter Fifty-Five

MacKlenna Farm, Lexington, Kentucky, August

ELLIOTT UNLOCKED THE mansion's front door, entered the house, and turned off the security alarm. "We're only staying a few minutes, so dinna run off," he said to Tate. The dog sniffed the air, and Elliott patted his head. "Nope. She's nae here." He'd said the same thing every night for the past two weeks, but Tate still sniffed for her. "Come on, let's go."

A nightly sweep of the premises had become a routine, not because it was necessary, but because he needed to know if anything had changed. And Tate, being Tate, always had to go with him. Tabor remained curled up on the sofa at Elliott's residence located on the other side of the stallion complex.

The critters had adjusted to Kit's departure. He couldn't say the same for himself. He missed her like crazy. Instead of getting easier, the pain of the separation seemed to be getting worse. Sleeping was difficult. No, it was damned near impossible. If only he knew what had happened to her, the nightmares might stop.

Sandy had received a few phone calls after the article appeared in the city-state section of *The Lexington Herald-Leader*, announcing Kit's decision to live abroad. Her friends were confused and concerned, but interest waned as plans for the September Yearling Sale and the three-week fall meeting at Keeneland peaked, just as Kit had predicted.

Elliott considered returning to Scotland as soon as live racing concluded at the end of October, and while there, decide whether to retire. With Sean and Kit both gone, his passion dwindled for both the farm and racing. After all, he wasn't a MacKlenna, and he certainly didn't need the money.

Tate trotted down the hallway, sniffing the floor, his tail flipping back and forth, Elliott followed, a small smile playing at his lips. The dog entered the office first and headed straight for the wet bar where he sat, whining.

Elliott flipped on the lights. "What will it be tonight, boy? A dram of whisky or a doggie treat?" Tate barked and Elliott laughed as he poured a drink for himself and gave the retriever a bone-shaped biscuit.

He tossed back his drink and walked to the bookcase, removed a handful of leather-bound volumes, and pushed the lever to open the secret compartment. It didn't open. He pushed again. Nothing. He broke out in a cold sweat. Was he having a heart attack? No, he didn't think so. Only stress. He took deep breaths. When he calmed, he pushed the lever once more. Again, nothing.

I will seal it so no one finds my journal.

He slapped the bookcase's edge. "She actually did it." With his hand shaking like an old man with palsy, he pulled his MacGyver knife from his pants' pocket and cut into the wood, loosening the seal. The door popped opened with a faint swish of misplaced air.

There sat Kit's journal.

He wiped the sweat from his forehead. Damn. Pictures of Kit from the time she was a toddler learning to walk to a perfect princess modeling her prom dresses played in his mind like a PowerPoint slideshow, each slide fading in and out.

He needed a few more drinks.

He returned to the bar and poured two fingers of scotch, gulped it down, and poured more. What was he trying to do, drink the whole damn bottle? He stared at the notebook nestled in the niche in the bookcase. Did Kit place it there within a year of leaving her time, or toward the end of her life? If she was ninety years old and dying, he didn't want to know. He lifted the bottle to his lips and took a swig, then wiped his mouth with the back of his wrist.

Suck it up, Elliott.

He returned to the bookcase, lifted the journal from the cubbyhole, and opened it to the last page. Kit had dated the entry June 1, 1853. His entire body relaxed with the exhalation of a long-held breath.

"Now, this will be a good tale." He turned out the light and left the room. "Come on, Tate, let's go home."

They walked down the hallway, passing the portraits of the MacKlenna men. When he reached the end, he noticed there was no longer a single female painting. There were two.

Tears burned his eyes. He brushed his fingertips across the newest portrait, and cleared his throat of the knot hanging there. God, he missed her, but life went on, and so must he. He pressed the control button for the home audio system, and a Bach Partita filled the mansion with glorious music.

"Good night, Kit. May God hold ye in the palm of His hand."

THE CELTIC BROOCH SERIES

THE RUBY BROOCH (Book 1)
Kitherina MacKlenna and Cullen Montgomery's love story

THE LAST MACKLENNA (Book 2 – not a time travel story)
Meredith Montgomery and Elliott Fraser's love story

THE SAPPHIRE BROOCH (Book 3)
Charlotte Mallory and Braham McCabe's love story

THE EMERALD BROOCH (Book 4)
Kenzie Wallis-Manning and David McBain's love story

THE BROKEN BROOCH (Book 5 – not a time travel story)
JL O'Grady and Kevin Allen's love story

THE THREE BROOCHES (Book 6)
A reunion with Kit and Cullen Montgomery

THE DIAMOND BROOCH (Book 7)
Jack Mallory and Amy Spalding's love story

THE AMBER BROOCH (Book 8)
Amber Kelly and Daniel Grant's love story
Olivia Kelly and Connor O'Grady's love story

THE PEARL BROOCH (Book 9)
Sophia Orsini and Pete Parrino's love story

THE TOPAZ BROOCH (Book 10)
Wilhelmina "Billie" Penelope Malone and Rick O'Grady's love story

THE SUNSTONE BROOCH (Book 11)
Ensley MacWilliam Andrews and Austin O'Grady

There are many more Brooch Books to come.
To read about the next few books, visit
www.katherinelogan.com/whats-next-2

ABOUT THE AUTHOR

Author Katherine Lowry Logan couples her psychology degree with lots of hands-on research when creating new settings and characters for her blockbuster Celtic Brooch series.

These cross-genre stories have elements of time travel, sci-fi, fantasy adventure, mystery, suspense, historical, and romance and focus on events in American history.

A few of her favorite research adventures include:

- attending the Battle of Cedar Creek reenactment and visiting Civil War sites in Richmond, Virginia (*Sapphire Brooch*),
- riding in a B-17 Flying Fortress bomber, and visiting Bletchley Park and the beaches at Normandy (*Emerald Brooch*),
- research in Paris, France, and Florence, Italy, with an art lesson in Florence (*Pearl Brooch*),
- a tour of New York's Yankee Stadium and several hours with their historian (*Diamond Brooch*),
- wine tours in Napa (*The Last MacKlenna*),
- and following the Oregon Trail for the first book in the series (*Ruby Brooch*).

Katherine is the mother of two daughters and grandmother of five—Charlotte, Lincoln, James Cullen, Henry, and Meredith. She is also a marathoner and lives in Lexington, Kentucky, with her fluffy Goldendoodle, Maddie the Marauder.

Website
www.katherinellogan.com

Facebook
facebook.com/katherine.l.logan

Twitter
twitter.com/KathyLLogan

I'm A Runner (Runner's World Magazine Interview)
www.runnersworld.com/celebrity-runners/im-a-runner-katherine-lowry-logan

If you would like to receive notification of future releases sign up today at KatherineLLogan.com or
send an email to KatherineLLogan@gmail.com and put "New Release" in the subject line. And if you are on Facebook, join the Celtic Brooch Series for ongoing book and character discussions.

*   *   *

Made in United States
Orlando, FL
24 June 2024

48255804R00211